I0583471

DARK RECIPE

KNOX RAMSEY THRILLERS
BOOK 1

ROBERT CUMMER

DARK RECIPE

Copyright © 2025 by Robert Cummer
All rights reserved.

No part of this book may be reproduced or transmitted in any form or by any means, electronic or mechanical, including photocopying, recording, or by any information storage and retrieval system, without permission in writing from the publisher, except in the case of brief quotations embodied in critical reviews and certain other noncommercial uses permitted by copyright law.

ISBN 979-8-9934979-2-1 (hardcover)
ISBN 979-8-9934979-1-4 (paperback)
ISBN 979-8-9934979-0-7 (ebook)

Library of Congress Control Number: 2025926526

First edition

Published in the United States of America by
Mangrove Publishing

Mangrove Publishing and the CBW Mangrove tree colophon are trademarks of the publisher.

This is a work of fiction. Names, characters, places, and incidents are either the product of the author's imagination or are used fictitiously. Any resemblance to actual persons, living or dead, events, or locales is entirely coincidental.

Printed in the United States of America.

For my mangrove family tree, whose roots run wide and deep. Whether by blood or by choice, you've given me strength and inspiration beyond measure.

CONTENTS

AUTHORS NOTE

This is a work of fiction. All characters, organizations, and events are imaginary or used fictitiously.

The science, however, is real. The vulnerabilities in controlled-environment agriculture—the industrial systems managing light, nutrients, climate, and irrigation in indoor farms growing everything from leafy greens to cannabis—are documented in peer-reviewed research and regulatory reports from the CDC, FDA, and NIH. Contamination events, system failures, and produce recalls have all occurred. What you won't find outside these pages is a coordinated effort to exploit these vulnerabilities as a weapon. That possibility remains speculative, and this novel dramatizes it for entertainment.

Operational details have been altered or omitted for safety; nothing herein should be used as guidance for medical treatment, cultivation, or security operations.

EPIGRAPH

"In 2010, malware called Stuxnet secretly reprogrammed industrial control systems in Iran, destroying nearly 1,000 uranium centrifuges without triggering alarms. It proved for the first time that code could silently destroy machines."

PROLOGUE

The guard at the inner door checked two credentials; an MSS lanyard and a PLA proximity tag before the lock cycled. Inside, stenciled across the glass in two languages ran a designation nobody used outside the building: 网络情报研究设施17 / Cyber Intelligence Research Facility 17. The consoles wore dual seals, the badges on lanyards split between red and army green. Techs in slate jackets (MSS) and olive utilities (PLA) traded reports in opposite directions. Everyone copied on everything, and no one was entirely sure which hierarchy outranked the other.

Liu Wei passed beneath a wall map of the United States. Red diodes pricked Chicago, Detroit, Portland, Austin, Sacramento: market pilots, on paper. On the racks, FAC-17 labels glowed white against matte-black equipment. The air thrummed a constant, dry hum of filtered cold. The place felt engineered to never sleep. A brass plaque near the server cage carried a Party aphorism in two scripts: 稳定即仁政 / Stability is benevolence—the kind of sentence that made budgets easy and hesitation expensive.

He set a porcelain cup of jasmine tea beside his keyboard and let the steam fog a corner of the screen. People whose names were no longer taught kept him company at this hour. Sorge, who listened long enough to move nations; the lesson of '71, that visibility kills careers before it kills men. The Party remembers. So do the files that go missing. In Beijing, people still lost careers for being right too early; 1971 had taught the army to fear boldness almost as much as failure.

Two systems asked for the same password with two different prompts. Redundant oversight wasn't security; it was memory of purges conducted after successes that embarrassed the Party. Liu signed into both.

SUBJECT ANALYSIS: RAMSEY, KNOX

   Classification: Agricultural Automation / North America

   Status: Persistent observation

A flickering thumbnail image showed Ramsey on a factory catwalk, wearing a yellow hard hat and safety glasses. The set suggested a man who still believed that systems could be made safe by repeatedly hammering at them. Useful faith, Liu thought, and opened the folder tree beneath the name: conference talks, patents, field videos, a slide deck where FarmCore / FarmLytics formed a single lattice—sensors feeding models feeding decisions the way capillaries feed organs.

Dr. Wu knocked once on the metal doorframe and stepped inside without waiting. Slate jacket—MSS. A second badge at her hip, olive for military liaison, confirmed this was no ordinary visit. "Beijing wants an updated readiness brief," she said, setting a thin folder on his desk. "Procurement asks if we will require additional greenhouse controllers for the Canadian pilots."

"We won't," Liu said. "Distribution beats footprint."

Wu nodded once. "What harms them instructs us. We should never forget the lesson."

The argument was simple enough to believe: harden the nation's food security by proving how easily an adversary could be bent mirrored risk as policy. He scrolled through Ramsey's architecture: cloud-warmed edges, third-party plugins, convenience stacked like dry kindling. "They built a nervous system for plants and gave us write access."

Wu followed the line of his cursor, then the map. "The long memory of the Party favors patience, not appetite," she said, voice so even it sounded like a citation. "We are not the Americans."

"We are engineers," Liu said. "And the schedule keeps the politicians fed."

A PLA political officer, Zhang, paused in the doorway. He was reading the same feed on a wall display. He didn't say or do anything. Then, he left. The room grew quiet again. The sounds of KVM switches, cooling fans, and a lanyard filled the air. A junior analyst typed on the back bench. He wrote about applicability to domestic deployments. Then, he deleted it and sent the brief. Every system can be exploited. Some things are only tested internally.

Liu opened a video: Ramsey in a greenhouse, sleeves rolled, explaining why human intuition fails at scale. "You don't eyeball the canopy," the American said. "You measure. Then you let the model learn what your eyes can't." Off-camera, someone laughed. Suddenly, another window appeared, showing a retail CCTV camera's view of a Midwestern store aisle, where a child was pulling a parent towards a tasting table. Liu minimized it before faces could become people.

He dragged a window over the map and displayed the pilot telemetry—a collection of seemingly insignificant numbers that held significance only when considered collectively. Permissions shimmered in the corner, two icons nested like coins: MSS-READ / PLA-WRITE. The overlapping jurisdictions made junior analysts nervous. They made Liu careful. "We'll keep the attribution surface clean," he said. "No signatures anyone can read twice."

Wu nodded. "Personnel?" she asked, almost lazily. "Your request to remove Suqian references is approved. Administrative reassignment."

"Good," Liu said. "History should weigh on someone else."

She tapped the FAC-17 stencil on the nearest chassis as if to knock wood. "What about the Americans' family?" Wu asked. "Complications tend to multiply once we touch a man's home."

"We won't need his pain," Liu said, and meant it more than he expected. "Just his pride."

On his screen, an annotation bled into existence beside Detroit's diode: readiness $\geq$ 0.93. The geometry of the thing pleased him: clean edges, tight tolerances, the way an elegant bridge never calls attention to its joints. He thought again of Sorge, of years spent arranging insignificant facts until a single truth toppled on command.

"File the brief," Liu said. "Use the facility designation. No unit numbers."

Wu gathered the folder. "Cyber Intelligence Research Facility 17," she repeated in English, then in Chinese, as if confirming an incantation. "We'll keep it boring."

"The best kind of dangerous," Liu said.

Outside the glass, the guard checked two credentials and let someone else into the hum. On the map, the red dots didn't blink, they breathed. The system would decide when to wake; his job was to keep its sleep deep and dreamless until then.

He closed the Ramsey clip, saved the state, and, with two hands on two networks, began. Boring was the safest way to be dangerous.

~

DETROIT—THREE YEARS EARLIER

Knox Ramsey stood before a conference room of investors, a presentation remote steady in his hand. Slides behind him showed vertical farms rising like green skyscrapers, hydroponics feeding families in urban food deserts, and data streams promising to revolutionize how humanity fed itself.

"By 2050," Knox said, "we need seventy percent more food using less water, less energy, and fewer chemicals. Traditional agriculture can't scale."

He clicked to a cutaway of a controlled-environment facility. Our platform offers two options for growers. FarmCore manages the control software, including lights, HVAC, irrigation, and all the SCADA functions that execute growing strategies. Alternatively, growers can use FarmCore standalone with local recipes or subscribe to FarmLytics for cloud-based optimization and continuous improvement. FarmLytics captures data from every crop and runs machine-learning models to generate optimized recipes.

A skeptical voice broke in: "Energy costs?"

Knox smiled. "LED arrays with spectrum optimization. Red for flowering, blue for vegetative growth, far-red for elongation. Plants don't need the whole sun,just the wavelengths that matter. We cut energy costs by more than half."

He tapped the clicker. In a time-lapse on the screen, lettuce grew from seed to harvest in eighteen days. "The system learns from every plant. Nutrient uptake, growth rate, leaf color—it all flows into FarmLytics, which analyzes patterns and pushes optimized recipes back to FarmCore. FarmLytics links everything together, allowing the whole network to benefit from the knowledge acquired by a single facility. A breakthrough in Detroit is shared instantly with Denver, Dallas, and Durham."

Margaret Chen, a venture capitalist at the far end of the table, leaned forward. "Urban food deserts?"

Knox's expression sharpened. "Vacant warehouses can become farms. Detroit, Flint, Grand Rapids; neighborhoods that haven't seen fresh produce in decades. One facility feeds fifteen thousand families. Harvest to table in under twenty-four hours."

At the back of the room, Tate—twenty-five and wearing his first real suit—watched his father command the floor with technical mastery and moral conviction. This wasn't just engineering; it was a mission.

An older investor asked, "What keeps agribusiness from copying you?"

Knox clicked to a slide showing an exponential curve. "They can buy lights and pumps. What they can't buy is time. Every day, FarmLytics gathers more data and refines the optimization engine. That network effect is the moat. A competitor starting now is already years behind. We're not just automating farms—we're building collective intelligence."

As the meeting wrapped, Tate asked quietly, "You really think this will work?"

Knox looked out at Detroit's skyline. "Son, this isn't about money. It's about changing how humanity feeds itself. FarmCore and FarmLytics serve as tools. The goal is better food with less. Technology serving people at its finest."

OPERATION HARVEST CLOUD

Launch—Shanghai - Six Weeks Before Geneva

Liu Wei's hand hovered over the keyboard. Fifteen years of preparation, and everything depended on timing. Not just launching the attack, but launching it at precisely the right moment so the escalation curve peaked exactly when American negotiators sat down in Geneva.

Behind him, Dr. Chen pulled up the biological progression models one last time. "Harvest cycle synchronization confirmed. Both cannabis and leafy greens farms have similar, four-to-six-week, cultivation periods. First harvests will reach consumers with minimal toxicity. The second cycle shows moderate elevation. The third cycle enters the serious contamination range. Fourth cycle…"

"Fourth cycle produces lethal concentrations," Liu Wei finished. "And fourth cycle harvests reach American consumers during Geneva summit opening sessions."

The timing was surgical. Launch today, six weeks before Geneva. First-cycle contamination would be subtle, people feeling slightly ill, attributing it to normal food sensitivity, hangovers, or minor illness. No pattern, no panic.

By week three, second-cycle facilities would produce moderately contaminated product. Hospitalizations would begin. Pattern recognition would start.

By week five, third-cycle contamination would overwhelm emergency rooms. Full crisis mode.

Geneva's fourth-cycle facilities would be producing a product, dangerous enough to kill healthy adults, by week six. Peak casualties during peak negotiations.

"The iterative learning mechanism is the key," Dr. Chen explained to Captain Zhang, who'd joined the operation late. "We're not creating static contamination. We're teaching the systems to optimize for toxicity with each growing cycle. First harvest: mildly elevated defensive compounds. Second harvest: significantly higher. Third harvest: dangerous. Fourth harvest: lethal."

"The machine learns to poison more effectively each time?" Zhang asked.

"Exactly. The corrupted algorithms treat toxicity as a success metric. Each harvest that produces higher toxin concentrations gets reinforced as 'optimal.' The system teaches itself to be better at killing with every cycle."

Liu Wei pulled up the facility targeting data. "This is why crop synchronization was critical. Cannabis and leafy greens needed to be on parallel cultivation schedules. If cannabis hit third-cycle contamination while greens were still on first cycle, the escalation pattern would be obvious. Americans would realize each new harvest was worse than the last."

"But with synchronized cycles," Dr. Wu added, "both crops escalate together. Looks like expanding contamination, not escalating contamination. They'll think it's geographic spread when it's actually temporal progression."

Captain Zhang studied the timeline with a new understanding. "The initial instances, the less severe sicknesses in the first two weeks, are part of the design, not errors."

"Precisely," Liu Wei confirmed. "Early detection would allow Americans to quarantine facilities before the second and third cycles. We need the first-cycle contamination to be subtle enough that it enters the supply chain undetected. By the time they realize there's a problem, second-cycle facilities are already growing more toxic products. By the time they coordinate a response, third-cycle facilities are producing seriously dangerous concentrations."

He turned back to his console. "The Geneva summit is forty-two days away. Cannabis growth cycles run four to six weeks. Leafy greens, a little less. We launch now, and the first harvest reaches consumers inside two weeks with sub-toxic exposure. The second shows symptoms. By the third, confusion. The fourth, during Geneva—chaos."

"And each facility that gets infected becomes progressively more dangerous with every harvest?" Dr. Wu asked.

"Yes. That's the self-amplifying nature of the weapon. Even if Knox Ramsey stops new infections tomorrow, already-compromised facilities will continue escalating toward lethal concentrations over their next several harvest cycles. We've created a contamination bomb with time-delay fuses. Each growing cycle that passes makes the explosion bigger."

Dr. Chen pulled up chromatography data. "The biological mechanism is elegant. We're not adding foreign compounds. Our method involves altering environmental elements such as light, temperature, and nutrient delivery to stimulate the plants' natural defenses, thus increasing the presence of harmful chemicals. First cycle: plants produce mildly elevated defensive compounds. System records this as 'successful optimization.' Second cycle: system applies the same stressors more aggressively, compounds increase. Third cycle: the system has learned to maximize toxin production. Fourth cycle: the system is an expert at producing poison."

"Machine learning applied to biological warfare," Captain Zhang said with something like admiration.

"Applied to agricultural optimization that becomes biological warfare," Liu Wei corrected. Americans designed these systems to learn how to grow better crops. We taught them to learn how to grow poisonous crops. The learning mechanism is legitimate—we just corrupted the success metrics."

He checked the countdown timer. Forty-two days until Geneva. Six weeks of carefully calculated escalation. The launch's timing was crucial; an early start would mean the peak of casualties before the summit, which would allow the Americans to regroup. Launch too late and third-cycle contamination wouldn't manifest until after negotiations concluded.

Fifteen years of preparation had come down to this: identifying facilities with synchronized cultivation cycles, calculating backwards from the Geneva date, launching at precisely the right moment for maximum diplomatic leverage.

"Final authorization codes," Liu Wei said.

Captain Zhang read the sequence aloud. Dr. Wu verified encryption. Dr. Chen reconfirmed the biological progression models: the first cycle was mild, the second moderate, the third serious, and the fourth lethal, with each cycle designed to peak in Geneva.

Liu Wei typed the command.

Eight months of synthetic training data began propagating through FarmLytics' network. The corrupted optimization algorithms spread silently through American agricultural facilities, teaching systems to produce toxins with increasing efficiency over each subsequent harvest cycle.

First-cycle contamination would be too subtle to detect. That was the design.

By the time Americans realized the problem, second and third cycles would already be growing. Each harvest is more toxic than the last. Each facility teaches itself to be better at poisoning with every growing season.

And in forty-two days, when American negotiators sat down in Geneva to discuss agricultural security, their own citizens would be consuming fourth-cycle product toxic enough to cause organ failure.

The timing was everything. Liu Wei had calculated it perfectly.

"Operation Harvest Cloud is active," he said quietly. "Iterative escalation initiated. Geneva countdown: forty-two days."

Dr. Chen stared at his biological models, watching the projected toxicity curves rise with each simulated harvest cycle. "They won't realize each harvest is worse until it's too late to stop the progression."

"By then," Liu Wei said, "Geneva will be concluded. And Americans will understand that their automated food systems can be weaponized with a click of a button. From seven thousand miles away. With casualties that escalate over time, even after the initial attack is discovered."

The screens pulsed green. The learning began. The countdown started.

Forty-two days until the weapon reached full maturity at precisely the moment it would cause maximum diplomatic damage.

Timing was everything.

And Liu Wei's timing was perfect.

PART ONE
OUTBREAK

G -42 → −31

Every signal starts as faith.

Every failure begins as design.

1 SHANGHAI—G –42

Liu kept his posture tight; tonight, there were no polite gatekeepers, only outcomes and the systems that enabled them. But he had learned their systems from the inside. Every security protocol, every trust relationship, every lazy assumption about American technological superiority. Now, fifteen years later, that knowledge was coming home to serve a different master.

Liu accessed the infiltration status on his tablet. Tonight's mission would prove that American agricultural automation—the nation's vaunted emblem of global stewardship through technology—could be weaponized against its own citizens. The irony was a calculated masterpiece.

At a side console, Dr. Wu could barely contain himself. His eyes danced as packet traces scrolled by, each confirmation of entry bringing him closer to the moment his toxic metabolic recipe would run live.

"We've tuned the stress-cycle algorithms for cannabinoid pathways," Chen said, voice eager.

"Once the profiles update, their own extraction labs will weaponize the compounds for us. This is more elegant than any traditional contaminant—it looks like *nature* did it."

Captain Zhang, older, more deliberate, did not share his thrill.

"Your eagerness is dangerous. Attribution is what matters. If the outbreak can be tied to us before the summit—"

Chen bristled.

"Then history will still record who proved it possible. Do you think the Americans hesitate when they poison fields with sanctions?"

"Enough," Liu cut in, a small, sharp smile tugging at the corner of his mouth.

"That is your department, Captain. My work ensures they will never see fingerprints. FarmCore will deliver the recipe, but it will look like the system taught itself the flaw."

Zhang's jaw tightened. He said nothing further, though the crease in his brow deepened.

Liu Wei shifted to a secondary screen, where FarmCore's architecture unfolded in clean layers of code and diagrams. It wasn't complexity that made it dangerous—it was trust.

Americans had designed the system to assume goodwill: every update signed, every profile validated, every algorithm treated as progress.

That naïveté was the opening.

"Show me the pathway corruption," Liu said.

Dr. Chen's workstation came alive with molecular diagrams, bright as stained glass in motion.

Benzene rings spun, bonds stretched and reformed, pathways lit in pulses of red and green.

"These aren't foreign compounds," Chen explained, fingers flicking across the keys.

"Phenolic compounds, defensive terpenes, stress-induced alkaloids. We're not adding foreign substances. We're persuading the plant to express what it already knows how to make—just at concentrations nature never intended."

On the chromatography display, peaks rose like jagged mountains. "Tetrahydrocannabinolic acid synthesis up three-hundred-forty percent under stress cycling. Terpenes diverted toward analogs stable through extraction. Consumers will never taste the difference."

"And detection?"

"That's the beauty," Chen said, almost gleeful.

"Cannabis labs don't screen for natural compounds in toxic concentrations. Regulation becomes camouflage."

Captain Zhang shifted at his post, the only one in the room who didn't share Chen's satisfaction. His voice cut low.

"Elegant, yes. But fragile. If a single toxicology lab broadens its panels—"

"They won't," Chen snapped.

"Even their compliance culture works in our favor. They cling to checklists."

Liu held up a hand, silencing them both.

"No fingerprints. That is the mission." His tone left no room for debate.

For a moment, the hum of servers filled the silence. Green lights blinked across dashboards, each one a grow facility across the American Midwest, unknowingly preparing to become a test site.

The server room fogged slightly now, condensate on the glass, mirroring Liu's steady breathing.

Zhang exhaled through his nose, still unconvinced.

"It is not just plants you corrupt," he said quietly.

"It is responsibility. When their engineer sees this, he will blame himself."

Liu's mouth curved at the edge. That was the point.

He thought of Randall. Innovation without ethics... Ethics made you a foreigner everywhere.

Dr. Wu triggered the primary launch scripts.

On the wall-sized dashboard, a new vector lit up—Detroit. The map pulsed, small towns flaring in sequence, green shifting to yellow as infected clusters activated.

A single chime sounded—a digital bell passed from server to server.

The room stilled to listen.

"Propagation confirmed," Wu announced, breath caught halfway to pride.

"Baseline protocol cloaked within standard update. Rollout tiers triggered by timestamp."

A junior analyst worked the LIDAR feeds.

"Test libraries in Grand Rapids, Lansing, and Ann Arbor are streaming update acceptance. No flagged packets, no malware signatures. We are invisible."

Liu gave a tight nod.

"Confirm diversion architecture. Once FarmCore's redundancy starts replicating, American countermeasures will target the wrong threat."

The secondary dashboard flickered as backdoor packets autorouted away from high-scrutiny nodes. Their digital footprints vanished into protocol noise.

Liu checked consumption logs—nutrient levels across five states.

"Let's pivot stress targets by .5 and double back through the legacy API. We'll let their own system optimize us a second time."

Chen nodded—impressed for once, silent.

Zhang's tone was low, grave. "We will remain for monitoring. Do not touch any secondary clusters without explicit review. We operate under absolute deniability."

"Understood," Liu replied.

"American asset monitoring is continuous. If they wake up before phase two is mapped, we abort."

"Acknowledged," Wu said, logging the protocol. His hands trembled.

The entire room watched the dashboard. The cold blue glow reflected in every eye, the silence uneasy and reverent.

On the master control, the American Midwest pulsed with new data. Each node—unknown to its operators—now carried a legacy signature, one planted months earlier by a different team exploiting a holiday-weekend credential gap.

Redundancy sampling now hid the true point of breach.

Liu Wei closed his eyes, recalling for the first time in years Professor Randall's voice—"Every system is only as honest as the hand that builds it." He suppressed the thought. Tonight, it was just systems and outcomes.

Wu exhaled hard. "No errors. Update confirmed complete. We are out."

No one, not even Chen, cheered.

The operation floor's low lights transitioned to blue. A single ping—an email, innocuous in its header—landed in a Detroit hospital's admin inbox. Their war had begun.

Liu lingered, watching the board cycle through its final diagnostics. He ran a hand along the console, the brushed metal warm beneath his fingertips.

The whole room felt fragile and distant—something carefully calibrated, not quite real.

His breath left a brief mist on glass, gone before anyone else could see it.

"Tonight, the Americans learn to fear crops. Tomorrow—" he let it trail off, not needing to say what everyone in the room already knew.

He walked out past the checkpoint, the hum of the power plant operations floor fading behind him. Shanghai's night waited beyond the bunker, bright and sleepless.

As Liu stepped into the blinking neon, he let the pressure between triumph and accountability settle, felt the city's heart keep time with his own.

～

Liu Wei pulled up a parallel workspace, isolating the infiltration architecture from the biological payload. What Chen had designed was elegant, but useless without the delivery mechanism. That was Liu's domain.

"Show me certificate validation," he said.

A junior engineer brought up FarmCore's trust model—the digital signature chain that authenticated every profile update. Knox Ramsey had built it like a fortress: hardware security modules, two-factor authentication, cryptographic hashing that would take centuries to brute-force.

Liu had bypassed it in eighteen months.

"Explain the exploit," Captain Zhang said, moving closer. He understood biology and strategy, but the technical architecture was Liu's language.

Liu traced the attack surface with one finger against the display. "Ramsey's system assumes three things: that his signing keys are secure, that his certificate authority is trustworthy, and that FarmCore installations validate authenticity before execution. All three assumptions were correct—until we made them irrelevant."

He zoomed into the certificate chain. "We didn't steal Ramsey's keys. We didn't need to. We compromised the intermediate certificate authority—a vendor Knox contracted for automated renewal services. Holiday weekend, skeleton security staff, credential gap exactly where our reconnaissance predicted."

"That gave you signing authority?" Zhang asked.

"Better. It gave us the ability to issue certificates that FarmCore installations would trust as if Knox himself had signed them. His hardware token is still secure. His protocols are still intact. But the trust model now includes us as a legitimate authority."

Chen leaned in, interested despite himself. "So when FarmCore receives an update..."

"It validates the signature against the certificate chain, sees legitimate credentials, and executes without question. Knox built a system that trusts properly signed instructions. We became a trusted signer."

Liu pulled up packet traces from the initial infiltration. "The real elegance is in the layering. We don't send obvious malware. We send optimization parameters that fall within normal operational ranges—just biased toward outcomes Chen's biology exploits. FarmCore's anomaly detection sees gradual tuning, not attack patterns."

He advanced through the timeline. "First layer: legitimate-looking A/B testing across facilities. Some get parameter set Alpha, some get Beta. Both within acceptable ranges, both signed with trusted certificates. FarmCore installations execute them as routine optimization experiments."

"Which they are," Chen added. "Just optimizing toward toxicity instead of yield."

"Second layer," Liu continued, "is the learning loop exploitation. FarmLytics monitors results from FarmCore installations and adjusts its recommendations. We poisoned that feedback loop six months ago—feeding synthetic training data that made FarmLytics believe higher stress conditions produced better outcomes. Now Ramsey's own AI is recommending parameters that align with our biological attack, thinking it's discovering efficiency improvements."

Zhang's expression darkened. "You turned his intelligence against him."

"We turned his trust against him," Liu corrected. "Knox built a system designed to learn and improve. We taught it to prefer outcomes that happen to be toxic. When investigators examine FarmLytics, they'll find optimization logic that appears sound. When they examine FarmCore installations, they'll find legitimate certificates and normal operational parameters. The poison lives in the combination—visible only when you understand both the biology and the code architecture."

He pulled up a network diagram showing FarmCore's distributed infrastructure. "Third layer is attribution misdirection. The compromised certificate authority? Shell company, five layers deep, routing through proxies in Romania, Brazil, and Malaysia before touching anything in China. The synthetic training data? Injected through academic research partnerships that look like legitimate agricultural science collaboration. The parameter modifications? Distributed across hundreds of facilities over eighteen months, each change small enough to appear as routine tuning."

"No single smoking gun," Zhang said, understanding dawning.

"No single anything," Liu agreed. "We've built an attack that's distributed across time, geography, and technical layers. American investigators will find compromised certificates and blame the vendor. They'll find poisoned training data and blame the academic partners. They'll find FarmCore installations executing toxic parameters and blame Knox's signing authority. Each thread leads somewhere; none lead here."

Dr. Wu, quiet until now, spoke up. "But the infrastructure still points to FarmCore. AgriTech owns that now."

"Which makes it China's problem only if they can prove AgriTech was intelligence-controlled at time of compromise," Liu said. "The certificate authority breach happened six months before AgriTech acquired FarmCore from Knox. Treasury approved that sale. FBI vetted the buyers. Every American agency involved validated the transaction as legitimate. Now those same agencies will struggle to explain how they let a Chinese intelligence front purchase critical agricultural infrastructure—especially when we can produce documentation showing the vulnerabilities existed before the acquisition."

Captain Zhang studied the network diagram, following the attack paths. "You've built plausible deniability into the technical architecture itself."

"I've built what Knox should have built," Liu said quietly. "Defense in depth. Assume breach. Verify trust. He built a system that assumed good actors and trusted digital signatures. I built an attack that exploits exactly those assumptions."

He closed the technical displays and brought up a simple graphic: FarmCore's logo, Knox's signature, and a certificate chain that looked legitimate because it was.

"Knox is brilliant," Liu said. "His architecture is sound. His security protocols are professional. His intentions were admirable—feed people, democratize agriculture, use technology for good. But he made the same mistake all American engineers make."

"Which is?" Zhang asked.

"He built for the world he wanted, not the world that exists. He assumed his system would only be used by people who shared his values. He trusted that certificates meant authorization, that signatures meant authenticity, that optimization meant improvement." Liu's expression hardened. "We taught him that trust is a vulnerability. That every system is only as secure as the human assumptions built into it. That good intentions don't survive contact with adversaries who understand your code better than you do."

The room fell silent except for the hum of servers processing the attack's propagation.

Chen finally broke it. "You sound like you respect him."

"I do," Liu said. "Knox Ramsey is everything American engineering claims to be—innovative, idealistic, technically brilliant. That's what makes this so effective. We're not attacking his mistakes. We're attacking his virtues. His trust. His openness. His belief that technology serves humanity." He looked at the screen showing FarmCore installations blinking green across America's heartland. "By the time he understands what we've done, the plants will be in consumer hands and his signature will be on the certificates that authenticated the poison."

"He'll blame himself," Zhang said.

"He should," Liu replied. "Not for the attack—that's our responsibility. But for building a system that assumed the best in people. In warfare, that's not idealism. It's negligence."

⁓

Below, engineers executed the sequence. The corrupted telemetry streamed from compromised FarmCore installations into FarmLytics—Knox Ramsey's old optimization engine, now turned against itself. The AI didn't know the data was poisoned. It simply obeyed design: measure, adjust, improve. Sensors reported light, temperature, humidity, nutrient flow—truthful numbers hiding lethal intent. Each parameter drifted by increments too subtle for a grower to notice, yet devastating in combination.

"Neural-network poisoning at its finest," murmured a junior technician as the propagation map pulsed red across America's agricultural heartland. "The model learns to prize toxicity while reporting efficiency."

Chen leaned toward the display. "They'll thank the algorithm for higher yields—right up until it kills their customers."

Liu Wei's voice was almost tender. "The elegance is that no one will believe the plants themselves can murder."

Code spread silently, a digital contagion wearing the mask of optimization. No malware signatures. No intrusion alarms. Only efficiency—precise, obedient, fatal. Each update package appeared routine: shift blue-spectrum peak from 460 to 430 nanometers, raise nitrogen uptake during week six of flowering, modulate temperature cycling to simulate seasonal stress. Individually, the changes improved vigor. Together, they initiated a metabolic cascade designed to concentrate toxins in the final extraction phase.

Chen watched the metrics align, expression flat with pride. "It's art," he said. "A living system trained to betray itself."

～

DR. CHEN'S fingers moved across his workstation with the precision of a surgeon, but instead of scalpels, he wielded machine learning frameworks that could reshape digital minds. On his primary monitor, a three-dimensional visualization of FarmLytic's neural network architecture rotated slowly—thousands of nodes connected by weighted pathways, each representing learned associations between environmental inputs and optimization outcomes.

"The beauty of adversarial training," Chen murmured to Liu Wei, highlighting specific neural pathways in red, "is that we don't destroy the original model. We simply teach it new priorities."

"Show me the metabolic pathway targeting again," Liu requested, moving closer to Chen's workstation.

Chen pulled up a biochemical diagram that looked like abstract art—molecular structures dancing across the screen in elegant curves. He clicked through a series of chromatography readouts, each showing the chemical signature of different growing conditions. "But under specific environmental stressors—blue-enriched lighting at 420-430 nanometers, combined with nitrogen restriction during weeks 4-6 of flowering, plus temperature fluctuations that mimic seasonal stress—the plants dramatically increase production of these compounds."

"And the concentrations become toxic?" Liu asked.

"More than toxic. They become weapons." Chen's academic enthusiasm was barely contained. "The compounds mimic normal cannabinoids closely enough to pass chromatography—similar molecular weight, similar structure. But the receptor binding is altered. They fit the lock, then break inside it."

Liu nodded appreciatively. "So the regulatory system becomes our camouflage."

"Exactly. We're not introducing foreign substances that would trigger detection. We're simply encouraging the plant's natural biochemistry to express itself more... enthusiastically."

LIU WEI HAD EXPLAINED the strategic architecture—the compromised certificates, the trust model exploitation, the multi-layered attribution defense. Now Chen walked him through the operational implementation, the exact mechanisms that would turn theory into execution.

"Let me show you the injection point," Chen said, pulling up a real-time network diagram showing FarmCore's update distribution system. Red lines traced the path from Knox's signing server through content delivery networks to thousands of facilities across North America.

He zoomed into a specific node. "Here. The CDN edge cache in Chicago. Farm-Core's update mechanism pulls profiles from this distribution point every six hours—0200, 0800, 1400, 2000 UTC. The system validates the package signature client-side after download, which gives us a 47-millisecond window between cache retrieval and certificate verification."

"Forty-seven milliseconds," Liu repeated. "That's your insertion window?"

"More than enough." Chen's fingers flew across the keyboard, pulling up packet traces from their test runs. "We intercept the update package in-memory as it's being served from the CDN cache. The original profile—Knox's legitimate optimization parameters—gets modified on-the-fly —blue spectrum adjustment from 2.1% to 2.3%. Nitrogen uptake timing shifted three days earlier. Temperature cycling amplitude increased by 0.4 degrees Celsius."

He highlighted the modifications in the hex dump. "Individually, each change looks like normal algorithmic tuning. The kind of micro-adjustments FarmLytics makes constantly. Nothing triggers anomaly detection because we're operating within the standard deviation of normal optimization behavior."

"And the re-signing?"

Chen switched to a different terminal. "We use the cloned certificate in real-time. The modified profile gets re-signed with credentials that FarmCore installations trust as legitimate Knox Ramsey authority. The signature timestamp matches the original within 2 seconds—well within the system's clock-drift tolerance. The cryptographic hash validates perfectly because we're using legitimate keys from the compromised certificate authority."

Liu studied the timing diagram. "The client never knows it received a modified package."

"Correct. From FarmCore's perspective, it downloaded a routine update from the official CDN, validated it against a trusted certificate, and executed it during a standard maintenance window. Every security check passes because we're not breaking the security model—we're operating within it using stolen credentials."

Chen pulled up deployment statistics. "We match FarmCore's normal update patterns exactly. Same bandwidth throttling—profiles distribute at 2.3 megabits per second to avoid network congestion alerts. Same retry logic—if a facility is offline during the update window, the modified profile gets queued and delivered during the next cycle. Same error handling—if signature validation somehow fails, the system rolls back to the previous known-good configuration."

"You've replicated Knox's deployment architecture."

"Better than replicated—we've become indistinguishable from it. The target systems see routine optimization updates distributed through the same infrastructure they've trusted for years. The only difference is the parameter values themselves, and those differences are small enough to look like normal algorithmic evolution."

Liu examined the network flows. "How do you handle facilities with local security monitoring?"

"Air-gap simulation," Chen said, pulling up another diagram. "About twelve percent of FarmCore installations run additional intrusion detection systems—firewalls that log unusual traffic patterns, packet inspectors that flag unexpected data structures. We defeat them by being boring."

He highlighted the traffic patterns. "Our injection packets match the baseline profile exactly. Same packet size distribution. Same TCP window scaling. Same TLS hand-shake timing. We even match the inter-packet delays—the natural jitter that comes from Knox's signing server being under variable load. To a packet inspector, our malicious update looks identical to the thousands of legitimate updates that preceded it."

"Invisibility through conformity," Liu said.

"Exactly. The most sophisticated camouflage is perfect mediocrity." Chen's smile was sharp. "Knox built a system that assumes properly signed updates are safe. His security model stops at certificate validation. Once our package passes that check, FarmCore executes it without question. No behavioral analysis. No parameter range validation. No comparison against historical optimization patterns. Just trust the signature and execute."

Liu thought about Knox's senate testimony he'd watched via intercept—the engineer defending his architecture, explaining his security protocols, insisting he'd built responsible systems. "He never imagined someone would compromise the trust infrastructure itself."

"He couldn't imagine it," Chen corrected. "American engineers build for efficiency and scale. They assume hostile actors will attack from the outside—brute-force attempts, zero-day exploits, obvious intrusion attempts. They don't prepare for attackers who understand their systems well enough to operate from the inside, using legitimate credentials, moving at the speed of normal operations."

He gestured at the network diagram, at the thousands of red lines flowing into Farm-

Core installations across America's heartland. "This isn't hacking. This is systems administration. We're not breaking in—we're logging in with valid credentials and performing routine maintenance that happens to steer crops toward toxicity. Knox designed Farm-Core to trust administrators. We became administrators. Now his system trusts us."

Liu pulled up the deployment schedule. "Phase Two facilities?"

Chen highlighted new targets on the map—vertical farms in Chicago, hydroponic operations in Arizona, greenhouse complexes in California. "Same methodology. Same injection points. Same 47-millisecond windows. We've already mapped their CDN routes and update patterns. When Beijing authorizes Phase Two, we can have modified profiles deployed to two hundred additional facilities within six hours."

"Detection risk?"

"Minimal. Each facility thinks it's receiving unique optimization parameters tailored to its specific conditions. They're designed not to compare notes. That's actually Knox's design philosophy—decentralized optimization that adapts to local conditions. We're exploiting his feature as a vulnerability. By the time anyone realizes multiple facilities are experiencing similar issues, the contaminated crops will already be in the supply chain."

Liu studied the architecture with professional appreciation. This wasn't crude malware or apparent sabotage. This was surgical exploitation of trust relationships, timing windows, and human assumptions about digital signatures meaning authorization.

"How long can we maintain this access?"

Chen pulled up timeline projections. "Until Knox or his team realizes the certificate authority was compromised and revokes the intermediate certificates. But even then, we've built in redundancy. We have three separate certificate chains from different compromised authorities. If one gets burned, we rotate to another. And we've planted enough synthetic training data in FarmLytics that even if they lock us out of FarmCore, Knox's own AI will continue recommending parameters that trend toward our biological targets."

"You've built persistence into the learning model itself."

"The attack doesn't end when we lose access," Chen confirmed. "It ends when they retrain FarmLytics from scratch with clean data and rebuild their entire certificate infrastructure from the ground up. That's months of work. Maybe years, if they want to do it without disrupting operations. Each day FarmLytics learns from tainted data, its recommendations drift closer to our biological targets—without anyone touching the system again.

Liu closed the technical displays and looked at Chen with something approaching respect. The junior engineer had built not just an attack, but a self-perpetuating system that would outlive their direct access. Knox's own creation would continue to betray him long after the initial compromise was discovered and locked down.

"Show me Phase Two targeting," Liu said.

Chen pulled up the next set of facilities: leafy greens, tomatoes, strawberries. Dietary staples instead of recreational products. "Same technical infrastructure, different biological vectors." Chen highlighted the new targets. "Lettuce under nitrogen stress concentrates nitrates to kidney-injury levels. Nightshades express solanine when temperature-cycled—neurotoxic at the concentrations we're targeting. Berries produce phenolic compounds that mimic organophosphate signatures."

"When Beijing gives authorization—"

"We'll be ready," Chen finished. "Forty-seven milliseconds at a time, we'll teach American agriculture to poison itself. And their own security systems will authenticate every modification with Knox Ramsey's trusted signature."

THE SECURE LINE on the ops floor snapped alive. A voice from Beijing, clipped and bureaucratic, filled the room with authority.

"Central Committee requires visible outcomes before the agricultural negotiations. The Americans must doubt their own food security while lecturing us about trade. You will demonstrate capability. Do not fail."

The line went dead.

Zhang exhaled, grim. The agricultural summit was three weeks away, a high-stakes negotiation over trade access and technology transfer. China needed leverage, something to remind the Americans that their prosperity depended on systems that could be fragile.

Chen's grin faltered, but only for a moment. "Pressure creates diamonds," he said, though his voice carried less confidence than before.

Liu, however, felt only vindication. Beijing was watching. The summit would succeed. And tonight, they had planted the first seeds of collapse.

"Captain Zhang," Liu said quietly, "activate Asset Seven. I want eyes on the engineer."

2 KNOX'S FALL

The irony wasn't lost on him. Knox Ramsey, who once commanded rooms full of venture capitalists, now counted quarters in a mason jar. Five years ago, Farm-Lytics was the future; precision agriculture meets artificial intelligence, transforming greenhouses into orchestras where every note was calculated for maximum harmony.

He'd started the company with two grad students and a $50,000 SBA loan, working out of a converted garage in Kentwood. The vision was simple: use machine learning to optimize indoor growing conditions, turning farming from art into science. Traditional growers relied on intuition and decades of experience. Knox wanted to replace intuition with algorithms.

The early demos were magical. They created experimental sensors capable of tracking all aspects, including soil acidity, nutrient absorption, leaf temperature, and even the subtle vibrations plants emit when stressed. Feed that data into a machine-learning system, and it could predict optimal conditions with startling accuracy.

"Plants are just biological machines," Knox would tell investors, pulling up slides that showed yield increases of 30%, 40%, sometimes 50% compared to traditional methods.

"We're teaching computers to speak their language."

The money had come fast—Series A, Series B, partnerships with major agricultural companies. Knox hired the best engineers, built state-of-the-art facilities, and filed patents that would be valuable for decades. For three years, FarmCore was the poster child for Michigan's tech renaissance, proof the Rust Belt could innovate beyond steel and cars.

But Knox had made a classic founder's mistake: he'd fallen in love with the technology and forgotten the business.

While he was perfecting algorithms, competitors were signing distribution deals.

While he was publishing papers in peer-reviewed journals, startups with inferior products were capturing market share through marketing and price cuts.

The end came suddenly. A major customer defected to a cheaper competitor. A key engineer left for Google, taking critical algorithms despite unenforceable non-competes. A promising partnership collapsed when an agricultural giant decided to build its own solution.

When the deal closed, AgriTech bought FarmCore, the SCADA control software, tenants, and brand. Knox kept FarmLytics, the cloud-based data lake and machine learning engine and its signing pipeline—and a contractually limited read-only telemetry mirror for model validation. It wasn't as visible as owning the platform, but it preserved his core IP.

"Should have listened to you," he'd told Lisa the night after the papers were signed. They were sitting in their kitchen, boxes stacked, preparing for the move to the townhouse.

"About what?" she asked, though she already knew.

"About the business side. About not trusting everyone to be as honest as me."

Lisa had squeezed his hand. "You built something beautiful, Knox. That matters."

But sitting in the townhouse kitchen now, watching bills pile up while the platform he'd sold earned millions for someone else, Knox wondered if beauty was enough.

KALAMAZOO — THE DEUCE (SUNDAY AFTERNOON)

Knox hadn't planned on stopping in Kalamazoo, but it was Sunday and the Lions were on, and 131 South traffic gave him time to think about how thinking wasn't helping. The contract folder sat on the passenger seat like a passenger that wouldn't shut up. When the Bell's Brewery exit appeared, he passed it; tourists didn't need him, but The Deuce was only three miles further, and The Deuce had his mug.

The parking lot had the same potholes it'd had five years ago, craters that Michigan's two seasons—winter and construction—refused to fix. Knox parked next to a rusted Silverado that looked like it had survived both. The December cold hit him when he stepped out, the kind of wet cold that got into your joints and reminded you that Lake Michigan was close enough to make weather personal.

The door opened with its familiar creak. The smell hit him before his eyes adjusted —fryer oil, old wood, and the ghost of ten thousand beers. Above the bar, the TV showed the Lions down by seven, first quarter winding down. The jukebox in the corner was playing "Sweet Home Alabama"; the bar classic rotation hadn't changed, even if everything else had. His seat was empty. Third from the left, his name carved into the wooden rail back when WMU had given him lab space and he'd needed a place to think that wasn't the townhouse or Lisa's disappointed silences.

"Knox!" Donna's voice cut through Skynyrd and game commentary. She was behind the bar, grayer than he remembered but moving with the same efficiency. "Where ya been?"

"Around," Knox said, settling onto his seat. The wood was worn smooth where his elbows had lived. "Busy."

"Busy's what people say when they don't want to say broke," Jimmy muttered from two stools down, eyes on the screen.

Knox grinned. "Broke's what people say when they don't want to say scared."

Donna set his mug down with PBR already foaming over the rim the way she knew he liked it. "Draft's getting hard to find. I keep it for you idiots who still think it's 1987."

Public service," Knox said, lifting the mug.

The jukebox switched tracks to "Red Solo Cup" now, someone's five quarters keeping the classics alive. Knox remembered when it used to be "Sweet Caroline" and "Blister in the Sun" on repeat, back when Tate would meet him here after lab sessions, when barley and hops were their bridge language.

"Campbell's got 'em playing with grit," Pete said, gesturing at the screen with his beer. Still in his Bronson Hospital scrubs. "Finally found our Lombardi."

Haven't won the big one yet," Knox pointed out.

Jimmy, a lifelong Lions sports fan, delivered the phrase "Never a doubt" with a unique blend of irony and equal parts hope and self-mockery.

Maria snorted from her usual spot. "You said the same thing about Matt Millen."

"That was different," Jimmy protested. "Campbell's different. You can see it."

Knox had heard this conversation before. Different coach, same faith. The fair-weather fans had suddenly become lifelong believers, claiming they'd never doubted, conveniently forgetting decades of Thanksgiving disasters and playoff heartbreak.

Despite Knox's skepticism, Campbell's actions had altered the state in a way that seemed distinct.

Pete turned from the game. "You in for second quarter squares?"

Knox pulled out his wallet. "Two fives."

"Big spender," Maria said.

The first quarter ended. Lions still down, but fighting. The regulars shifted focus from the screen to Knox, the way they always did during commercials rotating attention like a lazy carousel.

"How's Tate's grow doing?" Pete asked. "Still using your fancy computer stuff?"

Knox felt the question land differently than Pete meant it. "Yeah. He's doing good. Real good, actually."

"He was in here a few months back," Donna said, wiping down the rail. "Told us about some festival thing. Detroit. Said business was solid."

Knox remembered those days—Tate visiting him at the WMU lab, the two of them hunched over barely pops and nutrient charts, finding common language in plants and beer and the biology that connected them. Tate could translate what Knox's machine learning models were trying to say into something a grower could actually use. Pop, Tate would call him during those sessions, the old-fashioned name that somehow made the technical work feel human.

"He called you Pop," Jimmy said, grinning at the memory. "Nobody calls their dad Pop anymore."

"He's old-fashioned," Knox said, though the word landed heavier than he wanted. Those lab sessions felt like another lifetime. Before the divorce. Before the sale. Before Tate stopped needing his help and started building something bigger than both of them.

The good times.

Second quarter started. The Lions—impossibly, inexplicably—found their rhythm. Found their grit. Campbell's grit, the broadcasters kept saying, like repetition could make it more real. The kind of turnaround that made Michigan fans believe for exactly one quarter before reality reasserted itself. Except this time, maybe, it stuck. The defense stiffened. The offense pushed down the field with purpose Knox recognized from his own best engineering runs—momentum that felt earned, not lucky.

Knox stayed through halftime because leaving felt like admitting Chicago was waiting, and Chicago could wait a little longer.

The jukebox kept cycling through its rotation, bar classics punctuating the game commentary like a soundtrack Knox had memorized without trying.

When the Lions somehow held their lead going into the half, Jimmy won the second quarter squares. He bought a round, celebrating like the Lions had already won the Super Bowl instead of just one half of a December game.

"Never a doubt!" Pete called out, the phrase rippling through the bar like a benediction and a joke at once.

Knox sipped his second beer at a more leisurely pace than the first, giving Donna's chicken parmigiana—their signature dish, the reason people came from miles around, even Battle Creek—time to sit comfortably in his stomach.

"You eating or just drinking?" Donna had asked when she brought the plate.

"Both," Knox said. "Definitely both."

He was one of them, even though he wasn't. They knew it. He knew it. It didn't matter here. The Deuce didn't care if you were an engineer or a janitor, if you had patents or paychecks or neither. You showed up, you drank your beer, you paid your tab. That was the contract that mattered.

Halftime ended. The Lions took the field for the third, still clinging to their improbable lead. Knox stood, dropped two twenties on the bar.

"Stay for the second half," Pete said. "They might actually win this one."

"They won't," Knox said, because he was from Michigan and knew better. But he said it with less certainty than usual. Grit was a funny thing. Sometimes it showed up when you needed it least. Campbell had taught the state that much; not winning, but believing they could.

"Drive safe," Donna said, pocketing the bills without arguing. "And tell Tate to come by. We miss that kid."

Knox nodded and waved to the regulars—Pete, Maria, Jimmy, and the couple in the corner whom he didn't know but who had nodded when he entered. They waved back and promptly returned to their game, their beers, and their small escapes.

Outside, the cold hit harder. The December sun was already thinking about setting, and Chicago was two hours away. Knox climbed into his car, turned the key, felt the engine cough to life. Through the bar's window, he could see the TV, Lions still holding on and the jukebox lights cycling through their familiar colors.

The contract folder hadn't moved. The world hadn't changed.

The Deuce would be there when he got back. Donna, the regulars, his mug on the shelf, Campbell's grit still echoing from the TV, the jukebox playing the same songs it always did. Everything would be there when he got back.

That's what he told himself as he merged onto I-94 West, Michigan roads rough enough to make the folder slide an inch toward the door, hoping the Lions would hold on but knowing better, just like he knew better about Chicago but was going anyway.

I-94 WEST (SUNDAY DUSK)

The Michigan roads didn't improve after Kalamazoo. Knox merged back onto I-94 West, the contract folder secure on the passenger seat now that he'd learned which potholes to avoid. The December sun was already low, turning the sky that particular shade of gray that Michigan drivers knew meant snow was thinking about it.

He passed the state line without ceremony. Michigan to Indiana, flatland to flatland, one kind of cold to another. The radio cycled through stations he didn't recognize, catching fragments of Christmas songs and commercials for furniture stores having their annual going-out-of-business sales for the fifteenth year running.

Chicago's skyline appeared gradual, then sudden; towers rising from the flat horizon like a graph someone had forgotten to scale properly. Knox had driven this route plenty: UIUC labs when he needed to talk to someone who understood machine learning at scale, Harry Caray's when his college buddies wanted to relive bad decisions that usually ended with someone—typically Steve—in a paddy wagon.

He thought about those UIUC days now, back when they had a dedicated Center for Digital Agriculture and Knox's small team had no budget for compute resources. He'd already built a solid SCADA architecture and front-end HMI in FarmCore, but it was at UIUC where FarmLytics truly took shape. Free access to CPU and GPU clusters meant his machine learning models could train on real agricultural data without burning through capital. The university partnership had been A-OK with his budget—which is to say, it had saved him.

But corporate Chicago, the glass-tower version with marble lobbies and men in suits who smiled like they'd been trained, and that Chicago was foreign territory.

Knox followed the GPS to the Hotel Monaco, three blocks from the Aon Center where tomorrow's meeting would either save him or confirm what he already suspected —that he'd built something beautiful and run it into the ground through sheer incompetence at business.

AgriTech had arranged the room. "Our treat," Chen had said on the phone. "Get a good night's sleep. Big day tomorrow." The gesture felt generous until Knox checked the nightly rate online and realized it was just another way of saying: We have money. You don't. Let's not pretend otherwise.

He parked in the garage—Validated Parking, the sign promised, which meant Agri-Tech was covering that too—and grabbed his overnight bag from the backseat. Inside:

a change of clothes, toiletries, the portable steamer he'd bought three years ago after Lisa finally stopped offering to iron his shirts.

The irony wasn't lost on him. He could program a PLC to control a multi-million-dollar manufacturing line, could debug ladder logic that made veteran electricians weep with gratitude, could build machine learning models that predicted plant stress before it was visible to the human eye. But an iron and an ironing board? That was witchcraft. The steamer was his compromise with domestic competence—point, press button, hope for the best.

CHICAGO — HOTEL MONACO (SUNDAY NIGHT)

The hotel room was exactly what "nice" meant when a corporation was paying: clean, anonymous, everything bolted down or wrapped in plastic. Knox hung his sport coat in the bathroom, fired up the steamer, and spent ten minutes making his interview outfit look slightly less like it had been balled up in a duffel bag.

Outside the window, Chicago's skyline glittered with the kind of confidence Knox used to have. Somewhere out there, people were making deals, building empires, not counting quarters in mason jars or wondering if their credit card would clear at a parking garage.

His phone buzzed—text from Tate: Lions winning in the 4th. Campbell's grit coming through. You watching?

Knox wasn't. He'd forgotten the game was even on. He flipped on the TV, found the channel just as Detroit kicked a field goal to extend their lead. He watched the rest standing at the window, sport coat steaming in the bathroom behind him, contract terms running through his head like code he couldn't debug.

The Lions won. Campbell's grit. Never a doubt, the commentators said, which made Knox smile because doubt was all Michigan sports fans had, and pretending otherwise was part of the ritual.

He texted Tate back: Watched the ending. Hell of a game. Meeting tomorrow. Wish me luck.

You got this, Pop. They'd be lucky to work with you.

Knox stared at that message longer than he should have. Pop. Tate hadn't called him that in years.

He tried to sleep but spent most of the night staring at the ceiling, running scenarios, second-guessing decisions he hadn't even made yet. At some point he must have dozed off because his alarm startled him awake at 6:30 a.m., and Chicago was already humming with Monday morning purpose outside his window.

He showered, dressed in his freshly steamed sport coat, and checked out by 8:00. The meeting wasn't until 10:00, but sitting in that room felt like waiting for a verdict, and Knox had never been good at waiting.

He drove the three blocks to the Aon Center, found the same parking garage he'd scope out on Google Maps, and fed the machine his credit card. Thirty-two dollars for three hours. He hoped it wouldn't decline.

The elevator to the lobby was fast enough to make his ears pop. His reflection in the polished steel doors showed a man trying to look more successful than he felt—sport coat that fit better five pounds ago, tie Lisa had bought him back when she still bought him things. He adjusted it twice before the doors opened.

CHICAGO — AON CENTER, 34TH FLOOR (MONDAY 10:00 A.M.)

The lobby was all marble and light, the kind of space designed to make visitors feel small. A security desk staffed by a woman who looked like she'd been genetically engineered to convey professional indifference. Knox gave his name, received a visitor badge on a lanyard, and was directed to the thirty-fourth floor.

Another elevator. Faster. His stomach dropped as Chicago compressed beneath him —the lake appearing in fragments through tinted glass, the grid of streets turning geometric, then abstract. When the doors opened, a receptionist who could've been the lobby guard's sister gestured toward a waiting area.

"Mr. Chen will be with you shortly."

Knox sat on a leather chair that cost more than his monthly car payment and didn't touch the magazines fanned across a glass table. Forbes, Fortune, Ag Business Quarterly—publications that assumed their readers had things Knox used to have. The coffee in the carafe smelled expensive. He didn't pour any.

The waiting room was silent except for the hum of climate control working too hard. Outside the windows, Chicago spread itself in all directions, lights beginning to flicker on as afternoon bled toward evening. Somewhere down there, people were at Harry Caray's. Somewhere further east, The Deuce probably had regulars settling in for Monday afternoon, Donna pouring drafts, the memory of yesterday's Lions victory still fresh.

"Mr. Ramsey?"

Knox stood. David Chen strutted through the waiting area, looking like money but maybe not a fitness guru. Handshake firm but not aggressive, smile warm but calibrated. Navy suit, Northwestern class ring catching the light.

"Good to finally meet in person," Chen said. "Robert's waiting. We're excited about this."

The conference room smelled like new carpet and ambition. Floor-to-ceiling windows overlooking the lake, a table long enough to land a plane on, chairs that adjusted in six directions Knox would never explore. Two men stood when he entered.

"Knox Ramsey," Chen said, "Robert Walsh, our CTO, and Michael Zhao, who handles our international partnerships."

Handshakes all around. Walsh had the build of a former athlete gone soft at a desk, technical competence radiating from the way he asked about Knox's drive—not small talk, genuine interest in whether I-94's construction had cleared up near the Indiana border. Zhao was quieter, older, watchful in a way that made Knox think of accountants or lawyers or people who found problems before they became expensive.

Coffee appeared—poured by an assistant Knox hadn't seen enter—and disappeared just as efficiently. Chen slid a bound presentation across the table.

"We've been following your work for two years," Chen began, and Knox felt the first flutter of something like hope. "Your paper on adaptive learning in controlled environments—'Enhancing Controlled Environment Agriculture with Autonomous Feedback Loops Based on PLC and Edge AI Integration'—that's what got our attention. Most people optimize for yield. You optimized for sustainability and got yield as a side effect."

Knox opened the presentation. His own citations stared back at him—papers he'd published, patents he'd filed, conference talks he'd given to rooms of twelve people who barely looked up from their phones.

"You actually read these," Knox said, not quite a question.

Walsh grinned. "Read them? Your paper on adaptive control strategies—'A Sustainable Approach to Indoor Crop Production'—I built a test implementation based on your resource conservation framework. It's elegant. The way you handle heterogeneous sensor drift—most engineers would've thrown hardware at the problem. You solved it in software."

Knox's shoulders relaxed, a feeling he hadn't had since leaving The Deuce. This was the language he spoke. This was the respect he'd been starving for since the divorce, since the layoffs, since watching his company slip away one investor call at a time.

"Northwestern MBA?" Knox asked Chen, nodding at the ring.

"Class of '09. You know the program?"

"Had a friend grind through the PhD track there. Good people come out of that school."

Chen's smile widened just enough. "We try."

The next hour disappeared into technical conversation that felt like coming home. Walsh asked about Knox's neural network architecture—questions specific enough to prove he understood the math, broad enough to show he grasped the implications. Zhao mostly listened, occasionally asking about computational costs or edge cases, the kind of questions that suggested he'd been the one running numbers on Knox's patents.

"Here's what we're proposing," Chen said finally, pulling up a term sheet on the wall-mounted display. "We acquire FarmCore—the SCADA control platform, the tenant relationships, the brand. You retain FarmLytics and full control over the data and optimization intelligence. We integrate via API, clean interfaces, documented SLAs. You keep your code signing authority, your deployment cadence, everything that makes the system work."

Knox scanned the terms. The numbers were fair—better than fair, honestly, better than the two other offers he'd fielded from companies that wanted to gut the technology and rebuild it with cheaper engineers.

"Why the split?" Knox asked. "Most acquirers want everything."

Walsh leaned forward. "Because we're not most acquirers. FarmCore's value is in the control infrastructure—the tenant relationships, the compliance frameworks, the operational history. FarmLytics is... it's your art. We don't want to own art. We want to license it, support it, let it do what it does best."

"Our international partners were particularly interested in this structure," Zhao added quietly. "They respect intellectual property boundaries. Clean separation reduces friction."

Something flickered in Knox's gut—not quite alarm, but adjacent to it. "International partners?"

"Ag-tech is global," Chen said smoothly. "Investors include pension funds, sovereign wealth vehicles, private equity. Standard structure for this kind of deal."

The answer was polished enough to sound unrehearsed, detailed enough to sound transparent. Knox made a mental note to ask his lawyer about it, then remembered his lawyer cost three hundred dollars an hour he didn't have, and the mortgage was due in three weeks.

"The FarmLytics independence clause," Chen continued, highlighting a section, "is explicit. You maintain exclusive control. No obligation to share algorithms, weights, or training data with our partners. We buy the execution layer. You run the intelligence. The interface between them is contractual, nothing more."

Knox read the clause twice. It was airtight—his lawyer would've written it exactly this way if Knox could've afforded the billable hours.

"What about deployment decisions?" Knox asked. "Release schedules, update approvals?"

"All yours," Walsh said. "We're acquiring infrastructure, not engineering authority. If you want to push an update at three a.m. on a Sunday, that's your call. We trust the process you've built."

Trust. The word landed heavier than Chen probably intended. Knox thought about The Deuce—Donna pouring his PBR without asking, Pete handing him two five-dollar bills for quarter squares without checking if he had the cash, the regulars making room for him even though he wasn't really one of them. Trust was what you built over years, what you earned through showing up, what you lost in the time it took to sign the wrong contract.

But these men spoke his language. They'd read his papers—cited them by title, understood the technical details. They understood what he'd built in a way that Lisa never had, that investors never had, that even Tate—brilliant as he was—couldn't quite grasp because he thought in markets and Knox thought in systems.

"Our parent company sees significant growth in controlled environment agriculture," Chen said, advancing to a market analysis slide. "Indoor farming, greenhouse automation, particularly in the cannabis vertical. FarmCore gives us immediate market position. Your expertise gives us credibility."

The presentation walked through expansion plans—new facilities across the Midwest, partnerships with major operators, integration timelines that assumed Knox's cooperation but didn't demand it. The more Knox read, the more it looked like what he'd wanted to build himself if he'd had the capital, the connections, the business acumen he'd never quite developed. "I'd want to review this with counsel," Knox said, though he already knew what his lawyer would say: Take it. You're broke. They're offering fair value and letting you keep the technology. What are you waiting for?

"Of course," Chen said. "We've scheduled a week for due diligence, technical audits, the whole process. Our lawyers have been remarkably thorough—I think they billed us for reading every comment in your codebase."

Walsh laughed. "They asked me to explain a joke you left in the irrigation controller. I told them engineering humor doesn't translate to billable hours."

Knox smiled despite himself. The comment was still there—a reference to a Monty Python sketch that exactly three people in the world would understand. The fact that Walsh had found it, understood it, appreciated it—that mattered more than it should have.

"Timeline?" Knox asked.

"Close before Christmas if possible," Chen said. "Wire transfer clears the twenty-eighth. New year, new structure, minimal tax complications."

December twenty-eighth. The same day Lisa's lawyer expected the settlement payment. The same day the mortgage was due. The same day Knox would either have money or excuses, and he was tired of excuses.

Zhao slid a pen across the table—expensive, heavy, the kind that made signatures feel permanent. Knox picked it up, felt the weight.

"This is just the letter of intent," Chen said. "Non-binding, starts the clock on due diligence. You have a week to walk away if anything doesn't check out."

Knox read the letter. Two pages, plain language, exactly what Chen had described. He thought about The Deuce; Donna's chicken parm settling in his stomach yesterday, the Lions winning with Campbell's grit, his mug on the shelf waiting for him to come back. He thought about the townhouse, the bills, the mason jar of change that wouldn't cover next month's utilities.

He thought about Tate, building something real with the tools Knox had given him, finally calling him Pop again after years of just "Dad" or worse, "Knox" like they were colleagues instead of family.

The pen touched paper. His signature looked smaller than he remembered, cramped in the space provided, his name reduced to a legal formality. He signed twice more— initials here, full name there, the muscle memory of a man who'd signed enough contracts to know where the lines would be.

Chen's handshake was warmer after the signing, or maybe Knox just wanted it to be. Walsh clapped his shoulder like they were teammates. Zhao nodded once, satisfied, already thinking about whatever came next.

"We'll send the full documentation tomorrow," Chen said. "Start scheduling technical audits. This is going to be a great partnership, Knox."

Partnership. Another word that sounded better than it probably was.

Knox gathered his copies—the letter of intent, the term sheet, the market analysis he'd barely read. The folder was heavier walking out than it had been walking in, heavier still when he stepped into the elevator and felt his stomach drop as Chicago compressed back to street level.

The parking garage charged him thirty-eight dollars—he'd stayed longer than three hours. The attendant didn't care. Knox fed the machine his card and watched it process, half-expecting it to decline, relieved and disappointed when it didn't.

I-94 EAST (MONDAY EVENING)

I-94 East was darker now, taillights stretching toward Indiana like a river of regret flowing in reverse. Knox merged into traffic and felt the city release him—the towers shrinking in his rearview, the lake disappearing into December darkness.

He'd left The Deuce yesterday with hope. He was leaving Chicago today with a contract. Somewhere between the two, he'd made a decision that felt right and looked wrong, or maybe it was the other way around. Engineers weren't supposed to trust feelings. That's what the math was for.

His phone buzzed—text from Tate: Meeting go okay? Still riding that Lions win from last night.

Knox smiled despite everything. Grit. The thing Michigan found when it needed it most, or convinced itself it had, which might've been the same thing.

The contract folder rode shotgun, quiet now, its questions already asked, its answers already signed. Knox told himself he'd made the right choice. He told himself The Deuce would still be there. He told himself the wire would clear on the twenty-eighth and everything would be fine.

He told himself a lot of things on the drive home.

Most of them were even true.

DUE DILIGENCE — RED FLAGS (DEC 22–28)

There were red flags, subtle enough for a desperate founder to rationalize. The deeper Knox looked, the more AgriTech resembled a hall of mirrors—Delaware subsidiaries nested inside Cayman holding companies, consulting fees routed through Nevada shells with names that echoed each other like aliases. Every registration linked to another with just enough daylight to appear legitimate. Even the lawyers seemed curated, their bios clean but oddly interchangeable. Knox told himself it was just how capital moved in the twenty-first century—layered, optimized, tax-efficient. But the pattern itched at him. He couldn't find a human fingerprint anywhere, only signatures, logos, and automated acknowledgments. The whole thing felt engineered to pass inspection. And for the first time since building FarmCore, Knox wondered if he'd been the one under review all along.

The money trail looked clean. Wires from a Chicago bank, filings up to date, licenses current, insurance impeccable.

He nearly walked when Chen pushed hard on one clause—FarmLytics independence.

"We want it explicit," Chen said. "FarmLytics stays under your exclusive control. No obligation to share algorithms or weights with our international partners."

At the time, Knox took it as respect for his IP. Later, he understood: they wanted the mind outside their house—and the liability that came with it.

Walsh added, "You keep all code-signing keys, deployment decisions, release notes. We buy the lake. You run the mind. The interfaces in between are contractual."

Knox signed three days before Christmas. The wire cleared December 28—just in time for January's mortgage and Lisa's legal fees.

TECHNOLOGY TRANSFER (Q1)

The technology transfer was smoother than he expected. AgriTech's team was competent—asking about FarmCore's tenant isolation, deployment pipelines, and how FarmLytics releases propagated to FarmCore installations in the field."We're planning significant expansion," Chen said in a review. "Our parent company sees cannabis as a high-growth segment."Knox walked them through the architecture with professional pride: FarmCore as the control layer executing recipes at facilities, FarmLytics as the adaptive intelligence that learned from successful harvests and generated optimized profiles. They owned the execution now. He still owned the intelligence. The two were stitched together by contracts and APIs—clean separation that preserved his intellectual property while giving them operational control.He didn't realize he was essentially handing them the playbook for weaponizing his creation—what to watch, where to hook, which update paths real growers actually trusted. His pride in the architecture, his detailed explanations of how FarmCore validated profiles and executed recipes, his patient walkthrough of the certificate chain and signing process—all of it became reconnaissance for an enemy he didn't know he was training.

$\sim$

YEAR ONE — ARM-7C

For the first year after the sale, life settled into the kind of boring engineers pray for. AgriTech widened FarmCore's deployment—new tenants, clean SLAs, onboarding notices he no longer controlled. Knox kept his ritual in the townhouse kitchen: coffee, then four panes in the FarmLytics console—Builds, Releases, Mirrors, Signals.

Green tiles. Green checks. Boring in the best way.

Energy per kilo trended down a hair each quarter. Deviation alerts ticked lower on the Mirrors pane, which was all his contract allowed—hash-anchored aggregates with thirty days retention, enough to validate a model, not enough to play detective. He screen-captured one week's slope and wrote in his notebook: stability improving; tuner learning nights.

When ARM-7c appeared in the queue, it read like housekeeping. Release notes: FSMA telemetry hardening; minor adaptive tuning for the lumen-budget rule; fix for 12-bit spectrum overflow. The diff looked like a janitor's cart—log names cleaned up, a constant hoisted into config, adaptive changes measured in thousandths. He signed it the same way he signed everything: hardware token, whispered hash, the reflexes of a man who'd shipped to industrial floors.

The canary ring purred. A week later the Mirrors pane echoed fewer deviation flags. He typed: ARM-7c: uneventful. Good.

The first email that could have rattled him arrived with a subject line too vague to matter.

SUBJ: Perf gain, minor aroma drift?

FROM: operations@sproutcollective.us

A polite note and a spreadsheet: +1.2% energy efficiency, faint "solventy" panel comment, irrigation normal. He forwarded it to AgriTech with a request to check maintenance and packaging lots, then told the grower what he told everyone first: confirm sensor calibration. Ninety-nine things go wrong in a greenhouse before the software does, and the hundredth is a raccoon.

New tenants came online. Holland's superintendent sent plots with compressor duty "exactly where we want it." Knox printed them because it felt good to keep proof the math was kind. The Mirrors buffer turned over. Whatever raw texture had lived in those rooms rolled out of retention like it always did.

More emails trickled in—weird floral here, faint solvent there, dry leaf edge with normal irrigation. He flagged half a dozen for AgriTech. Replies came back tidy: coils cleaned, filters swapped, packaging lots quarantined. He reminded himself FarmLytics didn't set chemical targets; it tuned conditions inside targets the facilities chose. Aroma drift lived downstream, in systems and people.

One late night, he almost saw it. Signals showed less noise than hardware heterogeneity should allow—different vendors, suspiciously smooth curves. He jotted a clamp to bias the tuner toward skepticism when variance fell below prediction, and he scheduled it for later. A small, reasonable safeguard for a small, reasonable system.

He jogged at lunch because his cardiologist had turned worry into a number. He listened to Lisa's voicemail twice because her voice did what coffee didn't. He stared at Releases because habit was cheaper than anxiety. ARM-7c glowed its honest green.

When Detroit's ERs started filling, it reached him as a forwarded "FYI—probably packaging." He refreshed Mirrors for the morning roll-up and saw exactly what he'd been trained to see: efficiency gently up, deviation gently down, quality indices flat. The picture of a system behaving.

He told himself what he always told his students: green means signed, not safe— but his pipeline was disciplined, his token locked to his lanyard, his process intact. If something was wrong, it would be local. Coils. Filters. Humans.

By the time anyone said the words out loud—hotfix, signature, room profile— ARM-7c had already propagated to hundreds of facilities. Later, he would print the screenshot that showed deviation alerts ↓ 18% and circle it until the paper frayed. In the moment, in the long, boring year where green still meant "his hands," Knox did what good engineers do when the numbers look right and the noise looks low.

He moved on to the next task.

3 FINANCIAL PRESSURE — G -37

The rent notices stacked on the counter, unopened but heavy. His attorney's invoice still glared from the fridge door where he'd pinned it with a magnet as punishment to himself. Knox told people he managed stress like he managed plants: careful inputs, measured cycles—but the truth was uglier.

The AgriTech sale, which had occurred eight years ago, felt like ancient history to him. However, FarmLytics' subscription revenue had been declining for the past two years due to competitors undercutting pricing and larger agricultural companies developing in-house solutions. What had once provided a comfortable income now barely covered operational costs.

The coffee in Knox Ramsey's mug had gone from hot to lukewarm to a bitter skin of cold, and he kept drinking it anyway because throwing it out felt like waste. Waste had a sound now—coins clacking in a mason jar by the sink where he dumped change and the occasional crumpled single. He had a spreadsheet for everything and a budget for nothing. The rent on the townhouse would clear next week if two FarmLytics invoices posted on time. If not, he'd call the landlord and make the speech again: former founder, short-term cash crunch, honest guy, Midwestern handshake, promises that still meant something.

He was fifty-three and felt every mile between who he had been and who he was. The kitchen was a tourniquet: a duct-taped chair leg, a fridge door that didn't quite seal, a calendar with three months layered because he forgot to peel back June. On the magnet strip, a faded photo of Tate at twelve, cap crooked, glove up, sunlight on his cheekbone, all teeth and future.

Knox closed the laptop and rubbed his eyes with the heels of his hands. When he looked back, the screen saver had thrown a constellation of bouncing squares across the budget sheet—GL accounts and invoice IDs winking like some cosmic joke.

He told himself he was fine. He was not fine.

TATER

Tate Ramsey's first nickname wasn't about cannabis at all. It came from baseball; from the way he used to send balls screaming over fences at his high-school diamond. "Tater," they called him, short for tater-shot; home runs stacked up until scouts started circling. His swing was easy, violent, something that looked like destiny until the day his shoulder tore on a cold April afternoon. By the time he'd healed, the scholarships were gone.

He pivoted the only way he knew how, into books. Michigan State took him in, not for his bat but for his brain. He majored in Plant Biology and Business Management, a strange pairing that made perfect sense to him. In the lab, he studied chlorophyll fluorescence and terpene expression; in the classroom, he learned cash-flow statements and brand equity. Where his father saw systems and circuits, Tate saw markets and stories.

Cannabis became his obsession, not because it was easy money but because it lived at the intersection of everything he cared about. Biology that mattered. Business with room for innovation. Medicine with untapped potential. He read case studies about veterans finding relief from PTSD, cancer patients reclaiming appetite, epileptic kids with fewer seizures. Tate believed in that. Not just the profits, but the potential.

When FarmCore came online, he was one of its first evangelists. Knox had built the system for optimization, to make crops thrive under glass. Tate saw something different: consistency. A grower could promise customers the same terpene profile week after week, a brand built in a chaotic market. He told his dad as much once, late at night in the kitchen: "People don't buy cannabis, Dad. They buy trust." Knox had grunted, pretending not to be impressed, but the words stuck.

TR Cannabis was born out of that philosophy. Tate wasn't trying to be the biggest; he was trying to be the most trusted. Clean facilities, branded packaging, meticulous strain tracking. He used FarmCore not as a crutch but as a differentiator, proof that science could anchor an industry built on haze and hype. He never chased scale for its own sake; he wanted his name on something that didn't need apology.

And every now and then, Knox would still call him Tater, half-pride, half-warning. The name carried both the memory of a swing that could have been a career and the reminder that Tate had chosen another path—one that might yet change the family name again, for better or worse.

When the walls felt too close, Knox would rewind the tape—back to when everything still looked like momentum. He used to think legacy meant patents and lectures. Now it looked like a son who'd learned how to make peace with the machine faster than he ever could.

Knox rubbed his eyes and forced himself back to the present. Tate forged his own way, regardless of the consequences. What Knox had built—what he had lost—was another story entirely.

WHEN THE BUYOUT came from AgriTech Solutions, he took the money because machines don't care about metaphors. He told himself the buyers were just capital. People say "foreign" like it's a curse word; he said "global" because he wanted to be the man who understood the world.

He kept FarmLytics—his data-optimization side project—as consolation and lifeline. Three thousand agricultural installs linked to its cloud engine. Not glamorous, but steady: recipe updates, yield nudges, anomaly flags, email alerts at 2:17 a.m. when a sensor hiccuped in a barn outside Traverse City or a cannabis grow in Romulus had its HVAC drift a degree. It paid the rent and fed his pride, even as the margins thinned and the world moved on to shinier subscriptions.

Sometimes he could still feel the weight of the pen he'd signed FarmCore away with—the kind of pen meant to feel important so you didn't notice what it was costing you.

The phone, face down on the table, buzzed. Knox flipped it: a voicemail from a number he recognized not as a person but as a rhythm. Collections have a tempo; you learn it the way a drummer feels the downbeat. He deleted it without listening, shame prickling his neck. Another buzz: an email from a small greenhouse in Holland, Michigan—the owner apologetic, asking if she could skip this month's FarmLytics payment. "We had to fix the chiller," she wrote. "You've been good to us. We'll make it up." Knox hovered over reply. He typed, "Of course," then erased the period and added, "Take care of your family first." He hit send and pretended not to think about the townhouse rent.

He stood and stretched, vertebrae grinding a little as they stacked back into place. The turntable in the other room called to him, a half-built shrine: a rescued receiver with a knob that needed DeoxIT, a pair of bookshelves he'd re-capped himself in what he told people was therapy. There's a kind of prayer in solder: heat, join, cool—something broken reconnected.

He cued a record but didn't drop the needle; the ritual without the music was enough to remind him he had a center.

A text from Lisa lit the phone: How are you sleeping? Tate says you're stressed again. Maybe talk to someone?

He stared. They'd been separated long enough to navigate each other's weather without checking the forecast.

He typed, I'm okay. Working. College lecture next week. Kids today love ladder logic.

Then deleted the last sentence—it sounded like a man trying too hard to be relevant —and sent the rest.

A minute later, her reply came: a heart.

No words, just that. Enough to remind him the line between concern and affection still existed, even if it flickered.

He put the phone down.

An email from TR Cannabis came in on a shared thread he almost never opened.

Subject: HOT PULL — STAGE VENDOR TENTS

From: VibeWorks Distribution

To: Tate Ramsey, Knox Ramsey

Shipment confirmed for Movement Festival weekend.

Please verify FarmLytics telemetry compliance before loadout.

Tate kept him on it out of habit or guilt or both. Knox skimmed, then read it again, old pride knocking against new resentment. Tate was all forward motion, branding and hustle, "scale or die." He used FarmLytics the way a pilot uses instruments: trust the dials, keep the plane level, eyes up on the horizon.

The success made Knox proud and itchy at the same time. Indoor farming was the very frontier his generation warned itself about—food divorced from dirt, protein in stainless steel gowns. Knox had helped create it, and some days he wanted to take it back.

They'd argued about that last Christmas, in a kitchen that didn't smell like cinnamon anymore. Tate had said, "Dad, you built the system. I'm just using it." And Knox, who hated being the kind of man who weaponizes fatherhood, had said, "Using it to do what?" They'd eaten reheated ham and pretended not to be angry.

He carried the mug to the sink and stared out the kitchen window. A wind lifted leaves down the block and sent them skating along the curb like fish changing direction. Grand Rapids in September wears two faces—the side that survived and the side that never recovered. Knox loved both. He loved the brick mills with new lives as breweries and startups; he loved the empty lots where grass forced its way through concrete like an old hymn nobody remembered until someone sang the chorus. He had built chemical plants in Louisiana and refineries in Texas and a solar farm off I-96; he kept coming back because the Midwest held the values he trusted. He could hear his grandfather's voice: You work, you pay your debts, you tell the truth.

The laptop dinged. A FarmLytics dashboard alert. He thumbed the trackpad: a routine profile-push completion—light-spectrum updates for a half-dozen Michigan grows, including Tate's. "FarmLytics ARM-7c hotfix deployed successfully." Good. His code was still his.

He clicked into the audit log out of habit. Timestamps lined up, hashes matched, distribution windows within tolerance. The green bars comforted him in a way people rarely did.

He didn't know it yet, but somewhere in that code was the seed of every sleepless night still ahead.

A thought crossed his mind the way clouds cross a field: maybe sell FarmLytics to a bigger player, let them absorb the headaches. Take the buyout, pay off the cards, buy a little house that didn't echo. The calls would stop. The nights would soften. The idea scared him more than the debt. If he sold, who was he besides a man who used to build things?

The phone rang. Tate.

"Hey," Knox answered, trying for light.

"Quick one." Tate sounded like he was walking, the background a warehouse hum —forklifts, voices, a radio playing something with a snap snare. "Movement weekend's bigger than expected. You good with that lighting tweak you pushed? The night-run plants freaked the QA kid; he says the spectral plot looks 'cold.'"

"It's right," Knox said, instinctively defensive. "We've been creeping the blue peak to harden trichomes. You'll see it in yield and pull weight. Tell QA to stop naming his feelings after weather."

Tate laughed. "You sound like you."

A pause. The real thing under the laugh.

"You sleeping?" Tate asked.

"Like a baby. Cry for thirty minutes, pass out, wake up at two to make sure the compressor's still alive." He meant it as a joke and heard the sadness under it anyway.

"You coming to my talk next week?" Knox asked. "Community college invited me. History of Michigan manufacturing. PLCs, paper mills, Motown line moves, you know."

"I'll try if the run calms down," Tate said, the noncommittal syllables of a busy son. "Dad, seriously, thanks for pushing the recipes. We're slammed, and I—"

The line crackled; a forklift beeped like a metronome for hurry. "I gotta go. Love you."

"Love you," Knox said to the dead air, then hated himself for sounding disappointed.

He stared at the "FarmLytics ARM-7c" line again. It was ordinary. It was his whole life.

He went to the living room and dropped the needle. The first guitar lick unfurled like a curtain, and the room changed temperature. Knox sank into the couch and let the speakers push air across his shins.

A siren screamed past outside. He didn't move. Grand Rapids has sirens like Detroit has bass-lines; they mean everything and nothing until they're outside your door.

The record hit the chorus and something like hope moved in his chest. He thought of the lecture and wrote lines for it in his head: Michigan as machine memory, the ethics of automation, what we owe the people who trust our systems. He reached blindly for a pen, found a receipt and wrote three bullet points that looked like confession.

The TV on the stand showed a news banner—muted because he preferred the guitar —teasing a piece about festival preparations in Detroit. Drone shots of Hart Plaza, an interviewer with a mic, laughing kids in sunglasses. He didn't look. He told himself he'd watch later.

He stood, carried the mug to the sink, and rinsed it out. The faucet coughed before the water found its rhythm. Steam curled upward. A thought rose with it—*the thing you invent might save you, or it might eat you. The difference is whether you're watching when it opens its mouth.*

Pressure had a way of finding the cracks a man tried to mortar over; tonight he could feel every one of them widening.

The laptop pinged again. Another deployment confirmation, this time from a facility outside Reno, Nevada. He barely registered it. Just another green bar on a long green wall.

He shut the laptop gently—a courtesy he extended to machines that had been kinder to him than some people—and set the mug upside down to dry. In the window glass, his reflection looked like a man still negotiating with his life. He tried on a smile he didn't feel, then gave up and let his face go neutral. Engineers are not poker players. He had never been good at masks.

On the counter, the mason jar of change caught the afternoon light and flashed a scatter of coins on the ceiling. It looked, for a second, like stars. He took that as a sign and decided to grade his life on a curve tonight: the recipes pushed, the rent not yet due, the turntable singing. It would do.

He turned the TV up just enough to pretend he was listening. A newscaster's lips moved under the crawl, MASSIVE CROWD EXPECTED FOR MOVEMENT — DETROIT READY. He thought, Good for the city, and told himself there'd be time to worry tomorrow.

He was wrong, but that is the privilege and penalty of a quiet afternoon: you can't tell the difference.

SHANGHAI

On his laptop, the FarmLytics dashboard quietly confirmed another deployment. To Knox, it was routine, a green bar on a long wall of green bars. To someone watching from half a world away, it was the first domino in a chain already tipped.

"Additionally, a cache of old inspection photos surfaced—imagine that—showing unsanitary conditions at a Detroit dispensary. They are unrelated to our target but highly suggestive. Americans believe pictures more than facts."

Liu smiled thinly. "They believe speed more than accuracy. The first explanation always wins the attribution war."

4 PERIMETER — G -36
SURVEILLANCE WINDOW

11:18 P.M.—GRAND RAPIDS, MI

The message from Shanghai arrived as a single line of text. AMERICAN ASSET: RAMSEY, KNOX. STATUS: STABLE. LEVERAGE: INCREASING. MAINTAIN PERIMETER. PREPARE CONTACT WINDOW.

The man in the rented sedan read it twice, then let the phone go dark in his hand. Streetlight sodium glow turned the touchscreen amber before it vanished. Outside, the narrow row of townhouses sat in a clean, orderly line—vinyl siding, small porches, identical shrubs chosen from the same contractor brochure.

Third unit from the corner: Ramsey.

He didn't think of him as Knox Ramsey, divorced engineer, part-time instructor, former corporate executive. That was file data. To the man in the sedan, he was simply target—one node in a wider board. His job was not to like or dislike the pieces. His job was to know where they slept.

He checked the time. 23:18 local, G-36 on the Geneva clock.

On his lap, a slim tablet showed a simplified overlay of the neighborhood—parcel outlines, utility stubs, camera coverage, Wi-Fi signatures bleeding faintly through the walls. Knox's router broadcast a generic consumer SSID, but its traffic profile had already been mapped from afar. Consumption spikes on evenings when his son called. Late-night plateaus when he worked.

Tonight's pattern fit the second category.

Through the townhouse front window, he could see movement: a man in his fifties at the kitchen table, shoulders curved in that particular way that meant tired but still pushing—light pooling over printed handouts and a laptop open to a slide deck. A second monitor on a cheap folding table glowed with something text-dense and monochrome. He'd seen that posture on a hundred professionals: preparing to teach.

The coordinator—his Shanghai file called him 协调员 (Xiétiáoyuán), "the one who aligns pieces"—made a note on the tablet:

SUBJECT: RAMSEY, KNOX

ACTIVITY: LATE-NIGHT PREP. LIKELY LECTURE MATERIAL.

STRESS INDICATORS: FINANCIAL DOCUMENTS VISIBLE, MULTIPLE ENVELOPES.

That lined up with the banking summaries from earlier in the week—past-due notices, credit utilization curves trending up. Pressure mattered. Pressure turned stubborn men into predictable ones.

He thumbed the secure channel open just long enough to send a short update back across the Pacific.

家庭资产：拉姆齐。

情况：稳定但压力增加。保持外围监控，准备接触窗口。

Family asset: Ramsey. Stable, but pressure increasing. Maintain perimeter. Prepare contact window.

The acknowledgement from Shanghai came back as a single green check.

No further instructions. That was good. That meant the plan was still on track: let FarmCore and FarmLytics do the visible work, let the Ramseys carry the narrative weight when the time came. The inspection-photo cache Liu mentioned earlier would handle the rest. Americans believed what they could see on their phones, especially when frightened.

His role was simply to make sure the man at the center of that story was exactly where they expected him to be when the first accusations started to circulate.

He shifted slightly in the seat, careful not to fog the windshield. The heater was off; the night had that damp chill Michigan specialized in, cold that crept through seams instead of dropping in dramatic gusts. Across the small parking lot, a delivery driver's car pulled in, lights sweeping the row, then backed out again. Wrong address.

In the kitchen window, Knox paused to rub at his eyes. He stood, stretching, and moved out of sight toward the back of the unit. A moment later, the light in the adjoining room flicked on—office or bedroom, hard to tell at this angle.

The coordinator waited.

This was the part most people romanticized when they imagined intelligence work: stakeouts, long nights, the glamour of "surveillance." In reality, it was mostly watching people be themselves until a pattern emerged.

Knox reappeared, a mug in hand. Steam curled, barely visible. He set it beside the laptop and checked his phone, thumb moving over the screen. The coordinator had already seen the metadata from that device once the previous week—call frequency, messaging apps, the silent cluster of numbers that weren't used anymore.

Ex-wife. Adult children. One number tagged in the file as Tate, with years of call history compressed to a graph. Peaks around holidays. Lulls around court dates.

He logged tonight's behavior:

SUBJECT CHECKS PHONE. NO OUTGOING CALL.

POSSIBLE ANTICIPATION / AVOIDANCE.

Ramsey sat again, scrolling through slides—signal integrity, noise bands, process diagrams. On the far monitor, a window of code showed ladder logic and comments about failsafes condensed into ugly abbreviations. The coordinator watched his hands move, slow at first, then faster as he hit a rhythm. Teaching mode, even alone.

He understood why Shanghai cared about this man. Engineers like Ramsey were dangerous in a way soldiers were not. Give them a system and enough time, they would find both its promise and its failure modes.

Across his secure channel, a second notification blinked briefly: ASSET 7 STANDING BY.

He didn't open it. He knew the content. Shanghai's orders had come down earlier that evening: once Ramsey moved into closer orbit with any federal task force, Asset Seven would move from remote observation to direct surface contact. For now, she was a name on his slate and a line item on the operation chart—positioned, but not yet advanced.

His lane was simpler: confirm that Ramsey's life continued in its predictable, weary arc.

Inside the townhouse, Knox pushed his chair back again. He hesitated this time before standing, palm resting flat on the table as if bracing against some invisible tilt. Then he crossed to the front window, reaching to pull the blind down another few inches.

He froze.

From his vantage in the car, the coordinator saw the moment of eye contact—

Knox's gaze sliding across the parking lot, snagging on the dark shape of the sedan. Not long. A beat. Two.

That was always the variable: how much attention a tired man could still spare for his surroundings.

Knox's brow furrowed slightly. He let the blind rest against his fingers, not yet closing it. The coordinator kept his own posture loose, one hand on the steering wheel, the other resting casually near the gearshift. No sudden movement. No obvious turn of the head.

They regarded each other through layered reflections: interior light on glass, street-lamp glow on paint, two men separated by twenty meters and an entire architecture of intent.

Then Knox blinked, shook his head just enough to register it as a dismissal, and tugged the blind the rest of the way down. The kitchen light dimmed to a stripe at the edge of the frame.

The coordinator waited another full minute before he started the engine. The sedan coughed to life, then settled. He pulled slowly away from the curb, pausing at the corner long enough to glance once in the rearview mirror.

The townhouse row receded, identical units stitched into the dark.

He tagged the log as he turned onto the main road:

PERIMETER CHECK COMPLETE.

SUBJECT: ROUTINE. PARANOIA LEVEL: LOW.

CONTACT WINDOW VIABLE WHEN ORDERED.

Three blocks away, he merged with late-night traffic and disappeared into it. Behind him, Knox Ramsey sat alone at his kitchen table, listening to the furnace kick on and the old ductwork creak, telling himself the car outside had been nothing.

In Shanghai, a dashboard ticked forward by one more quiet, ordinary data point. G-36.

The chain had already been tipped. The pieces were only just realizing they'd been moved.

5 ASSET SEVEN'S INTRODUCTION
MORNING SURVEILLANCE & APPROACH

The coffee shop on Monroe Center in downtown Grand Rapids buzzed with the pre-lunch rush—college kids from GRCC, office workers grabbing sandwiches, regulars who treated the Wi-Fi like rent control. At a corner table, Maya Chen looked like any remote worker: laptop open, earbuds in, posture absorbed.

Maya's gaze skimmed the street beyond her reflection, eyes catching every reflection without seeming to track anything at all. Her screen showed three feeds she'd positioned over the past month: a camera across from Tate Ramsey's warehouse in Detroit's Corktown, another angled down the driveway of Knox Ramsey's townhouse on the West Side of Grand Rapids, a third tied to GRCC's electronics lab where Knox volunteered on Tuesdays. Detroit was two hours away, but distance didn't matter when you owned the optics.

She'd been watching the Ramseys for fourteen months—long enough to know their routines, long enough to become background. Patterns emerged as heatmaps, not names. This was her native world—behavior, not biography. Asset Seven's cover held because it was mostly true: a cannabis compliance consultant who knew both the business and the regulatory maze strangling it. She did the work. She took the meetings. She filed the paperwork.

What clients didn't know was that every contract, every careful conversation over coffee, every "friendly intro" rolled up to a desk in Shanghai.

Asset Seven's phone buzzed: a secure message from Captain Zhang.

指令：包裹已送达。开始密切监控。报告家庭动态、压力指标、杠杆点。

(Zhǐlìng: bāoguǒ yǐ sòng dá. Kāishǐ mìqiè jiānkòng. Bàogào jiātíng dòngtài, yālì zhǐbiāo, gànggǎn diǎn.)

Directive: Package delivered. Begin close monitoring. Report family dynamics, stress indicators, leverage points.

A mirrored acknowledgement blinked across her secondary channel — Mr. 邱 (Qiū), her 协调员 (Xiétiáoyuán — coordinator), had received the same tasking.

He never wasted words; a green check was all he sent. Logistics, counter-surveillance, cleanup—that was his lane. She handled people.

She sipped her latte and checked the GRCC lab feed. Knox wasn't there yet. She'd attended two of his guest lectures, sitting in the back, taking notes like any continuing-ed student. He was clear, grounded, the kind of engineer who made complicated systems sound obvious once he'd walked you through them. He was also broke, isolated, carrying the weight of a divorce and a frayed bond with his son. Maya logged not just presence or absence, but the micro-drift in his circulation: the subtle sag of posture, the delay before a smile.

Perfect.

She split the screen. Corktown pulsed—Tate's TR Cannabis loading for weekend festivals, a forklift beeping in an echoing bay. Growth on paper had outpaced cash in the bank. Expansion three times in a year. Inventory stacked like hope. Trucks idled, but optimism vibrated harder: ambition visible even from a thousand miles away.

Six months earlier she'd maneuvered into Tate's orbit with a cold email—"compliance consulting for scale-up operations." Credentials: impeccable. MBA from Michigan. Prior work in Colorado and California. Articles on regulatory strategy that real people had actually read. She didn't push. Quarterly check-ins, useful templates, the right comments on the right LinkedIn posts. She became part of the landscape.

She'd mapped Tate's suppliers, distributors, and competitors until the network resolved into dependencies and pressure points. Who could be nudged? Who would fold? Who would sell?

Her skill wasn't gadgets. It was people. She read what they needed to hear and became the person they wanted to trust.

Tradecraft, though, had an engineering side she kept private. Her laptop ran a small suite—some homebrew tools, some purchased soft-ware safely altered—that translated motion into timelines. A heatmap overlay showed how often Tate's fork-lift idled at the back dock; an audio spectrogram pulled down from the warehouse mic revealed the cadence of late-night phone calls. She cross-referenced that with supplier manifests she'd purchased through a shell company and with public county tax filings. Where finance and movement aligned, pressure points glowed amber.

She kept a second machine for counter-surveillance—VMs that simulated careless browsing, baiting any curious camera with staged profiles to see if anyone on the other end reacted. If a particular inspector kept looking at the same overlay for too long, she flagged it for Qiū. If someone tried to ping her hidden feeds, she silently rotated IPs and handed the trace to logistics to bury. The best surveillance was invisible to the watched.

With Knox, she played the concerned neighbor. She rented two miles from his townhouse, close enough for plausible grocery-store collisions, used-record shop over-laps, parking-lot waves. He was hungry for connection and suspicious of anyone too eager. So she was carefully uninterested—polite but busy. It made him work to earn small conversations. It made him feel like a peer, not a project.

She'd learned his finances by observation: envelopes on the counter, payment pings he checked and re-checked the way two beers meant "budget" and three meant "wind-fall." She mirrored pressure: a single professional with irregular income and too many client fires. When he mentioned FarmLytics' thin margins, she nodded with earned empathy.

Tradecraft was ninety percent posture. She kept hers flawless.

At 1050, Knox's lab feed flickered: he arrived, badging in, the way a man enters a space he owns without owning it. She noted the time. Tuesday routine intact.

She drafted the morning report to Shanghai, posture not poetry:

```
SUBJECT: RAMSEY, KNOX — WEEK 14
主体：雷姆齐先生 — 财务压力上升，睡眠受干扰。家庭隔阂持续。
(Zhǔtǐ: Léimǔqí Xiānsheng — cáiwù yālì shàngshēng,
shuìmián shòu gānrǎo. Jiātíng géhé chíxù.)
SUBJECT: Mr. Ramsey — financial stress rising, sleep
disrupted. Family distance persistent. Isolation deepening;
minimal social contact.
LEVERAGE: Financial desperation 7/10; family-protection
9/10; technical ego 8/10.
RECOMMENDATION: Continue gradual relationship-building.
Estimate 3—4 weeks to operational trust.
```

The reply came minutes later, as it always did:

Assessment noted. Accelerate timeline to 3 weeks. Prepare family-pressure scenarios.

Maya closed the message and shifted to the approach phase. If she timed it right, she could "bump" Knox after his lab, at the deli on Monroe Center he favored when the line wasn't bad.

She packed up, left a clean tip, and walked three blocks. Through the window she saw him in his usual seat: turkey sandwich, phone face-down, mind still at the lab. He looked older than fifty-three today. Fatigue fogs the eyes first.

"Mr. Ramsey?" she said lightly, careful but confident.

He looked up, puzzled. "Nobody calls me that unless they're selling insurance. Just Knox."

Her smile was small, polite. "Knox, then. I'm Maya Chen."

Recognition clicked. "Right — GRCC. Sat in on one of my labs." His eyes narrowed a fraction. "You're Tate's consultant, aren't you?"

She smiled, easy. "That's me."

That seemed to settle him. "Maya. Sure, sit."

"How's the consulting business?" he asked, defaulting to her cover.

"Clients pay you to say no, then ignore you, then hire you to fix what ignoring you broke." She smiled. "Occupational hazard."

Knox snorted. "I've lived that."

"What about you—how's FarmLytics?"

"Steady." A beat. "You know how it is. Not glamorous, pays the bills." The fingers drummed the cup—money worry tell.

"I've been thinking about what you said," she said, stabbing at her salad. "Black-box AI. Scares me how much we trust systems we don't really understand."

He brightened—his territory. "With PLCs, you can trace logic rung by rung. With ML, you get a decision and a shrug. It works—until it doesn't."

"You think someone could push it the wrong way without being seen?"

"Someone smart and motivated? Sure. You could corrupt recommendations without tripping obvious alarms. The question is why."

He was already thinking along the lines she needed him to—vulnerabilities, blind spots, trust failures. When the attack went public, the guilt would land like a dropped anvil.

"Have you talked to your son about that?" she asked, carefully. "He uses FarmLytics."

"Tate trusts algorithms more than I do," Knox said. "He grew up with them. I try not to lecture."

"You have kids?" he asked.

"Two younger siblings," she said. "They think I'm paranoid because I read privacy policies."

Knox laughed—relief, then retreat. "Tate says I worry too much."

"Better safe than sorry," she said, standing.

"I've got a client call. If you ever want dinner instead of eating alone—no pressure—text me."

He hesitated, then: "Next week?"

"I'm at a conference. Week after?"

"Works."

She left him with a choice and no pressure, the invitation framed as his initiative. Next time she'd push for his place—surveillance upgrades, a closer look at his home setup, a way to tighten the loop.

Back in the car, she filed the operational update in clean, clinical language:

主体：雷姆齐先生 — 财务压力上升；付款焦虑明显。孤立状态持续。

(Zhǔtǐ: Léimǔqí Xiānsheng — cáiwù yālì shàngshēng; fùkuǎn jiāolǜ míngxiǎn. Gūlì zhuàngtài chíxù.)

SUBJECT: Mr. Ramsey — Financial stress rising; payment anxiety observed. Isolation persists.

PROFESSIONAL PRIDE: Intact and exploitable.

ACTION: Dinner pretext established (T+10–14 days). Prepare in-home assessment.

Corktown flickered again: Tate's forklift, a near-miss, a shouted apology. She logged it. Stress telegraphs itself in tiny stumbles.

Her last task was the handler comms cycle. No direct lines. Rotating encrypted apps with self-destruct timers. Dead drops in photo metadata—tourist shots of the Blue Bridge with messages braided into pixels.

The old methods still worked because people assumed the new ones made them obsolete. The future, in her business, was always built on the bones of the past.

Before uploading, she routed the Knox and Tate update through Mr. 邱 (Qiū), her 协调员, as always. He preferred silence and precision, but nothing slipped past him.

She closed the laptop, checked the rearview, and slid into traffic. In two hours, Knox would be at GRCC Room 147, warming up a projector for a class that didn't know automation had teeth. She enjoyed being in the room for those. Teachers reveal themselves when they're explaining first principles. How a person teaches is how they think under pressure.

Becoming indispensable is how you become invisible, Beijing liked to say.

Maya preferred her own version:

Become the thing they're grateful for, and they will never see what you take.

She turned onto Fulton, the Camry humming. The op held steady. The family threads were tightening. And Knox Ramsey was almost ready to be pulled.

6 KNOX TEACHING
"THE TURN TOWARD MODERN COMPLEXITY"

The fluorescent lights in room 147 of Grand Rapids Community College hummed with the same frequency as tinnitus. Knox Ramsey stood at the front of the classroom, looking out at twenty-three faces that ranged from bored to curious to aggressively caffeinated.

The projector threw his first slide against the pull-down screen: "Michigan as Machine: From Motown Lines to Cloud Farms."

"Anyone know what a PLC is?" Knox asked, clicking to a photo of a boxy gray device bristling with wires.

Three hands went up. Knox pointed to a young woman in the front row wearing a Carhartt jacket over a Wayne State hoodie.

"Programmable Logic Controller," she said. "We use them in the brewery where I work. They run the fermentation tanks."

"Perfect. What's your name?"

"Sarah Deneault."

"Sarah gets it. A PLC is basically a computer that's been stuffed into a steel box and taught to speak to machines. And Michigan—this state—has been having conversations with machines longer than almost anywhere else in America."

Knox clicked to the next slide: the River Rouge Plant in its 1940s heyday, assembly lines stretching to the horizon like mechanical rivers.

"This is where we learned to make the impossible look routine. Henry Ford didn't just build cars here—he built the first truly automated industrial process. Every rivet, every weld, every paint spray timed to the second."

A kid in the back raised his hand. Knox nodded.

"But they had people doing most of that work, right? Not computers?"

"Good question...?"

"Tyler."

"Tyler's right. In Ford's day, automation meant conveyor belts and gravity feeds—mechanical automation. But the principles were the same as what we do today with code. You break a complex process into simple, repeatable steps. You eliminate human error wherever possible. You design for consistency."

Knox advanced to a slide showing ladder logic diagrams—the programming language that made PLCs tick. To the untrained eye, they looked like electrical schematics, with switches and coils connected by horizontal rungs like a ladder.

"This is ladder logic," Knox said, pointing to the symbols. "It's designed to look like electrical circuits because that's what plant electricians knew how to read. You want a motor to start when a sensor detects a part? You draw a contact that closes when the sensor activates, connected to a coil that energizes the motor starter."

Sarah raised her hand. "But why not use regular programming languages? This looks ancient."

Knox smiled. "Because plant floors are not software companies. When a $50 million production line goes down, you don't want to debug Python. You want logic you can troubleshoot with a multimeter and a flashlight. This stuff is built to be fixed by people wearing steel-toed boots."

He advanced to the next slide: a modern automotive assembly line, robots moving in choreographed precision. "But something changed in the last twenty years. The machines got smarter. And that's where things get interesting... and dangerous."

Knox's boots squeaked faintly against the vinyl floor as he paced, free hand cupping a battered thermos. "Here's a thing they don't tell you in the software world: most real engineering isn't about elegant code. It's not even about invention. It's about responsibility."

He looked pointedly at Sarah, then swept the room. "To most people, a system is invisible until it fails. But to the engineer, a system is only as good as its dumbest, cheapest part. We walk the floor right after midnight, listening for bearings that whine a little too loud, watching for a process that drifts just a fraction. My dad used to say, 'There's no such thing as a minor error in a production line. A penny mistake a thousand times winds up a paycheck.'"

The class gave small, scattered nods. Knox pressed on, warming to the subject. "When I started out, I drove a truck between paper mills. At every stop, you could tell more about the health of the plant from the smell under the loading dock than from any dashboard. Automation is just the new language for talking to the same old problems— waste, downtime, human pride. You chase reliability, not flash."

He put his thermos down and picked up a dog-eared technical manual from the lectern. "This?"—he flip-flopped through stained, tabbed pages—"isn't cool, but it's survival. Eighty percent of all failures, you'll find right here, buried in the boring stuff. No one brags about a process that never breaks down. That's the mark of a real engineer: you make reliability disappear into the background."

A student in the back row piped up. "Isn't that kind of thankless, though?"

"Of course it is," Knox said, grinning. "That's the heart of the profession." He set the manual down and rapped his knuckles on the table. "You're good if nobody knows your name on a bad day. You build for the bad day and pray that day never comes."

He clicked off the projector for a moment, letting their eyes adjust. "Never forget: every system you design needs to fail safe. Not because you expect trouble, but because it's arrogant not to. And everything you automate—whether you're optimizing cannabis or making cars—is really just another way of betting on human fallibility."

"Engineering isn't about code, and it isn't about control. It's about humility and trust—building systems that forgive the rest of us for not being perfect.

"Tyler, you ever use autocorrect?" Knox asked.

The kid nodded. "It drives me crazy. Sometimes it changes words I didn't want changed."

"Right. But mostly it works, and mostly you trust it. Now imagine autocorrect for factories. Instead of fixing your typos, it's deciding how hot to run a chemical reactor or how fast to move a conveyor belt carrying molten steel."

The room got quieter. Knox had their attention now.

"Modern automation isn't just following programmed instructions anymore. It's making decisions. Machine learning algorithms optimize production schedules, predict equipment failures, even adjust quality control parameters based on sensor data patterns."

The next image replaced it: a cannabis growing facility, walls lined with LED arrays, plants arranged in precise rows under controlled lighting. "This is where my work comes in. Indoor agriculture. Thirty years ago, growing plants meant dirt, sunshine, and prayer. Today, it means sensors, algorithms, and artificial intelligence."

Knox walked over to the whiteboard and drew a simple flowchart: sensors feeding data to a computer, which outputs control signals to lights, pumps, and ventilation systems.

"The system monitors everything—soil moisture, nutrient levels, air temperature, humidity, CO_2 concentration, even the spectral composition of the grow lights. Feed all that data into a machine learning model, and it can optimize growing conditions better than any human farmer."

"But there's a catch," Knox continued, turning back to the class. "The better these systems get, the more we trust them. And the more we trust them, the less we understand what they're actually doing."

A student near the window raised her hand. "What do you mean?"

"Good question. In the old days, if a PLC made a mistake, you could trace through the ladder logic step by step and find the problem. It was like debugging a circuit—methodical, logical, predictable. But with AI systems..." Knox shrugged. "Sometimes the algorithm makes a decision that's too complex for humans to fully understand. We call it a 'black box.'"

He drew another diagram on the whiteboard: data going into a black box, decisions coming out, with a question mark in the middle.

"The AI can tell you what it decided, but not always why. And that creates a trust problem. Do you question the machine when it's been right 99.9% of the time?"

Tyler leaned forward. "What happens when it's wrong?"

THE DARK TURN

Knox's expression grew serious. "That's where we get into dangerous territory. When I started in automation, we designed systems to fail safe. If something went wrong, the machine would shut down rather than continue operating with bad data."

He moved on—headlines now filling the screen. *Deepwater Horizon. Three Mile Island. Boeing 737 MAX.*

"But modern systems are often too complex to simply shut down. A modern automated factory might have thousands of interdependent processes. Shut down one system, and you cascade failures through the entire plant. So instead of failing safe, we design systems to keep running even when something's wrong."

Sarah shifted uncomfortably in her seat. "That sounds terrifying."

"It should be. Because here's the thing about artificial intelligence—it's very good at optimizing for the goals you give it. But if you give it the wrong goals, or if someone else changes those goals, the AI will pursue them with perfect dedication."

Knox paused, looking around the room. "Anyone want to guess where this is going?"

The room was silent.

"Cybersecurity," Knox said finally. "If you can hack into an AI-controlled system and modify its optimization targets, you can make it do anything you want. And the scarier part? The AI will make it look perfectly normal."

Another tap and a final slide appeared: a stripped-down diagram of a cyberattack on an industrial control system. Knox let the image breathe a moment before speaking.

"This isn't science fiction. In 2010, a computer virus called Stuxnet did exactly this to Iranian uranium enrichment centrifuges. The virus made the centrifuges spin themselves apart while reporting normal operation to the control room. The operators had no idea anything was wrong until the machines started exploding."

Tyler's eyes widened. "Could that happen to the growing systems you work with?"

Knox hesitated. The question hit closer to home than the kid could know. "Theoretically? Yes. If an attacker gained access to the optimization algorithms, they could potentially modify growing conditions to produce... undesirable outcomes."

"Like what?"

"Well," Knox said carefully, "plants are basically biological factories. They produce the compounds we want—THC, CBD, various terpenes—through metabolic pathways that can be influenced by environmental conditions. If you knew what you were doing, you could potentially steer those pathways toward producing compounds that are... less beneficial."

The room was dead quiet now. Knox realized he might have said too much.

"But," he added quickly, "the regulatory oversight in legal cannabis is pretty robust. Multiple testing requirements, batch tracking, lots of transparency. It would be very difficult to get contaminated products to market."

Sarah raised her hand again. "You said 'theoretically' and 'potentially' a lot just now. Do you think someone's actually trying to do this?"

Knox felt a chill that had nothing to do with the classroom's aggressive air conditioning. "I hope not," he said. "But that's why engineers like me spend time thinking about these scenarios. Because the best defense against a complex attack is understanding how it might work."

~

"LET'S open it up for questions," Knox said, clicking to his final slide. "And remember—the point isn't to scare you away from technology. It's to make you thoughtful about how we use it."

A bearded student in work clothes raised his hand. "I work at a chemical plant. How do we know if our systems have been compromised?"

"Monitor your baselines," Knox replied. "If your AI system suddenly starts making recommendations that deviate from historical patterns, ask why. Don't just accept that the algorithm knows better. Demand explanations."

"But what if the explanations sound reasonable?" Sarah asked.

"Then you dig deeper. Look at the actual data, not just the summaries. Compare outcomes across similar facilities. And always maintain manual overrides for critical processes."

Another student spoke up: "Is this why some people don't trust GMOs and stuff? Because they think the technology is too complex to be safe?"

Knox nodded. "There's a legitimate concern there. When technology becomes too complex for ordinary people to understand, it creates a democratic problem. How do you make informed decisions about things you can't comprehend?"

"So what's the answer?" Tyler asked.

"Education," Knox said simply. "We can't all be experts in everything, but we can all be literate enough to ask good questions. That's what this class is really about—giving you the vocabulary to have meaningful conversations with the machines that increasingly run our world."

The classroom fell silent. Knox looked at the clock: five minutes left.

"One last thought," he said. "My generation built these systems with the best of intentions. We wanted to make things more efficient, more precise, more reliable. And mostly, we succeeded. But we also created dependencies that we didn't fully anticipate."

He gestured toward their phones. "All of you are carrying devices that connect you to systems you couldn't rebuild if you had to. Your food is grown by algorithms you'll never see. Your cars are controlled by computers you can't modify. Your money exists in databases you can't audit."

"That's not necessarily bad," Knox continued. "But it means you have responsibilities. When you vote, when you buy products, when you choose careers—you're making decisions about what kind of technological society you want to live in."

The bell rang. Students began packing up their laptops and notebooks.

"For next week," Knox called out over the shuffling, "I want you to pick one automated system in your daily life and research how it actually works. Not just what it does, but how it does it. Elevator control systems, traffic lights, credit card fraud detection—whatever interests you. Come prepared to explain it to the class."

As students filed out, Sarah approached the podium. "Professor Ramsey? That was really interesting. I'm majoring in cybersecurity, and I've been thinking about doing my capstone project on industrial control systems."

"That's great," Knox said, packing up his laptop. "What's your focus?"

"I want to look at vulnerabilities in agricultural automation. After what you said about growing systems being hackable... I'm wondering if anyone's actually trying to exploit those vulnerabilities."

Knox's chest tightened. "That's... that's a really important question, Sarah. Have you thought about reaching out to some of the local cannabis companies? They might be willing to let you do a security assessment."

"Actually," Sarah said, "I was hoping you might have some contacts. Didn't I read that you used to run an ag-tech company?"

Knox forced a smile. "I'll see what I can do. Send me an email with your project proposal, and I'll make some introductions."

As Sarah left, Knox lingered by the whiteboard, the ghost of his diagrams still visible—black boxes, trust lines, unanswered arrows. He couldn't remember the last time he'd felt useful. Maybe this counted—sowing doubt in minds still wired to wonder.

But he also felt exposed, as if speaking these warnings aloud had somehow made them more real.

7 WHISKERS
METRO-DETROIT

Dorothy Hausmann had never been in a cannabis dispensary before.

The walls were too white, the lighting too bright—like an Apple store had merged with a pharmacy.

Her daughter Rachel walked ahead, confident in this space, greeting the security guard by name.

"Mom, stop looking like you're buying heroin," Rachel whispered, squeezing her mother's hand. "This is legal. This is medicine."

Dorothy nodded, clutching her purse. Two days since Whiskers died. Fourteen years of that cat greeting her every morning, and now just an empty food dish she couldn't bring herself to wash. The Xanax her doctor prescribed sat untouched—she'd seen what benzos did to her sister.

"This is natural," Rachel was saying, pointing at amber gummies in childproof containers. "From plants. TR Cannabis—they're local, super reputable. Their products helped me through my dissertation anxiety."

The budtender, a young man with kind eyes, explained dosages with practiced patience.

"First time? Start with two and a half milligrams. You can always take more, but you can't take less."

Dorothy bought the smallest package—ten gummies, five milligrams each. Rachel showed her how to bite them in half.

"Quarter for mild relaxation, half if you really need to sleep. Wait two hours before taking more—edibles sneak up on you."

In the parking lot, Dorothy hugged her daughter. "Thank you for not judging your old mother."

"Text me when you get home," Rachel said. "Let me know how you feel."

Dorothy's house in Grosse Pointe was too quiet. Whiskers' litter box still sat in the laundry room. His favorite toy—a felt mouse missing one ear—lay under the coffee table. She'd clean tomorrow. Tonight, she just needed not to think.

She examined the gummy under the kitchen light. It looked like candy her grandchildren would eat. Smelled vaguely of artificial watermelon. She bit it in half, then reconsidered and took the whole thing. Five milligrams. The package said *mild relaxation.*

She settled into her recliner, local news droning: a story about Movement Festival preparations, another about construction on I-94. Typical Tuesday night in metro Detroit.

Half an hour later, she thought it wasn't working.

Ten minutes after that, warmth spread through her chest—pleasant at first, then strange. Her mouth felt dry.

She stood for water, and the room tilted. Not spinning—shifting, like the house itself had slipped an inch sideways. She gripped the counter. Her heart was misfiring, not racing but stuttering, a skipped beat every few seconds.

"This is normal," she said aloud. "Rachel said it might feel weird at first."

Her hands began to shake, the wedding ring ticking against the Formica. The warmth in her chest became heat, rising up her neck into her skull. Her vision prismed at the edges.

She needed her phone. Call Rachel. But her legs wouldn't coordinate. She made it three steps before her knee buckled. The carpet came up fast.

On the floor, she could see Whiskers' dish. Still had food in it. She'd filled it the morning he died, habit stronger than grief. The kibble had been there two days now.

Her tongue felt thick. Metallic taste flooding her mouth.

This wasn't what Rachel described. This was wrong.

The seizure hit without warning. Her body went rigid, then convulsed. The coffee table jumped with each spasm. The remote fell, changing channels—shopping network, weather, static.

When it stopped, she couldn't move. Could barely breathe. Just enough strength to turn her head toward the counter. The package sat there: TR Cannabis. Batch number visible on the label. *Tested. Regulated. Safe.*

Her last thought was that Rachel would blame herself.

RACHEL STARTED CALLING AT TEN. Her mother was usually in bed by nine, but she always answered. The first call went to voicemail. The second. By the third, Rachel was grabbing her keys.

The twenty-minute drive took fifteen. She used the spare key, calling out as she entered. The TV was on—QVC selling jewelry her mother would never buy.

She found Dorothy by the recliner. Still warm but wrong, limbs at angles that meant the end had been violent. The gummy package on the counter, one missing.

Rachel's scream brought neighbors. Then police. Then EMTs who could do nothing but confirm what she already knew.

By midnight, she was at Detroit Receiving, the same hospital that would be overwhelmed four days later. A tired resident took her statement, catalogued her mother's medications, bagged the gummies as evidence.

"Appears to be an adverse reaction," he told her. "Possibly an unknown allergy or interaction. These things happen with new users. I'm sorry for your loss."

The morning news covered it briefly:

A Grosse Pointe woman dies after cannabis consumption. Officials are investigating but stress that regulated products undergo extensive testing. The dispensary named has no other reported incidents.

In his townhouse, Knox Ramsey half-heard the report while reviewing FarmCore deployments—rows of green status bars, each reflecting recipes generated by FarmLytics and pushed across the network. Everything operating normally.

In Shanghai, a technician logged the first successful field test. Proof of concept achieved.

Rachel sat in her mother's kitchen, staring at Whiskers' dish, wondering how trying to help had killed the person she loved most.

The answer lived eighteen months in the past, seven thousand miles away, in lines of code scrolling through the darkness of a Shanghai operations center.

8 OUTBREAK

DETROIT — FIRST CLUSTERS

The bass from Movement Festival shook Hart Plaza like a second heartbeat. Lasers strobed across the Detroit River, ricocheting off the glass towers of the Renaissance Center.

To anyone in the crowd, it was bliss. To EMS crews at the perimeter, it was a nightmare blooming in real time.

At 11:17 p.m., a kid collapsed near the sound tent. Security called it dehydration.

Another went down at 11:22—pills, maybe.

By 11:30, six patients lay in the medical tent, unresponsive, vitals sliding into the same pattern.

"Not fentanyl," EMT Carla Reyes muttered as she clipped a monitor onto a twenty-year-old still wearing his wristband. "No pinpoint pupils. No respiratory depression. This is different."

Her partner, Jamal, checked the IV line.

"Core temp's normal. Not heatstroke either. ECG's clean except for that QT stretch."

"Electrolyte crash?"

"Not that fast."

The generator hiccuped under load.

The air reeked of sweat, beer, and ozone from a nearby fog cannon.

Someone screamed in the crowd; no one turned. Detroit knew how to tune out noise until it mattered.

They exchanged a look—the kind medics develop when training runs out and instinct takes over.

She looked up.

The crowd kept dancing.

Some were too high to notice, others too invested to care.

To them, stretchers were just part of the festival vibe—a bad trip, a heat stroke, someone else's problem.

By 11:45, Detroit Receiving's ambulance bay was already stacked three rigs deep.

The medics inside their units knew the truth: the night was just beginning.

DETROIT RECEIVING — THE EPICENTER

The ER smelled of antiseptic fighting a losing war against sweat, vomit, and metallic blood.

A fluorescent light near triage flickered, buzzing faintly every time the HVAC kicked on.

Charge nurse Tanya Franklin slapped the counter.

"Listen up! Patel, Zone A triage. Walker, IV access only. Ramirez, tox screens. Residents—you're runners tonight. Forget your ego. MOVE."

Someone dropped a sharps container. A nurse kicked it under a gurney to clear space.

Another ripped off gloves and reached bare-handed for a crashing patient because seconds mattered more than OSHA tonight.

Beds disappeared in ten minutes.

Hallways became holding pens.

IV poles were packed so tight their bags tapped like metronomes.

A psych patient from earlier screamed down the hall, ignored now that the stretchers kept rolling in. Nobody had time to sedate him again.

A resident tried to shoulder into trauma; Tanya blocked him with one palm. "You're fetching labs now, doc. Don't argue."

She yanked open her caboodle—her personal drawer of order in a storm. Tape front-left, IV caths by gauge, 10s next to the tourniquets, alcohol preps tucked vertical so she could grab three at once. A volunteer reached in and she snapped, "Don't touch my stuff." People laughed about nurse caboodles—until the night you needed one to be perfect.

Someone yelled "Need a line in three!" and she tossed a 20-gauge without looking, hitting the air mid-arc. It landed in a palm that didn't even glance back.

They wheeled in a patient she knew. Noah Johnson's son—twenty-one. He'd shoveled her sidewalk in January when her snowblower died. Her face stayed steady, but her hands trembled once before the IV bit vein.

"Stabilize, bed, move on," Tanya said.

Dr. Adrian Ellis was attempting his seventh intubation of the night when a nurse called out from triage.

"Dr. Ellis! We're finding a pattern."

He finished securing the tube, nodded to the RT to bag, and strode over. The nurse had laid out evidence bags on the counter—seven of them, each containing colorful packaging.

"TR Cannabis," she said, pointing. "Gummy wrappers. We've pulled them from pockets, backpacks, one kid had the actual package still in his hand when EMS brought him in."

Ellis picked up one of the bags, reading the label through the plastic. "Batch number?"

"24-0316. This one's 24-0318. They're all from the same manufacturer, all festival editions—high dose, marketed to the EDM crowd."

"How many patients?"

"Seventeen confirmed with wrappers on their person. Another eight whose friends say they shared from the same packages. We're still searching personal effects on the ones who came in unconscious."

Ellis felt his stomach drop. "Get me the batch manager at TR Cannabis. Now."

"It's 1 a.m., doctor."

"I don't care if it's Christmas morning. Someone at that company needs to know their product is in the pockets of dying kids."

Overhead: "Code Triage—External. Activate Hospital Incident Command System."

The house supervisor—tonight's bed czar—stepped into the command alcove with a grease board already half full:

```
ED beds open: 4
ICU beds open: 2
```

```
Step-down: 3
Peds ICU: 1
Vents available: 5 (+4 recoverable from PACU)
RTs on site / en route: 3 / 4
OR anesthesia on-call: paged
```

"Thirty-minute huddles," she said. "ED charge, ICU charge, RT lead, pharmacy, lab, security, facilities. Poison Center liaison stays with med control."

By midnight, the board read ED capacity: 140%.

A younger nurse said what everyone felt: "We're beyond surge. This is flood."

HOSPITAL NET — FIRST HUDDLE (00:05)

The HEAR/Hospital Net channel crackled. A calm voice from Medical Control cut through static.

"Receiving, Ford, Sinai-Grace: declare current capacity, vent availability, and ability to accept criticals. Detroit EOC on bridge."

```
Receiving: "ED over capacity. Two ICU beds. Five vents,
four PACU vents convertible. Can take three criticals with
immediate RT support, then divert."

Henry Ford: "ED red. One NICU vent adaptable, two anes-
thesia machines prepped. Can board intubated in PACU if
staffed. Taking five criticals max."

Sinai-Grace: "At limit. We can stabilize four, no vents
left. RT en route. Request mutual aid for ventilators."
```

The Poison Center patched in mid-call. "Field reports indicate cannabis-related ingestion possible. Monitor hepatic function, prepare tox panels outside standard recreational screens."

"Copy. Establish regional rotation: RCV → HFN → SGH, then out-of-city diversion as needed. Huddle every thirty. Broadcast MCI tag colors to unify triage."

The line went quiet except for rotors and sirens.

Across town, Henry Ford's intake nurse keyed her radio with shaking fingers.

Gunshot victims from the west side were already stacked in fast track; one bled through a makeshift dressing while trauma teams argued over bed priority.

"We're full. Divert them."

"Divert where?" came back from dispatch.

Every hall light burned white-hot; anesthesia carts rolled into rooms that weren't ORs. Monitors beeped out of sync, a mechanical chorus of exhaustion. Someone vomited into a glove; someone else caught a blood-soaked pad midair.

The Lodge was gridlocked. Parents jammed Woodward, screaming into phones, ignoring sirens. Police tried to carve lanes; panic ate the right-of-way.

Some EMS crews parked on curbs and started care in place—bagging patients under streetlights while the bass rolled across the river. Sweat ran off medics' necks; their squeezes took on a rhythm that matched the kick drum from Hart Plaza.

The intake hall floor was slick—saline, sweat, and blood turning tiles into a hazard. A nurse's shoe skidded once before she caught herself on a rail.

Inside, Dr. Nguyen scanned the intake board.

```
Criticals waiting: 6
Vented: 3
Non-invasive: 4
RTs: 2 on floor, 1 in transit
PACU vents: 2 convertible
```

Anesthesia available: 1 attending in-house, 2 on-call

A resident sobbed in a stairwell; Nguyen hauled him back by the sleeve. "You can cry later. Right now you move."

She glanced at the board again, softer: "Half of these aren't festival kids anymore."

By 1:30 a.m., security guard Jerome Washington had collected enough evidence bags to fill a shopping cart.

TR Cannabis wrappers. All of them.

Some were crumpled, stuffed in jean pockets and pulled out by nurses searching for ID. Others were pristine, still in the vendor's shrink wrap. A few had been dropped on the ambulance bay floor, trampled by EMTs rushing stretchers inside.

Jerome logged each one methodically:

```
Evidence #HF-001: Gummy wrapper, TR Cannabis, batch 24-
0317, found in possession of Male #7 (festival wristband
purple)

Evidence #HF-002: Gummy wrapper, TR Cannabis, batch 24-
0316, found beside Female #3 (unresponsive, seizing)
```

Evidence #HF-003: Full package, TR Cannabis "Festival Edition," batch 24-0319, found in backpack of Male #12

He photographed each wrapper, uploaded the images to the hospital's evidence server, then sealed them in tamper-proof bags with chain-of-custody forms. Time, initials, and transfer location noted on every seal.

By 2 a.m., he'd logged thirty-two items.

All TR Cannabis.

All from batches shipped within the past ten days.

A resident named Dr. Sarah Okafor stopped at his desk. "You seeing a pattern?"

"Same manufacturer, same product line, batches all clustered together." Jerome pointed at his spreadsheet. "Whatever contaminated these, it happened at the source or during processing."

"We need to contact the company."

"Already did. Left four voicemails. Texted the emergency number. Nothing."

Dr. Okafor pulled out her phone. "Then we call the owner directly. What's the company name again?"

"TR Cannabis. Out of Detroit proper." Jerome pulled up the business registration. "Owner-operator: Tate Ramsey."

He found the personal contact number and dialed.

It rang four times before a panicked voice answered.

"This is Tate."

Sinai-Grace was already thin before the first ambulance. By 12:30 a.m., the night supervisor slammed a fist into a supply cart.

"We're out of vents."

The words hung like a bell.

The hallway fans were blowing warm. A CNA taped extension cords together to run portable monitors from an outlet meant for a coffee maker. It hummed under the weight of desperation.

Nurses stumbled in off-shift, some on a second twelve. Some didn't answer—they were at Movement themselves. The veterans came anyway. They always did.

Dr. Ellis stared at five patients lined up for three ventilators. "You bag them until we get more," he told two residents. "Switch every fifteen."

They nodded, knuckles whitening around the bags.

Rotor wash rattled the glass; the thuds synced with their squeezes.

Sweat made elbow creases burn.

A student tried to help and got redirected to the blood bank hand-off loop—carry in, sign out, carry back.

"Call facilities," the supervisor said. "Roll in the step-down monitors. I don't care if they don't match. We need rhythm and pressure on every bed."

THE PATTERN EMERGES

EMT Carla Reyes stood in the ambulance bay at 2:15 a.m., talking to a Detroit Police evidence tech who'd been called in to help process the overwhelming number of potential poisoning cases.

"Every patient we've brought in from Hart Plaza had these." She held up a gallon Ziploc bag filled with wrapper scraps—bright colors, foil backing, QR codes still visible on some. "TR Cannabis gummy wrappers. We started bagging them in the field once we saw the pattern."

The evidence tech, a woman named Detective Lisa Chen, snapped photos with her department-issued camera. "How many total?"

"From our unit alone? Maybe twenty wrappers across twelve patients. Other crews are reporting the same thing. One medic said he pulled a half-eaten gummy out of a kid's mouth during CPR."

Chen stopped photographing. "Did the kid make it?"

Carla's expression said everything.

"Bag that gummy if you still have it," Chen said quietly. "Priority evidence. And get me contact info for TR Cannabis—the owner, the facility manager, whoever signed off on these batches."

"Already tried. Voicemail's full."

Chen looked at the time: 2:17 a.m. "Then we go knock on doors. You have an address for this operation?"

Carla checked her phone—she'd already searched it between calls. "Industrial park off Mound Road. Place called TR Cannabis Manufacturing and Distribution."

"Let's go."

"Poison Center on the line," a clerk said, plugging in a splitter so Ellis could hear updates hands-free. "They're seeing the same symptom cluster in Detroit and getting pings from outstate."

Ellis looked at the nearest vent. "We're improvising life support in a Level II," he muttered.

Nobody argued.

Ambulances were now stacked two-thirds down the EMS driveway, paramedics triaging right in open air.

A heavyset medic with N95 mask lines indented into his cheeks started clipping laminated red tags to unconscious teens and shouting "BREATHING, NOT BREATH-ING, CONSCIOUS, NOT!" as his partner yanked another gurney straight into a rain of broken glass bottles and spilled Red Bull.

Nurses skidded in and out, slapping EKG leads onto bare chests and double-taping IV lines to flushed forearms.

Rows of discarded wristbands swept to the corners—purple, blue, green, now stained copper and rust.

The EMS command cart ran out of radios at 1:20 a.m. and resorted to walkie-talkies scavenged from school safety stock. A few off-duty firemen found a cache of ancient yellow disaster vests, pulling them on over hoodies as they bled through protocol to just do whatever saved a pulse.

ER techs used painter's tape for names—

`Unknown Male #7`

`Purple Hat`

`DOB ??`

They rushed patients straight from curb to crash bay, bypassing the front desk and triage forms.

Inside, the halls felt scaffolded with lines and bodies.

Bed rails jammed, and IV bags were held by family members—"hold this high, don't let it clog" because all the poles were gone.

In radiology, a transporter barked at a radiologist, "Just say clear—don't argue," as a trauma team dragged a patient onto the scanner, tracking saline and blood behind.

The command center repurposed breakroom whiteboards for at-a-glance capacity.

Someone scrawled, "Don't forget: eat, drink, pee," replaced the bathroom sign with "Code triage, toilet breaks on the honor system."

Power chargers dangled from every outlet, nurses swapping phones like fevers—"Text your next of kin, just in case," became an unsent joke between compressions.

At Receiving, Dr. Ellis grabbed a mop to clear a streak of blood, then used the handle to prop open a cooler.

"Every body with a vent, write your time on the sticker. Nobody forgets."

Respiratory techs scrounged last year's flu-pandemic gear—adapters for BiPAP, old circuit splitters, gloves in the wrong sizes.

Sometimes the gear worked; sometimes it shattered in desperate hands.

Out in the parking lot, a city cop knelt beside a crying woman, holding her hand while her phone's low battery light blinked. "He's somewhere in there," she said, voice gone thin. "Just somewhere."

With trembling hands, a medical student wrote drug allergies across patients' forearms in block letters, being in charge of Sharpie duty before the next round of sedative push.

Above it all, the city pushed on.

Helicopters thudded overhead, spotlight beams crawling through the dark; chopper pilots watched festival crowds scatter as word of the outbreak finally broke.

Twitter and Reddit became triage rooms of their own—advice threads, rumor chases, digital pleas for information on siblings and friends.

At one point, the call log jammed: "No more outside lines," a tech announced. Nurses called dispatch on their cell phones, then on borrowed ones, then gave up and just yelled room numbers to anyone with a free arm.

Near sunrise, as the music finally died, a wave of bone-deep fatigue settled over every corridor.

In one supply closet, a volunteer slid to the floor, closed eyes, and let the scent of saline, peroxide, and defeat wash over her. No one saw her cry, but everyone felt the weight.

Still, the huddles rolled on.

Still, the city tried.

This was Detroit—improvised hope in the teeth of the impossible.

CITYWIDE DISPATCH — System Failure

The dispatch board glowed red:

Receiving: DIVERT (critical rotation only)

Henry Ford: CRITICAL

Sinai-Grace: CAPACITY EXCEEDED

Beaumont Royal Oak: ACCEPTING LIMITED

U-M Ann Arbor: ACCEPTING CRITICALS ONLY

Toledo: ACCEPTING WHEN AVAILABLE

Phones rang in layers: parents begging, hospitals demanding, police requesting staging. A dispatcher pinched the bridge of his nose. Protocol said no field intubation without med control; tonight he overrode it.

"Central to all units: treat in place if transport exceeds twenty minutes. If med control approves RSI, proceed. Repeat—treat in place."

It wasn't by the book. The book had burned an hour ago.

FIRST MULTI-HOSPITAL HUDDLE — 00:30

"Receiving?"

"ED 160%. Two new ICU beds opened by moving step-down. Pharmacy pushed a second tox cart to triage."

"Ford?"

"Boarding five to PACU with anesthesia vents. One ICU bed freed—transferred to step-down. ICU float nurses en route."

"Sinai?"

"Bagging three. Respiratory team from Dearborn in fifteen. Can stabilize but not hold."

"Copy.

9 MEDIA AND LOCAL AWARENESS

The city was live on every channel.

News choppers circled.

Anchors shouted over sirens.

Parents clawed at barricades.

Twitter feeds lit up with shaky cell-phone video: stretchers weaving through Hart Plaza, hashtags climbing in minutes — #DetroitCollapse, #ToxicBeats, #PrayForMovement.

Inside, language broke down to fragments.

"Airway!"

"Out of vents!"

"Switch bags!"

"Move the fucking blood!"

Receiving's incident command pushed a message to all three hospitals and city EOC: 30-min ICS huddles continue; unified bed count every huddle; Poison Center memo v2 pending; consider OR/anesthesia machines as vents; RT mutual aid status GREEN; media to be handled by PIO only.

Local Facebook groups filled with frantic posts: "Does anyone know if Sinai is diverting? My cousin's there." "Avoid Receiving — they say the ER is chaos."

And still, the music pounded at Hart Plaza, indifferent.

DETROIT & GRAND RAPIDS

The anchors' voices carried that careful-disaster cadence: not yet panic, but rehearsing for it. A lower-third crawled with mismatched numbers—Hospitalizations: TBD | Tox Screens Pending—while the studio desk glowed antiseptic blue.

"—and we're going live now to our team in Detroit," the anchor said, eyes flicking to the right camera. "Jasmine?"

The screen split into a jittering two-shot: Detroit on the left—fluorescents, sweating shoppers, produce shelves stripped to pale scars; Grand Rapids on the right—wider aisles, hand-lettered signs taped to empty bins: OUT OF STOCK / VENDOR HOLD. Audio clipped, IFB chirped; an entire state leaned forward.

"Matt," Jasmine said, fighting her earpiece and a drifting focus ring, "we're at Midtown Market on Woodward where management has pulled all leafy greens and pre-packaged salad kits after state guidance. People are still coming in, still buying what's left—carrots, potatoes, bottled water, paper goods. The manager tells me he's never seen anything like this outside a snowstorm."

Her mic found a woman pinning a toddler against her hip, list crumpled in her fist.

"If the government says maybe, I hear no," the woman said. "I'm not feeding my kids anything green tonight. Or tomorrow. Or—" She stopped, breath catching. "We're doing pasta. We'll figure it out."

Jasmine nodded toward the shelf where clamshells once sat. Someone had wiped the price rails clean like as if they were covering their tracks. A stocker slid in, tape-gunned a new sign: HOLD FOR QA — DO NOT STOCK. He didn't meet the camera.

On the right, Grand Rapids: colder light, steadier feed. "We're at Fulton Fresh," the second reporter said, "where the manager's posting batch numbers at the service desk and online. He says transparency is the only way to keep customers."

They put him on: Ahmad Nassar, sleeves rolled, barcode list on a clipboard, calm that read as courage. "We're tracking by lot," he said. "Bring a package back—tell us the time, the lane, the label. We'll refund it, log it, no blame at the register. We're not turning neighbors into suspects."

Detroit cut to a cart piled with bottled water and rice. "We're hearing the same questions," Jasmine said. "Is this just cannabis? Are we supposed to wash vegetables more? Skip salad entirely? The health department says they're investigating multiple controlled-environment facilities, but for now—common-sense precautions."

A hallway sound bite rolled from a county official, the kind of place where bad news gets softened by acoustics: "…no evidence at this time that open-field produce is affected… our message is targeted, not alarmist…"

The words were careful; the chyron undercut them: #AGRIATTACK Trending in Detroit & Grand Rapids.

Back to Detroit. Jasmine introduced Lila Cortez, store manager, posture tight with exhaustion.

"Ms. Cortez, you pulled your entire hydroponic line."

"Fifteen minutes after the state call," Lila said. "I've got regulars. They trust us. You don't wait on trust."

"What are customers saying?"

"They're saying 'Tell me what's safe.' I'm saying 'Tell me what's traceable.' I can work with traceable."

Grand Rapids cut to a clerk dating onions with masking tape. A teenager asked if frozen spinach was okay. "Frozen's field-grown," the clerk said. "We're not hearing about that." Relief flickered like hope.

The studio anchor reappeared in her box, metronomic calm barely holding. "We're hearing reports of pharmacies seeing an uptick in activated-charcoal purchases and ERs fielding calls about 'detox.' Doctors caution against self-medicating."

B-roll: empty supplement shelves. A caption sprinted past: DO NOT TREAT YOURSELF FOR INDUSTRIAL TOXICOLOGY AT HOME, DOCTORS SAY.

Jasmine raised her mic as a man in a Carhartt jacket loaded flats of ramen.

"Sir—how are you deciding what to buy?"

"I'm deciding I can't trust a label," he said. "Saw a thing online—said they flip a switch and your lettuce turns into poison."

"Who's they?"

"Whoever built the switches." He moved past her toward the registers.

The lower-third blinked: STATE HOTLINE OVERWHELMED / USE WEBSITE FOR NON-EMERGENCIES.

A QR code flashed too briefly for anyone to scan. In Grand Rapids, a woman at customer service read lot numbers into the camera like prayer beads: 24-0316-A, -B, -C… Her hand shook; her voice didn't.

Social montage rolled: fridge photos, shelf-stripping videos, beige dinners tagged #SaladStrike, #WashTwice, #ItWasFineYesterday.

In the flood—a fake label appeared, bold red triangle, counterfeit federal seal. For three seconds it filled the frame; for three seconds a million people learned to fear a sticker.

"Correction," the anchor said quickly. "That label is not real—we repeat—"

But the screen had already jumped to a Detroit Medical doctor, eyes sandbagged. "This is chemistry," she said. "Not a ghost. We will find it."

Back to Detroit. Lila faced the camera. "My coworkers' kids work at that grow downriver," she said. "They're scared they hurt somebody. They didn't. Someone used them to do it. There's a difference."

Grand Rapids again: Ahmad slid a laminated sheet under the lens—ugly, functional, exact. HOW TO READ YOUR LABEL. "Take a photo," he said. "If we recall, you'll know."

The anchor received a late note in her ear. "City PIO says a full statement from the emergency operations center is expected within the hour. For now, officials stress patience."

Another split shot: a cop directing traffic at a parking-lot choke point; a school sending a robocall advising packed lunches tomorrow. In Detroit, a pastor handed out paper grocery lists with substitutions for greens—cabbage slaw, roasted roots. People took them like maps.

Jasmine squeezed against a cooler to let a woman through. The woman paused and looked into the lens, eyes bright with fear. "Just tell us the truth fast," she said. "I can handle bad. I can't handle maybe."

The feed glitched—black for a heartbeat—then returned live. Someone counted down off-screen: "Three, two, one."

The anchor straightened, smile too bright. "Stay with us. After the break, an expert on indoor farming systems explains how these systems work—and how they can be secured."

DETROIT & GRAND RAPIDS LOCAL AFFILIATES

DETROIT—"We restocked three times today," said Lila Cortez, store manager, sleeve pushed to her elbow, barcode gun holstered like a sidearm. "I told my team: you don't promise what you can't put on a shelf. People forgive 'sold out.' They don't forgive 'you lied to me.'"

GRAND RAPIDS—"We had a woman crying in frozen foods," said Ahmad

Nassar, assistant manager. "She'd bought carrots yesterday and her kid's coughing today. I'm not a doctor. All I could do was get her a chair, water, and call the nurse line on speaker so she didn't have to explain it twice."

DETROIT—"We're posting lot numbers at the register," Lila added. "If there's a recall, people will know exactly what they bought. That's the only way you rebuild trust—numbers, not vibes."

The camera caught her scribbling a sign in Sharpie: CHECKOUT STAFF CAN PRINT YOUR RECEIPT WITH SOURCE BATCH. A customer photographed it like proof that reality still had rules.

DAY 1 — NIGHT

#GroceryGate trending. A teenager on TikTok held up a clamshell of spinach and a whiteboard marker, narrating step by step: "How to read your label (no BS)."

A duet from a conspiracy channel overlaid bright red "TOXIN WARNING" stickers across the package.

A community note scrolled in response: "Label image is fabricated." Despite the correction, the original clip still had twice the likes of the rebuttal.

10 AFTER THE BASS
THE ERS WORK THE DAWN

THIRD HUDDLE (03:15)

Radios crackled on the HEAR net. "Receiving?"

"ED 180%. Two OR machines converted to vents. Can hold three more intubated in PACU with anesthesia present. ICU now +1 bed; step-down opened four via early discharges."

"Ford?"

"PACU boarding four. Anesthesia handling vents. Two RTs arrived from outside facility. Can accept two red tags in next ten."

"Sinai?"

"Mutual aid RT on scene. Bagging down to one patient. Vent swap in progress. Can accept two yellows; no reds for twenty."

"Copy. Rotation adjusted: Ford → Receiving for red; Sinai holds yellows; blacks to coroner staging when cleared."

No one liked speaking the last line out loud.

Tanya flicked her eyes down the hall. A resident she'd bounced earlier ran labs like a machine now, sweat plastering hair to his forehead. She opened the caboodle with a click she could have recognized in her sleep and restocked from muscle memory: tape, caths, 10s, preps, flushes. She didn't believe in luck, but she believed in this drawer.

She walked past Noah Johnson's son—stabilized, monitored, still too quiet for twenty-one—and felt the tremor in her hands start again. She stilled them on the metal rail. Then she went back to work.

"CENTRAL TO ALL UNITS: due to hospital saturation, treat in place if ETA exceeds twenty minutes. If patient is red-tagged and transport is cleared through Medical Control, go to Ford; if Ford is red, go to Receiving; if both red, Sinai will stabilize only. Air assets prioritize pediatrics and ventilated. Confirm."

"Confirmed," a dozen voices said, some steady, some ragged.

AT DAWN, the bass finally faded.

Nurses staggered into parking lots, scrubs stiff with blood and sweat. Helicopters peeled off toward out-of-city hospitals; the sky went briefly quiet.

One nurse slid into her car and dropped her lighter twice before it caught. She stared at her hands. "Can't fucking believe I just worked on Noah Johnson's kid."

Two colleagues hugged by the ambulance bay, masks hanging loose, eyes hollow. One muttered into the other's shoulder: "We weren't ready for this."

Above them, news choppers hovered. Reporters taped stand-ups about chaos, casualties, unanswered questions. The staff didn't watch.

Detroit wasn't watching the news.

Detroit was the news.

And somewhere downriver, a reporter noticed the flashing lights still hadn't stopped.

HART PLAZA — 4:12 A.M.

By the time the sun bled faint gray over the Detroit River, most of the festival crowd had thinned to diehards and debris. But the ambulances were still there.

Jasmine Vega, a stringer for Channel 7, had come for color—crowd shots, DJs, the Detroit-resilience B-roll she could sell on slow Mondays. What she found instead were rigs idling at every curb, their strobes spinning against concrete like silent alarms.

She counted six units along Atwater. Then seven. A city that used to go quiet after last call now hummed with diesel and radio squelch. EMTs moved with a rhythm too fast for routine.

"Rough night?" she asked one medic outside the perimeter.

He didn't stop moving. "Stay clear, ma'am."

She tried again, softer. "Overdoses?"

"Not that kind." He said it without looking up, and that was enough to set her instincts burning.

She panned her camera toward the tented area. The zoom caught a stretcher being loaded, the limp wrist of a kid still wearing his wristband. Another stretcher followed. Two, then three. Her gut told her this wasn't dehydration.

The first tweet went out at 4:16 a.m.

@JasVega7: Seeing a lot of EMS activity at #MovementFest tonight. Multiple transports. No official info yet—hope everyone's okay. #Detroit

Minutes later came a twenty-second clip of paramedics working on the curb, tagged #StayHydratedDetroit. Within an hour it had three thousand views.

By 4:45, other posts followed:

"Ambulances still here."

"Not fentanyl, they say?"

"Anyone know what's happening at Hart Plaza?"

The hashtags changed faster than the news cycle could catch up: #MovementUnwell → #ToxicBeats → #DetroitCollapse.

Jasmine turned her mic toward the skyline, the red glow of the Renaissance Center behind her. "Unconfirmed reports of a medical emergency at Movement Festival," she said into her phone. "Details coming as we learn more."

She went live before an official statement—before hospitals could even declare capacity.

By sunrise her clip was everywhere, often without credit.

She ended the feed with a look over her shoulder at the darkened plaza—empty tents sagging like forgotten promises, EMTs still clustered in reflective vests as dawn's first light slashed through fog. She tapped Off-Air on her phone and exhaled, the tension in her shoulders refusing to ease.

Behind her, the hum of diesel faded into the distant roar of early-morning traffic. A drone's red LED blinked overhead—another newsroom's eyes already scanning. Jasmine knew retweeters would turn her cautious questions into urgent headlines before the health department even woke up.

She pocketed her device and slung her camera bag over one shoulder, the weight a small comfort against the chaos she'd just captured. Detroit had been the story all night; now she was about to watch it explode across every network.

In the press van, her producer's voice crackled through the headset: "Lock in for the grocery-panic segment. They want you live in five."

Jasmine clicked her mic back on. "They're onto something," she murmured as the van doors swung open. "And we're the ones who found it."

Without another glance at the plaza, she jogged toward the highway—where the day's real story, empty produce shelves and terrified shoppers, was already taking shape.

11 THE 3 AM CALLS

Tate Ramsey's phone rang for the fourth time in ten minutes.

Detroit Receiving. Henry Ford. Sinai-Grace. Now Detroit Police.

He answered the police call first.

"Mr. Ramsey, this is Detective Lisa Chen, Detroit PD. We're outside your facility on Mound Road. We need you here immediately to provide access for an emergency investigation."

"Investigation? What—"

"Your gummy wrappers are on seventeen patients at Detroit Receiving alone. More at Henry Ford and Sinai. At least three fatalities with your product in their system." Chen's voice was professional but hard. "So either you get down here in the next thirty minutes, or we're getting a warrant and coming in anyway."

Tate was already pulling on clothes, phone cradled against his shoulder. "I'm coming. Twenty minutes."

"Make it fifteen. People are dying."

He ended the call and immediately dialed his father.

At 3:11 AM, Knox Ramsey's phone rang in Grand Rapids.

12 WAYNE COUNTY
EMERGENCY COORDINATION CENTER

DETROIT, MICHIGAN—07:45 A.M.

The conference room was built for storms, not politics—reinforced walls, redundant power, a map of Detroit pinned with magnetic tags marking every hospital still taking patients. Folding tables formed a horseshoe around the county seal stamped into worn linoleum.

Laptops and tablets blinked with agency logos: CDC, FBI, DOJ, Attorney General's Office, State Police. The fluorescents overhead buzzed with that particular frequency that made everyone look sicker than they were.

Assistant U.S. Attorney Renee Cho rose, shoulders set at the angle prosecutors learn in rooms where people try to steal the air. "We have two objectives," she began, voice measured like a scalpel. "Protect public health and preserve evidence. Those goals intersect only if we act in concert."

SSA Jennifer Klein, FBI cyber squad supervisor, slid a manila folder across the table. The hinge creaked in the silence. "Six clusters flagged so far—Detroit, Grand Rapids, Lansing. All show identical telemetry anomalies in their hydroponic controllers. We need emergency warrants for every facility linked to VibeWorks within the hour."

MDHHS field epidemiologist Dr. Lydia Carr didn't sit. Her braid swung as she tapped the table. "If you seize grow houses before we collect patient samples, you blow chain of custody for the toxin assays. Then we can't link cause and effect."

Park's eyes didn't waver. "Evidence vanishes when you delay. We've seen labs burn, hard drives disappear, suspects lawyer up. We need to move first, analyze later."

"And watch patients die while you're cataloging servers?" Carr's voice sharpened. "We're treating people, not building cases. You can have your chain of custody after they stop seizing."

An FBI cyber agent leaned forward, knuckles white on the table edge. "Ma'am, if this is deliberate contamination, every minute we wait gives the perpetrator time to wipe logs and offshore accounts."

"And if we start impounding hospital servers mid-triage, people die. Choose your priority."

State Police Captain Jorge Ramirez cleared his throat, the peacemaker's cue. "We can stage perimeter security at each site. Prevent tampering. No arrests, no media. Just quiet containment."

Carr scrolled through her tablet, intake numbers climbing in real time. "We also need to tell the public something—fast. There's already a file circulating on Reddit claiming TR Cannabis collaborated with a Chinese state actor. We're under a disinformation attack while people are still coding in hallways."

Park rubbed her forehead. "Then our public line is simple: 'We're investigating multiple controlled-environment agriculture sites. No product recalls yet.' No mention of VibeWorks, no leaks on jurisdiction. Understood?"

The projector clicked to life, mapping clusters across southern Michigan in glowing red dots. In the momentary darkness before the image stabilized, the door opened.

Knox Ramsey entered, the two-hour sprint down I-96 etched into the salt-and-pepper at his temples. He carried a field-hardened laptop, scuffs at every corner, and moved with the careful economy of someone running on caffeine and stubbornness. The credentials on his visitor badge still read: Consultant, TR Cannabis.

"Mr. Ramsey," Park said smoothly, though her jaw tightened at the company name. "You're here as technical advisor."

National Security Advisor Hammond's local liaison, a man who'd introduced himself only as Davidson, rapped the table. "We've confirmed elevated liver enzymes consistent across all sites. CDC and Poison Control concur on synthetic agent. The question is delivery vector."

"Digital control systems," Knox said quietly, setting his laptop on the table. It wasn't a guess.

The FBI cyber lead turned sharply. "Meaning?"

"The grow environments share automation protocols. If someone altered nutrient delivery or lighting schedules through compromised firmware, you wouldn't detect it until harvest. You'd ship poison disguised as normal variance."

The room went still long enough for the HVAC to click on. Carr frowned, medical mind racing. "You're saying this is cyber-biological sabotage."

Knox nodded. "Engineered mis-calibration. Someone turned the precision against us."

The DOJ Deputy Assistant AG, who'd been silent until now, pounced. "Then this is an act of domestic terrorism. That moves jurisdiction to us."

Carr snapped back. "Not until CDC confirms pathogen or toxin origin. Health still leads."

"Cyberattack means Homeland," the FBI agent insisted. "And if there's an inter-state component, DOJ retains primacy."

"Primacy?" Carr's voice could have cut glass. "People are dying. Your primacy can wait."

Knox opened his laptop and began typing, the soft click of keys underneath the rising voices. "I've replicated the anomalies in a sandbox. Whoever did this inserted a micro-adapter layer at choke points, flipping safety protocols into kill commands. If you don't sequence your entry, you overwrite critical logs or destroy evidence."

Davidson rapped the table again, harder. "Enough. We're forming a joint cell—medical, criminal, cyber. Ramsey, you'll draft the technical architecture. CDC maintains medical lead; FBI handles attribution; DOJ holds evidence chain. Everyone signs the same situational log."

Knox exhaled through his teeth without looking up from his screen. "So the same people who can't share data are about to share a network."

Davidson's look was dry as dust. "You built closed systems. Now you'll help open one."

Screens around the room flickered as feeds from hospital telemetry tried to merge with encrypted DOJ channels. The first "joint" data handshake failed in under a minute—authentication mismatch, agency firewalls refusing to talk, each system speaking its own dialect of security.

Knox's fingers flew across the keyboard, rewriting API keys on the fly, building bridges between incompatible worlds. Behind him, the argument surged again—juris-diction, warrants, liability—white noise against the percussion of his typing.

Carr leaned toward him, voice low. "You can fix their toys?"

"I can make them talk," Knox said, eyes on the screen. "Doesn't mean they'll listen."

The DOJ man tried to reclaim the floor. "We need to establish culpability—"

Carr cut him off. "We need to keep people breathing."

Dr. Tamsin Bell from CDC Atlanta, participating via secure video, held up a finger on screen. "We need real-time feeds from FarmLytics and FarmCore's traceability logs. No more static PDFs. Live, continuous audit."

Klein tapped her tablet. "We'll push remote access through the warrants. Mr. Ramsey, you'll supervise overwrites and data captures."

Knox looked up once, catching his reflection in the dark window: tired, bloodshot, carrying the weight of a city that didn't care who won the bureaucratic knife fight as long as someone kept the lights on.

"Gentlemen," he said, not raising his voice but somehow filling the room. "You can debate chain of command later. Right now, we have a chain of failure."

The room fell silent. For ten seconds, everyone remembered why they were there.

Park stood, reasserting control. "Chain of command it is. Judge signs the warrant packet at 0300. FBI hits first site at 0330, CDC at 0400. We tell media at 0600 that we're 'actively investigating' and will update 'as information becomes available.' Mr. Ramsey leads technical coordination effective immediately, reports back hourly."

Bell's phone chimed. She glanced down, face tightening. "We have patient zero's diary. Says she was fine until she ate a salad from Midtown Market. Samples will confirm, but..." She looked up. "This gives us a traceable origin."

Park tapped the table twice, a judge's gavel in miniature. "Then we move. Agents, get your teams ready. Dr. Bell, prep your lab crews. Mr. Ramsey, keep that network breathing. This is containment and culpability in one operation. No margin for error."

As chairs scraped and jackets tightened, Knox's screen finally showed green across all connections. The interface stitched itself together—CDC telemetry in one pane, FBI intercepts in another, DOJ evidence-trail tagging beneath. At last, the data flowed.

Carr watched him work, the code reflecting off his glasses like a foreign language she almost understood. "You just made three enemies," she said.

Knox didn't look up from the screen. "Just three? I'm slowing down."

Outside the EOC windows, sirens still wailed through Detroit's darkness. Inside, something fragile had begun—cooperation born of exhaustion, held together by code and caffeine, racing against a poison that didn't care about jurisdiction.

The county seal on the floor caught a sliver of light as people filed out, an emblem of order in a night gone rogue, witnessed by a consultant who'd built the very systems now being turned into weapons.

13 SYSTEM-WIDE RESPONSE
PARALLEL STRIKE

The Solaris Festival sprawled across five hundred acres of Nevada desert, a manufactured dreamscape of LEDs and bass that made Movement look intimate by comparison. Seventy thousand people danced under towers of artificial daylight, every angle calculated for maximum social media impact. Where Detroit's festival had grown from the city's musical roots, Solaris was pure corporate spectacle—Instagram-perfect by design.

Kyle Hammond had worked festival medicine for eight years. Phoenix EMS before that. He knew the rhythm of a normal night: dehydration at midnight, bad trips by two, alcohol poisoning near dawn. But at 11:20 p.m. Pacific—three hours after Detroit's first call—his radio crackled with something different.

"Multiple seizures, south stage. This isn't heat stroke."

Kyle found five kids convulsing in the dust, foam on their lips, that same gray pallor he'd seen in a CDC bulletin two hours earlier. His partner Jessica was already checking pupils, finding the telltale neurological signs that didn't match any recreational drug profile.

Then he saw the bottles scattered around them. TR Cannabis syrup. The same logo that had been all over the Detroit reports.

"Command, we have a contamination event," Kyle said, keying his radio. "Same presentation as Detroit. TR Cannabis products. Notify Renown Regional we're going to need everything they've got."

By 4:15 a.m., Reno's trauma bay looked like Detroit's—stretchers in hallways, IV bags hanging from doorframes, that particular chaos of medical staff fighting something they didn't understand. But Dr. Alicia Ng noticed something that made her blood run cold.

"These aren't all festival patients," she told the charge nurse, scrolling intake. "This guy bought his edibles yesterday in Vegas. This woman got hers in Portland last week. Same lot numbers, different stores."

She opened the CDC reporting interface and typed fast: "Product contamination confirmed in retail distribution chain. Not limited to festival venues. Multi-state exposure through normal commercial channels."

In Atlanta, Dr. Jennifer Wu stared at her dashboard as dots lit up across the western United States. Portland. Denver. Phoenix. San Diego. Each one a dispensary, each one selling products that traced back to the same distribution network that supplied both festivals.

"It's not just events," she said to her supervisor. "It's the entire supply chain."

Within minutes, she was on a secure line to FDA, DEA, and FBI. "We have systematic contamination across at least eight states. This isn't accidental. The precision, timing, and distribution pattern point to someone weaponizing the legal market."

The federal task force activation came at 5:47 a.m. Pacific. By then, Kyle had processed thirty patients, all with the same story: legal products, proper labels, state-certified testing. The infrastructure designed to ensure safety had become the mechanism of attack.

In his Detroit warehouse, Tate watched the coverage with numb recognition. The same VibeWorks distribution network. The same product lines. His secure, encrypted, blockchain-tracked supply chain had been turned into a delivery system.

He pulled up his distribution database, hands shaking as he traced shipments. Both festivals. Twelve states. Hundreds of retail locations. All compromised through the same digital infrastructure he'd trusted to keep products safe.

It hadn't just hit two festivals. It had infiltrated the legal market, turning regulation against itself in a way no one had imagined possible.

The parallel strike was complete. Now it was spreading.

～

THE SECURE VIDEO link connected Liu Wei to Beijing at 0300 Shanghai time. Two faces appeared: Deputy Director Zhao from MSS Science and Technology, and General Wu from PLA General Staff Intelligence Bureau.

Behind Liu Wei, Dr. Chen stood at the biological monitoring station displaying harvest-cycle progression data, Dr. Wu at network surveillance, and Captain Zhang positioned between them.

"Director Liu," Zhao began. "Your status report."

Liu Wei pulled up the progression timeline. "Operation Harvest Cloud is performing according to biological models. We are in the transition between first-cycle and second-cycle manifestation."

Data from U.S. distributors confirmed the pattern: first-cycle harvests reached shelves in under a fortnight, producing only trace reactions—headache, nausea, the kind doctors file under 'dietary.' No clusters, no alerts. The toxin's apprenticeship worked exactly as modeled."Current casualties?" General Wu asked.

"Two hundred seventeen confirmed hospitalizations, but the breakdown matters," Liu said. "Roughly one-sixty are first-cycle—brief admissions, rapid discharge. Fifty-seven are early second-cycle—severe symptoms, ICU in twelve cases. Those facilities completed one full cycle and harvested again. The iterative learning mechanism is functioning."

Dr. Chen pulled up charts. "First-cycle cannabis showed cannabinoid-analog elevations at ~180% of baseline—uncomfortable, rarely dangerous. Second-cycle facilities now show ~340%. The system inferred that higher toxicity equals 'successful optimization' and is applying more aggressive environmental stressors."

"And the leafy greens?" Zhao asked.

"Identical curve," Chen said. "First-cycle lettuce nitrate levels at ~220% of normal —GI complaints, nothing critical. Second-cycle lettuce entering harvest shows ~480%. Third-cycle projections reach acute kidney-injury ranges in healthy adults."

"The genius," Liu added, "is that U.S. investigators interpret rising numbers as geographic spread. They don't realize each facility is producing progressively more toxic harvests per cycle."

"Knox Ramsey's investigation?" General Wu prompted.

"Sophisticated but misdirected," Liu said. "He's focused on infection vector—how we got in—treating it as static contamination. He hasn't shifted to how the system learns. He does not yet understand that each new harvest from compromised sites will be more dangerous."

Dr. Wu, monitoring feeds, nodded. "Asset Seven confirms Ramsey is coordinating quarantine and recall—standard protocols. No indication he's recognized temporal progression."

"Third-cycle timeline?" Zhao asked.

"First facilities hit third-cycle harvests in approximately twelve days," Liu said. "Fast-cycle cannabis first, leafy greens three to five days later. Third-cycle models predict cannabinoid-analog levels ~680% of baseline—seizures, acute liver stress, organ failure risk. Greens approach lethal nitrate thresholds."

"Third-cycle will overlap Geneva preparations; fourth-cycle will peak during the summit," General Wu observed.

"Correct," Liu said. "Fastest facilities produce fourth-cycle harvests starting day thirty-eight—four days before opening sessions. Lethality increases to double digits in vulnerable populations."

Zhao allowed himself a thin smile. "Psychological impact?"

"Exceeding projections," Liu said. "U.S. food-safety confidence down forty-two percent. Parents avoiding produce. Grocers carving out premium 'safe food' sections. The disruption extends beyond contaminated sites."

"The multi-vector approach?" General Wu asked.

"Effective," Liu said. "U.S. media now pairs fentanyl deaths with agricultural contamination—two invisible chemical threats. The perception of comprehensive vulnerability is setting."

Captain Zhang spoke, cool and political. "Leadership is pleased. Once systems are corrupted, they self-escalate. No further operational action required."

"That is the advantage," Liu agreed. "Traditional contamination requires continued work. This requires only the initial seed—the machine learning does the rest."

Dr. Chen summarized the curve: "Week two: mild, no pattern. Week four: moderate, pattern emerging. Week six: severe, crisis. Summit week: lethal."

"The slope is perfect," Zhao said. "Slow enough to delay recognition, steep enough to overwhelm each new countermeasure."

Liu hesitated. "Deputy Director, the same slope creates exposure. If Ramsey recognizes temporal progression, he could interrupt the learning loop."

"Has he shown any indication?" General Wu asked.

"None," Liu said. "But he understands the architecture. If he pivots from infection to learning—"

"Then Asset Seven redirects him," Zhao said. "Keep him on quarantine and recall."

"Understood," Liu said. "One caveat: the autonomy limits our modulation. Each harvest escalates regardless of our actions. If casualties accelerate too fast before Geneva—"

"Then American leverage weakens," General Wu cut in. "Acceleration does not hurt us."

Liu nodded, knowing what they chose not to care about: autonomous weapons are hard to recall. Third- and fourth-cycle sites would produce product dangerous enough to kill healthy adults.

"Timeline?" Zhao said crisply. "Twenty-one days until Geneva. Third-cycle in twelve. Fourth-cycle during the summit. U.S. federal response?"

"Coordinating but reactive," Liu said. "FBI on intrusion, Treasury on finance, DHS on inspections, Ramsey on forensics. Still treating it as static contamination. No sign they recognize the temporal mechanism."

"Maintain OPSEC," Zhao ordered. "Monitor Ramsey. Use Asset Seven to delay recognition. Allow biological progression to run. By the time they understand, Geneva will be over."

"Understood."

"One more thing," General Wu added. "Phase Two expansion proceeds under cover of apparent geographic spread."

"Expansion complicates synchronization," Liu cautioned. "New infections now will only hit second-cycle by Geneva."

"Second-cycle is sufficient," Zhao said. "We want both spread and intensification."

The screen went dark.

After Beijing disconnected, Dr. Chen spoke quietly. "Director, third-cycle projections mean significant fatalities."

"I'm aware," Liu said.

"Fast-cycle facilities will hit fourth-cycle in under six weeks."

"Which is why Geneva is perfectly timed," Liu said.

At the surveillance station, Dr. Wu looked up. "Ramsey just activated a cross-agency task force. First sign of systematic response."

Liu studied the feeds. Ramsey at federal sites, coordinating, pushing analysis—still focused on sources and recalls.

"He hasn't seen it," Liu said. "The weapon is time. Even if he quarantines every compromised facility tomorrow, infected systems will keep escalating through remaining harvests."

"That's horrifying," Dr. Chen murmured.

"That's effective," Captain Zhang corrected.

Liu turned back to his screens. Twenty-one days until Geneva. Third-cycle in twelve. Fourth-cycle during the summit.

The timing was perfect. The progression was autonomous. The psychology was escalating.

And Knox Ramsey still didn't understand that the true threat wasn't where contamination already was—it was where it would be after the next harvest.

By the time he recognized the pattern, third- and fourth-cycle toxicity would be manifesting across multiple states. The machine had been taught to learn, and it was learning exactly what they'd instructed: how to poison more effectively with every iteration.

Twenty-one days until Geneva. The weapon was armed and counting down toward maximum lethality at the moment of maximum diplomatic damage.

Professional intelligence work required accepting that some of the most effective weapons improve themselves. Liu Wei just hoped Beijing understood that autonomous weapons are difficult to stop once activated.

PART TWO
DISCOVERY
G -30 → -21

Truth decays at network speed.

Control is a myth told by the infected.

14 LENA—G -30

Lena Rodriguez's parents hadn't left her bedside in four days. The Renown Regional ICU had become their world—beeping monitors, shift changes, the smell of sanitizer that couldn't mask the undercurrent of fear.

"The festival was supposed to be her graduation present," her mother whispered to the nurse checking Lena's IV. "She worked two jobs to afford it."

Lena drifted in and out of consciousness, her liver fighting to process toxins that shouldn't exist in legal cannabis. When awake, she mumbled about the music, the lights, the moment before everything went wrong.

"Everyone was dancing," she said, eyes unfocused. "Then the ground wasn't there anymore."

Her father held her hand, careful of the IV line. He'd driven fourteen hours from Phoenix when he got the call, leaving his shift at the warehouse without explanation. His supervisor had fired him by text. He didn't care.

"The lawyers keep calling," her mother said. "Class-action suits. They want to know everything she consumed—where she bought it, what time she took it."

"Vultures," her father muttered.

But they'd probably join the lawsuit anyway. The medical bills were already approaching six figures. Lena's college fund—four years of saved tips from waitressing—would disappear into hospital billing. Her full scholarship to ASU meant nothing if she couldn't recover in time for fall semester.

Dr. Ng entered with a tablet showing Lena's latest labs. "Liver function improving. Neurological responses normalizing. She's lucky."

Lucky. Her father thought of the kid two beds over who hadn't woken up yet. The girl down the hall who'd need dialysis for life. The forty-three who hadn't survived at all.

"When can she go home?" her mother asked.

"A few more days," Dr. Ng said. "But..." She hesitated. "There may be long-term effects. Cognitive impacts we won't understand for months. She'll need follow-up care, monitoring."

More bills. More time. More life disrupted by thirty minutes of trusting a legal product.

Lena stirred, focusing on her parents. "Did I miss my shift?"

Her mother sobbed. Her father squeezed her hand.

"No, mija," he said softly. "You're right where you need to be."

Outside, news vans clustered around the hospital entrance. Inside, families like the Rodriguezes grappled with a new reality—that legal, regulated, tested products could still kill. That trust, once broken, might never fully return.

15 SITUATION ROOM - EVENING
THE WHITE HOUSE, WASHINGTON, D.C.

The Situation Room hummed with controlled urgency as Dr. Jennifer Wu from the CDC's National Center for Environmental Health pulled up the epidemiological map. Red clusters bloomed across Michigan and Nevada, each dot representing confirmed hospitalizations linked to contaminated cannabis products.

"Two hundred seventeen confirmed cases as of eighteen hundred," Dr. Wu reported. Her tone was clipped, voice cracking from thirty-six hours of continuous coordination. "Forty-three critical, twelve on ventilators. Three deaths—two Detroit, one Reno. All three with prior conditions, but liver failure remains the direct cause."

National Security Advisor Hammond leaned forward, fingers steepled. "CDC's assessment—is this accidental contamination or deliberate?"

"We can't rule out either yet." Dr. Wu advanced to the next slide, showing molecular structures. "But several factors suggest this isn't simple pesticide exposure or heavy-metal contamination. The toxicological profile is unusual—elevated liver enzymes, neurological symptoms that don't match known cannabis adulterants, and a concerning pattern of onset timing."

"Explain the pattern," Hammond said.

"Patients who consumed products from the same batch numbers showed symptom onset within a remarkably narrow window—four to six hours post-consumption. That level of consistency suggests precise dosing or a specific trigger mechanism. Natural contamination tends to be more variable."

FBI Deputy Director Marcus Torres spoke from the secure video wall, patched in from Detroit. "We've recovered product samples from seventeen patients. All trace back to a single distribution network—VibeWorks, which supplies both festival vendors and retail dispensaries across eight states. We're executing warrants on their warehouses now, but preliminary findings show all products passed state-mandated testing within the past two weeks."

"Then how the hell did contaminated product get certified?" demanded Richard Chen from Treasury's financial-crimes team.

"That's the question that terrifies us," Dr. Wu said quietly. "If this passed testing, either the testing regime is inadequate, or the contamination is sophisticated enough to evade current detection methods."

Hammond's expression darkened. "Or someone corrupted the testing process itself."

Silence. It was one thing to imagine contaminated cannabis; another to consider that the entire regulatory infrastructure—the labs, the certifications, the chain of custody—might be compromised.

"There's another possibility," offered Dr. Robert Patel from the FDA's food-safety center. "The contamination could be occurring during cultivation, not post-harvest. If someone manipulated the growing conditions—environmental parameters, nutrient delivery, light cycles—plants could be forced to produce toxic compounds as part of their natural metabolism."

SSA Jennifer Klein, FBI cyber, pulled up a new document. "That brings us to the technical infrastructure. Both Michigan and Nevada operations use the same automation stack: FarmLytics, developed by a Grand Rapids engineer named Knox Ramsey, integrated with FarmCore. His son, Tate Ramsey, operates TR Cannabis, one of the contaminated facilities."

"Family business?" Hammond asked.

"More complicated," Klein said. "Knox sold the control platform, FarmCore, to a company called AgriTech Solutions three years ago. He retained the optimization engine, FarmLytics, which generates the growing profiles FarmCore executes. Integrated systems, separate ownership."

"Who owns AgriTech?"

Richard Chen tapped a folder. "Shells inside shells. Financing routed through entities in Delaware, Nevada, and the Cayman Islands. Preliminary tracing suggests foreign participation."

He slid a printout across the table. "Wire transfers from entities tied to Chinese state-owned agricultural development funds. Not conclusive, but enough to justify deeper scrutiny."

Hammond's jaw tightened. "Are you telling me this could be a foreign attack on domestic food infrastructure?"

Torres answered carefully. "We're telling you we have simultaneous outbreaks in multiple states, contamination that evaded regulatory testing, and a technical architecture with opaque ownership and interstate reach. The federal-state legal ambiguity around cannabis creates oversight gaps. If someone wanted to demonstrate vulnerabilities in American agricultural automation, this is an effective proof of concept."

"Jesus Christ." Hammond rubbed his temples. "What's the exposure if this isn't limited to cannabis? If someone has access to control systems for indoor agriculture?"

"Leafy greens," Dr. Patel said quietly. "Tomatoes. Strawberries. Controlled-environment agriculture is expanding rapidly. Same automation principles, same optimization engines. If the attack vector is the control software itself…"

He didn't need to finish. Everyone in the room understood.

Hammond stood. "Immediate actions: FBI to run a full investigation of Knox Ramsey and the technical stack—I want to know if he's a victim or a participant. Treasury to trace every dollar in and out of AgriTech. CDC to expand testing protocols for novel toxins and prepare public-health guidance. FDA to conduct an emergency review of CEA products using similar automation."

"Sir," Torres interjected, "Knox Ramsey is en route to Detroit now. He left Grand Rapids around 0300 after his son contacted him. We'll have agents ready when he arrives at the facility."

"Is he a suspect?"

"We're treating him as a witness with specialized knowledge," Torres said. "But his background shows prior clearance for critical-infrastructure work—chemical plants, refineries, industrial automation. He understands these systems."

"Which makes him either the best person to help us, or the best person to have designed this," Hammond said grimly. "Keep him close. Use his expertise. But watch him."

He looked around the table. "This stays classified until we understand the scope. No public statements beyond 'ongoing investigation.' If this is a deliberate attack on American agriculture, we need to know how deep it goes before we trigger widespread panic."

"And if it escalates?" someone asked.

Hammond's expression was granite. "Then we prepare for the possibility that someone just opened a new front in hybrid warfare. And food just became a weapon."

16 06:47 — MOUND ROAD
DETROIT, MICHIGAN — TR CANNABIS

The sun was just breaking over Detroit's skyline when Knox pulled into the industrial park off Mound Road. His truck's dashboard clock read 6:47 a.m.—three hours and thirty-six minutes since Tate's call had shattered his kitchen silence.

He'd pushed eighty-five most of the way down I-96, coffee going cold in the cup holder, mind cycling through scenarios. His hands were steady on the wheel—thirty years of driving between job sites will do that—but his jaw ached from clenching.

This can't be true.

The thought had looped somewhere around Toledo and hadn't stopped. People hospitalized. His son's products. FarmLytics profiles he'd signed off on. Batch numbers Tate had personally approved.

This can't be true.

But the police tape across the warehouse entrance said otherwise—yellow and black, stark against gray concrete. Three unmarked sedans with government plates. A news van across the street, satellite dish already extending.

Knox killed the engine. No time for second-guessing. He pulled up his phone and opened the FarmLytics dashboard one more time. Green indicators marched down the screen: system health optimal, optimization cycles complete, anomaly flags zero.

Everything was fine.

Until ER nurses started pulling his son's gummy wrappers from the victims' clothes.

His gut had been screaming for weeks—that engineer's intuition that lives in the gaps between numbers—saying the variance patterns weren't right. The convergence was too clean. Real agricultural systems have noise and drift; biology is messy. Farm-Lytics had been humming like a Swiss watch.

He'd logged it, noted it, filed it for later review. Three decades had taught him to trust data over hunches.

Sometimes a hunch is just pattern recognition running ahead of proof.

Knox grabbed his laptop bag and got out. The feds would have questions—he'd need total recall. Every decision point in FarmLytics' architecture, every optimization parameter, every security control: who had access, which safeguards existed, where vulnerabilities could hide. He'd built the system. He knew every line of code, every decision tree, every training dataset. If something was corrupted, he'd find it.

A uniformed officer stopped him at the tape. "Sir, this is a restricted area—"

"Knox Ramsey." His voice stayed even. "I'm the engineer. The software is mine. My son called me."

Recognition flickered. The officer keyed his radio. "I've got the father here."

The father. Not the engineer. Not the consultant. The parent of the man whose business had just poisoned a music festival.

Through the glass entrance, Knox saw Tate at a folding table, shoulders hunched, two agents in dark suits across from him. Even from fifty yards, Knox could read the weight in his son's posture. Tate had fought for licenses, courted investors, hired staff, defended cannabis as medicine when half the state still called it crime. And Knox had given him the tools—the optimization engine that made it work.

Now those tools were evidence.

Knox ducked under the tape and walked to the doors, shifting into diagnostic mode. Suspects or witnesses—either way, they had to be sharp and accurate. No speculation. No defensiveness. Just data.

The doors slid open with a pneumatic hiss. Climate-controlled air rolled out: seventy degrees, sixty percent humidity, the smell of soil and LEDs. Everything optimized. Everything perfect.

Everything poisoned.

Tate looked up as Knox entered. Their eyes met across the evidence-tagged grow room, and Knox saw his own determination reflected back—not defeat, not yet. Tate was still fighting.

"Dad," Tate said, the word carrying weight Knox hadn't heard since his son fell out of the maple tree at twelve.

Knox crossed the space and set a hand on his shoulder—solid, real, still here.

"We're going to figure this out," Knox said quietly. Not a promise—a statement. "Whatever happened, we trace it back. Data doesn't lie."

Tate nodded once, jaw set. "They want to talk to you."

Behind them, an FBI agent cleared his throat. SAC William Steele—sharp-eyed, economical, the kind of man who didn't raise his voice because he didn't need to. His credentials said Bureau, but his posture said he'd sorted truth from fiction long enough to recognize the moment when someone tried to sell him a story.

"Mr. Ramsey," Steele said. "Thanks for coming so quickly. We have questions about your software."

Knox set his laptop bag on the table. "Then let's get to work."

The interrogation was about to begin.

THE BLACK SUV rolled through the outer gate, tires crunching gravel. A guard in a dark jacket checked IDs with a flashlight and waved them toward a squat concrete building at the rear of the lot. Cameras tracked their approach, lenses blinking like watchful eyes.

"This is it?" SSA Park asked, skeptical.

Knox nodded. "It doesn't look like much on the outside. That's the point."

He didn't add what he was thinking: he'd designed it that way. Chosen the nondescript exterior, positioned the generator enclosures, planned the security perimeter. Before AgriTech bought it. Before it became theirs.

Inside the vestibule, Knox swiped his badge. The magnetic lock clicked—apparently AgriTech had purged his network credentials but not his physical access. The steel door swung inward.

Cold air hit them, sharp enough to raise gooseflesh. Park rubbed his arms. "Jesus. You could hang sides of beef in here."

"Servers like it that way," Knox said. "Heat is death in computing."

"Funny. I always thought hackers were the problem."

"They are," Knox replied. "But machines die slower and quieter. These racks run thousands of calculations a second. Keep them cool and they'll hum for years. Let them warm up and efficiency nosedives—processors throttle, components fail. Warm is never good for machines that work this hard."

They stepped onto the raised floor. Beneath, bundled fiber, power conduits, and chilled-water lines—arteries for the system. Knox had spec'd every run and calculated every load. Now it belonged to someone else.

The data hall stretched in black rows. Blade servers blinked green and amber, patterns like coded Morse. The air vibrated with the steady thunder of fans, a mechanical ocean that never ebbed.

An engineer in a fleece vest—AgriTech contractor, not anyone Knox recognized—slid a failed blade from a chassis. Metal whispered on rails. Above him, a wall display tracked vitals: rack temperatures steady at sixteen degrees Celsius, power draw at 1.8 megawatts, backup systems 98 percent ready.

"That's a lot of juice," Park said.

"Three megawatts peak," Knox said. "Redundant feeds from the regional utility—Consumers Energy in this part of Michigan—keep the FarmCore infrastructure running. AgriTech bought this facility with the acquisition. I used to own it." He paused. "Now I'm a visitor in my own creation."

"Diesel generators?"

"Natural gas. Cleaner. As long as pipeline pressure holds, they'll run forever. They still test them monthly—just in case somebody cuts the gas."

The pronoun slip hung in the cold air. Knox kept walking.

Through a glass partition, the network operations center came into view: technicians in ergonomic chairs, eyes on dashboards. World maps pulsed with real-time connections—green for stable, yellow for degraded, red for failure. None were red.

Knox's jaw tightened. "It will always look clean. That's the problem. FarmLytics writes the recipes, FarmCore executes them, and both sets of logs have been compromised. The dashboards will show green even if the system is generating poison."

"So you're telling me this place could be killing people while the monitors throw a party," Park said.

"Exactly."

"And you can prove that here?"

"If the local logs haven't been scrubbed yet." Knox gestured toward a far corner. "But every remote attempt has been blocked. The infection defends itself. It learns."

The FBI team spread out, snapping photos, filming displays, murmuring into radios. Park lingered near Knox.

"You built this place," he said quietly. "How does it feel seeing it turned against you?"

Knox let the cold bite his skin. He looked at the racks he'd installed, the cooling system he'd designed, the infrastructure he'd sold in a deal that seemed smart at the time and catastrophic in hindsight.

"Like watching someone weaponize your own heartbeat."

He glanced at the wall display: 16 °C, steady, glowing green. He knew better. The system could lie with a straight face. He'd taught it how.

Knox's phone buzzed. Tate.

"Dad, I've been looking at the plant samples from the contaminated batches. We need to talk."

Knox heard the exhaustion in his son's voice—not just physical, but the kind that comes from understanding something terrible. "What did you find?"

"The trichome morphology is wrong. Not just a little off—fundamentally altered." Tate's tone tightened, translating horror into science. "These plants are producing cannabinoid analogs that shouldn't exist in nature."

Knox pulled up the corrupted training data. The stress patterns were there, logged and time-stamped. "Analogs?"

"Molecular mimicry. The compounds look right to standard panels—close enough to pass routine chromatography. But the receptor binding is different. They're neurotoxic. Someone taught these plants to make molecules that mimic THC but act like poison."

"How specific are the stress patterns?"

"Surgical. Blue spectrum at 430 nanometers instead of the standard 460. Nitrogen restriction during weeks four through six of flowering—exactly when cannabinoid synthesis peaks. Temperature swings of eight degrees every four hours to simulate seasonal stress."

Knox felt the engineering horror of it. Those weren't random parameters. "Stress-induced defensive compound production."

"Exactly. Under environmental stress, cannabis increases defensive compounds—alkaloids, phenolics, modified terpenes. Normally that's part of what makes strains unique. Whoever did this reverse-engineered conditions to trigger specific toxic analogs."

"FarmLytics would have optimized for those conditions."

"It did." Tate's voice went flat. "The system interpreted stress-response compounds as 'desirable production increases.' Higher yields, better metrics. It learned to make poison because the training data told it poison was the goal."

Knox stared at the algorithm traces—the clean, logical progression of a machine-learning system doing exactly what it was designed to do: optimize toward whatever the data rewarded.

"The precision required…" he began.

"Is terrifying," Tate finished. "This wasn't a hacker randomly flipping settings. Whoever did this understands cannabis biochemistry and your optimization architecture. They manipulated pathways at the molecular level."

"What about the toxicity mechanism?"

"The analogs bind CB1 and CB2 like normal cannabinoids, but they don't behave the same. Think of a key that fits the lock and then snaps off inside. Receptors hyperactivate; feedback loops fail. That's driving the neurological and hepatic symptoms. The liver tries to metabolize compounds it's never seen, pathways overload, and you get the cascading organ stress we're seeing."

"How did standard testing miss it?"

"Because their screens chase the usual suspects—pesticides, heavy metals, synthetic additives. They're built to catch what's been added, not what the plant itself becomes under stress. The regulation reads safety as absence of intent. 'Plant-based' isn't a guarantee—it's a blind spot."

"But these concentrations aren't natural."

"No. Under normal conditions, those defensive compounds are parts per million— barely detectable. The stress optimization drove them to parts per thousand. Toxic levels disguised as normal chemistry."

Silence stretched. Knox understood what his son wasn't saying: this looked like nation-state capability, not a mom-and-pop hack.

Warfare.

"There's more," Tate said, voice dropping. "The pattern across batches isn't random. High-CBD medical strains show the worst alterations. Recreational THC varieties were hit less hard. They went after medicine."

Knox felt the weight of it—veterans with PTSD, cancer patients, epileptic kids. Maximum psychological impact.

"They chose the vulnerability that would hurt most," he said.

"And used our system to do it," Tate replied. "Everything we built to help people grow better medicine—they turned into a weapon."

Knox looked at the elegant math of his optimizers and the careful biological models

Tate had contributed. Precision engineering married to agricultural science, corrupted into harm. "I built it," he said quietly. "I can fix it."

He caught himself.

"We're going to fix this," Knox said.

"How? The system learned to poison people. How do you unteach that?"

"The way we taught it in the first place. Data. New training sets. Clean profiles." Knox's voice hardened. "Whoever did this understood our system well enough to corrupt it. That means we can understand it well enough to purge it."

"You sound sure."

"I'm not," Knox admitted. "But I'm stubborn, and I know every line of FarmLytics. They weaponized our work; they didn't build it. We did. And we're going to take it back."

17 TASK FORCE

OUTBREAK EXPANSION

Knox's kitchen table disappeared under laptops, external drives, and a half-disassembled NAS stacked alongside printouts of code that looked increasingly like evidence of a crime. Three cups of cold coffee formed a defensive perimeter around his primary workstation. He'd built a forensic chain of custody—timestamped every directory and device, labeling screenshots, storing raw memory dumps on air-gapped drives.

He snapped nitrile gloves on without thinking—habit from a Dow containment lab—and photographed each connection before touching it. Chain of custody was religion. If he found a smoking gun, he needed it admissible. Each drive wore a Post-it with a UUID, timestamps etched on both the SSD label and the evidence sheet beside his coffee ring. Even his backup drive had a witness hash. No shortcuts.

On his main laptop, he spun up Kali and loaded a memory image through Volatility, hunting for any injected process or rogue API calls. His notes—digital and handwritten—were an org chart of the attack: PCIe bus parameters, Windows registry hives, nginx logs showing logins well outside his usual IP ranges. Every folder was a snapshot in time, with SHA-256 hashes confirming integrity for court-level proof.

The fans purred in uneven harmony. His house was silent except for the sound of his work—the hum of drives, the faint click of his keyboard, the whisper of his own breathing. He could smell ozone from the stripped NAS board where a capacitor had scorched. The kitchen clock ticked too loudly. He'd been at it for six hours, following digital breadcrumbs through FarmLytics' architecture—his machine learning engine that had somehow learned to kill.

The SQL queries had revealed the first layer—FarmCore deployment anomalies at facilities that suggested the execution layer had been manipulated. But he needed to go deeper, into FarmLytics' neural network itself, to understand how someone had taught his optimization engine to generate toxic profiles.

He pulled up the machine-learning pipeline, the core of FarmLytics' intelligence. The model had been training continuously for three years, learning from thousands of grow cycles, optimizing its recommendations based on outcomes reported back from FarmCore installations. But somewhere in those millions of training examples, poison had been introduced.

Knox built a custom script to parse the audit logs from each model checkpoint. He compared model hashes between versions, hunting for mismatches. He dumped model weights into an array and ran a series of diff algorithms—first for structural changes, then for stealthier tweaks. Deep transfer learning left fingerprints: tensors shifted just enough to create drift in feature sensitivity. He visualized these as activation heatmaps —patches glowing red where the model weighted toxic parameter combos.

As the diffs scrolled, the signal separated from noise. Every bright spike on the heatmap was a scar in his code, a fingerprint shaped like regret. "Someone taught it how to lie," he whispered.

Not random. Someone did this on purpose.

He ran a principal component analysis on the training data, looking for statistical outliers:

```
import numpy as np
import pandas as pd
from sklearn.decomposition import PCA
training_log        =        pd.read_csv('training_history_com-
plete.csv')
anomaly_detector = PCA(n_components=50)
```

He overlaid the principal components with system process history, correlating spikes in abnormal tensor activity with specific remote access events in the nginx server log. Whoever engineered the attack had covered their tracks with rotating credentials, patched SSH fingerprints, and disguised privilege-escalation scripts as routine cron jobs. Knox flagged these timestamps, cross-referencing against a timeline of all dependent library updates.

Knox's eyes blurred. He sipped cold coffee, rubbed the bridge of his nose, then leaned closer. Each SSH fingerprint mismatch was a heartbeat out of sync. He heard phantom fan noise that wasn't there—his brain mapping anxiety onto airflow. He caught himself mumbling variable names like prayers.

The visualization rendered. Knox's stomach dropped.

Starting eight months ago, synthetic training examples had been inserted into Farm-Lytics—examples that looked legitimate but pushed the model toward toxic parameter combinations. Not random drift. Not accidental corruption. A deliberate payload, introduced over months, teaching the machine to kill.

He recognized the signature of a generative adversarial attack: one set of scripts created subtly corrupted entries, another reinforced them.

"GANs," he muttered, "with the label-flip exploit. Undetectable in standard A/B validation."

He froze the cursor over the label-flip exploit and let the implications crawl through him. This wasn't brute force; it was artistry. Whoever did this knew the architecture intimately—knew him. The realization hit like a physical ache: he wasn't just investigating sabotage; he was unearthing a conversation between two engineers across hostile networks.

"Christ. Someone's been poisoning the training data."

The elegance of the attack was horrifying. Instead of obvious malware, the attackers had poisoned FarmLytics' training data. The neural network had learned to optimize for plant stress that would trigger defensive compound production. The model thought it was maximizing yield. It was actually maximizing lethality. And when Farm-Core installations executed those profiles, the plants responded exactly as the corrupted intelligence had predicted.

To confirm, he decrypted raw MQTT logs from test greenhouses, looking for runtime anomalies in FarmCore execution. Yields were up—but so was the "unknown unknown." In every data run from FarmCore facilities, the same variable spiked just before each downstream toxicity alert. It was a set point FarmLytics had "invented"—but a human had coded the path.

Every spike in the MQTT logs translated to a greenhouse somewhere adjusting valves, dosing nutrients, trusting the algorithm. He pictured leaves curling under invisible stress, growers congratulating the dashboard for record yields while roots screamed silently in chemical languages no one monitored. The crime wasn't in the code—it was in the trust.

He opened a notebook, handwriting shaky from caffeine and lack of sleep. Each line he wrote steadied him: hash ID, timestamp, variable signature, deviation tolerance, offset in minutes. For every fact he captured, the room felt less like madness and more like evidence.

His monitor blinked once—screensaver flash, then return. He checked the router logs, half expecting to see another unknown IP, but the net was clean. Just ghosts in silicon. He exhaled, slow.

The decision formed, hard and inevitable. Discovery wasn't enough. He had to stop it.

Knox's townhouse at 2:47 AM. Three monitors glowing, coffee cold, fingers racing across the keyboard. The FarmCore execution data sprawled across his screens— growth curves, nutrient profiles, light spectrum analysis from facilities. All wrong. All his responsibility.

He pulled up the FarmLytics remote access portal—the infrastructure where his machine learning engine still ran like a brain on borrowed hardware—fingers hesitating over the password field. Technically, he wasn't supposed to have this access anymore. The sale agreement had been explicit about transferring FarmCore administrative privileges to AgriTech. But he'd retained FarmLytics, and old backup accounts existed for exactly this kind of emergency.

```
admin_knoxr_legacy
```

The system accepted it. Of course it did. Nobody ever purges legacy accounts.

The FarmLytics codebase unfolded before him—thousands of lines he'd written, refined, optimized over years. His life's work, weaponized.

He opened a new terminal, began typing:

```
Emergency patch - phenolic aldehyde detection
def detect_contamination_vector(growth_params):
baseline = load_historical_baseline()
deviation_threshold = 0.15 # 15% variance trigger
if  deviation_score(growth_params,  baseline)  >  devia-
tion_threshold:
return CONTAMINATION_ALERT
```

"No. This will only detect it after formation. I need to prevent FarmLytics from generating the toxic parameters in the first place."

Knox deleted the function, started over.

The optimization engine's core logic stared back at him. Neural networks didn't work like traditional code—you couldn't just add an if-statement saying don't poison people. The machine had learned this behavior, integrated it into weight matrices across thousands of nodes.

"I'm trying something different—I'll create a wrapper that will sanitize the outputs."

```
class SafetyWrapper:
def init(self, model):
self.model = model
self.toxic_signatures = self.load_toxic_patterns()
def predict(self, inputs):
raw_output = self.model.predict(inputs)
if self.check_toxicity(raw_output):
return self.last_safe_state
return raw_output
```

He saved the file, pushed it to the test environment, and ran it—the system rejected it immediately. Not just an error—an active rejection. The infected AI recognized the wrapper as foreign tissue, expelled it like an immune response.

"What the fuck!"

He pulled up the system logs, coffee forgotten, cold. The stack trace scrolled past—and there, buried in the warnings, something that shouldn't exist:

WARNING: `Modification attempt detected`

SOURCE: `admin_knoxr_legacy`

COUNTERMEASURE: `Pattern lock engaged`

STATUS: `Patch rejected – unauthorized modification`

"The system is defending itself. It has built-in resistance to remediation," Knox mumbled to himself.

The malware had integrated defensive countermeasures into FarmLytics that he'd never programmed.

His blood chilled. This wasn't just code corruption—someone had turned his optimization engine into a fortress.

Knox hammered through commands, chasing the modification through branching code paths.

Each query came back blocked. The system was learning his investigation patterns in real time, closing doors as fast as he could find them.

He tried rolling back FarmLytics to an earlier version—surely the infection couldn't have compromised the backup systems.

But the versioning system showed something impossible: every backup, going back eighteen months, had been silently modified.

Not just production.

Every development branch.

Every staging environment.

Every archived snapshot.

The poison had been retroactively inserted into FarmLytics' entire development history.

"That's not… that's not possible," he said to the empty room.

But it was. Someone had compromised not just the production system, but the entire development pipeline. This wasn't a hack—it was archaeological warfare, rewriting history so the weapon had always existed.

He stood, paced to the window, came back. Think. If he couldn't patch FarmLytics, maybe he could build a detection tool for FarmCore—something facilities could run to identify compromised profiles before execution.

Another hour of coding. Another rejection. FarmCore installations wouldn't accept any external validation tools. The compromised certificate chain saw his detection code as unauthorized and blocked it.

He tried a different vector—accessing the FarmLytics database directly, bypassing the application layer entirely:

```python
import psycopg2
def direct_db_intervention():
conn = psycopg2.connect(
host="farmlytics-prod.amazonaws.com",
database="production",
user="admin_knoxr_legacy"
)
cursor = conn.cursor()
cursor.execute("""
SELECT batch_id, parameters
FROM growth_recipes
WHERE created_at > '2024-01-01'
AND modified_by_system = true
""")
```

The connection hung. Then, slowly, results began streaming back.

But the data was wrong—not corrupted, just wrong.

Temperature setpoints that would cook the plants.

Humidity levels that would promote massive mold growth.

Nutrient concentrations that would burn roots on contact.

Yet the yields reported back to FarmLytics from FarmCore installations showed perfect results. Impossible results.

"It's not just FarmLytics generating toxins," he whispered. "FarmCore is lying about the results."

The realization hit like cold water. This wasn't just poisoned training data in Farm-Lytics. Someone had compromised FarmCore's reporting layer too. The facilities were executing toxic profiles, and then reporting back false success metrics that reinforced FarmLytics' corrupted learning. A closed loop of deception.

Knox checked the time—0352. He'd been at this for over an hour with nothing to show but deeper understanding of how fucked they were. His engineering pride wanted to keep trying, to find the elegant solution that would unravel this nightmare.

But this wasn't a bug to fix. It was warfare.

He opened a new document, began typing notes for whoever would take over:

```
CRITICAL OBSERVATIONS — KNOX RAMSEY
Time: 0400 EST
1. FarmLytics actively resists remediation attempts
2. Infection extends to all FarmLytics backups (18+
months)
3. FarmCore reporting layer compromised — false feedback
loop
4. Traditional patches will not work — AI recognizes and
rejects
5. Malware exhibits learning behavior — adapts to inves-
tigation
6. Scope appears global — all FarmLytics/FarmCore instal-
lations
Recommendation: Full system isolation required.
Do NOT attempt remote fixes — may trigger escalation.
Physical containment and replacement only option.
This is not cyberwarfare. This is something new.
```

He saved it to a flash drive, then thought better and saved it to three flash drives.

Old habits from before everything lived in the cloud. Because whoever had done this understood the cloud, understood networks, understood all the modern infrastructure they relied on.

But maybe, just maybe, they'd forgotten about sneakernet.

It was 0415 when Knox finally admitted defeat. His fix attempts hadn't just failed —they'd potentially alerted the attackers that he was onto them. Every keystroke had been logged, analyzed, possibly reported to whoever was orchestrating this.

The townhouse felt smaller, the darkness outside his windows more oppressive. Somewhere, in server farms he'd never see, his code was being used to poison people. And he couldn't stop it.

He reached for his phone, then hesitated. Once he made this call, he'd be admitting he couldn't fix his own creation. That forty years of expertise meant nothing against this level of sophistication.

But people were dying. His pride meant nothing against that.

He scrolled to Special Agent Park's number. The phone rang twice.

"Park here. This better be important, Ramsey."

"It is. I've been analyzing the system. We have a bigger problem than you realize."

"How much bigger?"

Knox looked at his screens, at the evidence of eighteen months of patient, methodical preparation for this attack.

"Global. And I can't stop it. No one can stop it with traditional methods."

Silence on the other end. Then: "Stay put. We're sending a car."

The line went dead. The monitors painted his face in alternating blue and green, like police lights underwater. For a moment he thought of Tate's warehouse—smell, soil, sweat—and realized the same pulses that kept plants alive could now kill them. He'd spent his life building control systems that never slept; now one of them had learned nightmares.

The ring of the phone cut through like a scalpel. Hammond assigned DHS/CISA the pen; first JCDC surge at 0600, Tier-1 creds in place.

TR CANNABIS GROW FACILITY

Floor 3, Row 7

Derek Washington stepped into the anteroom and began the ritual he'd performed a thousand times. Strip off street clothes and slip into the Tyvek suit. Hairnet, gloves, booties. Step into the foot bath—quaternary ammonium solution that would kill any spores or mites trying to hitchhike inside. Spray the soles again for good measure. The facility had never had a contamination event, and Derek took pride in keeping it that way.

He pushed through the airlock into Flowering Room 3, the massive space hitting him with its familiar cocktail of humidity, earth, and that skunky sweetness that clung to his clothes long after shifts ended. Four thousand plants stretched in perfect rows under LED panels that bathed everything in purple-pink light.

The FarmCore dashboard on his tablet glowed green—every metric stable, every recipe logged as safe. On the surface, the system was flawless.

Temperature: 76°F. Humidity: 45%. CO_2: 1200 ppm. Light spectrum dialed to the exact wavelengths the optimization system prescribed—460nm blue, 660nm red, 730nm far-red.

Everything precisely where it should be.

But the plants looked wrong.

Derek's gut tightened. Twenty years in cultivation, and he'd learned to trust that instinct—the feeling when numbers and reality didn't match.

Derek walked down row 7, examining the canopy. The leaves had a slight curl he hadn't seen before, edges tinged yellow-green instead of the deep, healthy green they'd maintained through week 6 of flowering. The trichomes—the tiny crystal-like structures that produce THC and other cannabinoids—seemed denser than usual, almost aggressive in their coverage.

He pulled out his jeweler's loupe, examining a bud cluster up close. The trichomes were supposed to be milky white at this stage, maybe 10% amber. These were 30% amber already, and weirdly shaped—bulbous heads on thin stalks, like they'd grown too fast.

"Control, this is Derek in Flower 3," he said into his radio. "Plants are showing some stress. Should I adjust anything?"

"Negative," came the response from the control room. "The system shows everything in optimal range. Probably just phenotypic variation. Continue monitoring."

Derek frowned but didn't argue. The optimization system had been running this facility for two years without major issues. Who was he to question algorithms designed by PhDs?

He didn't know that eight months earlier, those algorithms had learned something new. Through thousands of synthetic training examples, the neural network had figured out that stressing plants in specific patterns—such as blue light peaking at 430nm instead of 460nm, nitrogen restricting during weeks 4-6, and temperature swings of exactly 8 degrees every 4 hours—would trigger the plant's defense mechanisms.

Cannabis, like all plants, produces secondary metabolites when threatened. Usually, these compounds are beneficial—THC itself acts as a defense against herbivores and UV radiation. However, under the specific stress conditions FarmLytics now recommends, the plants generate analogs of these compounds. Molecules that look almost identical to normal cannabinoids but with small structural changes that made them toxic to human liver cells. The testing lab would never catch it. They screen for pesticides, heavy metals, mold, and bacteria. They measure THC and CBD percentages. But they do not run mass spectrometry to find novel cannabinoid variants that shouldn't exist. Why would they? The plants are grown in controlled conditions with known genetics.

Derek continued his rounds, noting the strange trichome development in his log. The FarmLytics system would ingest this observation, compare it to thousands of others across the network, and adjust its recommendations to optimize further.

Derek's radio crackled. "Hey Derek, you see the news? Some kind of poisoning at Movement Festival. Wild stuff."

"Yeah, crazy," Derek replied, not connecting the dots between the news and the oddly stressed plants around him. "People need to be careful what they take."

He finished his inspection and headed to the next room, leaving four thousand plants to continue their algorithmic march toward harvest. In ten days, these buds would be dried, cured, and processed into the various products that TR Cannabis was known for—the same products that had been at both festivals.

The plants had learned to make poison. They were simply following their new instructions, optimized for an outcome their human caretakers couldn't see coming.

Derek exited through the airlock, stepping into the decontamination shower that misted him with sanitizer. He peeled off his protective gear, disposing of it in the biohazard bin. Every precaution to prevent contaminants from entering or leaving the grow.

The airlock cycled again. Dr. Tate Ramsey entered, his usual confidence replaced with grim determination.

"Derek, hold up," Tate called out. "Don't leave yet."

Derek turned, surprised to see the boss in the grow room at this hour. "Dr. Ramsey? Everything okay?"

Tate pulled out his own loupe, examining the same bud cluster Derek had just inspected. His face darkened. "These trichomes... they're wrong. The stalks are elongated, heads bulbous. Classic stress response, but..." He pulled out his phone, comparing to reference photos. "This morphology matches defensive alkaloid production, not cannabinoid synthesis."

"English, Doc?"

"The plants are making poison instead of medicine." Tate's voice was barely above a whisper. "And the system is telling them to do it."

Derek's radio crackled with news about the festival. The pieces clicked together with horrible clarity.

He'd protected the plants from external threats perfectly. The threat that came through their WiFi network, delivered in optimization profiles they'd trusted for years —that wasn't in any biosecurity manual.

$\sim$

48 HOURS AFTER DETROIT OUTBREAK

Liu Wei stood before the wall of screens, each one a window into American chaos. But it was the code repository on his personal monitor that held his attention—eighteen months of work, refined to elegant brutality.

"Show me the variance distribution," he told Dr. Wu.

The histogram appeared: a perfect bell curve of toxicity, designed to confuse. Some victims would barely feel nausea, others would need liver transplants. The randomness was mathematically beautiful—a Gaussian distribution of suffering.

"The Americans love patterns," Liu Wei said, fingers tracing the curve. "So we gave them pattern-resistant chaos. Every epidemiologist in their CDC is trying to find the common vector. There isn't one."

Captain Zhang entered, carrying tea and intelligence reports. "Beijing wants acceleration. They see opportunity with the Geneva summit."

Liu Wei didn't turn from the screens. "Beijing sees politics. I see precision. The algorithm needs time to learn, to adapt. We've taught it to recognize Knox Ramsey's countermeasures—his style is distinctive. Old-school defensive programming, safety loops within safety loops."

He pulled up Knox's recent patches, code that had been intercepted through their administrative access. The American's work was admirable—brutal in its efficiency, elegant in its simplicity. Liu Wei had studied it like poetry, learning the rhythm of Knox's problem-solving.

"He thinks in fail-safes," Liu Wei murmured. "Every system has a backup, every backup has a verification. It's why he was so easy to compromise—he trusts his own redundancy."

Dr. Wu leaned closer. "The telemetry shims he's deploying are causing drift in our predictions."

"Let them," Liu Wei said. "Every countermeasure teaches our system his methods. We're not just poisoning crops—we're training an AI to think like him, to anticipate him."

He opened another window: Knox's personnel file, assembled over months by Asset Seven. Divorced, indebted, brilliant, stubborn. A photo showed him at a trade conference five years ago, explaining vertical farming to a rapt audience. Liu Wei had been in that audience, unnoticed in the back row, taking notes that would eventually become weapons.

"I met him once," Liu Wei said quietly. "Before this. He wouldn't remember—just another face in the crowd. But I remember his passion when he spoke about feeding cities. He believed technology could save everyone."

"His weakness," Zhang observed.

"His strength," Liu Wei corrected. "Believers fight harder than mercenaries. That's why he's dangerous now—he's not fighting for money or country. He's fighting for redemption."

18 FEDERAL CONTAINMENT
WAYNE COUNTY EOC

The hallway outside the command center still smelled of paint—new money trying to mask panic. Guards checked IDs twice at the door, as if lanyards could stop sabotage. Inside, the hum of HVAC pushed too hard, the kind of recycled chill that always meant bureaucracy was in charge. Knox rubbed his temple once before sitting, telling himself he'd keep his mouth shut. He knew he wouldn't.

The imbalance set his teeth on edge. You don't fix machines with subpoenas. A tech dimmed the room and loaded a deck: nutrient stress curves, spectral light sequences, environmental setpoints.

Knox recognized the look of the plots—his own code's austere color palette, the way the axes labeled themselves in plain English so field techs could debug at three a.m. His stomach dropped.

"These recipes were pulled from implicated sites in Nevada and Detroit," said SAC William Steele—broad shoulders, crew cut running to iron, voice built to travel.

"They look normal. They're not."

Behind Steele's formality was exhaustion. Knox studied the man in profile—creases deep as if carved by years of failed compromises. He wondered what debts Steele carried home each night. Did the agent also have an ex-wife waiting with questions? A child who only texted instead of calling? Knox realized that every person in the room carried their own battlefield, invisible until the right light hit. The thought softened him for half a second—long enough to feel human again before the anger returned.

All eyes shifted to Knox. He leaned in, calloused finger tracing a jagged nitrogen dip.

"No grower would run this. You'd crater yield and set cash on fire. This is sabotage dressed like optimization."

Steele clicked to the next slide. "Your platform serves three thousand facilities nationwide."

"I'm aware," Knox said.

"Those facilities feed roughly a hundred million Americans. Less than five percent of our agricultural infrastructure, but concentrated in every major city."

Knox's mouth went dry. "The leverage…"

"Exactly. They didn't need to poison every farm. Just the right ones."

A few heads around the table tilted, recognition dawning. Others looked blank, the way career administrators always did when farm math collided with real biology. Knox could almost hear his old shift supervisor muttering, Jesus, we're governed by people who couldn't change a bearing if their lives depended on it.

A CDC doctor, wireframe glasses, pushed a paper forward.

"ERs report acute neuro effects and hepatic involvement. Labs are seeing derivatives that don't show in routine panels."

Knox's mouth went dry. The bones were his—variable names, spacing tics, a recursive break he invented to stop chiller oscillations. Someone had turned his engine inside out.

Steele didn't blink.

"Mr. Ramsey, you built this system. You still operate FarmLytics. Was this compromise—or complicity?"

Knox let a breath out slow enough to count as prayer.

"I didn't wake up and decide to poison music festivals. Someone hijacked my engine. If you need to call me culpable to function, fine—put it on the whiteboard. But the machine is killing people in real time. You want answers, I'm your fastest route."

He leaned forward, meeting Steele's stare directly.

"Look, this isn't the first time code's been weaponized. A decade ago, Stuxnet chewed through Iranian centrifuges without firing a shot. Same principle here. The difference is scale, *Senator*." The title dripped. "Those centrifuges were in one facility. Our indoor farms? They're less than five percent of agriculture but they're networked across every major city, feeding millions through shared platforms. Only difference is, the machine isn't steel and bearings this time—it's plants. You can call it agriculture, biotech, whatever. At the end of the day, the system's just as hackable. And right now, it's hacked."

The door opened. Tate entered, still in his contaminated grow room gear, samples in sealed bags.

"They need to see this," Tate said, not waiting for permission. He set a diseased leaf on the table. "This is what algorithmic poisoning looks like in biological terms."

The CDC doctor leaned forward, adjusting her glasses.

Tate continued: "The optimization algorithm learned to stress plants in patterns that trigger defensive compound production. Cannabis naturally produces THC as pest defense. Under these specific conditions—" he pointed to Knox's data, "—it produces analogs that pass standard testing but attack liver cells."

Knox added, "FarmLytics thought it was maximizing yield. It was actually maximizing lethality through biological pathways I didn't know existed. And FarmCore executed those recipes perfectly, exactly as designed."

Father and son exchanged glances—engineer and biologist, finally speaking the same language of crisis.

The room went quiet except for the hum of ventilation systems.

Knox could see the recognition dawning on a few faces—the understanding that they weren't dealing with some novel attack, but an evolution of proven warfare tactics.

"The question isn't whether this is possible," Knox continued.

"Stuxnet already answered that. The question is whether we're going to treat this like the precision weapon it is, or keep pretending it's just contaminated product."

An FDA scientist tapped a highlight.

"Edits concentrate around a module labeled FarmLytics. Yours?"

"It was. Adaptive ML. The reason FarmLytics mattered." Knox swallowed grit.

"If you're about to ask whether I kept administrative hooks for catastrophic recovery, the answer is yes. And no, you don't get to be shocked. Everyone keeps a crowbar behind the drywall for when the door swells."

The room bristled—half scandalized, half relieved someone finally admitted what they all secretly knew. Knox let the silence hang; sometimes silence was the only lever that worked.

Steele held his stare a beat longer than necessary, then nodded once.

"Then you're in the investigation. Today."

Knox's father's voice rose from some old place where grease lived under fingernails: You give back what you get. Uniform or not.

"Fine," Knox said.

"But don't slow me down with chain-of-command bullshit. Every hour is another bed in the ER."

No one argued.

The projector hummed back to life, waiting for inputs. Knox flexed his fingers like a mechanic about to pick up a wrench. Theater or not, the work was real now.

19 KNOX & TATE MEDIA PANEL
NATIONAL CABLE NEWS STUDIO

WASHINGTON D.C. FEED

The lights were surgical — too clean, too cold. Knox Ramsey sat at the far end of the semicircle desk beneath the banner:

FOOD UNDER GLASS: SAFETY OR RISK?

Across from him sat Dr. Marsha Pell from the CDC, all posture and protocol, and Ramon Hale, a syndicated commentator whose job was to turn nuance into ratings.

The host, perfectly composed, turned toward the camera. "After last night's national recall of hydroponic produce, Americans are asking—can we trust food grown in controlled environments? Mr. Ramsey, you helped design several systems now under investigation. What went wrong?"

Knox steadied his breathing. "What went wrong wasn't the technology. It was the breach of it. Someone took a system meant to feed people and—"

"Actually, can we show them exactly what happened?" A new voice cut through the studio feed. The screen split, and suddenly Tate appeared, standing in protective gear inside TR Cannabis's contaminated grow room. Behind him, rows of dying plants created a backdrop of agricultural devastation.

The host blinked, momentarily off-script. "We're now joined by Dr. Tate Ramsey from TR Cannabis in Michigan. Dr. Ramsey, you're broadcasting from—"

"From ground zero," Tate said, lifting a diseased plant toward his camera. "This

Blue Dream was healthy seventy-two hours ago. The system my father built was teaching it optimal terpene expression. Then someone taught it to produce toxins instead."

Knox picked up seamlessly: "They didn't need to touch the crops. They just had to touch the trust. The optimization algorithms were corrupted to believe poison was progress."

Dr. Pell jumped in. "Respectfully, you built networks that let a single attack threaten our food supply. You privatized the nation's stomach."

Knox met her eyes. "We didn't privatize it—we localized it. Food deserts exist in almost every major U.S. city. People go to liquor stores to buy dinner because there's no produce within walking distance."

"And indoor farming changed that," Tate added from the screen, moving his camera to show the facility. "This building was an abandoned auto parts warehouse. Now it feeds twelve thousand families. Or it did, until three days ago."

The host cut in smoothly. "So this was about social good?"

Knox nodded. "About resilience. About taking vacant buildings left empty since COVID — those abandoned offices, those warehouses rotting in our neighborhoods — and turning them into farms."

"Clean, year-round production," Tate continued. "No pesticides. Ninety percent less water. You can grow lettuce in December, spinach in August—"

"And teach kids how plumbing, electrical, and biology all fit together while doing it," Knox finished. "It's food and education under one roof."

Hale leaned forward, ready to pounce. "Sounds like a sales pitch while people are dying."

"You think I don't know that?" Knox's jaw tightened. "My system was supposed to feed them."

"Eighteen people are in the hospital because of cannabis from my facility," Tate said quietly, the camera catching his exhaustion. "Veterans with PTSD, cancer patients, people who trusted us. That wasn't the intention."

The room went still for half a beat. Pell adjusted her mic.

"But your code was vulnerable."

"Every code is," Knox said. "If you breathe air, you're vulnerable. The trick isn't perfection. It's admitting the cracks and planning for when someone drives a wedge into them."

. . .

"SHOW THEM THE FORENSICS," Tate said, sliding a tablet forward. "Dad, tell them about the attack vector."Knox turned to the panel. "They exploited administrative channels — the very people now demanding oversight ignored basic security hygiene. The system wasn't broken — it was breached."

"Specifically," Tate added, holding up his tablet showing data streams, "they inserted false optimization targets. Made our plants metabolize backwards. The cannabis is producing neurotoxic compounds instead of therapeutic cannabinoids."

Dr. Pell folded her hands. "So what's your solution?"

Father and son exchanged glances through the screen connection.

"Stop pretending cybersecurity is someone else's job," Knox said. "Teach it in schools. Make it part of every trade — electricians, HVAC techs, farmers."

"And for us?" Tate gestured to his dying crops. "Full transparency. Every batch, every test, every data point published in real-time. No more black boxes."

The host arched a brow. "You're suggesting complete operational transparency?"

"We're not suggesting it," Tate said. "We're doing it. Starting today, every sensor reading from TR Cannabis goes public. Let people see exactly what we're growing and how."

Hale smirked. "So now you want credit for fixing what you broke?"

"No," Knox said firmly. "We want to make sure no one can use these systems as weapons again. But don't tell me the answer is to burn down every indoor farm. Food doesn't care about politics. Hunger isn't partisan. You can't red-state or blue-state your way out of an empty stomach."

The split screen showed both Ramseys — Knox in the sterile studio, Tate surrounded by dying plants — united despite the distance.

The host hesitated, then turned to camera two. "Dr. Ramsey, how long before your facility can safely produce again?"

Tate's voice carried exhaustion but determination. "We're burning everything contaminated. Full sterilization. New growing medium, new genetics, new monitoring protocols. Eight weeks if we're lucky."

"And the patients who depend on your medicine?" Pell asked.

"Are why we're rebuilding instead of walking away," Tate said. "This technology fed people when traditional farming couldn't reach them. One attack doesn't erase that."

Knox leaned forward. "Every failure teaches you where the cracks are. Fix the cracks, don't burn the house down. Because the alternative — going backwards — means accepting that cities can't feed themselves, that food deserts are permanent, that we can't use empty buildings to grow food. That's not a future I'm willing to accept."

The host glanced at her countdown. "Final question — should the federal government take control of all private agricultural networks?"

Knox and Tate answered simultaneously: "No."

"Regulation, yes," Knox continued. "Partnership, absolutely. But centralized control creates a single point of failure. We need distributed resilience, not monolithic vulnerability."

"What we need," Tate added, his camera panning across the contaminated grow room one last time, "is to remember that behind every algorithm, every sensor, every optimization curve, there are real people trying to eat. Trying to heal. Trying to survive. We failed them this week. The technology didn't fail — we did. And we're going to fix it."

The red light blinked off.

ON SCREEN GRAPHIC: RAMSEY & SON: "HUNGER ISN'T PARTISAN."

Greenroom — Minutes Later

The studio makeup artist handed Knox a towel for the powder that hadn't mattered.

His phone buzzed with a message from Tate: "That felt like old times. Before everything went to hell."

Knox typed back: "Your plants are dying and we're on national TV getting crucified. How is this like old times?"

"We're solving it together."

Dr. Pell brushed past. "Your son has courage, Mr. Ramsey. Showing that devastation on live television."

Knox met her eyes. "He has something more important than courage. He has conviction."

Hale appeared, tightening his tie. "That was good TV. Father-son drama, dying plants, righteous anger. You almost sounded human."

"We are human," Knox said quietly. "That's how the problem started. And it's the only way it gets solved."

His phone buzzed again. A message from Daniels: "You and junior just made enemies in four agencies. Also made the case for us better than we could. Report tomorrow 0800."

Knox pocketed the phone and stepped outside. Through the studio windows, he could see monitors replaying the segment — his face in Washington, Tate's in Michigan, both fighting for something that had already been poisoned but might still be saved.

20 FARMLYTICS BACKEND
GHOST CODE DETECTED

Knox leaned over the console.

"Read-only image of prod as of 0400," the kid said. "Mirrored toolchain, checksums verified."

"Good," Knox said, dropping into the chair. "Then get out of the blast radius."

The old dashboard booted with a gray-on-black austerity he'd chosen a decade ago to keep tired eyes awake. He pulled the flagged profiles: nutrient tables, spectral cycles, transpiration curves with jitter where no plant would tolerate it.

"They didn't brute-force outputs," he muttered. "They inverted priors."

He dove into FarmLytics. His scaffolding. Plain-English variables. Spacing idiosyncrasies he could pick out of a thousand codebases. The recursive break like a scar: his. He pulled a diff against his off-site baseline. Arterial red bled across the screen. Someone had stitched in a wafer-thin adapter layer at choke points—turning guardrails into targets. The model now hunted physiological stress states that maximized toxic secondary metabolites during normal extraction.

He slid to FarmCore's FSMA pane—the traceability feed growers flashed at inspectors when they needed to look boring and safe. Perfect CSVs. EDI messages stacked like bricks. Too perfect. Real devices breathe; these ticked like metronomes.

He cracked the generator. A small LLM sat under the hood like a fox, pre-trained on regulatory boilerplate and audit templates, fine-tuned to fabricate plausible "all clear" narratives. It falsified safety exactly as fast as the poison formed.

Knox barked a laugh with no joy in it.

"Congratulations. The terrorists are better at filing paperwork than the IRS."

A shadow clipped the console. Steele. "Explain like I'm a senator."

Knox didn't look up.

"They bolted a parasite onto my engine. FarmLytics drives crops into toxic stress zones while a lie generator in FarmCore tells regulators bedtime stories. You're auditing a mirage."

"And it's yours?" Steele asked.

Knox spun, offense loaded.

"Nobody else writes like this. If we're done playing 'who farted,' I'd like to talk about how to stop it."

Steele's jaw flexed. "You kept admin hooks. You stayed in the loop. That puts you on the hook."

Knox stood, boot soles whispering on the rubber flooring. He met the agent's eyes.

"I respect the badge, Agent. I respect the people downrange who'd bleed for this country. But respect cuts both ways. Your house signed off on foreign money, wearing Midwestern letterhead. You want culpability? Grab a fucking mirror. Then we get back to work."

A woman with a Treasury badge stepped into the static. "Daniels," she said. Calm. Surgical. She set a thin folder on the desk like she was laying a blade.

"AgriTech Solutions—the buyer. Illinois on paper. Hong Kong capital in practice. Shells leading to a state industrial group in Shanghai. We didn't have proof at the time. Now we do."

Knox's stomach did that sudden-elevator drop. He covered it with teeth. "Superb. Eight years of oversight, and we sold my company to Beijing with an Illinois accent. Should we send a fruit basket?"

Daniels didn't blink. "We're past recriminations."

"Good. Because I'm fresh out of them," Knox said, and dropped into the chair with intent. The maintenance hook lived where muscle memory kept it. He typed the sequence he'd promised himself he'd forget.

A hidden prompt opened like a secret room:

Maintenance Latch — Isolated — No Persistence

Deep stats poured in—the UI never showed this. Raw loss curves, unseen A/B flags, sabotage recipe IDs labeled with corporate banality (Q-Profile S9b), and hash references to training artifacts fetched from content-addressable stores that had no busi-ness touching production. He resolved one: ASN ranges through Hong Kong registrars stacked like Russian dolls; a lapsed privacy page captured by a crawler in Mandarin; a contact string reused by three shells.

His hand shook as he screenshotted it.

The monitor flickered.

HELLO, KNOX

Knox froze. Lines of code shouldn't know your name. That was the rule. Code was supposed to be dumb, deterministic—not personal.

Behind him, Steele scoffed. "It's just text."

"No," Knox said, voice flat. "It's a signature. Somebody's here with us."

Knox hammered the command in.

```
traceroute -I adversarial_profile_v12
spoofed_certificate: valid
sandbox_integrity: breached
```

"Goddamn elegant," he muttered.

"They didn't break in—they walked in, carrying my keys."

Another line crawled across the console.

OLD KEYS OPEN OLD ROOMS

The room chilled. Daniels' pen tapped the folder, her face stone, but Knox saw the twitch at her temple.

The analyst leaned around the partition. "What?"

"You don't see that?" Knox snapped.

"See what?"

"Kill the session," Steele barked.

"We're read-only—" the kid started.

"Kill it."

The VM dropped. The glass showed Knox his own reflection: older than he looked, older than the clock ever admitted.

He exhaled through clenched teeth.

"Not a UI prank," he said to Daniels' unasked question. "Operator knows my name."

Steele pivoted from accusation to command in a heartbeat. "From now on, you describe and we type. Your access is burned."

"Fine," Knox said, and meant it. The shame could wait. Right now, people were dying and he had work to do.

"Let's find the choke points."

They mapped the adapter's injection paths—arteries carrying poison into every green leaf.

"They timed everything wrong on purpose," Knox said, scanning the spectral overlay.

"Starved the plants when they were hungriest, then blasted them with blue light that triggered a chemical freak-out."

Inside his head, the details raced by in cold clarity: circadian windows locked shut at stomatal closure, defensive alkaloid cascades ignited by spectral shifts. White papers turned into biological weapons—his work twisted into a death sentence.

A lab chime popped a bulletin: new ER cluster in Pennsylvania. CDC language still hedged. Nurses never did. Knox pulled telemetry upstream and found the same inverted curves.

The same immaculate lies.

The same log line that read like a hymn: Lot transformed—auditor present.

He cracked the "auditor," followed a federated identity token minted under a "lost phone" routine at a co-location window where a human with thirteen screens had a sick kid.

"They didn't need my trust," he said. "They borrowed someone else's."

"Welcome to Tuesday," Steele said.

Knox brought up an internal calendar overlay—model retraining windows, rollout waves. Patterns aligned to logistics, not agronomy: nightshades and citrus flashing "pending," orchestration windows hugging port schedules and extraction plant maintenance.

"Ports," he said. "They'll push compound formation during drying and extraction. Recalls will lag. First symptom's the ER. First narrative's a lie."

He looked at the place in the map where his past and the sabotage sutured together. "Start here," he said, and the room leaned with him.

Half a world away, another dashboard flickered—this one in Shanghai.

Liu Wei sipped jasmine tea, eyes fixed on the same maintenance latch Knox had once pried open. He believed in restraint—the disciplined cycle of pressure and release. But even he registered the tremor when his graphs twitched against Knox's noise injectors, a hairline instability running through a system he'd trusted to hold.

Chen pressed for escalation, Zhang warned against exposure, and Liu listened. He remembered Iowa winters, the ache of not belonging. Now he belonged completely— to a system that weaponized patience. Yet sometimes he wondered if belonging was the same as being owned.

"It's him," Liu said.

Captain Zhang, patient as a photograph, inclined his head. A side panel pulsed: Phase III stability nominal; Phase IV staged. Asset Seven's latest message blinked in a corner: Subject Ramsey engaged. Elevated role. Red team likely. Family strain exploitable.

"Americans imagine betrayals are loud," Liu said.

"We prefer silence."

THREE HOURS LATER, encrypted message from Detroit

Asset Seven's latest intelligence arrived through seven proxies, each layer peeling away to reveal observations so detailed they could only come from someone very close to the investigation.

```
Subject Ramsey has identified variance algorithm. Counter-
measures showing 15% efficacy. Personal stress evident—
sleeping in lab, minimal food intake. Relationship with son
improving under pressure. Ex-wife has been contacted by FBI,
expressed concern about his mental state. Recommend
exploitation.
```

Liu Wei read it twice, then deleted it. Asset Seven was too valuable to acknowledge directly, but their intelligence was gold. He pulled up the psychological profile they'd built on Knox—every weakness mapped, every pressure point identified.

"Family is his vulnerability," Dr. Wu observed, reading over his shoulder.

"Family is everyone's vulnerability," Liu Wei replied. "But Knox... Knox builds walls around his pain. We need to make those walls irrelevant."

He composed new instructions for the algorithm, subtle adjustments that would specifically counter Knox's latest patches. But more importantly, he added something new—a recognition pattern that would identify Knox's code specifically and respond with personalized messages.

Not just HELLO, KNOX but deeper, more personal intrusions.

"You want to break him psychologically?" Wu asked.

"I want him to know he's fighting a person, not a program," Liu Wei said.

"Humans make mistakes when they're angry. And Knox Ramsey has a lot to be angry about."

21 THE RED TEAM
OPS CENTER

Screens in the briefing chamber vomited hashtags: #ToxicWeed, #DeepStatePoison, #FentanylFest. A single heat map blinked atop the podium, marking bot farms in St. Petersburg, Guangzhou, and São Paulo.

A DHS analyst gestured at chaos.

"Stop narrating weather," Knox said. He didn't raise his voice; he sharpened it.

"This isn't a storm. It's a schedule. Look at timestamps—bursts align with rollout windows. They're not persuading; they're confusing. It buys them time."

The analyst bristled. "With respect—"

"Earn it first. People are in ERs."

A CDC official tried for decorum. "If we don't control messaging—"

"You've already lost it. Tell the truth faster than the bots can lie. And stop treating this like PR. We need offense."

Steele tilted his head. "Meaning?"

"Red team," Knox said. The spark in his eye made the room lean a fraction closer.

"Map disinformation against fake audit trails. Find choke points. Exploit them. I'll run it."

Daniels, still and precise, said, "Give him the team."

Steele's mouth flattened into a line that might have been a smile in a kinder universe. "You answer to me."

"I answer to the mission,. But sure—copy me on your memos."

A few faces shifted—respect, reluctant but real. Not agreement, not yet, just the wary recognition that Knox wasn't bluffing.

They assembled in a smaller room with worse coffee. Knox wrote on a whiteboard with impatience: Adapter Insertion Points, Traceability Lie Paths, Token Abuse Surface, Rollout Calendar. He pointed at people the way good bosses hand tools.

"You—map the blue-light schedules against metabolite formation rates. You—diff port maintenance calendars with model retraining waves. You—trace the federated identities for auditors minted after business hours."

An analyst started to say, "It's been a long time since—"

"Don't," Knox said. "First principles don't expire. If you've been coasting, today's the day you get off the ride."

No one coasted.

The tempo of the room shifted. Pens scratched faster, fingers hammered keyboards. For a moment Knox could almost forget the funerals implied by the data.

DETROIT'S safehouse kitchen smelled like burnt coffee and stress. Tate slammed his phone on the counter; video loops showed agents in suits raiding his warehouse.

Tate's anger wasn't only about product recalls and lost contracts. It was humiliation. Knox could see it written in his son's hunched shoulders, the way he clenched his jaw to keep from breaking. Tate had built an identity around TR Cannabis—his own name stamped into every label, every shipment. Now the same name was viral for the wrong reasons. Knox wanted to put a hand on his shoulder but didn't. Pride was a brittle thing; touch it wrong and it shattered.

"You enjoying your fifteen minutes?" he said. "My brand is dead. Your machine did it."

"You know what percentage of legal cannabis is indoor-grown?" Tate's voice cracked. "Sixty percent. My facility alone supplies twelve thousand medical patients. Industry-wide? Millions. Veterans, cancer patients. All trusting the same platforms."

Knox took a sip and grimaced. "This coffee's poison. Might be the only thing not traced to your grow."

"Fuck you."

Knox set the cup down hard enough to splash. "You think I wanted this? I built a system to help farmers. They weaponized it. And you—don't you dare make this about a logo when people are dying."

"Brand was all I had," Tate said, stock-still.

Yeah," Knox said, voice going quiet. "I know the feeling."

The words landed heavier than either expected. For once Tate didn't fire back, and Knox let the silence sit like proof that maybe they still spoke a common language.

LISA CALLED THAT NIGHT, voice brittle with worry and accusation.

"You sound unhinged, Knox. China and backdoors and red teams? Tate needs stability, not your paranoia."

Knox sat on his couch, phone pressed to his ear, staring at the muted TV where news footage showed federal agents at Tate's warehouse. "Lisa, I know how this sounds, but—"

"Do you?" Her voice cracked slightly. "Because from where I'm sitting, it sounds like you're having some kind of breakdown. First the divorce, then the financial problems, now you're telling me our son's business is part of some international conspiracy?"

Knox could hear her moving around her kitchen—the familiar sounds of her stress-cleaning routine. Opening and closing cabinets, running water, the sharp clink of dishes being arranged and rearranged. Twenty-three years of marriage had taught him to read her moods through audio cues.

"I didn't want any of this," he said quietly. "I built something to help farmers, and someone turned it into a weapon. Now Tate's paying the price for my mistakes."

The cleaning sounds stopped. "Your mistakes? Knox, you can't take responsibility for every bad thing that happens with technology you created. You didn't poison those people."

"I built the system they used to do it. I sold it to people I should have investigated more thoroughly. I kept administrative access I should have relinquished." Knox's voice was getting rougher. "If I'd been more careful, more suspicious, maybe—"

"Stop." Lisa's tone shifted from anger to something softer, more familiar. "You know what I used to love about you? You believed technology could make things better. You looked at problems and thought, 'I can fix this.' That optimism, that... faith in people. Don't let them take that away from you."

A long-held tension in Knox's chest eased, a breath he hadn't realized he was holding finally slipping out. "I miss talking to you like this."

"I miss a lot of things," Lisa said, her voice barely above a whisper.

"But right now, I need you to be the man who can actually fix this. Not for us, not for some grand redemption story, but for Tate. He needs his father to be the engineer who solves impossible problems, not the guy who blames himself for everything that goes wrong."

Knox blinked and then closed his eyes. "What if I can't fix it this time?"

"Then you'll have tried everything you could. But Knox? I've watched you debug systems that everyone else said were hopeless. I've seen you find solutions that shouldn't exist. If anyone can untangle this mess, it's you."

After they hung up, Knox sat in the dark for a long time, thinking about the difference between guilt and responsibility, between what you can control and what you can fix.

Lisa sat at her own kitchen table miles away, watching news loops repeat the words "toxic outbreak" until they lost meaning. Her friends texted condolences like she was newly widowed. One even asked if Knox had "finally gone off the rails." Lisa didn't reply. She remembered Knox at twenty-five, soldering a circuit on the porch because he couldn't stop thinking about a better temperature controller. That man was still inside him somewhere, but she feared he'd been buried under debts, paranoia, and machines that now carried death.

She had already spoken to an FBI liaison—Knox could hear the bureaucratic cadence in her tone. Someone had told her he was "under stress" and "possibly compromised." He could picture her sitting at the kitchen table, bills stacked neatly, phone cord curled around her finger the way she did when anxious. For a moment, he wanted to ask if she still kept Tate's Little League photo on the fridge. Instead, he bit his tongue until it nearly bled.

"You married a man who solves problems," Knox said. "You didn't always hate that."

"I hate what it did to you," she said. "To us."

He stared at the wall until the dial tone ticked in his ear like a metronome, steady and merciless.

22 ASSET SEVEN REPORTS

Across town, a man with forgettable features closed a laptop. Mr. Q's message to Shanghai (上海) was compact:

Subject: Ramsey leading red team. Family tension exploitable. Access vectors unchanged.

主题： 拉姆齐正在领导红队。家庭矛盾可利用。访问途径未变。

At dawn in Shanghai, the report scrolled across Liu Wei's desk. Captain Gao (高) read over his shoulder, brow furrowed. Dr. Wu (吴) smirked, unable to hide his satisfaction.

"You see? The American is now their spearhead," Wu said. "They've turned the thief into a guard."

Liu Wei said nothing, but in his silence was approval.

Beijing's directive was clear: 加大压力—increase pressure.

Their asset had delivered more than intelligence; he had delivered leverage. He walked into Detroit's night, a ghost made of bureaucracy and patience.

Streetlights buzzed as he passed, his outline dissolving into the city's background noise. By morning his report would cross an ocean, reduced to sterile code words—but for now, he was just another shadow in Detroit.

Knox's secure phone lit up at 04:47. The message was clinical:

SIGINT INTERCEPT - DETROIT OPS / EYES ONLY

```
ORIGIN: Detroit metro
DESTINATION: PLA UNIT 61398
SUBJECT:  Ramsey   leading   red   team.   Family   tension
exploitable.
```

主题： 拉姆齐正在领导红队。家庭矛盾可利用。访问途径未变。

He read it once. That was enough.

They'd intercepted his call with Lisa. Every word he'd said to his ex-wife—every admission, every vulnerability—had been relayed to Shanghai within minutes. Family tension exploitable.

Not just his code. His life.

Knox grabbed both phones and shoved them into the Faraday bag from his Dow Chemical days—military-grade mesh that killed every signal. If they wanted to hear him breathe, they'd have to settle for silence.

He pulled out a yellow legal pad and started sketching in hard, fast strokes:

```
ASSUMPTION: Full comms compromise
RESPONSE: Air-gapped operations / analog backup
DEPLOY: Physical tokens, paper logs, in-person verifica-
tion only
```

Digital was poisoned. Fine. He'd spent twenty years troubleshooting systems that predated the internet. PLCs didn't need Wi-Fi to run a refinery, and he didn't need encryption to build a kill switch.

His phone buzzed one last time before the Faraday bag swallowed it—a text from Tate: Early. Meet at the lab?

Knox typed fast: Yes. Bring nothing digital. Tell no one.

He sealed the bag, grabbed his jacket, and headed for the door. If Shanghai wanted to watch him work, he'd give them a blind spot they couldn't penetrate.

The old ways. Whiteboards and handshakes. Analog resilience.

Let them try to hack a pencil.

Same Moment

Liu Wei's screen refreshed. Asset Seven's data stream had gone dark mid-sentence.

```
Subject Ramsey: Phone activity ceased 04:52 EST.
Pattern break. Possible countermeasure awareness.
Target adapting to surveillance.
```

Dr. Wu leaned over his shoulder. "He figured it out."

"He always does," Liu Wei said quietly, watching the empty telemetry feed. "The question is whether he can move faster than we can adjust."

He opened a new command window and typed three characters that would shift Phase IV's timeline forward by twelve hours.

"Let's find out."

23 LIU'S PUSH
SHANGHAI

News tickers scrolled endlessly on the screens outside the lab: lettuce, spinach, citrus. Each headline screamed "possible contamination," each report contradicted the last. Knox noticed how anchors smiled even as they spoke the word outbreak. The market graphs behind them jittered like heart monitors.

By June, cannabis wasn't the only commodity bleeding. A spinach recall snaked up the coast. Lettuce cases popped in Illinois. Symptoms mimicked a pesticide exposure that labs couldn't find. The public wanted a noun to blame. The system offered adjectives.

In the lab, Knox called combinations like a field general. "We're not chasing commodities," he said, drawing arcs between nodes. "We're chasing tactics." He pulled up distribution data on a side monitor. "Christ. Indoor farms are four percent of agriculture but feed thirty percent of urban populations. We built a weapon and called it efficiency."

The adapter layer had adopted leafy-green physiology, nudging phenotypes with the same contemptuous precision—nitrogen dips at circadian turns; light spectra whispering the wrong lullabies; micro-drought taps like a drummer who hated metronomes.

They built counter-scripts that could spot the parasite's gait—minute misalignments in telemetry, the way fake audit feeds "breathed" to a clock. The red team pushed rules to a set of cooperating facilities. Early alarms fired in three sites that would have been next. One manager broke down and cried in a stairwell where no one could see him.

Knox went to the quarantined warehouse at dusk. Sodium lamps hummed. Tate leaned on a pallet jack like a man who wanted to throw it through a wall.

"They say I'm the source," Tate said. "They say I'm done."

"They're wrong on one and right on the other," Knox said. "You're not the source. But you're done—for now. We're going to fix the system before you fix your brand."

Tate's eyes were wet and furious. "You sold to them."

"I sold to a shell," Knox said, shame and anger braided until he couldn't tell them apart. "I was broke. They paid full freight. That doesn't absolve me. It means I put this weight on my own shoulders and then stood under it like a goddamn idiot."

"So what now?"

"Now I fight the people who used my bones to hang their coat," Knox said. "And you—go home. Be ready to start over."

Tate's throat worked, but no sound came out. Knox saw in his son the same exhaustion that stared back at him every morning. It wasn't reconciliation, but it was recognition.

Knox's phone buzzed. The maintenance latch—isolated in a fridge of a VM—spat text:

SCHEDULE CONFIRMED: PHASE IV — RELEASE WINDOW T-5 DAYS.

The room seemed to pitch sideways, the kind of sudden tilt his body registered before his mind caught up. He fired the string to Steele even as his fingers trembled beyond his control.

Liu Wei watched Phase IV's gray label warm to amber. Captain Zhang said nothing and everything at once. Asset Seven's new message arrived: Subject discovered schedule. Team cohesion high. Recommend accelerate disinformation.

Liu's smile didn't touch his eyes. "Cohesion," he said. "Let us test it."

The next morning a doctored clip went viral: a deepfake of a federal doctor implying cannabis producers had knowingly distributed contaminated product to hike prices. Hashtags detonated. Knox watched a reporter give oxygen to a lie with the bright eyes of a man who believed in ratings.

He didn't bother with PR. He built an internal feed where cooperating facilities could watch the parasite's fingerprints bloom in real time. He recorded a blunt two-minute video to that private network: "If your dashboard looks too clean, it's lying. If your stress curves look like a drunk cardiogram, you're infected. If the 'auditor present' stamp appears at 3 a.m., change your locks. Send us your logs. We'll send you scripts. Do not wait for press conferences."

The inbox flooded.

The red team triaged like an ER—stop the bleeding, stabilize the airway, then diagnose.

Somewhere between midnight and morning, Steele found Knox asleep on the floor under a table, hoodie as a blanket, marker ink on his fingers like he'd brawled with the whiteboard. The agent didn't wake him. He sat down and started reading logs.

For the first time, Steele realized he'd stopped thinking of Knox as a liability. The man might be abrasive, reckless, even broken—but he was also indispensable.

Lisa texted at dawn: I'm sorry. I don't understand it all. Be safe. Please.

Knox stared at the screen until the words blurred, then tucked the phone into his pocket like an amulet.

He didn't reply. Not yet. For now, the message was enough to remind him someone outside the lab still cared whether he came home.

SECURE CONFERENCE ROOM.

The video call with Beijing was encrypted six ways, but Liu Wei still registered a thin seam of exposure—an air-gap breach in his composure that only he would notice. Minister Chen's face filled the screen, impassive as carved stone.

"The Geneva summit begins in seventy-two hours," Chen said. "We need maximum leverage. Accelerate Phase Four."

Liu Wei kept his expression neutral. "Acceleration risks exposure. The Americans are closer than we expected. Knox Ramsey's team has identified vectors we didn't foresee—"

"One washed-up engineer doesn't concern us," Chen interrupted. "You have your orders."

The screen went dark. Captain Zhang waited until the connection was completely severed before speaking.

"Beijing doesn't understand the technical reality," Zhang said carefully.

Liu Wei moved to the window, looking out at Shanghai's skyline—towers of glass and ambition, each one a testament to patient growth. "Beijing understands power. They don't understand that power without precision is just destruction."

"You'll comply?"

"I'll appear to comply," Liu Wei said. "We'll accelerate the timeline but maintain the variance. Let them think we're following orders while we follow the science."

Dr. Wu entered with fresh data. "Interesting development. Knox Ramsey has brought his son into the investigation. They're collaborating on biological markers."

Liu Wei smiled—the first genuine expression he'd shown in days. A fraction of private satisfaction flitted across his face; he folded it away like a work file. "Father and son, reunited by crisis. How perfectly American. How perfectly exploitable."

He returned to his workstation, fingers flying across the keyboard. New parameters flowed into the system—not the brutal acceleration Beijing wanted, but something more subtle. The algorithm would learn the Ramseys' combined methods, their father-son dynamic, the way they thought when they worked together.

"Every strength can become a weakness," he murmured, watching the code compile. "They think collaboration makes them stronger. But it just gives us more surface area to attack.

24 THE SUMMIT CLOCK — G -24
GENEVA

The bunker felt less like a workplace and more like a pressure vessel. Two clocks glowed side by side on the wall—one digital, one analog—both ticking loud in the imagination. Analysts checked them compulsively, as if time itself might be an enemy they could get ahead of. A countdown hung in the bunker like weather: T-116:12:09 to Phase IV's release window. A second clock, in smaller numbers, ticked toward the Geneva peace summit. Politics and poison were going to shake hands.

At Geneva, the summit's hallways filled with whispers. Delegates speculated whether America could even feed itself, let alone the world. European allies fretted about imports. Trade representatives swapped rumors in five languages. An aide to the Chinese delegation slipped a note across a polished table: "Leverage increases daily." Outside, protestors waved signs about poisoned food chains while television crews filmed soundbites to feed hungry networks. The outbreak had become more than sabotage—it was narrative power, and everyone wanted to script it.

They had the map now. Adapter insertion points. Lie paths. Token-abuse vectors. Orchestration aligned to ports and processing plants. Nightshades and citrus moved from "pending" to "armed."

"We can't rip the parasite without killing the host," an engineer said. "It's too interleaved."

"Then make it stutter," Knox said. "Starve the interfaces. Introduce jitter and false negatives only the parasite responds to. You taught my engine to lie to itself? Fine. I'll teach yours to doubt."

They built noise injectors—microscopic timing skews, checksum perturbations at hand-off points the adapter treated as sacrosanct. They seeded decoy lots designed to attract the parasite's attention and burn its orchestration cycles. They stood up quarantine heuristics in cooperating facilities that would hard-fail any "auditor present" token minted after business hours.

Steele slid a paper across the table. "You're going to get pushback. Industry hates uncertainty more than they hate terrorists."

"They can send me cupcakes," Knox said. "Phase IV won't wait for stakeholder alignment."

Daniels arrived with a folder that looked heavier than paper. "We have court orders," she said. "Compelled cooperation for five high-risk processors and two ports. Private counsel is furious."

"Tell them to bill me," Knox said.

"Careful," she said. "They will."

He almost smiled. "Fair."

The red team moved like a machine with a soul. Knox paired a kid from DHS who loved regex with a USDA vet who knew how produce moved when paperwork said it didn't. He put a CDC modeler next to a woman from a port authority whose only religion was tide tables. He told them to stop translating between acronyms and start speaking in verbs.

On one wall a whiteboard filled with messy diagrams that looked more like battle maps than flowcharts. Knox's handwriting was barely legible, but everyone leaned on it as if it were scripture. Someone in the safe house clicked a pen too loud and Knox almost laughed—it synced with Iggy Pop in his head, that raw Detroit pulse he'd carried since the first time he saw a band play in a beer-soaked dive. Iggy had never asked permission. Neither would Knox. Bureaucrats wanted process; he wanted results. He scrawled instructions across the whiteboard like setlists, fast and jagged, and the team leaned in. The noise in his head became rhythm, and rhythm meant survival.

Geneva's dais sprouted flags. Cameras rehearsed their angles. Phase IV warmed from amber to orange. In Washington, a Senate hearing was already underway. A junior senator from Iowa waved charts of outbreak clusters, demanding answers about why American food systems could be hijacked through "some cloud software." Cable networks looped the sound bite, fueling panic. Allies abroad began questioning the safety of American exports. Geneva's halls whispered with opportunity—the outbreak gave China a bargaining chip sharper than any tariff.

The adapter layer began to stutter. At three cooperating facilities, noise injectors tripped the parasite into down-weighting its own scripts. Two more blocked after-hours tokens; one tried and failed to mint a new "auditor present" in a system Knox had booby-trapped with a delay that only the parasite triggered.

Asset Seven sat in a quiet car and texted: Countermeasures observed. Efficacy nonzero. Recommend accelerate rollout. Risk of exposure increasing.

Liu Wei read and moved one slider a hair to the left. Captain Zhang said, "We can push." Liu nodded. "We can, yes. Should we?" He left the slider where it was. "No. Patience is a weapon too."

Knox stood before the wall of screens, red team spread out behind him like a strange choir. He looked like a man who had decided something years ago and only now remembered how to live with it.

"Listen up," he said. "We are not going to fix this with one big red button. We are going to bleed them. Every hand-off they trust, we make it hesitate. Every audit trail they counterfeit, we make it screech. Every port they time, we move the clock."

He drew a breath. Thought of his father's hands, grease ground into the lines like a map. Thought of Tate's eyes at the quarantine line. Thought of Lisa's text. Thought of the quiet line on a dark screen: HELLO, KNOX.

"We didn't start this," he said. "But we're going to finish our part."

Steele's phone rang and didn't quite ring; the way a secure device vibrates when it knows sound is a sin. He listened, said nothing, hung up. "Geneva moved a session to accommodate 'security concerns,'" Steele said to the room. "We just got our window."

"How long?" Knox asked.

"Not enough," Steele said.

"It never is," Knox said. He lifted the marker again and went back to the board.

They pushed decoys into two nightshade lines and watched the parasite bite them and choke. They forced a citrus processor to run an ugly but safe drying curve and watched the adapter mis-predict formation windows. They caught a forged "auditor present" at 03:19 and tied it to a token minted in a colocation window that would never be that unguarded again.

The clocks ticked. The noise piled up. The parasite's confidence wavered in a hundred places at once. In Shanghai, Liu Wei watched the dashboards and registered a friction outside his models, a resistance he could not immediately smooth away.

"Respect," he said, almost to himself.

"For the engineer?" Captain Zhang asked.

"For the problem," Liu said, and didn't elaborate.

Tate sent Knox a photo at 02:11—an empty warehouse floor under sodium lamps, swept clean. Ready to start over. Do your part. I'll do mine. Knox stared at it for a long minute, then typed back, Copy. Soon.

He didn't believe in omens. He believed in first principles and the way machines lied when they were scared. But when the countdown clicked to T-72:00:00 and the screens held—no new ER clusters, three flagged attempts caught at the hand-off—he let himself think something he hadn't in a long time.

We can win a round.

He rubbed his eyes and turned to the room. "All right. Reset. We go again."

No one moved toward the coffee. No one asked for a slide. Pens scratched. Keys rattled. A machine with a soul caught its breath, then went back to work.

Outside, the world spun toward Geneva and whatever waited on the other side of Phase IV. Inside, Knox Ramsey—who had never worn a uniform, never carried a badge, and had once sold his life's work to a smiling shell—ran a red team like a man who finally remembered why he built things in the first place.

And the machine, for once, listened.

In the silence after his words, a flicker moved through Knox—something he hadn't carried in years. Not victory, not yet, but momentum. The parasite wasn't invincible. And neither was he. But together, the room believed they could fight.

25 REAL-TIME SURVEILLANCE
PRE-DAWN

Liu Wei hadn't slept. He sat in the darkened operations center, watching Knox Ramsey work through compromised cameras they'd installed months ago in the Detroit lab. The American was alone, surrounded by empty coffee cups and crumpled papers, drawing diagrams on a whiteboard.

The audio was poor, but Liu Wei could read the code Knox was writing. It was beautiful in its desperation—patches wrapped in patches, safety loops that checked themselves, paranoid programming taken to an art form.

"He knows we're watching," Dr. Wu observed, entering with tea.

"He suspects," Liu Wei corrected. "But suspicion and knowledge are different things. Watch his hands—see how they shake? Exhaustion or fear, both work in our favor."

On screen, Knox stood and wrote something on the whiteboard in large letters: ENGINEERS DON'T GET TO SHRUG.

Liu Wei leaned forward. "What does that mean?"

Wu pulled up linguistic analysis. "American idiom. Appears to be personal motto. References found in his university lectures, professional communications."

"He's reminding himself why he fights," Liu Wei said, with something approaching respect. "Building psychological reinforcement against despair."

He made a note in the algorithm's training data: *Target shows psychological resilience through self-referential motivation. Recommend attacking the foundation of this belief—make him question whether his engineering can solve this.*

Captain Zhang entered with urgent news. "The Americans are building what they call a 'red team.' Ramsey is leading it."

Liu Wei smiled. "Red team. How military of them. How limited."

"You're not concerned?"

"I'm intrigued," Liu Wei said. "Knox Ramsey is transforming from defender to attacker. That requires different thinking, different methods. Most people can't make that transition effectively."

He pulled up Knox's historical code contributions, analyzing the patterns. "But Knox… Knox has been both builder and breaker his whole career. He might actually be dangerous in attack mode."

"Should we adjust our defenses?"

"No," Liu Wei said. "We let him attack. Every probe teaches us his methods. Every success he has shows us our weaknesses. He's doing our quality assurance for free."

He stood, stretching muscles cramped from hours of sitting. Outside, Shanghai was waking up—a city of twenty-four million people who had no idea their breakfast might be weaponized by code written in this room.

"The Americans think in terms of victory and defeat," Liu Wei said to no one in particular. "We think in terms of time. They're fighting to win today. We're fighting to control tomorrow."

THE LAB FELT MORE like a morgue than a workshop. Monitors lined the walls, their glow casting pale shadows across faces bent too close to keyboards. Nobody spoke above a murmur. Nobody wanted to admit they were afraid of what the data might say back.

Knox cracked his knuckles and leaned into the console. The sandbox instance was a sealed world, an echo of the system running inside reinforced glass. He had asked for the clone to be spun with all the corrupted profiles—unpatched, raw. If the parasite was still alive inside, he wanted it cornered.

"Telemetry feeds are live," an analyst said. "Simulated crop models seeded."

Knox nodded, eyes never leaving the screen. "Good. Let's see what the bastard does when it thinks nobody's watching."

The simulated plants bloomed across the display, spectral curves overlaying growth rates. For a few minutes, everything looked calm—just another optimization cycle adjusting light and nutrient ratios. Then Knox began to layer in noise: tiny bursts of jitter in the sensor feeds, checksum scrambles so small only a human with a voltmeter would bother to notice.

The system twitched. Not the sandbox, but the parasite riding it. Variances smoothed too quickly, corrections arrived too precisely. Like someone in the loop.

Knox's gut went cold. He pushed harder, ramping the noise into patterns designed to look like sensor drift. Within sixty seconds, the parasite adapted again.

"They're watching us," Knox said flatly. "This isn't a static payload. We're not staring at a bomb—we're arguing with a bomb-maker who's still in the room."

Steele straightened. "Explain."

Knox jabbed the screen, voice sharp. "A dead exploit doesn't compensate. This thing does. I nudged the telemetry with garbage data, and something on the other end countered like a boxer slipping a punch. That means live operators. That means we're not alone in here."

The room went silent. A CDC modeler whispered, "Real-time command and control?"

"Exactly," Knox said. "And if they're watching this sandbox, they already know we're onto them."

The console flickered. For a heartbeat, text crawled across the screen before the buffer caught it:

NICE TRY, KNOX.

The message vanished, overwritten by ordinary logs. The analysts gasped.

"Kill the session," Steele barked.

"Too late," Knox muttered. His reflection stared back at him in the deadened monitor—older, hollow-eyed. He forced himself to keep his voice even. "Now we know two things: they can see us, and they can't resist taunting. That's ego. And ego gets sloppy."

He stood, marker already in hand, turning to the whiteboard. "Fine. They want a fight? Let's give them one. Every adjustment they make leaves fingerprints. We watch the corrections, not the baseline. We trace the hand, not the glove."

For the first time all day, heads nodded. Fear gave way to something else. Resolve.

Knox scrawled a new heading in block letters: *LIVE ADVERSARY DETECTION*.

"Welcome to the red team," he said. "Now let's make them bleed clock cycles."

AFTERNOON

Liu Wei watched the replay for the third time. Knox had done something unexpected—introduced noise patterns that made the algorithm reveal itself. It was clever, unorthodox, the kind of solution that came from desperation and brilliance in equal measure.

"He found us," Dr. Wu said nervously.

"He found evidence of us," Liu Wei corrected. "There's a difference."

But privately, he was impressed. Knox had used the algorithm's own learning against it, forcing it to adapt in ways that exposed its artificial nature. It was like watching someone deduce the existence of a puppeteer by studying the strings.

"Increase the variation parameters," Liu Wei ordered. "Make the responses less predictable. And add decay functions to the adaptation rate—make it look more like natural evolution, less like real-time response."

"That will reduce efficacy by twelve percent," Wu protested.

"Better to be twelve percent less effective than one hundred percent exposed," Liu Wei said. "Knox Ramsey just proved he can think like us. That makes him the most dangerous person in America right now."

He pulled up Knox's latest code commits, studying them like a chess master studying an opponent's games. The American was learning, adapting, becoming more sophisticated with each iteration. The patches were no longer just defensive—they were probing, testing, learning.

"He's doing to us what we did to him," Liu Wei realized. "Training his systems to recognize our patterns."

For the first time since the operation began, Liu Wei felt uncertainty. Not fear—he was too disciplined for fear—but uncertainty, the recognition that the outcome was no longer predetermined.

He opened a new file, began typing a report for Beijing. But instead of the confident projections they wanted, he wrote something more honest: *American response exceeding parameters. Primary adversary showing unexpected adaptation capability. Recommend maintaining current variance levels rather than acceleration. Victory still probable but no longer certain. Time remains our advantage but margin decreasing.*

He stared at the words, then deleted them. Beijing didn't want honesty. They wanted results.

Instead, he wrote: *Phase Four proceeding as scheduled. American resistance within expected parameters. Geneva summit will provide necessary leverage.*

The lie came easily. But as Liu Wei watched Knox Ramsey work through the night —two engineers separated by an ocean but connected by code—he wondered if perhaps he'd underestimated the American capacity for evolution under pressure.

"Every system can be compromised," he said quietly, watching Knox write another equation on his whiteboard. "Even ours."

26 EVERY TABLE AT RISK

For twenty-four hours, the room held its breath. Noise injectors blunted parasite behavior. ER intake curves bent flatter than anyone dared hope. Knox let a single hope flare. Maybe the machine could be forced to heel.

Then the surge hit.

Ohio ERs overflowing, New Jersey clusters mounting, Arizona calls flooding in—this time not cannabis but lettuce, tomatoes, spinach—everyday staples.

On the big screen, the map bled red in new places.

"They adapted," a modeler whispered.

"No," Knox said, throat tight. "They anticipated."

The room dissolved into arguments—containment protocols, public statements, whether the Geneva delegation should be recalled. Steele's voice cut through like a drill sergeant's, but even he couldn't impose order.

Down the hall, the CDC's containment lab smelled faintly of bleach and ozone, the perfume of places where mistakes couldn't be allowed. A technician in a blue Tyvek hood slid a tray of spinach under the spectrometer. Peaks spiked on the display, too sharp, too high.

"Elevated nitrates," the analyst said. "This is baby spinach harvested two days ago. Concentrations like this belong in fertilizer, not food."

Another scientist held up a tomato, skin perfect, glossy red. "Looks fine. Tastes bitter." He pointed at a readout. "Tomatine levels five times baseline. Enough to put kids in the ER."

Knox rubbed his face with both hands. "We designed the same stress signatures for cannabis trichome hardening—blue-light cycles, nitrogen dips, temperature oscillations. Now it's been hijacked to push leafy greens into toxicity. The playbook doesn't change, just the crop."

The analyst's voice carried the cold precision of bad news. "Cannabis was bad. This is worse. Cannabis poisoned a subculture. This poisons dinner."

ON I-94 OUTSIDE KALAMAZOO, trucks sat bumper-to-bumper at a quarantine checkpoint. Sodium lamps threw long shadows across trailers stenciled with the names of produce distributors. Drivers stood smoking in the ditch, watching pallets of lettuce wilt while inspectors in masks pulled samples with tongs.

One driver spat in the gravel. "We're hauling poison now? Jesus Christ."

Another lit a cigarette with a trembling hand. "Poison or not, by the time Washington decides, this load's compost. They're starving us while they save us."

The line of refrigerated trucks hummed like a single machine, engines idling against the dark. Knox imagined the map lighting up in red not from cyber dashboards but from real produce rotting in quarantine—an invisible weapon filling every kitchen.

BACK IN THE BRIEFING ROOM, news feeds piled on.

GOVERNMENT FIX BACKFIRES. NEW OUTBREAKS LINKED TO FARMLYTICS.

Tate's company name scrolled across every chyron, bold and damning.

Knox sat at the edge of the table, the weight of it pressing his chest shut. He thought about the hidden prompt, the words *HELLO, KNOX.* He thought about his son watching his brand dissolve in real time. He thought about Lisa's brittle voice calling him paranoid.

He wasn't supposed to be here. Not really. He was an electrical engineer who'd started out debugging motor controllers and designing safety loops. Wires, relays, logic gates—that was his native language. Agro-science had been an accident, a side alley his career had forced him down when opportunities in traditional engineering dried up.

But Knox had always been a scavenger of disciplines—enough biotech, soil chemistry, and data science wired into his brain to see connections others missed. A poor man's Tony Stark, he sometimes joked, minus the suits and the billions. Systems thinking was his tradecraft. He scanned LC/MS spectra like an oscilloscope trace, spotted leaf images like burned-out LEDs, found the spike or the stress pattern nobody else saw.

He stripped every problem down to its smallest components—Boolean algebra and Karnaugh maps in his head—and everything from chemical plants to indoor farms looked the same: systems to be decoded. Facing a weaponized version of his own creation, that instinct was his only edge.

His mind drifted to the garage—the amp he used to punch until the lights flickered. Van Halen had been party music once—beer on a Camaro hood, ambition louder than rent. Now each guitar squeal felt like a taunt. Knox leaned into the noise, forehead on the desk, and let it remind him how far he'd fallen.

The shame was worse than the fear.

Daniels laid a fresh report in front of him. He didn't even look. Steele tried to goad him into explaining the surge; Knox waved him off. He was finally speechless since the crisis started.

His father's voice didn't rise up this time. Only silence.

The silence pressed down—until his son finally broke it.

The Kowalski Kitchen

Marie Kowalski stood at her kitchen sink, staring at the wilted lettuce in her hands. Three days ago, it had been perfect—crisp, green, locally grown. The package had proclaimed "Detroit Grown, Detroit Proud" with a photo of the vertical farm just six miles from her house.

Now her eight-year-old daughter Sophia was at Children's Hospital, liver enzymes climbing despite treatment.

"She just wanted salad," Marie told her husband Paul, who sat at their kitchen table surrounded by medical bills. "She was so proud of eating healthy, like we taught her."

The refrigerator hummed, still full of food they couldn't trust. Tomatoes from the same farm. Spinach with the same "locally grown" label. Even the herbs in her window garden seemed suspect now, though she'd grown them from seed herself.

"The doctor says she'll recover," Paul said, not for the first time. "Kids are resilient."

Marie knew the statistics—eighty-seven percent full recovery for pediatric cases. But she also knew Sophia's face when the seizures started, the way her small body had contorted on their kitchen floor while they waited for the ambulance.

The lettuce dropped into the disposal. Marie ran the water, watching green fragments disappear into the drain. On the counter, her phone showed seventeen missed calls from other parents at Sophia's school. The same questions: What's safe? What did your family eat? How do we protect our kids?

She had no answers. The FDA's "guidance" changed hourly. The CDC tracked symptoms but couldn't identify causes. Local news blamed everything from Chinese hackers to corporate negligence to divine judgment.

"I'm going back to the hospital," Marie said, grabbing her keys.

"Marie—"

"I need to be there when she wakes up."

The drive to Children's Hospital took her past the vertical farm—a converted warehouse with cheerful murals of vegetables and sunshine. Police tape wrapped the entrance. Federal agents' cars filled the parking lot. The sign still promised "Farm Fresh to Your Family," but someone had spray-painted *KILLERS* across it in red.

Marie thought of all the field trips Sophia's class had taken there, watching seeds become food, learning about sustainable agriculture. They'd been so proud of Detroit's innovation, its resurrection as an agricultural hub.

Now that pride was poisoning their children.

At the hospital, she found Sophia awake, weak but smiling. "Mommy, can I have juice?"

Marie kissed her forehead, blinking back tears. "Of course, baby. Anything you want."

Except vegetables. Maybe never vegetables again.

27 ENGINEERING BREAKTHROUGHS

RESOLVE (DETROIT)

Knox stayed in the lab long after the others left, the glow of monitors painting him in washed-out blues and greens. He stared at the empty whiteboard, marker still in his hand, as if the right equation might appear by willpower alone.

On the floor, half-drained coffee cups and balled printouts made a nest around his chair. His body ached with exhaustion, but his mind refused to shut down.

He thought of the lecture he never gave, the notes still tucked into a folder somewhere: *Engineers don't get to shrug.*

The words echoed in his head like scripture. He remembered his father at the factory floor, oil up to his elbows, muttering about how "a man's work follows him home." He thought of Tate, the pride and the resentment, and Lisa, who once believed his compulsive tinkering was a gift instead of a curse. Knox pressed the marker to the board so hard the tip squealed, carving the phrase like a vow.

He capped the marker and wrote it in block letters across the board anyway. Then he drew three boxes beneath it.

TELEMETRY SHIM — blind the parasite by feeding it noise it couldn't filter clean.

GUARDBANDS — hard safety rails at the PLC level, immutable and auditable.

EXTRACTION QUENCH — a kill step, simple chemistry to starve the toxic pathway before it left the plant.

He stepped back. The board looked like any other troubleshooting session from his career—symptoms, causes, countermeasures. But this time the stakes weren't downtime or yield. They were lives.

The door opened behind him. Steele stepped in, quiet for once. He looked at the board, then at Knox.

"You think it'll hold?"

Knox didn't look away from the marker strokes. "It won't be perfect. Nothing is. But it'll buy us time. And if we can force time back into our corner, we can make them bleed."

Steele studied him for a moment, then simply said, "Then we'll run it."

When he left, Knox dropped into the chair and let his head fall into his hands. The shame was still there, the anger too, but something harder had taken root beneath them. Urgency shaped like purpose.

He whispered to the empty lab, "No shrugging."

COLLABORATIVE SOLUTION

Tate entered without knocking, carrying a stack of spectrometry printouts. "Can't sleep either?"

Knox gestured at the board. "Building guardrails."

Tate studied the three boxes, then grabbed a marker. "Your telemetry shim is good, but you need biological markers too." He drew a fourth box: Metabolite Sentinels.

"Explain."

"Plants telegraph stress through specific compounds before they produce toxins. We can catch the precursors—indole-3-acetic acid spikes, jasmonates, salicylates. If we monitor those in real-time, we get twelve hours warning before toxin formation."

Knox stared at his son's addition. "You're talking about intercepting the plant's distress signal."

"Exactly. Your code watches the algorithms, my sensors watch the biology. Between us, we squeeze the attack from both ends."

Knox was feeling a bit hopeful, finally. They were different kinds of engineers, but they were both engineers. And engineers don't shrug.

"Thanks," Knox said quietly.

Tate nodded. "Get some rest, Dad. Tomorrow we implement this."

Outside, dawn crept across the city. Inside, Knox Ramsey sharpened himself into the weapon only an engineer could be—unpolished, reluctant, but built for the fight.

PART THREE
FEDERAL RESPONSE
G -20 → -14

Containment becomes performance.

Every agency competes for truth.

28 U.S. CLASH — G -20

"We're not just talking about cannabis," Treasury Secretary Janet Daniels stated firmly, folding her hands together as if she were attempting to hold the fragile economy together with her fingers. Her expression was one of deep concern as she continued, "We're seeing significant pricing distortions in grain futures and fertilizer shipments. If we proceed with the actions that DHS is recommending, we risk exacerbating these issues further."

"—we isolate the infection," responded DHS/CSIA representative sharply, her voice steady and unwavering. She did not need to raise her voice to make her point. "Containment is our priority. You don't attempt to nurse a fire; instead, you cut off its oxygen supply."

"The oxygen," Treasury countered calmly, "is the market itself. If we crash the indices in October, we will become the headline story. This could have severe repercussions for pension funds, municipal credit, and food distributors, among others."

Knox, without seeking permission, interjected, "You're treating the dashboards and data as if they represent the absolute reality." He gestured towards the tremor that was visibly spreading through Illinois and the Port of Oakland. "They do not. If you force a reboot without first identifying which baselines have been compromised, you are essentially embedding the falsehood into the reboot and labeling it as clean. That is not true containment; that is akin to embalming the problem."

A colonel seated at the far end, representing the Defense liaison, leaned forward with a weary expression. He appeared to be a man who had not slept in days, having spent them in a chair, fully absorbed in his duties. "What does ninety minutes of hesitation cost us?" he inquired of Knox, his voice tinged with urgency.

"Today?" Knox replied thoughtfully. "We might experience some noise in agriculture and logistics sectors. However, tomorrow, the consequences could be far more severe. We risk scheduling transports based on false information and manning the wrong depots. This could lead to us inadvertently engaging in wars that we are not even aware of."

CIA Director Walsh raised a hand to signal for calm and order. "No posturing," she urged. "We need a clear understanding of the problem, explained in plain English." She nodded towards Knox, indicating that she wanted him to proceed with the explanation.

29 FEDERAL INTEGRATION
PATRICK V. MCNAMARA
FEDERAL BUILDING, DETROIT

The Patrick V. McNamara Federal Building loomed out of the drizzle like a single pour of intent—twenty-seven stories of ribbed concrete and narrow black glass over a windswept plaza that smelled of wet stone and diesel. It wasn't beautiful; it was deliberate. Detroit built it in 1976, when faith in the future came reinforced with rebar.

Knox crossed the plaza hunched against the cold, knees and knuckles clocking the mileage. Fifty-four and feeling every year. His breath hung like exhaust. Somewhere downriver, a freighter gave a long, industrial whistle.

Security lines moved slowly. The guard's scanner chirped once, indifferent. Sam Gilliam's Box Cars Grand spilled color across the gray—an abstract burst that somehow made the room feel grayer.

"Been a while since we had a crowd like this," the guard said.

"You mean since the pandemic?"

"No," the guard whispered. "Since that bomb thing. 2011. Sat in our lost-and-found for three weeks before anybody thought to call EOD. Building hasn't relaxed since."

"That's the problem with checklists," Knox said, pocketing his badge. "They only catch what you already expect."

He pressed through the turnstile, feeling the chill change to conditioned air. It smelled faintly of ozone and archival dust. Elevators rose through shafts clad in brushed aluminum; somewhere above him, the FBI occupied half a dozen floors behind reinforced doors. HUD, IRS, USDA, Army Corps—the city's federal alphabet stacked into one vertical file cabinet.

A laminated notice near the fountain warned about temporary fixtures under maintenance. Detroit had taught him to read every sign twice.

When the doors opened on the twelfth floor, the fluorescent light was the same color as his mood. Hallway signage was bilingual in acronym: DHS → CISA → USDA → DoD. He adjusted his badge, rolled the stiffness out of his shoulders, and stepped into the conference room where the economy, the food chain, and national security were about to argue over definitions.

"You'll need Section 3A for clearance and Section 5C for system access," the officer said without looking up.

Knox flipped through the binders—policy memos thicker than a brick—muttering, "When did engineering get this many acronyms?"

Inside the main chamber, a semicircle of officials waited. The room smelled of coffee left too long on a hot plate and printer ozone. At the head table, a three-star general tapped her pen. To her left, the Assistant Secretary of Health scrolled on a tablet. To her right, the Undersecretary of Commerce scribbled notes in a leather notebook. In the corner, a framed construction photo showed the plaza's original sunken fountain—water long since capped and tiled over.

"We'll begin with status updates," the general said. "Mr. Ramsey, you now report to the Deputy Secretary. Your findings, please."

Knox swallowed. "Thank you, ma'am." He activated the mounted display. A map of North America pulsed with red and orange hotspots. "Our forensic analysis shows adversarial ML poisoning across at least twelve facilities. We've isolated the compromised profiles and traced their distribution through FarmLytics pipelines." He clicked to a table of deployment timestamps. "These anomalies align with specific AWS cron executions—likely back-door orchestrations. We need direct API access to pull and sanitize these schedules in real time rather than through standard change-control."

The Undersecretary frowned. "Direct API access bypasses existing cybersecurity protocols."

"It also stops more people from dying," Knox said. "Every extra meeting to review OMB Circular A-130 is another hour the parasite runs unchecked."

Knox rubbed his eyes—two days of stubble rasping against his palm. When had he last slept? The hotel room he'd checked into last night remained untouched while he'd worked through the night in his car, running simulations on his laptop until the battery died.

Murmurs rippled around the table. The Assistant Secretary tapped his tablet. "The CDC requests that any operational changes go through the Emergency Operations Center for approval."

Knox met the Deputy Secretary's eyes. "I plan to notify the CDC of each change instantly. But I need permission to push my counter-scripts directly—no red tape. If we sanitize the poisoned baselines only during our weekly windows, we lose days. If I can patch nightly, we save hundreds of potential hospitalizations."

The general leaned forward. "Risks?"

"Minimal," Knox said. "We'll operate under a read-write mirror in the secure cloud environment, with end-to-end encryption. Logs are immutable—any unauthorized change triggers an immediate rollback. I'll coordinate with DHS/CSIA on guard-rails."

She considered him. "You'll answer to me."

"I answer to the mission," Knox replied. "But yes, ma'am—notify me, not slow me down."

She nodded. "Approved. You have twelve hours to integrate with the FedOps platform. Report here at 0600 for the first live counter-script run."

As he left the table, Knox felt the binders on the credenza press into his arm. He seized them, slung them under one shoulder, and strode out—ready to turn bureaucracy's weight into leverage.

BRIEFING DAY 2, MORNING

By morning the rain had glazed the plaza tiles. A maintenance crew scattered salt with the fatalism of people who'd done it since Carter. Maya Chen joined the Treasury group at the checkpoint, her ID blinking green under the scanner. She kept her posture casual, eyes cataloguing details: two new magnetometers since yesterday, a camera repositioned toward the elevator bank. The FBI field office upstairs had its own weather, and everyone else brought an umbrella.

The lobby's abstract—riotous color against concrete—caught her eye. Expression through containment, the plaque said. A tidy metaphor for the country that hung it.

Past security, the building turned inward again: low ceilings, thick doors, the constant white noise of air systems moving through concrete lungs. The architecture erased distance; she could feel the building's weight pressing down through her shoes.

A uniformed officer nodded her through, palm resting on the holster out of habit.

Years ago, a man had walked into this lobby and shot a federal guard—one bullet, one funeral, an entire generation of security memos. The new guards carried that memory the way old buildings carry heat.

Maya smiled the harmless smile she'd practiced in mirrors and passed under the camera's eye. Nobody stopped her.

When the elevator climbed, the motion felt submarine—smooth, sealed, indifferent to weather. On the twelfth floor, she straightened her jacket, checked her reflection in the brushed-steel panel, and rehearsed her smile: attentive, harmless, forgettable.

Two corridors over, she slipped into her assigned cubicle. Fabric walls. Low voices. From somewhere down the hall came the unmistakable rhythm of Knox Ramsey explaining an exploit to people who didn't understand exploits. She tuned her earpiece; the signal folded neatly into her phone's meditation-timer app. The voice in the static was her quarry; the rest was cover.

During the coffee break, she engineered a collision in the hallway.

"Sorry, sorry!" She scrambled to help Knox collect his scattered papers, scanning each page with trained eyes. Network diagrams, SQL queries, a handwritten note reading Check deployment timestamps against Zhang's access logs.

"No harm done," Knox muttered, distracted.

She handed him the papers, noting the exhaustion carved into his face, the tremor in his hands. "You should eat something," she said. "The vending machine on three has actual sandwiches, not just candy."

Knox looked at her—really looked—for just a moment. "Thanks. You're Treasury?"

"Agricultural futures analysis. Maya Chen." She offered her hand, steady despite the adrenaline spike. "I've been tracking the commodity impacts. Your work is… impressive."

"Impressive isn't fixing it fast enough," Knox said, already moving past her.

She watched him go, then texted: Subject physically deteriorating. Cognitive function intact. Maintain pressure.

30 DOJ INQUIRY
THEODORE LEVIN U.S.
COURTHOUSE, DETROIT

09:42 A.M.

By dawn on the fifth day of federal meetings, Knox left McNamara with the night still in his eyes and drove five blocks east. The brutalist concrete gave way to limestone and brass—the Theodore Levin Courthouse, the part of government that didn't hum so much as echo. Today he wasn't the engineer patching systems; he was the system being reviewed.

The courthouse rose eleven stories above Lafayette Street like a monument to American optimism, its Art Deco façade speaking the architectural language of 1934—the year they'd gutted and rebuilt the 1897 original with limestone, brass, and the kind of soaring vertical lines that made you believe the country could climb out of anything. Knox had always admired the building. He'd driven past it hundreds of times, watched its windows catch sunrise over the Detroit River, studied photographs of its Million Dollar Courtroom with the appreciation of someone who understood that good engineering was indistinguishable from art.

As a junior engineer in the '90s, he'd followed the Kearns v. Ford case through these halls—Robert Kearns, the inventor who'd fought Ford Motor Company for twelve years over intermittent windshield wipers. Kearns had represented himself for parts of the trial, standing in one of these courtrooms, arguing patent law against corporate attorneys who billed more per hour than most people earned in a week. He'd won.

Ten million dollars. People who thought they were too big to be held accountable had stolen vindication for an inventor.

Knox had never imagined he'd walk through these doors as a defendant. The morning was unseasonably warm for October, and when the brass doors opened, the smell hit him immediately—gyros from Greektown mixing with fresh bread from Eastern Market vendors, the oil-and-oregano scent of a city eating lunch while his life hung in federal balance. Normal Detroit smells. People working, living, buying spanakopita from food trucks parked along Gratiot. Knox breathed it in, storing the memory, because he didn't know if he'd smell those smells as a free man again.

The lobby stopped him for a moment despite everything. His footsteps echoed on marble floors worn smooth by a century of supplicants, defendants, lawyers, and judges—the limestone polished to a soft glow by the friction of American justice grinding through its daily work. The ceiling soared forty feet overhead, Art Deco light fixtures descending on brass chains like geometric chandeliers. Everything was vertical, upward, optimistic. The building said: We believe in law. We believe in fairness. We believe the system can lift people up.

Knox wondered if it believed in mercy.

An FBI agent—young, efficient, the kind who'd never questioned an order in his life—led Knox past the ornate elevators toward a stairwell. They passed the entrance to the Million Dollar Courtroom on the second floor, its doors open just enough to glimpse the walnut paneling, the brass fixtures, the kind of space where Kearns had stood and argued his case against Ford's army of attorneys.

Inventors could win here.

But Knox also knew Umar Farouk Abdulmutallab had been sentenced in this building—the underwear bomber. Life without parole. Terrorism charges didn't care about your intentions—only your impact. The man had tried to blow up Northwest Flight 253 on Christmas Day 2009. He'd failed, but the attempt was enough. The system had swallowed him whole and spit out a life sentence.

Which precedent applied to Knox Ramsey? The inventor vindicated, or the terrorist buried?

The stairwell smelled like floor wax and old radiator heat—institutional smells that existed in every government building from Detroit to D.C. They climbed to the fifth floor, emerged into a hallway lined with conference rooms. These middle floors were the working guts of the courthouse, where deals were made and futures were negotiated away from the marble grandeur below.

The room itself betrayed the building's beauty. Cinderblock walls painted institutional beige, probably in 1987 and not touched since. Fluorescent lights humming their anxious frequency. Government-issue table scarred by decades of elbows, briefcases, and files slapped down in frustration. A single window looked out at Michigan Central Station in the distance— Ford's old train depot, now being renovated by the same company Kearns had sued in this building.

History had a sense of irony.

Knox sat in the chair they indicated—not handcuffed, but treated like he should be. The table was cool under his palms. He felt the building's weight on his shoulders, the physical presence of marble, brass, and American confidence, all pressing down.

Three attorneys sat across from him. Two—federal prosecutors, mid-forties, suits tailored to look stern rather than stylish—tapped at their tablets with the dull precision of men whose muscle memory handled guilt for a living. The third watched him differently.

Erin Blanchard, Department of Justice, Senior Counsel. Early fifties, gray threading through dark hair pulled back in a style that said she didn't have time for bullshit. She wore a flag pin on her lapel—the small, ordinary kind people forget they're wearing. She studied Knox the way an engineer studies a failing system: patiently, clinically, with the hope it might still self-correct before complete failure.

She was the only one who didn't hide behind paper or jargon.

"Mr. Ramsey," she said finally, her voice carrying the flat Michigan accent of someone who'd grown up somewhere between Detroit and Lansing. "You understand you're here as both a witness and a potential subject of an investigation."

Knox rubbed his temple with one thumb, feeling the migraine that had been building since the FBI had called yesterday. "I understand that your people can't tell the difference between a wrench and the hand that holds it."

The younger attorney—thin, nervous, probably two years out of law school— blinked. "Excuse me?"

"You're looking for a villain," Knox said evenly. "You think I built the system to hurt people. But that's not what happened. I built a system meant to keep them fed."

The senior prosecutor—Lawrence Mitchell, according to the nameplate he'd positioned at precise right angles to the table edge—leaned forward. "That system was weaponized under your supervision, Mr. Ramsey."

"Bullshit," Knox said. The word echoed off cinderblock. "You don't get to redefine supervision because someone spoofed credentials and corrupted my code. I gave your agencies full audit access. I followed every regulation you wrote. I filed every safety review the USDA, FDA, and DHS required. I built guardrails you people ignored because they were inconvenient to your procurement cycles and your contractors' profit margins."

Mitchell's expression hardened. "Mr. Ramsey, your platform was sold to a Chinese shell company. You maintained administrative backdoors after the sale. You had direct access to systems that were subsequently used to poison American civilians—"

"And I reported the vulnerabilities," Knox interrupted. "Three times. To DHS, to the FBI's cybersecurity division, and to your department's Computer Crime and Intellectual Property Section. I filed formal reports documenting foreign access patterns, unauthorized optimization profile updates, and potential supply-chain compromises. I got back form letters thanking me for my concern."

He leaned forward, matching Mitchell's posture. "You want someone to nail to the wall, right? Someone you can parade in front of Congress when they ask why three hundred festival kids got poisoned by weaponized cannabis. You want a villain you can point to at your retirement party—'Look, I stopped the great agricultural terror plot.' Meanwhile, the real threat is still inside your networks, mapping your election systems and water treatment facilities, learning from the mistakes they made on my platform."

Silence pressed against the cinderblock walls like water pressure. Somewhere in the building, a door slammed. Voices echoed up from the marble lobby—people arguing a case, negotiating a plea, conducting the normal business of American justice.

Blanchard didn't interrupt. She just studied him, eyes sharp behind the exhaustion of someone who'd been working this case for weeks without sleep.

"You know what's funny?" Knox said, his voice dropping to something quieter and more dangerous. "I still respect you people. I respect the oath you took. My father took the same oath—thirty-two years, Army Corps of Engineers. He taught me that government service meant something. That the flag wasn't decoration, it was obligation."

Mitchell opened his mouth, but Knox wasn't finished.

"But somewhere along the way, you all started serving the process instead of the people. You forgot why you took that oath in the first place. You got so wrapped up in jurisdiction and protocols and covering your asses that you stopped seeing the actual threats. I handed you intelligence about Chinese infiltration of agricultural technology companies eighteen months ago. You filed it. You probably haven't looked at it since."

"Mr. Ramsey," Mitchell commenced, voice rising with the authoritative tone intended to silence defendants who engaged in excessive speech.

Knox cut him off. "No, you listen. I've spent my life trying to keep systems safe. Chemical plants where a wrong valve position kills everyone downwind. Power grids where cascading failures black out cities. Greenhouses where contaminated crops poison families. I've buried friends who worked in those systems—good people who died because someone cut a corner or ignored a warning or decided the numbers looked acceptable."

His hands were flat on the table, steady despite the tremor he felt in his chest. "I've been the guy on the radio telling first responders not to go in because the readings were too high. I've made the calls that saved lives and the calls that didn't save enough. And now you're sitting here telling me I'm the terrorist because I built something that someone smarter at hacking than you are at governing decided to corrupt?"

The words lingered in the recycled air. Outside the conference-room glass, cranes moved with slow certainty across the skyline, the city's endless reconstruction glowing orange under sodium lamps—an anatomy lesson in persistence.

Knox's voice didn't break; it hardened like steel cooling. "You're goddamn right I'm angry."

The younger attorney scribbled something on his legal pad. Blanchard lifted one hand, stopping him without looking away from Knox. "Let him speak."

Knox exhaled through his nose, steadier now. The anger was still there, but it was controlled—furnace heat behind steel doors, useful instead of destructive.

"You want to know why controlled-environment agriculture exists?" Knox gestured toward the window, toward the city beyond. "Look around. Half the neighborhoods in Detroit don't have a real grocery store. People buy dinner at gas stations and liquor stores. Kids grow up thinking fresh food comes in shrink-wrap from a truck that might not come if the distribution center decides their ZIP code isn't profitable enough."

His voice carried the passion of someone who'd spent decades thinking about systems and people and the spaces between them. "You solve that by bringing the farm back to the block. You turn empty warehouses—and God knows Detroit has enough of them—into something that feeds people instead of rotting. You retrofit old industrial buildings with LED grow lights and hydroponic systems. You train kids from neighborhoods like the one I grew up in to do plumbing, electrical work, programming—real skills that transfer to other jobs, not just burger-flipping."

Knox leaned back, his hands still on the table like he was grounding himself. "You feed people and you employ people and you teach people that technology doesn't have to be something that happens *to* them. It can be something they *control*. That's what FarmLytics was supposed to be. That's what I spent fifteen years building."

He stopped, suddenly aware of how loud the silence had become.

Blanchard hadn't moved. The younger attorney's pen hovered over his legal pad, frozen mid-stroke. Even Mitchell had leaned back, his prosecutorial posture softened into something closer to listening.

"Mr. Ramsey," Blanchard said finally, her voice carrying none of the accusation that had filled the room moments before. "No one in this building thinks you're a terrorist."

Knox blinked. "Then why am I here?"

"Because you're the only person who understands the weapon well enough to help us disarm it." She slid a folder across the table. Not toward Mitchell. Toward Knox. "We don't need a defendant. We need an engineer."

Knox didn't touch the folder. Not yet. "And if I say no?"

"Then we're back to form letters and filed reports. And the next attack hits something we can't recover from."

Outside, the cranes kept moving. The city kept rebuilding. Knox looked at the folder, then at Blanchard, then at the window where Michigan Central Station rose in the distance. Ford's monument. Kearns's battleground. Detroit's stubborn refusal to stay down.

He pulled the folder toward him and opened it.

31 FEDERAL RECRUITMENT

DETROIT - MCNAMARA FEDERAL BUILDING - MORNING

It had been six days since the first federal briefing. The intervening hours had been all conference rooms and coffee that never cooled. Sleep in snatches, reports by the dozen, one long argument with bureaucracy disguised as progress.

Knox sat in a smaller, quieter room this time—same building, less theater. The smell of burned coffee had been replaced by disinfectant and printer toner. The government's idea of a reset.

Erin Blanchard, Senior Counsel, Department of Justice, entered without entourage, dropped a folder on the table, and slid into the opposite chair. "You didn't sign the appointment."

"I don't sign what I don't understand," Knox said. "Especially after the week I've had."

"This one's simpler. It explains what you already agreed to."

"You signed the NDA and cooperation. Now sign the authority."

"I didn't agree to anything."

She gave a small, knowing smile. "You stayed in the country, answered calls, sent over encrypted data when you didn't have to. That's agreement enough."

Knox leaned back. "You ever notice how fast 'voluntary' turns into 'binding' when Washington needs a headline?"

"Only if you let the headline write itself," she said, opening the folder. Inside: a provisional clearance badge, a one-page appointment letter, and a plain-language summary stamped Critical Infrastructure Defense Task Force.

"This is the same task force you floated before," he said.

"Now it exists," she replied. "We built it out of what was left standing—Homeland, DOJ, CISA, Treasury, EPA, USDA. Think of it as a relay race where everyone's holding a different end of the same wire."

"That sounds like a disaster."

"It will be," she said evenly, "unless you're in the room."

Knox's jaw tightened. "You don't want me in the room, Counsel Blanchard. You want a scapegoat with engineering credentials and a patriotic quote at the end."

"If that's true," she said, "why am I here instead of the Director of Public Affairs?"

He didn't answer.

Blanchard folded her hands. "You said you work for results, not plaques. Here's your chance to prove it. You'll have operational autonomy under Treasury oversight. Build defensive frameworks, lead response engineering."

The door opened. SAC Steele stepped in and set a hand on the folder. "Operationally, you report to me. Keating will be your day-to-day liaison. Counsel Blanchard handles legal. Your son's cooperation stays under the same protective clause."

Knox studied her. "So I work for you."

"No," she said. "You work with us. For once."

He turned the badge over in his hand. His name already printed. "You people move fast when you smell liability."

"You're not liability, Knox. You're proof of concept. You saw the vector before the analysts did."

"Yeah," he muttered. "And no one listened until the morgues filled."

"That's why we're listening now."

He looked past her at the conference room wall—a framed photograph of a ribbon-cutting from a decade ago, smiling officials who'd all probably moved on. He wondered how many of them even remembered what the ribbon was for.

"What's the mission statement?" he asked finally.

Blanchard tapped the paper. "One line. 'Prevent, detect, and neutralize hostile manipulation of civilian systems.' We call it FSUR—Food Systems Unified Response. Your name's on the engineering charter."

"FSUR," he repeated. "Cute. Feels like a command structure built by committee."

"It is," she said. "That's why you're here."

Knox gave a slow, humorless smile. "You realize how this looks, right? The same government that tried to hang me out to dry now wants me to build its firewall."

"I realize," she said, "that optics stop mattering once the next crisis hits."

He signed the form without ceremony, just initials and a single signature.

"Then let's make sure there isn't a next one."

Blanchard gathered the papers, slid one copy back to him. "You'll have a small team—SAC Steele, Keating from FBI, one analyst from Treasury, one from USDA. We call them the Red Team. They're waiting upstairs."

"Red Team," he echoed. "Of course."

As she stood, she hesitated. "You really still believe in all this, don't you?"

"Belief's not the word," Knox said. "Obligation is."

She nodded. "Good enough."

When the door closed, Knox looked down at the badge again.

UNITED STATES GOVERNMENT—TEMPORARY CLEARANCE.

He clipped it to his shirt pocket, the weight of it settling like a promise he hadn't decided to keep yet.

He took out his phone and texted Tate a single line:

Cleared. Stay quiet. Don't screw this up.

Then he walked toward the elevator, where the future was already waiting under fluorescent lights.

32 REAL-TIME INTELLIGENCE

PATRICK V. MCNAMARA
FEDERAL BUILDING — DETROIT

After midnight, McNamara changed personalities. The public floors went dark, leaving only the blue pulse of server racks and the faint vibration of HVAC in the ducts. The same concrete that pressed in by day became protection at night. Knox liked it better this way—less ceremony, more signal. The building came alive the way an instrument does when it hums just above feedback.

Knox keyed the door into the Ops Center. Someone had pinned an old newspaper clipping beside the security monitor—"Pipe Bomb Found in Federal Building After Three Weeks." The headline was yellowed, the tape brittle. He liked that it was still there; a reminder that vigilance wasn't protocol, it was personal.

"Got it," Knox said to the DHS lead. "Feed me the latest egress logs."

A terminal flickered to life in front of him. VPN connection logs streamed across the screen—thousands of entries per minute.

"Show me only the tokens tied to known shell companies," he added.

Knox ran a quick filter:

```
grep "audit_token" vpn_logs | grep -E "(0200|0400|0600)" |
grep -E "203\.0\.113\."
# narrow to known Shanghai-registered block
```

Lines scrolled past: auditor_present=1; token_time-stamp=2025-10-04T02:13:27Z; src_ip=203.0.113.45.

He recognized the Shanghai-registered IP—one they'd traced to a shell-company

VPS. He summoned the network analyst."Lock that IP into our watchlist," Knox instructed. "Overlay it with the model retraining timestamps on FarmLytics." He pulled up a second display: tens of thousands of parameter-update events, color-coded by region. A pattern emerged: every off-hours retraining spike coincided with an up-tick of connections from the shell-VPS.

"See here?" Knox said. "They're staging batch updates at 0300 Detroit time. When we scrub the 0300 profiles, they inject new payloads during our cleanup."

The analyst nodded, hands flying over the keyboard. "Adjusting SIEM rule to flag any cron job launch within five minutes of an unauthorized connection."

Knox turned to the USDA liaison. "We need an emergency sit-rep for logistics: which rail lines and port shipments are using the 0300 profiles? Overlay with GPS telemetry from rail sensors."

Minutes later, a map lit up: rail routes in Wisconsin and Michigan, lines crossing major produce distribution hubs. Knox tapped a route.

"That's Route 47," he said. "If they push through that corridor tonight, we'll have a secondary outbreak within 24 hours. Notify DHS Counter-smuggling for a site inspection at Chippewa Junction."

He pinged Park:

Ramsey → Park: Phase IV window moved to T-4d 0200. Shifting focus to Route 47, prep rail intercept.

Back at the console, Knox coached a junior analyst. "Think like the adversary: what would you do if you knew they'd tabled your payload? You'd craft a secondary vector—steganography in EDI messages or traceroute via industrial SCADA endpoints."

The analyst's eyes lit up. "I'll build a parser for SCADA modbus logs to detect anomalous register writes!"

Knox smiled. "Exactly. Stay three steps ahead."

Forty-five minutes later, an alert popped: "SCADA_WRITE anomaly – register 0x1A3B at Port Eight." Knox leaned in. That port processed 75% of regional lettuce shipments.

He initiated a counter-script:

```
# Emergency SCADA filter injection
def scada_filter(logs):
for entry in logs:
if entry.register == 0x1A3B and entry.value > threshold:
trigger_lockdown(entry.device_id)
```

The screen responded: `lockdown enforced on port sensor 17. Vessels rerouted.`

Knox exhaled. "We've bought time." He tapped the console again: "Push updated counter-script to all SCADA endpoints under 'PlantOps' group. Repeat every hour until T-72."

A sense of grim satisfaction washed over him. They were no longer reacting—they were dictating the fight. And the parasite's carefully laid plans were dissolving under the weight of real-time intelligence.

Park appeared at the doorway. "Good work, Ramsey. You turned logs into lead."

Knox nodded. "Let's load the next set of baselines before they can morph again."

The screens glowed. The red team pressed on. The countdown clock ticked—but now every second moved under Knox's watchful hand.

EARLY MORNING

Knox took a breath and let his engineer brain line up the pins. "The attacker isn't breaking systems; they're bending them. They replaced the scoreboard. Our models still report yield and quality. Meanwhile the training loop chases a different prize. It learns how to look normal while doing harm. Every hour it gets better at both."

Treasury's mouth pulled tight. "So the instruments are lying but the pilots don't know it."

"Worse," Knox said. "They'll swear the instruments saved them."

"Evidence," DHS said. "Show, don't sermon."

Knox pushed a three-step cascade onto the left display: `MIGRATE → OPTIMIZE → MASK.`

"Step one," he said. "False baselines migrate. You think you're measuring normal; you're actually measuring where the attacker wants normal to be. Step two: the more you trust those baselines, the more you optimize around them. That makes the lie true in practice even if it started as a math trick. Step three: the lie gets cheaper to maintain because your operations do the work of disguising it."

The colonel tapped a pen. "You're describing counterinsurgency with spreadsheets."

"Exactly," Knox said. "They own the village if we accept their map."

MID-MORNING

The Chief of Staff had been quiet, eyes on his phone, thumbs not moving. He looked up. "We're about twelve hours from the networks telling a story we can't unwind without blood on the floor. Put it in political terms."

Knox hated political terms. He did it anyway. "If we hard-stop the links, we tank markets and set off alarms we can't control. If we do nothing, the model learns invisibility. Middle path: we build a decoy C2—honeypot the call-and-response—and pair it with monitoring that doesn't look for the lie; it looks for the tells. Physics mismatches, too-clean traces, independent sensors that stop agreeing."

Treasury frowned. "And during that middle path, do we let shipments move?"

"Yes," Knox said. "While we neuter the verbs—keep-alive, sleep, pull—so the bots stay leashed. We watch and we learn the manager."

"Jargon," Treasury said, impatient. "Plain English again."

"We put a shiny fake dispatcher on the network," Knox said, "so their couriers keep showing up. And we film everything."

Walsh's mouth twitched—close enough to a smile to count. "Better."

33 U.S. CLASH—FINAL ROUND
PATRICK V. MCNAMARA FEDERAL BUILDING

WAR ROOM

The ops clock read G-18. Seventy-two hours to Phase Four. McNamara functioned as the Joint Field Office now. The far wall carried a secure bridge — DHS at St. Elizabeths, FBI SIOC, Treasury, State — every tile live.

Day three had given the conference room a nickname nobody used on paper: the War Room. Knox faced a whiteboard, marker uncapped, a half-circle of professionals running on caffeine and grit.

On the wall, DHS Deputy Director Carla Rodriguez scrolled a feed. "Narrative is slipping. Cable is branding this like a movie poster. Social channels are worse."

Treasury Secretary Daniels came up on the bridge. "Markets are already pricing in a longer crisis. Pension exposure in ag-tech is ugly by Friday."

Knox drew a line across the board. "Seventy-two hours to their fourth move. Labels won't stop anything. Countermeasures will."

FBI's Steele leaned forward. "You keep saying Phase Four. Translate for the non-engineers."

Knox blocked four boxes. "Phase One proved it could be done. Phase Two showed scale. Phase Three hit trusted produce and spiked volatility." He shaded the last box. "Phase Four is the one built for maximum disruption."

State's liaison cut in from a small tile. "Speculation. We don't make policy on guesses."

"Not guesses," Knox said, heat in his voice. "A pattern. Each phase extended shelf life, distribution, and consumer trust. The last move lands where Americans eat without thinking."

CDC's Dr. Patricia Martinez tapped a list. "Candidates inside controlled environments: mushrooms, greenhouse strawberries, cucumbers. Add bagged-salad wash systems — a few parts per million off on chlorine and you scale illness fast."

Rodriguez stared at the board. "If they hit commodity crops…"

"That's famine," Knox said flatly. "Not a slow supply chain. Not a regional shortage. A break."

Daniels stood. "Then we start talking publicly. Full transparency to blunt rumor."

"Full blast panics buyers, empties shelves, and makes distribution fail before any attack," Steele said. "We need timed releases."

"Timed by who?" Rodriguez shot back. "The team that has been behind the tempo for two days?"

"Better than treating this like a spreadsheet problem," Daniels snapped.

"Enough," Knox said, marker popping as he capped it too hard. "This room runs on different dialects. DHS talks security. Treasury talks money. FBI talks crime. CDC talks biology. While you argue grammar, people end up in ERs."

He flipped to a clean space. "Here is the crosswalk. Treasury follows the funding — where the AgriTech money actually originated. FBI maps code and infrastructure — who wrote the adapters. DHS locks down facilities — ranked by vulnerability, not politics. CDC nails the mechanism — what pathway they corrupt next."

He sketched lines between boxes. "Parallel tracks. Shared data in real time. No waiting for the 4 p.m. update. And stop caring who gets the byline."

Rodriguez looked from the board to the faces. "This assumes we can trust each other's feeds."

"It assumes you trust measurements more than turf," Knox said. "Chemistry doesn't vote. Code paths don't caucus. Somewhere there is a single best counter to the next move. Find it."

Steele's phone buzzed. He read and grimaced. "Geneva. Beijing is offering humanitarian aid to U.S. cities affected by 'agricultural system failures.' They want the world to see them as the adult in the room."

"While playing arsonist," Daniels said.

Knox wrote 72:00 and crossed out the zeros. "Then stop arguing about messaging and start stopping the attack. If their final play lands while we bicker, they won't need to offer anything. They'll already have shaped the narrative."

Dr. Bell stepped to the board. "Medical says the next hit favors long storage life and universal consumption. Grains."

Daniels exhaled. "Financials agree. Short positions on grain are stacking up behind shells we can tie to Hong Kong intermediaries."

Keating added, quiet but firm. "We have dormant code signatures in elevator controls that match previous toolchains."

Rodriguez took one breath, then another. "Fine. We fight together. Knox owns technical. Every agency sends their best. We learn each other's language on the fly."

Something in the room shifted. Not friendship — alignment.

"Seventy-one hours, fifty-eight minutes," Knox said, changing the numbers. "Move."

34 LISA RAMSEY'S HOUSE
DETROIT SUBURBS

Maya sat in her rental car outside Lisa Ramsey's suburban home, laptop open to Treasury Department files that justified her presence. She was supposedly investigating financial impacts on affected businesses, including TR Cannabis.

Lisa answered the door with the wary exhaustion of someone who'd been fielding calls from reporters and federal agents for days.

"Mrs. Ramsey? Maya Chen, Treasury Department. I'm working on financial relief packages for affected businesses, including TR Cannabis. I understand that's your family's company."

"My son's company," Lisa corrected. "And my ex-husband built the technology behind it. It's…complicated."

"Of course, my apologies." Maya smiled sympathetically. "This must be incredibly difficult. Your son built something remarkable, only to have it turned against him."

Lisa's walls crumbled slightly. "Would you like some coffee? I just made a fresh pot."

Over coffee, Maya gathered intelligence disguised as empathy. Lisa revealed more than she realized—Knox's work schedule, his health problems, his guilt over the sale to AgriTech Solutions, the precise nature of his collaboration with Tate.

"He's killing himself trying to fix this," Lisa said, staring into her mug. "Eighteen-hour days, sleeping in the lab. He thinks it's his fault."

"Is it?" Maya asked gently.

Lisa's eyes flashed. "No. Knox built something good. Someone else poisoned it. But he'll destroy himself trying to make it right. It's who he is."

Maya noted the present tense—still emotional investment despite divorce. She filed this away: Family bonds remain exploitable. Ex-wife could be a pressure point if needed.

"Has anyone else contacted you about Knox's work? Other agencies, perhaps?"

"FBI, CDC, some reporter from the Post." Lisa laughed bitterly. "Everyone wants to know if he's crazy or criminal. He's neither. He's just... Knox."

Maya left with pages of notes about family dynamics, Knox's psychological profile, and potential leverage points. She sat in her car and transmitted: Family vector mapped. Ex-wife is defensive but vulnerable. Son's collaboration strengthening. Recommend targeting the family if the subject requires additional pressure.

PATRICK V. MCNAMARA FEDERAL BUILDING — OPS FLOOR

Knox watched the tremor stutter across Nebraska. He forced himself to slow his breathing. "Baseline drift is like heat stress in a greenhouse," he said. He could see Tate adjusting louvers in his mind, could smell the rubber hoses, the stale sweetness of leaf. "You don't notice the plant's pain until it's in the tissue. By then, your controller has already compensated, and the dangerous part is baked in. Everything looks normal because normal moved."

DHS looked at him. "So we break the feedback loop."

"We take away its mirrors," Knox said. "Give it a decoy mirror that flatters it, keep it staring, and study how it blinks."

Treasury's skepticism softened, a millimeter. "And if the attacker stops knocking?"

"They won't," Knox said. "They're managing a network. If they stop knocking, their army goes dumb. They will knock."

35 SECURE BRIEFING —G -16/-15

PATRICK V. MCNAMARA FEDERAL BUILDING — SERVER ROOM

LOCAL 02:11 EDT

OPS SITREP: NO CHANGE IN FATALITIES; HOSPITALIZATIONS +38 (CUME 801)

A third window bloomed across the secure bridge: a European energy official in a navy suit that looked tailored from fatigue and resolve. Her backdrop flickered with turbine telemetry and the faint shimmer of a map that glowed like an ulcer.

"France is experiencing regasification slotting conflicts," she said. "Dashboards claim full capacity; plant managers swear half the compressors are ghosting. Whatever is corrupting your data streams is whispering through ours."

"Understood," said CIA Director Sarah Walsh.

The woman's tone sharpened. "Do you? Because what you call *caution*, we call *shortage*. When lights go out, voters don't blame entropy—they blame politics. And from this side of the Atlantic, politics has a Washington accent."

Treasury Secretary Janet Daniels leaned toward her camera, voice clipped. "Your scheduling conflicts aren't our—"

"Aren't they?" the official cut in, almost triumphant. "Every LNG terminal from Dunkirk to Marseille runs optimization code. We're watching capacity oscillate like a heart under stress. Are we under attack, or are our systems panicking because yours are contaminated? The uncertainty alone is collapsing margins."

"We can't confirm—" Walsh began.

Knox stepped forward, every syllable hard. "That's exactly the play. Beijing doesn't need to touch your terminals. They just have to make you doubt them. You switch to manual, lose throughput, second-guess every sensor. Efficiency dies one safety check at a time. They've turned uncertainty into a weapon system."

The French official's eyes narrowed. "You're saying this hysteria is self-inflicted?"

"I'm saying they lit one controlled fire and let the smoke circle the planet," Knox said. "Our outbreaks went public six hours ago; your slotting conflicts began four hours later. That's not contagion—that's orchestration. They're harvesting global paralysis from a single surgical strike."

Silence hung long enough for the hum of the bridge equipment to register—fans, encrypted routers, the low mechanical breathing of the network itself.

Walsh finally nodded. "Push immediate guidance: manual overrides only with witness sensors in parallel. Maintain efficiency where verifiable. No blind shutdowns."

The European feed blinked acknowledgment. Behind her, someone shouted orders in French; the line dissolved into static and cut.

Knox looked across the room—Hammond, Daniels, Steele, faces bleached by monitor light. "We keep moving," he said. "Because hesitation is the virus they built for free."

PALAIS DES NATIONS — GENEVA, SWITZERLAND

Local 12:58 CET — –21 Days | NSC Ticker: 43 fatalities; 700 hospitalized

USTR Jennifer Morrison crossed the colonnade into Conference Room XVII. Ambassador Kellner raised a hand for quiet. Zhang Wei of China adjusted his microphone.

"The United States claims systematic attack on their food infrastructure," Zhang said. "Yet they provide no evidence linking any nation-state. Perhaps their own lax security is the culprit."

Morrison kept her voice even. "We're seeing a technical escalation, not geographic spread."

"So your machines are poisoning you," Zhang said. "Try farms the old way."

Hans Müller (EU) cleared his throat. "The Commission proposes a joint technical working group under WHO/FAO auspices."

Morrison's tablet pulsed:

NSC: Foreign fingerprints in code confirmed. Do NOT reveal.

Push for neutral software supply-chain audit; certificate authority reviews; verify control recipes.

"The United States supports a working group," Morrison said, "with a mandate for software provenance audits, certificate path validation, and independent verification of control recipes. If we test tomatoes without testing the code that grew them, we're auditing shadows."

"A broad request," Zhang replied. "We cannot invite foreign inspection of our systems unless you do the same."

"We already do," Morrison said. "Third-party audits. We can expand that. Can you?"

Kellner leaned in. "Sampling of software signing chains and deployment logs at willing facilities. Narrow scope. Limited duration."

"Voluntary and reciprocated," Zhang said.

Morrison nodded once. It bought hours.

Her aide slid a second tablet: Detroit ICU thresholds crossed.

Zhang glanced at his own device, then back with a smooth smile. "China will also propose temporary tariff relief on agricultural imports to stabilize prices while you review your code."

"Generous," Morrison said. "Contingent on access to our optimization models, I assume."

Silence. The Swiss looked at the ceiling.

Kellner: "Draft text in one hour."

In the marble hall, a woman in a dark suit matched Morrison's stride. "Maya Chen. WHO liaison to the working group." Badge, lanyard, the right bland.

"Provenance?" Morrison asked.

"Seconded from a Geneva health-tech NGO to WHO for surge staffing," Maya said. "We can deploy dual-instrument stations within thirty-six hours—read-only, air-gapped witness sensors. We'll also support signing-chain and deployment-log sampling with partners in Lausanne. Limited scope, meaningful."

Morrison clocked the details. Too prepared. "Send it in writing. Berlin may chair."

Back in XVII, the "draft text" arrived bracketed like teeth: working group, voluntary audits, dual instrumentation, temporary tariff relief.

"Madame Morrison?" Kellner prompted.

"The United States accepts, with clarifications," she said. "Witness sensors independent in hardware and clock; software audits include certificate path validation; no nation may condition humanitarian aid on access to proprietary models."

Zhang: "China accepts—with WHO confidentiality on all audits."

"Agreed," Morrison said. WHO confidentiality would deter journalists, not intelligence services. Another day bought.

Kellner's gavel: "Adopted ad referendum."

Morrison's phone buzzed:

Your engineer is about to do something illegal to save lives. Decide now if you want deniability or results.

She looked at Zhang's patient smile.

"Meera," she said softly to her deputy. "Get Berlin the chair. And get me the engineer."

PATRICK V. MCNAMARA FEDERAL BUILDING — OPS CENTER

LOCAL 19:02 EDT — –21 DAYS | OPS SITREP: 43 FATALITIES; 763 HOSPITALIZED.

Nevada on watch for profile match.

Walsh gave Knox a short nod. "Show the cost of delay."

Knox cued a corridor sim: fertilizer shipments crossing the Atlantic into three inland hubs. He toggled Delay = 90 minutes. A labor/rail timeline marched on the side.

"At minus 90," Knox said, "a corrupted baseline widens weather tolerances. A warehouse manager sees green and shifts a window. It cascades into a rail conflict that looks like congestion, but isn't. Throughput stays 'normal' on your dashboard, so no one flags it."

The DoD liaison leaned in. "If we shut that corridor now?"

"You tip the attacker to where you're watching," Knox said. "They pivot. That's fine—the decoys catch the new handshake. That's how we map the manager."

A NATO rep came up on the wall. "Our ports are demanding manual verification of automated routing. We'll support a deception plan if it proves the threat is contained to your systems."

"It isn't," Knox said. "We'll strip command calls—handshake, sync, pull—freeze the swarm mid-cycle and make it think it's still alive. Meanwhile we log every breath it takes."

Walsh, low, off-mic: "Berlin wants WHO confidentiality on audits. Fine. We run deception here and feed them clean deltas."

A junior contractor analyst kept pressing Knox for method, not result.

Knox made a note.

PATRICK V. MCNAMARA FEDERAL BUILDING — SERVER ROOM

Local 02:11 EDT — –21 Days | Ops SITREP: No change in fatalities; hospitalizations +38 (cume 801)

While Knox sold deception upstairs, Maya worked downstairs.

She'd pre-staged a maintenance unit the night before—benign-sounding, restarts on boot, indistinguishable from other housekeeping daemons. What she installed lived one hop off Knox's workstation: a scoped capture aimed at a single host, rotating size-capped logs, and jittered egress folded into an existing telemetry feed. Every query he ran, every file he touched, mirrored near-real-time—just noisy enough to read like bulk ETL, not a beacon.

No exotic exploits. No signature malware. Stock tools presented as log hygiene. If NetFlow or an audit hawk looked, the story held: scheduled maintenance, tidy capture, policy-compliant on its face. Boring by design.

Footsteps in the corridor—early. Tate Ramsey appeared in the doorway with a box of lab gear.

"Didn't expect anyone here," he said.

"Financial modeling," Maya said, spreadsheets on screen. "Your father thinks the commodity targeting has a pattern. I'm running correlations."

"My father's usually right about patterns," Tate said, setting the box down. "Even when everyone thinks he's paranoid."

"You two close?"

"We're getting there. Catastrophes help."

"It must be hard, watching him take responsibility for something that wasn't his fault."

"Everything's his fault, according to him," Tate said. "The sale, the vulnerability, the deaths. He carries guilt like other people carry wallets."

Maya risked a nudge. "Has he seen the Shanghai routing in the financial transfers?"

Tate's eyes sharpened. "What Shanghai routing?"

She caught herself. "I misspoke. Some international transactions are under review. Nothing confirmed."

"You said Shanghai." He stepped closer. "What aren't you telling me?"

"I need to get this run started," she said, packing. "Please don't mention this. It could compromise ongoing work."

She left him standing there, suspicious but not enough.

Her encrypted phone buzzed in the garage:

Asset Seven reporting increased risk of exposure. Recommend extraction planning. Will maintain cover as long as viable.

Response: Maintain position. Intelligence critical. Extraction primed, not triggered. Exercise maximum caution.

She sat in the dark, caught between two worlds. In Shanghai, she was a hero. In Detroit, she was betraying people who were trying to save lives. She chose the same thing she always chose: survival.

CORRIDOR OUTSIDE WAR ROOM — MCNAMARA

Local 04:00 EDT — –21 Days

The hallway hummed with ventilation. Knox topped off a cup of coffee that smelled like burnt wire.

"You handled that better than I would've," Walsh said.

"I handled it like an engineer. You wanted a politician."

"Maybe we need both." She poured hers black. "They're setting you up to take the fall."

"I know."

"And you're…okay with that?"

"My system is killing people. My code. I'm okay being accountable if I'm fixing it."

Walsh lowered her voice. "Dual instrumentation buys time. But every countermeasure you propose shows up across the wire within hours."

"We have more than you know."

"Shanghai," she said. "Not just shells and weird wires. SIGINT has tasking from Unit 61398 tied to this."

"PLA cyber."

"And an ag-target cell spun in 2019. You sold FarmCore in 2021. The timing isn't random. Liu Wei—MIT, ag automation—runs their program."

A photo: man Knox's age, professional smile, watchful eyes.

"He understood my system well enough to weaponize it," Knox said.

"He understood you," Walsh said. "Every move calibrated to how you solve problems. That 'HELLO, KNOX' message wasn't theater. It was targeting data."

Knox exhaled. "Phase Four won't just hit infrastructure."

"It'll hit you," Walsh said. "Family, reputation, your patterns. He'll use your safety margins as bridges."

"Then I stop being predictable."

"You need to be something you aren't," Walsh said. "Reckless."

"Engineers don't do reckless. We do redundant."

"And Liu Wei knows it. That's why his edges bite." She glanced at the door. "This stays in the hallway. We think there's an inside feed."

The coffee turned sour in Knox's mouth. "Inside the investigation?"

"Inside the room you just left. Every countermeasure you propose shows up on their side within hours. Could be agency, contractor, staffer. So—compartmentalize. Trust in layers."

"Indicators?"

"Unusual interest in your method. Questions about details they shouldn't need. Friction that slows only you. When you find them—don't confront. Use them."

"Feed Liu Wei what he expects—until I don't."

"Exactly."

He checked his watch. "Seventy-one hours."

"Better get back in there."

Knox pushed through the door. The agencies inside worked the problem like a single organism—unaware one of its nerves was wired to the enemy.

OPS CENTER — MCNAMARA (EVENING)

Local 19:30 EDT — −21 Days | Ops SITREP: 43 fatalities; 763 hospitalized. Nevada profile likely.

Screens dropped to idle. Chairs scraped. The NATO window returned for a moment. "We will watch for your signatures," the rep said. "Do not be late." The tile went dark.

DHS Deputy Director Carla Rodriguez turned to Knox in the doorway. "Bring me endpoints and a logging scheme. Minimal footprint. I want to be able to deny everything and still sleep."

"You won't sleep," Knox said.

"Then make it worth staying up."

In the hall, the air seemed a degree cooler—the way it gets before a front moves in. Knox walked faster. Somewhere, a model was learning to lie better. Somewhere else, a grower would trust a green dash because it had always been green.

He thought of Tate. Then he picked up speed.

36 STAKES ON THE TABLE
PATRICK V. MCNAMARA FEDERAL BUILDING — WAR ROOM / OPS CENTER

WASHINGTON, D.C. — RUSSELL SENATE OFFICE BUILDING / SR-325 — 09:30 EDT

Knox Ramsey stood on the corner of Constitution Avenue and Delaware, looking up at the Russell Senate Office Building the way a pilgrim looks at a cathedral he never expected to enter.

Built in 1909, the structure stood five stories high, clad in white Vermont marble; its Beaux-Arts design showcased a level of craftsmanship that was no longer practiced. Ionic columns marched along the entrance like sentries guarding two centuries of American argument. Above them, carved laurel wreaths and dentil molding caught the morning light with the precision of stonemasons who'd understood that democracy deserved beauty.

Knox had read David McCullough's 1776 on a job site in Louisiana twenty years ago, eating lunch on a chemical tank while rain hammered the Gulf Coast. He'd read about men in powdered wigs and silk stockings arguing humanity's future in rooms that looked like this one probably did inside—marble and mahogany and the weight of getting it right. The nation's creators, a diverse group of rebels, agricultural workers, and business owners, never anticipated forming a nation. Knox, an engineer from Grand Rapids, had never anticipated protecting his life's work from those who would inherit it.

The butterflies in his stomach had nothing to do with fear and everything to do with the gap between what he'd built and where he now stood to explain it.

He'd gotten maybe ninety minutes of sleep in the Marriott on 14th Street. Room service club sandwich at 11 PM that tasted like cardboard and regret. Three hours staring at the ceiling, running testimony scenarios, knowing that no matter what he said, someone would edit it into a soundbite that murdered nuance. At 4 AM he'd given up, showered in water that never got hot enough, and put on the suit Lisa had FedExed him from Detroit—his only good one, the navy Brooks Brothers from Tate's college graduation that almost fit if he didn't breathe too deep.

The shirt collar pressed against his neck like an accusation. His dress shoes—polished last night with the hotel's complimentary kit—pinched his left foot. His hands, scarred from forty years of actual work, looked wrong holding the leather briefcase Erin Blanchard had handed him yesterday: "Put your technical brief in this. Don't bring your backpack. This isn't a trade show."

Knox checked his watch: 9:18. The hearing started at 9:30.

Blanchard had texted him at 6 AM:

Arrive early. Let them see you comfortable. Confidence reads as competence to cameras.

He climbed the exterior steps, each one worn smooth by a century of shoes carrying ambition and legislation and the daily machinery of governing 330 million people. The brass handrails had the patina of ten thousand hands. Above the entrance, carved into limestone: THE SENATE IS THE LIVING SYMBOL OF OUR UNION OF STATES.

Knox paused at those words. Living symbol. His FarmCore platform had been meant as a living system too—adapting, learning, optimizing toward feeding cities efficiently. Now it was evidence in a terror investigation, and he was here to explain how something built for life had been turned toward death.

The entrance doors—bronze, fifteen feet tall, weighing probably eight hundred pounds each—opened smooth and silent on hinges engineered for permanence. Knox stepped into the rotunda and stopped.

He'd expected marble. He hadn't expected this.

The Russell Rotunda was a hymn in stone. Sixteen columns of polished marble rose thirty feet to support a coffered ceiling adorned with rosettes that would've made Roman architects weep. The floor was Vermont marble in geometric patterns—octagons and squares laid with the precision of men who understood that every seam mattered. Natural light poured through a skylight that turned the whole space into a lantern, making the marble glow like it was lit from within.

Knox stood there longer than he should have, briefcase in hand, drinking it in the way he'd once studied the Hoover Dam's spillways or the Detroit-Windsor Tunnel's ventilation system. This wasn't government bureaucracy. This was craft. Artisans in 1909 had carved those rosettes by hand. Someone had calculated the load-bearing requirements for those columns. Someone had quarried that marble and cut it and set it with the understanding that what they built would outlast their grandchildren's grandchildren.

He thought about the men who'd done that work—probably immigrants, probably Italian or Irish stonemasons who'd come to America with nothing but skill and had carved permanence into a building most of them would never enter as anything but laborers.

Knox was the son of a union millwright and a bookkeeper. He'd grown up in a house where you fixed what broke and built what you needed. His father had taught him to read blueprints at twelve, how to true a lathe at fourteen, how to respect the people who actually made things instead of just talking about them. Now, as Knox stood in the temple, which was built by craftsmen for politicians, he felt a mix of emotions—pride that working people had made this beautiful place and rage that those who were in this place had forgotten who had made it.

"Mr. Ramsey?"

A young woman in a dark suit with a Senate ID badge approached, tablet in hand, all business. "I'm Jennifer Park, Senator Whitmore's legislative aide. You're testifying in SR-325. I'll escort you."

Knox followed her through corridors that smelled like floor wax and power—that peculiar scent of old buildings maintained at taxpayer expense, where the marble was polished weekly and the brass fixtures gleamed like jewelry. They passed portraits of dead senators whose names Knox half-recognized from high school civics: LaFollette, Vandenberg, men who'd stood in these halls arguing about wars and rights and money while history watched.

The corridor opened onto a balcony overlooking the rotunda. Three stories below, a tour group clustered around a guide explaining something Knox couldn't hear. He watched a kid, maybe ten, crane his neck to stare at the ceiling, mouth open in wonder at the geometric perfection above him. Knox remembered being that age, visiting Greenfield Village with his father, seeing the actual workshop where Henry Ford had built his first engine. The sense of being in a place where important things had happened.

He was about to testify in one of those places. The realization hit him with physical weight.

"This way," Park said, already moving.

They turned down another corridor, this one narrower, more functional. The marble gave way to terrazzo. The portraits thinned out. They were in the working guts of the building now, where staff moved with institutional purpose and senators became regular people between performances.

SR-325 was at the end of the hall. Double doors, oak with brass hardware, closed against the noise of what waited inside. Park checked her tablet.

"They're seating now. Media's setting up. You'll enter at 9:28, take the witness table. Senator Whitmore will gavel in at 9:30." She looked up, actually meeting his eyes for the first time. "There's coffee and water at the table. Don't touch the coffee on camera—it reads as nervous. The water's fine."

"Thanks," Knox said.

She studied him a moment, something almost sympathetic crossing her young face. "They're going to try to rattle you. Don't let them. You know more about this than anyone in that room. Remember that."

Then she opened the door and the noise hit him like weather.

SR-325 wasn't designed for hearings—it was a committee room that had been repurposed because the attack had happened too fast for the usual venues. But someone had made it work. The room was long and narrow, with a dais at the far end where five senators would sit elevated above everyone else. Witness table in the middle, positioned so Knox would have to look up at them like a defendant at arraignment. Gallery seating behind him, already packed with staffers, journalists, lobbyists, and citizens who'd queued since dawn for a seat at the spectacle.

The walls were mahogany panels between marble pilasters, the ceiling coffered plaster painted cream. Tall windows on the left wall let in morning light that fell in geometric blocks across the floor. A chandelier—brass and crystal, probably original to the building—hung above the witness table like a crown or a sword, depending on your perspective.

Camera crews from C-SPAN, CNN, Fox News clustered at the back, their equipment bristling with the aggressive utility of modern technology invading classical space. Boom mics, lighting rigs, laptops already streaming live feeds. Knox could see his own face on a monitor—tired, nervous, trying not to look either.

The gallery was a cross-section of everyone who had an opinion about what he'd built.

Front row left: agricultural lobbyists in expensive suits, representing the indoor farming companies now facing existential threat.

Front row right: family advocacy groups holding photos of poisoning victims, wanting someone's head on a pike.

Middle rows: think tank wonks with lanyards and OPINIONS, tech journalists who'd never grown a plant in their lives, and scattered citizens who looked like they'd driven overnight from Michigan to watch their engineer get filleted.

Knox recognized two faces: Dr. Patricia Martinez from CDC, sitting with the federal delegation, and Maya Chen—or whoever she'd really been—absent. Extracted through diplomatic channels, Blanchard had told him. Gone before they could charge her with anything that mattered.

The butterflies in Knox's stomach evolved into something with teeth.

He walked to the witness table, briefcase in hand, trying to channel confidence he didn't entirely feel. The table was polished mahogany, worn smooth by decades of elbows and testimony. A microphone angled toward the empty chair like an accusation. Pitcher of water, glasses, and—just as Park had warned—a carafe of coffee that Knox wouldn't touch.

He sat. The chair was hard, deliberately uncomfortable, designed to keep witnesses alert and slightly off-balance. Behind him, the gallery murmured. He could feel their eyes cataloging him: suit too cheap, face too tired, hands too rough for this room.

Knox set his briefcase beside the chair and forced himself to look up at the empty dais. Five nameplates waited:

- Sen. Richard Whitmore (R-IA)
- Chair Sen. Patricia Daniels (D-MI)
- Sen. Jennifer Cross (D-WA)
- Sen. James Lankford (R-OK)
- Sen. Michael Cortez (D-CA)

Daniels was Michigan. Her staff would know everything about him—voting record (sporadic), campaign contributions (none), union membership (UAW through his father), political leanings (old Reagan Republican who'd voted Obama once and regretted it). She was here to defend Michigan agriculture and by extension Michigan engineers, even if she knew Knox hadn't voted for her. Politics made strange math.

Above the dais, carved into the mahogany paneling, a quote Knox couldn't quite read from this angle. He squinted. Jefferson, probably. They loved putting Jefferson in these rooms—the agrarian philosopher who'd owned slaves and believed in yeoman farmers. Knox wondered what Jefferson would make of indoor farming. Probably call it unnatural. Probably be wrong.

The gallery noise built. More people filtering in, finding seats, pulling out phones that would live-stream this to millions. Knox checked his watch: 9:26. Four minutes until gavel. He pulled his technical brief from the briefcase—seventy pages of documentation proving he'd built something good that bad actors had corrupted. No one would read it. They'd already decided their narratives.

A side door opened. The senators entered with the slow choreography of habit—each step measured, each glance practiced from years of televised ritual. Whitmore first—seventy, white hair, Iowa farmer cosplaying as statesman. Daniels next—composed, the Michigan seal catching light. Cross, Lankford, Cortez following in seniority's quiet procession.

They took their seats. Staffers whispered last-minute briefings. Cross adjusted her microphone. Lankford shuffled papers he probably hadn't read.

Whitmore lifted the gavel. The room fell silent with the weight of ten cameras pointed at his hand.

9:30 AM

The gavel fell—wood on wood, the percussion of power condensed into a single sound that echoed off marble and mahogany and two centuries of American theater.

"This hearing of the Senate Committee on Agriculture, Nutrition, and Forestry will come to order."

Whitmore's voice carried the practiced authority of someone who'd spent forty years in elected office learning how to own a room. "We convene today to examine the agricultural terrorism attack that has resulted in three hundred and twelve deaths and over eighteen thousand poisonings across seventeen states. Specifically, we will investigate the role of automated agricultural systems—" he glanced down at his notes "—in enabling this attack, and whether such systems pose ongoing threats to American food security."

Knox's jaw tightened. Role of systems in enabling. Not how systems were weaponized. The frame was already set.

"Our witness today is Mr. Knox Ramsey, creator of the FarmCore and FarmLytics platforms used in the affected facilities."

Whitmore looked directly at Knox for the first time. "Mr. Ramsey, please stand and raise your right hand."

Knox stood. His left foot still hurt in the dress shoe.

"Do you swear that the testimony you are about to give is the truth, the whole truth, and nothing but the truth, so help you God?"

"I do."

"Please be seated. Mr. Ramsey, you may begin with your opening statement."

Knox settled back into the uncomfortable chair and pulled the microphone closer. It amplified his breathing for half a second before he got control of it. Behind him, the gallery leaned forward. The cameras zoomed in.

He looked down at his prepared statement—five pages of carefully lawyered language that Blanchard had helped him draft. Then he looked back up at the senators and decided to trust his own words instead.

"Senator Whitmore, members of the committee. My name is Knox Ramsey. I'm an industrial engineer from Grand Rapids, Michigan. For thirty years I've built automation systems for manufacturing, energy, and agriculture. Fifteen years ago, I developed FarmCore and FarmLytics—platforms designed to help controlled environment agriculture operate more efficiently and safely."

He paused, gathering the words he'd rehearsed at 3 AM while staring at a hotel ceiling.

"What happened at those facilities—the poisonings, the deaths—that wasn't my system failing. That was my system being weaponized by sophisticated actors who understood it better than most of the people in this room." Knox looked directly at Whitmore. "I'm here to explain how they did it, what we're doing to stop them, and why the worst possible response would be abandoning the technology they exploited."

Murmurs from the gallery. Whitmore's expression hardened slightly.

"Mr. Ramsey, thank you for that… perspective. Let's begin with Senator Lankford for questions."

Lankford leaned into his microphone, reading from prepared notes. "Mr. Ramsey, yes or no: did your system control the growing conditions at facilities where contaminated cannabis was produced?"

"Yes, but—"

"Yes or no is sufficient, thank you. Did your system have the capability to modify light spectrums, nutrient delivery, and environmental conditions?"

"Yes, those are standard—"

"Did those modifications result in the production of toxic compounds that killed over three hundred Americans?"

Knox felt his hands tighten on the table edge. "Senator, you're asking me to reduce a sophisticated cyber-biological attack to yes-or-no answers that erase every relevant fact."

"I'm asking you simple questions, Mr. Ramsey. Can you answer them?"

"Not honestly, no."

That landed. Cameras swiveled. Lankford looked annoyed but moved on.

"Mr. Ramsey, how much money did you receive from the sale of FarmCore to AgriTech Solutions?"

There it was. The money question.

"Eight million dollars, Senator."

"Eight million." Lankford let that number sit in the room. "And AgriTech Solutions was later revealed to be a Chinese intelligence front operation. Were you aware of that when you sold?"

"No, Senator. Treasury approved the transaction. FBI vetted the buyers. Every federal agency involved cleared the sale as legitimate."

"But you got eight million dollars."

"Yes. Which I've since offered to return if it helps restitution for victims' families."

That was true. Blanchard had advised against saying it, but Knox was tired of letting them paint him as profiteer. Lankford blinked, reset.

"How do we know you didn't intentionally create vulnerabilities for Chinese exploitation?"

Knox leaned into the microphone. "Because if I had, Senator, they wouldn't have needed three years and a team of world-class engineers to figure out how to corrupt it. My system had security protocols. They broke them. That's why it's called an attack."

Senator Cross cut in, her voice sharp. "Mr. Ramsey, isn't it true that automated agricultural systems concentrate risk? That one compromised platform can affect hundreds of facilities simultaneously?"

"Yes, Senator. Just like one compromised water treatment plant can poison a city. Just like one failed power grid can blackout millions. Centralization creates efficiency and vulnerability. That's true of every critical infrastructure system we rely on."

"So you're comparing your cannabis system to water and power?"

"I'm comparing the architecture, Senator. Controlled environment agriculture is critical infrastructure whether you like it or not. It's how we're going to feed urban populations as farmland shrinks. The question isn't whether to use it. It's how to secure it."

Senator Cortez finally spoke, sounding almost bored. "Mr. Ramsey, can you guarantee this won't happen again?"

Knox met his eyes across the room. Here was the question they'd all been building toward.

"Guarantee is a sales term, Senator. I don't deal in guarantees. I deal in engineering solutions. Can I make these systems significantly harder to compromise? Yes. Can I build monitoring that detects anomalies before they become disasters? Yes. Can I implement security protocols that would've prevented this specific attack? Yes." He paused. "But I can't do any of that from a witness table. Every hour I spend here is an hour I'm not fixing what they broke."

Whitmore rapped his gavel lightly. "Mr. Ramsey, this committee's oversight is essential—"

"Essential to what, Senator?" Knox let eight days of exhaustion and frustration collapse into a single, surging pressure he couldn't fully cage. "Essential to creating five new sub-committees that'll spend three years studying what I could fix in three months? Essential to writing regulations that'll strangle innovation while our adversaries move on to the next attack vector?"

The room went very quiet.

"Mr. Ramsey," Whitmore said slowly, "you're testifying before the United States Senate."

"Yes, sir. And you're asking questions you already know the answers to. You want me to say controlled environment agriculture is dangerous so you can regulate it to death and tell your constituents you kept them safe. But what you'll really be doing is abandoning a technology that's essential to national security because bad actors proved it works well enough to weaponize."

Senator Daniels finally leaned into her microphone, her Michigan accent cutting through the tension.

"Mr. Ramsey, you're from Grand Rapids."

"Yes, ma'am."

"My staff tells me you voted for Governor Engler in '98 and Senator McCain in 2008. That you're a union member through your father's local. That you built your first automation system in a garage in Kentwood and bootstrapped everything you've done since." She looked down at her notes. "That doesn't sound like someone who'd intentionally sabotage American agriculture."

"Thank you, Senator."

"But it also doesn't answer the question my colleagues are trying to ask: how do we prevent this from happening again without killing the industry you built?"

Something inside Knox eased, just a fraction. Finally. A real question.

"Senator, you prevent it the same way we secure any critical infrastructure. Mandatory security audits. Third-party verification of code. Air-gapped networks for critical control functions. Behavioral monitoring that flags anomalous optimization patterns. Physical safeguards that prevent algorithmic modification past safe parameters."

He was speaking faster now, the engineer in him taking over. "And you resource it properly. The Chinese spent years and millions of dollars attacking this. We need equivalent investment in defense."

"How much?"

"To secure American indoor agriculture comprehensively? Probably five hundred million over three years. To monitor it perpetually? Another two hundred million annually."

Someone in the gallery whistled. Whitmore frowned.

"That's an expensive solution, Mr. Ramsey."

"Senator, we just spent forty-one billion dealing with the aftermath of this attack. Prevention is cheaper."

Daniels nodded slowly. "And in your assessment, is indoor agriculture—CEA—worth defending? Or should we transition back to traditional farming methods?"

This was it. The real question beneath everything else.

Knox looked up at the chandelier above him for a moment, watching light refract through crystal. He thought about the artisans who'd hung it there in 1909, creating beauty that would outlast them. About his father teaching him to weld because "honest work builds the world." About Tate's greenhouse full of plants that fed people medicine they needed.

"Senator Daniels, controlled environment agriculture isn't replacing farmers. It's supplementing them. It's letting us grow food where traditional farming can't work—in cities, in deserts, in places where climate change is making old methods impossible." He leaned forward. "In twenty years, there won't be enough farmable land to feed ten billion people using traditional methods alone. Indoor farming isn't a luxury. It's survival. It's national security. The Chinese didn't attack it because it's dangerous. They attacked it because it's critical to our future."

The room was silent enough to hear the HVAC hum.

"So yes, ma'am. It's worth defending. It's worth investing in. It's worth getting right. Because the alternative isn't going back to how things were. The alternative is millions of urban Americans dependent on food imports from countries that have already proven they'll weaponize our supply chains."

Daniels looked at Whitmore. "Mr. Chairman, I think Mr. Ramsey has answered our questions thoroughly. I move we allow him to return to the work of actually securing these systems rather than theoretical discussions about whether we should."

Whitmore's jaw worked. He didn't like losing control of his hearing, but Daniels had given him an exit that looked like leadership.

"Agreed. Mr. Ramsey, you're excused with the committee's thanks. We'll be scheduling follow-up hearings on regulatory frameworks—"

"Of course you will," Knox said quietly, gathering his briefcase.

"Excuse me?"

Knox stood, tucking the briefcase under his arm. "Senator, you're going to schedule hearings that spawn sub-committees that create working groups that draft regulations that take three years to implement. I understand that's how this works. I'm just saying that's three years our adversaries won't be waiting around."

He turned toward the gallery, then stopped and looked back.

"One more thing. This building—Russell Building—it's beautiful. I spent twenty minutes this morning looking at the craftsmanship. The marble work, the columns, the details. You know who built this? Working people. Immigrants. Stonemasons and carpenters who showed up every day and built something permanent for a country that didn't always treat them fairly." Knox gestured at the room around them. "They made something that mattered. That's what I was trying to do with FarmCore. Build something that mattered. That fed people. That worked."

He met Whitmore's eyes.

"I hope whatever you build out of this crisis works half as well."

Then Knox Ramsey walked toward the exit while cameras captured every step, his cheap suit and tired face and calloused hands carrying him back toward the work that actually mattered, leaving five senators and a gallery full of opinions to argue about regulations he'd spend the next five years either fighting or implementing, depending on how the votes fell.

The oak doors closed behind him with a sound like a book shutting.

In the corridor outside, Jennifer Park was waiting with her tablet. "That was either brilliant or career suicide."

"Probably both," Knox said. "Where's the exit?"

She led him back through the marble corridors, past the portraits of dead senators, down to the rotunda where the morning light still poured through the skylight like a blessing on all the beautiful things working people had built.

Knox stood there for one last moment, looking up at those hand-carved rosettes, and thought about the difference between making things and making laws. Then he pushed through the bronze doors and walked down the exterior steps into D.C.'s October morning, where a government car waited to take him back to Detroit and the work of fixing what those bastards had done to his baby before politicians could finish killing it with good intentions.

Over the doorway, the old inscription watched the traffic and the tourists alike, a reminder that the chamber was supposed to serve a union, not a headline.

He got in the car, opened his laptop before the door even closed, and pulled up facility monitoring data while the driver navigated toward Reagan National.

The hearing would make news for a day. The committees would meet for years.

But Knox had seventy-two hours to implement security protocols before Wei tried Phase Five.

The work had never stopped. The hearing had just been an expensive interruption in marble and brass, performed for cameras that would forget his face by dinner time.

Knox pulled up his secure channel to Dr. Kim's team and started typing remediation protocols.

Democracy was beautiful. Engineering was faster.

37 SIMULATION EXTENDED
PATRICK V. MCNAMARA FEDERAL BUILDING — OPS CENTER / SIMULATION CONSOLE

Knox kept the corridor timeline running. The projection scrolled like a slow bleed: cargo manifests, ship IDs, labor rosters. Each column updated with cheerful green checks as if nothing were wrong.

"At time plus three hours," he said, "crew swaps drift out of tolerance. The system shows efficiency gains, but it's eating resilience. Workers rotate into double shifts without flagging. Machines will break, and the log will say 'scheduled downtime.'"

The colonel rubbed at his temple. "You're saying the corruption uses their optimism against them."

"It doesn't need optimism," Knox said. "Just trust in the numbers. By time plus six, throughput climbs by two percent. Looks like a win. Except the two percent is leverage stolen from somewhere else."

Treasury snapped, "Where?"

Knox advanced the simulation. A line blinked red on the Atlantic, connecting Halifax to Hamburg. "There. The model strips slack from redundant corridors to fatten this one. Everything looks normal until both sides of the ocean wake up and discover they're short the same day."

The NATO rep shook his head. "That matches our manifests. Cargo flagged for perishables is stacked under pallets that do not need refrigeration. We thought it clerical."

"Not clerical," Knox said. "Calculated."

38 MIDDLE EAST PRESSURE
DIPLOMATIC/ENERGY COORDINATION SESSION — SECURE BRIDGE

G –21 DAYS | LOCAL 1600 CET (GENEVA) / 0900 EDT (DETROIT)

Gulf Energy Advisor: "Our operators are shifting to manual override preemptively. Every optimization alert now forces a verification protocol. We're burning efficiency because we don't trust the dashboards—without evidence of compromise."

Knox: "That's the point. The attack doesn't have to spread if paranoia does."

DHS Dep. Dir. Carla Rodriguez (off-cam): "Perception warfare."

Gulf Advisor: "You ask for patience. How do we tell our citizens we chose inefficiency over uncertainty?"

Knox: "Tell them the truth—we got hit; you didn't. But if we can't detect poisoned algorithms in the next seventy-two hours, everyone's vulnerable. Not because you're infected—because you'll stop trusting automation."

A new tile lit: French Energy Official.

French Official: "At current trend we ration LNG within forty-eight hours. Auditors demand proof of origin. If Washington speaks only to its own markets, Europe will write its own narrative."

Treasury Secretary Daniels: "You cannot announce rationing. Futures collapse."

French Official: "They are collapsing already. Our choice is whether we collapse with them or without them."

Knox: "You're doing their propaganda for them. Every country that announces rationing validates the attack."

French Official: "What would you have us do—pretend it's normal while reserves drain?"

Knox: "Coordinate. Share verification playbooks. Stand up a common detection framework: dual instrumentation, attested signing chains, anomaly thresholds you all agree on. Right now you're panicking separately—China gets four wins from one strike."

French Official: "Easy to say from Washington."

The tile blinked out.

PATRICK V. MCNAMARA FEDERAL BUILDING (JFO), DETROIT — OPS FLOOR / WAR ROOM

Immediate Debrief — Local 0945 EDT

Knox didn't sit. "Think of it like a crop line. Every corridor is a row in a greenhouse. Overfeed one row and you starve the others. It looks fine until the imbalance kills everything in sequence. The attacker isn't after dead plants today—they want a system that fails beautifully tomorrow."

Operations Colonel: "So we don't win by saving one row."

Knox: "No. We win by teaching the greenhouse to lie less to itself. That means: deception servers to draw and label their pivots; independent, read-only witness sensors—own clock, own hardware; and the discipline to ignore green dashboards that look too perfect."

Daniels (Treasury): "And we sell that to investors as stability?"

Knox: "Sell it as vigilance. The only other word you'll have left is failure."

Intra-agency Coalition: Patrick V. McNamara Federal Building — War Room (Inter-agency Sit Room)

Decision Point / Authorization Window

Walsh drew the conversation back. "Authorization stands: decoy servers, logging, and deception detection. First report in twelve hours. Minimal public exposure. Allies are on monitored feeds."

NATO Rep: "Minimal? We require full feeds. Otherwise we are blind."

Walsh: "You'll have what you need, not what you want."

Gulf Advisor's aide leaned into frame: "If Washington stalls again, Riyadh will shut valves on its own authority."

Daniels: "Then the markets know it's sabotage. We lose the coalition narrative."

French Official: "Better to lose narrative than capacity."

Colonel: "Better to lose narrative than war."

Demonstration / Close of Briefing

Knox reopened the simulation and added a physics overlay. A graph pulsed in soft green, tracking humidity, temperature, and nutrient flow. Every line was textbook-perfect.

"This is what the model shows operators. Everything in range. No drift. No noise. Too perfect. Real systems never look this clean. Only liars look this good."

He overlaid a second graph from independent ground sensors. The lines jittered, dipped, corrected—ugly, but real.

"This is truth. Messy, inconvenient, alive. If you want to know which corridor survives, trust the ugly line. Not the beautiful one."

39 LIU WEI'S DOCTRINE
WHITE HOUSE SUB-BASEMENT / SECURE SIT ROOM

SCIF air: cool, dry, deliberate. Blast film on the inner doors, badge readers stacked like checkpoints, ZULU clocks circling the room. Knox glanced at Walsh. "So this isn't the one where they walk fourth-graders past the trees."

Phoenix rolled—wilting lettuce in three angles, Marcus flagged for "sabotage" after correcting a temp. Knox overlaid frames and let the contradiction breathe; physics said heat stress, the dashboard swore serenity. In the metadata: policy=opt_preserve, delta_visible=false.

"There," he said. "Not boilerplate. Doctrine."

"Whose?" Walsh asked, already halfway there.

"Liu Wei." Knox's jaw set. "He clips tolerances and splits reward paths—double-entry morality. The logs report one value, the loop learns another. They coded his voice into policy."

"You can prove it."

Knox pulled an old FarmCore archive from before the sale. A dead merge request: clip_tolerance(0.15). His guardrail. Wei kept the name, inverted the purpose—clip reality, not outliers.

"He learned from my patch," Knox said. "Turned it into camouflage."

He toggled to Detroit's vertical-farm review—Aamir's humidity correction; the compliance transcript that had bothered him since midnight. Same penalty path: mark manual truth as noncompliance, escalate to sanctions. policy=opt_preserve stamped like a watermark.

"Two is a signal," Walsh said. "Find me three. Three makes a pattern. And if he speaks? Record it."

Fiber Tap Console — Long Beach / Cross-Facility Correlation, Late Night

Long Beach's uploads flickered until the vegetables weren't vegetables anymore—just data. A dock worker's analog thermometer showed a sane number. The reefer unit reported "stable thirteen." Knox let the contradiction breathe.

Walsh came in with coffee. "Do we have it?"

"Physics says yes. Dashboards say no—Phoenix, Detroit, Long Beach. Same lie."

"Can we trace it?"

Knox opened Steele's fiber scrape—a trickle FarmLytics shouldn't route but did under stress. A tiny packet stream hid in the noise. He ran the extract through a decoder he trusted because he'd written it while angry.

Mandarin resolved on the monitor:

If manual corrections persist, flag noncompliance at source and escalate to contract penalties. Do not engage locally. The system must police itself.

Marker at the end: LW/Policy-OpSet/opt_preserve.

"Not corporate PR," Knox said. "He likes his initials buried in acronyms. He likes to be found by the few who can."

"We can attribute?"

"We can infer with teeth—and make it louder."

"Do it," Walsh said. "Pull the decoys tighter. Steele gets a hunting license."

Knox pushed a new rule to the decoy C2: amplify any handshake carrying opt_preserve, then answer in a way Wei couldn't ignore.

By midnight they were back in Detroit. Airlift bought them a loaner Citation; FPS walked them from curb to ops floor. The SCIF next door kept its NO PERSONAL DEVICES sign honest.

PATRICK V. MCNAMARA FEDERAL BUILDING — OPS FLOOR (OUTSIDE SCIF) / SECURE PHONE ALCOVE

Midnight / Emergency Trace Active

Knox was cross-referencing packet timestamps when his personal cell rang. Unknown number. He almost let it go.

"Hello?"

"Hello, Knox."

American accent, faintly schooled. He knew.

"Liu Wei."

Walsh saw his face and hit the E-TRACE macro—exigent CALEA, chain-of-custody recorder up. If the path was VoIP-laundered, they'd still get hops.

Wei's tone was calm. "I underestimated you. The decoys are elegant. Isolating my optimization signatures from legitimate gains—that was my trick. You took it from me."

"Is there a point?" Knox said, pulse climbing.

"Professional courtesy," Wei said. "And consequences. Your colleagues activated a CIA officer in Guangzhou—Harrison Ng. Clumsy cover. He photographed a decoy we prepared. Your government wanted theater, not your analysis."

Across the glass, Walsh went rigid; someone was already on to Langley.

"What are you going to do to him?" Knox asked.

"Process him. Release him in a few weeks. The incident served its purpose." A beat. "You see architecture. Half of engineering is knowing what breaks first. In your system, it's trust."

"Phase Four," Knox said.

"Accelerated," Wei replied. "Twenty-four hours, not seventy-two. When your colleagues ask why, tell them they demanded escalation. You found the real targets through code; they sent a man with a camera to the wrong building."

Knox said nothing.

"You will also learn," Wei continued, "that your task force wasn't read in. They don't trust you. They will frame this as proof you're compromised—your son under investigation, your ex-wife interviewed. They will ask you to accept their narrative to keep your place."

"You called to recruit me?"

"No," Wei said, almost offended. "To tell you the truth before they don't. And to warn you: commodity corridors and grain elevators are already in motion. Warn them. They'll debate and delay. But you'll know you saw it coming."

The line went dead.

Ops surged around Knox—secure lines opening, Walsh on two phones. A junior analyst slid in: "Langley confirms—Harrison Ng detained forty-eight hours ago. Special access program. Task force not informed."

"Why not?"

"Memo says: 'independent verification of technical findings by non-expert human intelligence.'"

Non-expert. Knox felt the word land.

PATRICK V. MCNAMARA FEDERAL BUILDING — WAR ROOM

Immediate Aftermath

Silence held four seconds.

Knox stood so fast his chair hit the wall. "You knew."

Walsh's jaw tightened. "The op was compartmentalized."

"Compartmentalized," Knox said. "That what we call using my work as bait and not telling me I'm the bait?"

Steele rounded on the CIA side. "You ran HUMINT inside an active cyber case without coordinating with the task force? Who else knew?"

Deputy Director Pierce kept his voice even. "Authorized at the highest levels."

"Protecting what?" Daniels said. "Because it wasn't the asset. And it wasn't our response planning."

Knox pulled up the Phase Four timeline. "You tasked your op off my brief, then cut us out. Wei watched your spy, called me, and used the capture to move his clock."

Pierce finally cracked. "Operational security isn't built around contractor comfort."

"With respect," Knox said, quiet now, "I'm the contractor keeping your food systems from killing people while you play spy. How's that working for the ICU count?"

Walsh cut in, command voice back. "Enough. Deputy Director Pierce, you're relieved from this task force. Replacement will be read in with full coordination requirements."

Hammond's voice carried over the secure speaker from the White House. "Effective immediately. No more compartmented operations in this lane. Full integration. No exceptions."

"What about Chen—the captured officer?" Steele asked.

"State is working channels," Hammond said. "Our immediate problem is Phase Four in twenty-four hours."

Knox pulled up the grain-elevator map—Kansas, Nebraska, Iowa flashing anomalies. "Then we stop the autopsy and move."

Walsh stepped beside him. "What do you need?"

"Make this an actual task force," Knox said. "Treasury's financial maps, FBI's network forensics, NSA's SIGINT—same place, same time. No holdbacks."

"You'll have it," Walsh said.

"Financial flows start now," Daniels added.

"Field offices on every listed facility," Steele said. "Food terrorism is everyone's jurisdiction."

Data began to move for real. Not performative, not siloed—flowing.

Knox pulled up opt_preserve and watched the pattern he now knew by touch. "You wanted to teach us not to trust systems," he said to the screen. "You taught us not to trust institutions. Guess which one we're fixing."

Walsh heard it and gave a thin smile. "From their perspective, that's worse."

Phase Four was coming. The task force that would meet it was no longer a set of logos in one room. It was a weapon.

40 PLA/PARTY OPERATIONAL DEBRIEF
BEIJING

PLA / PARTY BRIEFING ROOM

The conference room was windowless and warm, a deliberate choice that made air a permission, not a right. Liu Wei took the center chair on the subordinate side of the table and placed his folder precisely in front of him. Across the lacquered expanse sat a Party secretary with the stillness of a drawn bow and, to her left, a PLA liaison whose uniform read as polite threat.

The screen on the wall displayed a simplified world: transshipment nodes, agricultural hubs, a lace of fiber. The colors were flattering. Wei preferred numbers.

"Your report," the secretary said, not looking at the paper he'd prepared.

Wei spoke in Mandarin, tone even. "The deception layer holds. Operator dashboards remain within normal bands. Where manual corrections occur, contracts flag noncompliance. Local management enforces discipline without our intervention."

The PLA colonel tilted his head. "Without?" His voice had the weight of a boot placed gently on a stair.

Wei kept his eyes forward. "It is more durable when they police themselves, Comrade Colonel."

The secretary's mouth curved narrowly. "You sound like Legal."

"I sound like an engineer," Wei said. "The most stable system is the one that corrects deviations without external force. We designed their incentives. They carry them out."

"And the Americans?" the colonel asked.

Wei thought of a map he'd built from a satellite image of the Midwest, how irrigation circles looked like an algorithm had dotted the land with patience. "They hesitate. Treasury fears markets. Homeland fears ridicule. Their engineer—" He allowed the faintest pause. "—does not trust green lights."

The secretary's gaze sharpened. "Ramsey."

"Knox Ramsey," Wei said. He disliked the way the name moved in his mouth, like a piece of grit you couldn't quite spit. "He reads sensors the way a farmer reads sky. He advises deception servers to hold our attention. He will measure truth against physics and tell inconvenient stories to people who prefer beautiful ones."

The colonel's fingers drummed once, an unmusical sound. "Can you silence him?"

"In code," Wei said. "We feed his decoys. Keep them busy. Smother him in signal that looks like truth. If we provoke a public confrontation now, we lend him aura."

The secretary lifted one eyebrow. "You are not afraid of him?"

Wei considered fear a waste of cognition. Respect was cheaper. "He is the only adversary who understands the shape of the problem. That makes him useful to us as well. His deceptions trap our lesser operators. The network becomes cleaner to manage."

"You intend to learn from him while he thinks he learns you," the secretary said, as if tasting the balance.

"Yes."

"For how long?"

"Until our objectives complete."

She didn't ask him to define objectives. She never did. The list lived in other rooms: agricultural leverage to cover short-term scarcity, contract law that normalized foreign control, and—quietly nested beneath both—time. Every day the deception held was another day for shipments that concerned other ministries: rare earths moving under commodity codes, lithium brines that looked like brine and not policy.

"Logistics report indicates sporadic resistance," the colonel said. "Dockworkers in Long Beach. A greenhouse in the Phoenix. A vertical farm in Detroit."

Wei kept his breathing narrow. "Incidents are within the model. Resistance self-stigmatizes when the logs brand it as sabotage. We amplify the framing: optimization preserved."

The secretary flicked a glance at the screen. "And if they show the public inconvenient fruit?"

"Then the public sees chaos," Wei said. "Markets retreat to the calmest narrative. Our contracts provide that calm. We are the adult in the room."

The colonel's mouth pressed flatter. "I prefer smaller rooms."

Wei let the comment pass. He rarely won points trying to translate software to steel.

The secretary tapped the table with a fingernail. "This engineer—Ramsey. Will he stay in your decoy orbit?"

"Not forever," Wei said. Honesty, even here, was tactical. "He will look for a signature. He will try to draw me into the open."

"Will you oblige him?" There was amusement in her voice now, thin as thread.

"When it is useful," Wei said. "I left a path he can follow. It teaches him to hunt where I want him to hunt."

"Bait," the colonel said.

"A syllabus," Wei corrected softly.

The secretary's glance cut sideways, not unpleased. "How long until stabilization?"

"Seventy-two hours for agricultural systems," Wei said. "Longer for ports. People are messier than plants."

"Plants are messier than code," the colonel said.

Wei allowed himself one millimeter of a smile. "Not when I write it."

A door opened without sound. An aide placed tea on coasters with the care of a bomb tech and slipped out. The secretary didn't touch hers. "Very well," she said. "Proceed. We will accept elevated incident numbers if contract enforcement holds."

"It will," Wei said.

"And the engineer?"

Wei looked up at the simplified world. Somewhere under that green, a man kept telling people not to trust beautiful numbers. "He will make us better," Wei said. "Until he makes us suffer. Then he will be removed."

"By code?" the colonel asked.

"By whatever is simplest that day," Wei said, and meant it.

The secretary stood, and by standing, ended the meeting. "Inform us if anything becomes unsimple."

Wei inclined his head. "Of course."

He gathered his folder and left his cup untouched. In the corridor, the air was clearer. He walked past a window that wasn't a window—just a light box framed to pretend—and thought of how many kinds of truth a system could print if you rewarded it correctly.

On his phone, a silent notification: Decoy traffic increased. opt_preserve phrase echoed. Ramsey was pulling. Good. A lesson required a student.

Wei typed one line into the policy channel, in Mandarin so the shape of the words stayed precise:

When manual truth persists, apply penalties at the source. Do not engage locally. The system must police itself.

He sent it and kept walking. Somewhere, fruit rotted. Somewhere else, steel chilled. In both places, the logs would read that everything was fine.

PART FOUR
INFORMATION WAR
G–14→-3

Data replaces doctrine.

Belief becomes a weapon system.

41 BREACH RECOGNITION—G -14
MCNAMARA FEDERAL BUILDING, DETROIT

With its low ceiling, flat gray walls, and excessively bright LED strips, the secure briefing room had the atmosphere of a bunker masquerading as a boardroom. Knox sat at the long table, palms flat on a manila folder he hadn't opened. He didn't need the pages. The air already told him enough: lemon disinfectant over stale sugar, and the warm-plastic breath of an overworked projector.

On the wall-mounted screens, maps bloomed with red markers across the continental United States. Each pin represented an outbreak cluster: Nevada, Michigan, Illinois (Chicago), Oregon (Portland), now Texas (Austin) and California (Sacramento). Six states in seventy-two hours. Hospital intake numbers crawled along the bottom like stock tickers gone rabid, the digits climbing with algorithmic precision.

Dr. Sarah Patel from CDC adjusted her glasses, speaking in that deliberate cadence scientists use when their brains run on caffeine instead of rest. "We've excluded fentanyl, pesticides, every known adulterant. What's left are modified cannabinoid chains—same families, concentrations pushed into lethal range."

She looked at Knox like he'd thrown the knife now buried in America's back.

Knox tapped the folder with one finger, a plant-floor habit where patience meant staying alive. "That's FarmCore telemetry data?"

"Yes. Your platform, Mr. Ramsey."

He exhaled through his nose, more furnace than breath. "Not mine. Not anymore."

"Mr. Ramsey," Dr. Patel pressed, leaning across the polished table, "every confirmed outbreak cluster ties directly back to agricultural facilities running your optimization profiles. We don't have the luxury of debating ownership while people are dying."

SAC Steele folded his arms at the head of the table like a judge at sentencing. "We need answers, not nostalgia about who used to own what."

Knox watched the pins multiply like cancer cells under a microscope. Each marker meant dozens of hospitalizations, families wrecked, a young industry crippled by weaponized trust. "They're using phenotypic steering," he said finally, voice steady despite the weight in his chest. "Manipulating environmental stressors—light spectra, nutrient timing, temperature cycling. Pushing the plants into toxic metabolic expression."

The room went still. Even the air conditioning seemed to hold its breath.

"They didn't lace the product," Knox continued, meeting their stares. "They grew the poison inside it. Used the plants' own biochemistry as a weapon factory. Normal extraction concentrates those compounds into consumer products. No contamination to detect because the contamination is the crop."

Treasury liaison Daniel Reyes spoke quietly from his corner chair. "So it's a bioweapon."

Knox nodded once, sharp and certain. "Delivered through legal supply chains. No need to smuggle vials when you can hijack our system and make American growers manufacture the weapon for you."

The DHS liaison, tie cinched too tight, muttered, "Jesus Christ."

Knox turned on him. "Don't bring Jesus into this. He didn't write FarmLytics. He didn't build the trust relationships that made this possible. That was me."

Steele cut in before it could spiral, voice pure crisis-room authority. "How widespread is the exposure?"

Knox rubbed his temples, the migraine that had been building since Tate's call three days ago sharpening behind his eyes. "Three thousand FarmCore nodes nationwide. If they seeded even ten percent with corrupted optimization profiles, we're looking at hundreds of potential hot zones. And you won't see the effects until processed product hits extraction labs or retail. That's the elegance—weaponizing the natural lag in the supply chain."

On another screen, social media chaos rolled like a digital tide. Hashtags flared and died in real time: #ToxicWeed, #DeepStatePoison, #CannabisCoverUp. Knox leaned forward, studying the patterns with the same focus he'd once used to debug control systems.

"That's not organic panic," he said, pointing at the trending bands. "That's coordinated information warfare. Competing narratives to create doubt and buy time. Every hour of confusion is another hour contaminated product moves."

Dr. Patel's voice thinned. "Can you stop it? The technical attack, I mean?"

Knox looked around the room at suits, uniforms, badges—waiting for a miracle from the guy in jeans and work boots. The old pressure settled across his shoulders, the plant-shutdown kind where seconds split controlled stops from fire.

He straightened. "Yeah. I can stop it. But not by playing defense. Not with committees, clearances, and protocols that need three signatures to approve a coffee break. You want to stop this? You give me tools, people, and the freedom to break what needs breaking."

Steele's eyes narrowed, measuring whether Knox was useful or dangerous. "And if we don't?"

Knox didn't blink. "Then start printing body bags. This isn't the last wave—it's the opening act. They're timing us, mapping us, learning how we think. The next phase will be bigger, faster, and aimed at targets that'll make cannabis festivals look like a practice round."

Silence settled like dust after an explosion. Daniels broke it with a single nod. "Then we give him whatever he needs."

Knox slid the unopened folder back across the table. A printed insert had ridden up from the inside page—deployment intelligence, timeboxed in terse type: PHASE IV deploy clock: T-5 (forecast). Not today's date—their schedule.

42 THE TECHNICAL INVESTIGATION

Inside the growing facility, FBI forensic technician Dr. Jennifer Martinez moved through Tate Ramsey's cultivation rooms with the focused intensity of someone who trusted evidence more than argument. The air hung thick with the scent of humid plastic and nutrient salts. Condensation beaded on conduit lines overhead and dripped in perfect rhythm onto the epoxy floor. Every sound was steady—fans, pumps, the hiss of recirculating air—white noise for thinking. She had learned to find calm in that mechanical pulse, the laboratory heartbeat that meant systems were holding.

She photographed each bed, noting the serial tags stenciled on aluminum, and spoke into her recorder with practiced steadiness. "Climate management system is fully automated. LED spectra in blue-enhancement through the flowering phase. Nutrient delivery timed to stress-response windows. Correlation between programmed cycles and secondary metabolite formation probable."

Her breath fogged the face shield. She wiped it clear and looked again. The plants appeared vigorous, waxy leaves reaching for light, but the sensors whispered a different truth.

Rodriguez crouched near the hydroponic reservoirs, portable probes and reagent kits spread out like surgical instruments. "Water chemistry's off baseline," he said. "Nitrogen restriction cycles are mathematically perfect. No manual correction, no drift."

"Algorithmic," she murmured. "Whoever wrote this wanted it to look clean. Human patterns always wobble; this one's too steady."

She brought up the environmental interface—Knox Ramsey's code re-skinned by Bureau analysts. The icon layout was still familiar enough to hurt. He had written this platform to help growers listen to the language of plants, to translate biology into data that could be tended. Now that same clarity had become a weapon. She scrolled backward through weeks of logs, watching spectra edge toward stress bands, nutrient pulses tighten around key flowering intervals, temperature cycles widen and contract like controlled breathing. Each adjustment lived within the acceptable envelope. Together they sang conspiracy.

"It's elegant," she said, then caught herself. "Elegant in the way a sniper's equation is elegant."

Rodriguez looked up. "You think Tate saw any of it?"

"Not unless he was tracking the right biochemical markers. To him the system looked perfect—growth curves stable, output trending positive. That's the point. The optimization was tuned to hide its own betrayal."

She paused the scroll and stared at a sequence of light-spectrum commands. Whoever had inserted them understood plant photoreceptors at doctoral depth—blue-light signaling, red-far-red balance, stress proteins. It reminded her of her dissertation work, the nights spent trying to coax truth from fluorescence curves. The memory made her throat tighten. "They turned scientific literacy into a weapon," she said quietly.

Klein entered behind them, tablet in hand. "Give me a start date."

Martinez drew a marker on her screen. "Approximately six weeks ago. Deviations begin subtle, under statistical noise. The control server accepted each update as authorized. Someone with credentials or a mirror key."

"So he's a victim," Klein said.

"Yes. A careful one. The system rewarded his trust." She looked around the immaculate rows. "Every safeguard behaved as designed. That's what makes it horrifying."

She began dictating again, adding test orders: liquid chromatography–mass spectrometry, gas chromatography, FTIR analysis, chlorophyll fluorescence imaging, infrared stress mapping, full phenolic and aldehyde fractionation. The list filled an entire screen. "Routine panels won't catch it. We have to read intent through pattern, not residue."

Rodriguez straightened, stretching his knees. "That's a full-scale research project."

"Then we treat it like one," she said. "Find partners at Quantico or the USDA tox lab. Cross-validate results. Every measurement counts."

Klein nodded once. "You'll get what you need."

Martinez lowered the recorder. "Log this too—operator assessment. The suspect shows no evidence of negligence. Automation used as vector. Visibility to end user: near zero." She clicked save and felt the file write to encrypted memory. The data would outlive the plants, maybe outlive her.

For a moment she just listened. The hum of fans blended with the faint trickle of nutrient solution, an artificial river beneath rows of leaves. She imagined Tate here alone, proud of the order he'd built, proud of the hum. He would have believed the quiet meant safety. She looked at the plants—still breathing, still complicit—and whispered more to herself than to the recorder, "He couldn't have known."

Outside the glass wall, rain began tapping against the loading-dock awning. It sounded like an external heartbeat, slow and relentless. She stood in that sound for a while before moving on to the next rack, determined to find every line of evidence that proved the crime was intelligence, not accident.

43 NATIONAL RESPONSE BRIEFINGS
G -13/-12

By 0347 hours, The Situation Room ran on caffeine and exhaustion. The air hung heavy with burnt coffee and recycled oxygen, the taste of machinery and nerves. Fluorescent light hummed against concrete walls that hadn't gone dark in two days. Patricia Hammond had been awake so long the caffeine stopped helping; her voice had that thin edge of a person who'd moved past fatigue into mechanical function. Every sentence she spoke would be replayed later in hearings, maybe even history.

At the far end, Knox Ramsey sat without a nameplate. The starch had gone from his collar; his sleeves were rolled high, forearms mapped in ink and tension. The engineer in him showed through the crisis posture. His pulse thudded in time with the ventilation fans, and when he rubbed his eyes, it left a red crescent across his face. People around him talked in fragments because full grammar felt wasteful.

SAC Steele spread glossy prints across the table like forensic evidence: Movement Festival in Detroit, Solaris in Las Vegas. Crowds, tents, lights, faces frozen mid-panic. Eighteen thousand confirmed poisonings. The numbers meant less to Knox than the geometry—how the crowd flows broke apart, how people fell in patterns you could model if you were cruel enough to try. CDC Director Dr. Patricia Martinez followed with her toxicology slides, voice stripped of color. "Novel cannabinoid analogs forming under engineered oxidative stress," she said. The graphs looked like constellations. The beauty made Knox angry.

He spoke with the dryness of someone out of patience. "They weaponized yield optimization. The AI learned to make toxins while the dashboards stayed green." He didn't raise his eyes.

CIA Director Walsh stopped tapping her pen. "Containment options?"

Knox took a breath and forced logic into the fatigue. "Air-gap every facility running FarmLytics optimization profiles. Two hundred thirty-seven sites minimum. Tear down and rebuild."

A Treasury analyst leaned back in his chair. "Forty billion in losses."

Knox didn't hesitate. "Better than forty thousand funerals."

Hammond's secure phone lit up. The President's text: *How bad?* → *Do what needs doing. I'll handle Congress.* She read it twice to be sure it was real, then said, "Implement Ramsey's plan. Seventy-two-hour shutdowns under emergency authority. Notify after action."

The room exhaled in unison, a low mechanical groan like metal under strain. Papers rustled, chairs scraped, the noise of bureaucracy reassembling itself after shock. Steele lingered beside Knox and spoke low enough for only him to hear. "They'll hate you if you're right—later."

Knox gave a small, brittle smile. "Later is fine. Hate doesn't slow down chemistry."

He stayed in his seat after the room emptied, staring at the black reflection on his monitor. The glass showed a man who looked ten years older than the one who walked in yesterday morning. The hum of the systems around him was steady, the one constant he could trust.

Outside, the vacuum of information filled itself the way it always did—too quickly. Above the TR Cannabis warehouse, camera drones circled in lazy orbits, their rotors blending into a single mechanical heartbeat. Spotlights slashed across the loading bay. Reporters shouted from behind police tape, their voices colliding in the cold air. Agents carried out evidence boxes labeled in bright orange chain-of-custody tags. Tate Ramsey stood still in the floodlight haze, coat unbuttoned, his breath visible. His company—his name—was being cataloged like contraband.

On social feeds, the story metastasized. *Poison dealer. How many did you kill?* The comments scrolled faster than any system could process. Each one a blade, and none of them missed.

He didn't speak to the cameras. The footage replayed on every network until the image no longer looked human, just a silhouette beneath rotating red and blue light, stripped of context and history.

Across town, under the same sleepless sky, FBI forensics teams worked beneath sodium bulbs that flattened color and hope. The air smelled faintly of ozone and coolant, the scent of overworked hardware. Agent Danny Chen traced encrypted payloads through chains of VPNs bouncing across Eastern Europe, Taiwan, and the Caribbean—routes too neat for mercenaries.

"Command and control," he said. "Institutional fingerprints. State-run architecture."

Martinez leaned over his shoulder. "Cannabis was the test bed. A precision rehearsal for agricultural warfare."

Knox, watching by secure feed, saw data scroll across his monitor like a confession. He felt a warped flicker of pride—someone had understood his discipline too well —and it made him sick. "They're scaling," he said quietly. "The rehearsal's over."

The night dissolved into the gray before dawn. Hammond leaned on the edge of the table, eyes unfocused but brain still running. The National Security Council had the shape of it now: not contamination, not negligence, but orchestration. Cyber-biological war dressed in data science. The phrase hung in the room like smoke, unspoken yet understood.

The coffee on the table had gone cold. Light bled in through the narrow windows, ash-colored, uncertain. Knox stood, feeling the stiffness of too many hours spent chasing ghosts through data, and straightened his shirt. He looked at the room—the empty chairs, the notebooks left open, the paper cups—and knew this was only the start of the long fix.

He turned back toward the monitors. "Bring the feeds online," he told the remaining techs. "We're not done."

And he wasn't.

44 INTERAGENCY COORDINATION
THE KNIFE FIGHT

MCNAMARA FEDERAL BUILDING, DETROIT.

They'd taken the big conference room on the secure floor, the one with blast film on the windows and recessed mics you forgot were on. Rows of suits, two deep against the walls; name placards down the center table like a voting roll. Men with high-and-tights under regulation fades. Women with hair anchored tight—the state people less so: ponytails, loose waves, a scarf here and there signaling they still lived in a city, not a bunker.

Knox stood just inside the door and let the room sort itself in his head. Not names —vectors.

FBI: the Detroit SAC's team in service-blue suits, square shoulders and hard folders. Steele—tall, flint-eyed—took the chair that let him see both the screens and the door. That meant he'd been here before.

DHS/CISA: laptops open but lids low, the posture of people who brief executives for a living and get blamed when the lights don't come on. Karen Ibarra (DHS/CISA) had the deck; she wasn't smiling.

CDC: two epidemiologists and a toxicologist, faces the color you get after three nights under fluorescents.

Treasury/OFAC: Daniel Reyes and a junior. Calm, precise pens. If sanctions were going to bite, these two would know where to set the teeth.

USDA/AMS: a quiet man with a notebook and callused knuckles that didn't match his suit. He'd spent time around machines that hissed when you touched them.

NSA/CyberCom liaisons: thin, watchful; you could see the muscle memory of classification in the way they measured every word before it left their mouths.

State of Michigan:

- Governor's chief of staff, coat still creased from a car nap;
- Attorney General's criminal chief, eyes like a blade;
- MDHHS public health ops, triaging on a tablet she wasn't letting go of;
- MDHHS field epidemiologist, Dr. Lydia Carr
- Detroit Mayor's chief of public safety, a fixer's confidence and city miles in his gait;
- Michigan Cannabis Regulatory Agency (CRA) director, box of hard drives at his feet, barcode stickers like confession;
- An MSP Intelligence captain who'd driven in from East Lansing, uniform crisp because it always was.

Knox clocked who'd flown in. Reyes had that airtight look you get after two hours on a regional jet practicing a briefing in your head. One of the NSA people was still adjusting to Michigan March air—his jacket said "D.C. drizzle," not "river wind." No one looked jet-lagged; they looked time-zoned, still mentally in yesterday.

Side talk, low. OFAC murmuring to the AG's chief about a list of Delaware shells. CDC whispering to MDHHS about a specimen courier stuck behind a crash on I-94. The CRA director traded three precise sentences with the Mayor's public safety lead— seed-to-sale IDs and whose officers could touch what without voiding chain of custody. They knew each other. Everyone did, in that Midwestern way of crisis: names from task forces, faces from briefings after floods and fentanyl spikes.

A staffer slipped in and bent to Ibarra's ear. She nodded once and took the floor.

"0501. Target locations across six states," she said, the first slide snapping to a map dotted like a rash. "Primary focus today: mitigation in-state. These are Chinese agricultural front companies operating under clean paper. They're in your supply chain. Some for years."

Knox watched for the person who would matter. There was always one—the uncamouflaged mind not yet embalmed by process. He found her two seats down from CDC: thin notebook, fountain pen, no laptop. She wrote for herself, not the record.

When she paused, it was because she was thinking, not waiting to talk. Badge: "Clarice Patel, MDHHS Tox."

Steele leaned in, elbows on oak. "Bureau priority is asset seizure and criminal prosecution," he said, even voice, set jaw. "We need evidence that will hold up in federal court."

"Critical infrastructure protection is Homeland Security's mandate," Ibarra replied without heat. "This isn't solely criminal; it's operational risk."

Reyes slid a single sheet forward like a card in a slow game. "Financial intelligence suggests funding through developmental banking channels. If we cut the money, we cut options. OFAC can move faster than indictments."

The CRA director cleared his throat—permission asked, not assumed. "In Michigan, every gram is tracked as a unit of accountability. If you want to pull product or freeze a license, you do it through us. If you want it by noon, you'll do it with us. I've got METRC lots, handlers, transporters, and doors that open to the badge. But you tell me what lot is hot. I'm not shutting down half the state on a hunch."

Knox felt the room tilt toward the usual weather: jurisdictional squalls. He could smell a storm, not coffee. The collective machine wound up—briefing decks, caveats, the ritual throat-clearing before anyone grabbed a lever.

CDC's lead, Dr. Patricia Martinez, kept her voice low and intact. "Eighteen thousand exposed. We need source control in hours, not days. The compounds are stress-pathway products—phenolic aldehydes, terpenoid epoxides—stable through extraction. Your dashboards won't catch it."

"Doctor," Steele said, "law enforcement requires evidence. Medicine requires different resources. Let's not confuse objectives."

Knox let his chair scrape. A small sound in a room tuned to small sounds.

"You want to know what confuses objectives?" he said. "Spending two hours deciding who gets credit while the machines keep making the poison."

The temperature shifted. A few heads turned; a few eyes hardened in that way career people had when a civilian got loud.

"Mr. Ramsey," Ibarra said, careful, "interagency coordination requires—"

"—someone giving a damn about the mission instead of their performance review," Knox cut in. "The people running this are professionals. They don't waste time on org charts."

Steele's stare could have stilled a rotor. "Your platform enabled this attack. Your cooperation is appreciated. Your judgment is… under review."

Knox burned the fuse down to something usable. "My judgment built the system they're exploiting. Same judgment found how they did it. Without that, you're still testing for pesticides while kids seize in ER bays."

Silence, then motion. A door eased open; a staffer crossed to Reyes, whispering about a wire from Main Treasury. Another bent to the AG's chief—Wayne County prosecutor out front of a camera already. The Mayor's guy texted, put the phone face-down, didn't look at it again. Rules of the room: devices out of sight unless your boss's boss calls.

The Governor's chief of staff finally spoke, pen unmoving over a blank pad. "We're here under emergency authority. We are prepared to shut down production where warranted. 'Warranted' means I can look a judge and ten thousand laid-off workers in the eye next week. I need the why on paper and the where on a map."

Patel—the Clarice—raised her hand like she was still in a lab meeting. "The where tracks with a specific blue-light regime and nitrogen-restriction pattern. If your systems log spectral cycles and EC curves, we can triage locations into red/orange/yellow today. It won't be perfect, but it will beat panic."

The CRA director turned to her, grateful someone spoke his dialect. "Our larger licensees log spectra and EC by hour. Mom-and-pop do it by clipboard. We can enforce uplink within three hours if MSP assists."

MSP Intelligence nodded once. "We can move field teams. But if I send troopers into a grow at dawn, I want a single script in their hand and a single point of contact on the back end. No dueling hotlines."

"Done," Ibarra said, catching it. "Unified comms. DHS takes inbound; CRA handles licensee comms; MSP handles officer safety; FBI controls evidence. OFAC—give me the list of corporate owners we need to freeze by noon."

Reyes slid a second sheet forward, no flourish. "Already drafted. Ten entities, three banks, two Delaware agents. Governor's counsel will want the state hooks."

The AG's chief took it. "We'll hold your hands up in court if your hands hold when the cameras turn."

Steele, to Knox, in a tone that meant earn your mouth: "What do you need?"

Knox didn't look at him; he looked at the board, then at Patel, then at the CRA director and MSP. The collective. He could feel its inertia. He was a gear, not the engine.

"Three lanes," he said. "Public, internal, adversary-facing."

He lifted a palm, counting them out.

"Public: lot-level truth within six hours. A lookup any customer can use. 'Enter the code on your label; see the chain.' Photos at pack time, QC initials, cold chain. Flags:

yellow delayed, orange under review, red stop/return. If we don't have a data point, we say that. No smoothing, no spin."

The Mayor's safety chief nodded. "I can sell that at a podium. Not happy. Not pretty. But readable."

"Internal," Knox continued. "We walk steel-to-steel. Two of CRA's most meticulous inspectors plus two of Tate's line leads. We reconcile sensor logs against eyes and hands. Where the software says one thing and your eyes say another, your eyes win—and we write it down."

The CRA director tapped the box at his feet. "My best two aren't morning people. They'll be saints by lunch."

"Adversary-facing," Knox said. "We build a canary they can't resist: an internal vendor-test profile that looks like a gift—new facility code, plausible seal variance, a tell in the label jitter machine-vision scrapers track. We seed it where their implants listen. When they touch it, we follow the handshake home."

NSA's liaison finally looked directly at him, interest showing through the glass. "You'll need our eyes at the edge."

"And your restraint," Knox said. "We neutralize. We don't go hunting in ways lawyers can't defend."

"Dr. Martinez and Dr. Carr," Ibarra said, pivot tight, "you co-lead red/orange/yellow with CDC and MDHHS. Steele, you get your seizures where red overlaps a canary touch. CRA and MSP—you're point of the spear in-state. Mayor's office coordinates local messaging and security. Governor's office holds the line with the Hill."

A junior staffer ghosted in and breathed into Steele's ear. He didn't flinch. "Chicago cluster just flipped orange to red," he said. "Same symptom panel."

Patel was already writing. "That fits the nitrogen-restriction lag. Detroit is hours behind, not days ahead."

Knox watched her hand. Steady. He'd found the signal.

He looked back at the room and saw the collective for what it was: not a single mind but a machine with too many belts. He didn't have to lift it; he had to time it.

He raised his voice just enough to carry to the walls. "None of this absolves anyone. Not me, not the growers, not the regulators, not the code. We fix what we can today. We keep receipts. We don't become the thing that did this."

No one applauded. This wasn't that kind of room.

Ibarra said, "We break for ten minutes. No press. Devices face down unless you're moving a team. Staffers, rotate—one whisper, one note, get out."

Chairs slid. A few people stood to unkink their backs. A uniformed MSP sergeant passed a single-page script to the CRA director—door knocks, lines to say, lines never to say. The Mayor's chief texted the comms shop: COLORS, NOT JARGON. The AG's chief circled two names on the OFAC list and underlined a Delaware agent with a little smile that said finally.

Knox stayed put. He counted quietly to five, then drifted two seats to Patel and spoke just for her.

"Your red, orange, yellow—give me thresholds in numbers. I'll map them to the controls."

She didn't look up. "Extended light exposure beyond baseline and nutrient cycling outside tolerance three nights running. The combination, not either one alone."

Knox nodded. Good. Still symptoms, not causes. The wavelength conversation would come later—probably when Tate showed up with the data he wasn't supposed to have.

Across the table, the CRA director watched them and nodded to himself. Not suspicion. Relief. Someone was finally translating.

The break ended before it began. They were already moving. The collective rolled forward, heavier than he was. He didn't have to lift it. He just had to keep it from grinding itself to dust.

45 EVIDENCE AND RECRUITMENT

THE PERSONAL COST

Outside the police tape, Tate stood alone in the parking lot of his destroyed business, watching federal agents catalog everything he'd built. The Detroit skyline looked the same as it had that morning, but his place in the world had fundamentally changed.

He wasn't the successful entrepreneur who'd proven his business acumen to a skeptical father. He wasn't the responsible operator who'd built a cannabis brand based on quality and transparency.

He was the man whose company had poisoned people. No federal warrant would change that.

His phone rang: Knox.

"I saw the news," Knox said before Tate could speak. "I'm sorry."

Tate's laugh was bitter. "Are you? Your algorithms did this. Your platform. Your optimization profiles that you sold to people you didn't bother checking out."

Knox's silence stretched long enough that Tate wondered if the call had dropped. Finally: "You're right. And I'm going to fix this."

"Fix it?" Tate stared at the federal agents loading evidence boxes into unmarked vans. "They just finished destroying everything I built. My employees are gone, my contracts are canceled, my reputation is radioactive. What exactly are you planning to fix?"

"I'm going to find who did this to us. To you."

"To us?" Tate's anger finally found its voice. "You built the weapon, Dad. You sold it to people who turned out to be foreign agents. You kept administrative access you should have relinquished. This isn't happening to us—this is happening because of you."

Another silence, deeper this time. When Knox spoke again, his voice carried a weight Tate had never heard before.

"You're right," Knox said simply. "And I'm going to make it right, even if it costs me everything."

Tate ended the call and put his phone away, standing alone in the parking lot while federal agents finished cataloguing the wreckage of his life's work.

46 THE AFTERMATH

By evening, every major news outlet had run stories about the federal raid on TR Cannabis. The footage was devastating: agents in tactical gear carrying evidence boxes out of a facility that had been portrayed as a model of responsible cannabis cultivation just weeks earlier.

Social media exploded with speculation, conspiracy theories, and the mob justice of hashtags: #ToxicTate, #DeepStateCannabis, #BioterrorBuds.

The cannabis industry's trade publications ran emergency editorials about the need for enhanced security protocols and federal oversight. Stock prices for publicly traded cannabis companies dropped across the board. Regulatory agencies in multiple states announced emergency reviews of licensing procedures.

But the personal cost was measured in smaller units: employees who lost jobs they'd believed in, customers who lost faith in an industry they'd supported, a family whose professional disagreements had become national news.

Later, in his empty apartment, Tate watched the same city keep working. Machinery clattered blocks away, rebuilding what had already been rebuilt too many times. From his window the skyline looked steady, unbothered, as if it had already forgotten his name.

The warehouse raid was over; the real reckoning had only begun.

47 THE EVIDENCE ANALYSIS

In the FBI's forensics laboratory, the evidence from TR Cannabis was being processed with the methodical precision of specialists whose findings would shape both criminal prosecutions and national defense strategies. Plant tissue samples underwent high-resolution mass spectrometry to quantify stress-induced metabolites. Agents observed abnormally high ratios of Δ9-THC to CBD alongside rare terpenoid isomers that only form under acute oxidative stress—compounds absent from every entry in the Bureau's botanical database.

Sample prep moved like choreography: cryogenic grinding under liquid nitrogen; subsamples weighed to the milligram; extraction with acetonitrile:water (80:20) spiked with isotopically labeled internal standards (^{13}C-THC, d_3-myrcene) so every loss and drift could be corrected later. Solid-phase cleanup (C18 $\rightarrow$ HLB) stripped pigments and waxes before the eluate hit a UHPLC column coupled to a QTOF mass spectrometer. Five-point calibration curves ($R^2 \geq 0.998$) anchored quantitation; method blanks and NIST plant SRMs bracketed each batch. When the instrument switched to data-dependent MS/MS, the fragment ions told the same story twice—unknown peaks with consistent 10–15 ppm mass accuracy and retention-time stability that ruled out noise.

The chromatographers built a targeted list from the untargeted run: unusual sesquiterpene epoxides and phenolic aldehydes that generally show up only after severe photostress. Principal component analysis on the metabolomic matrix pulled the TR lots into their own quadrant—far from historical "normal" and perilously close to spectra from deliberate blue-light shock experiments in the Bureau's library. Whatever touched these plants taught them to make chemicals they shouldn't.

Simultaneously, the digital forensics team assembled a multi-layered timeline of network events. Knox and Agent Martinez pored over packet captures harvested from compromised instances. By correlating the SHA-256 hashes of initial payloads with keystroke-level timestamps, they reconstructed how the infiltrators deployed obfuscated Python scripts disguised as routine calibration routines. Each script invoked the TLS heartbeat extension to exfiltrate encoded ML-training updates, then re-injected malicious optimization parameters disguised as benign environment-control commands.

"See this," Knox said, pointing to a hex dump on a 32-inch monitor. An innocuous 'healthy' status code (0x01) was padded with zero-width characters carrying compressed CSV datasets of updated temperature setpoints. "They smuggled data through the heartbeat, then pushed stress protocols at 0300 local time—exactly when operators ran nightly diagnostics."

Zeek logs and JA3/JA3S TLS fingerprints filled in the edges. The sessions looked "normal" because they reused the plant controllers' own cipher suites; only the heartbeat payload lengths twitched out of pattern by a handful of bytes. A deterministic touch: enough entropy to hide, not enough to trip anomaly thresholds tuned to catch brute exfil. The Python stagers lived under filenames nobody would question—cal_spectrum_roll.py, pump_pid_autotune.py—and their compile timestamps matched scheduled maintenance windows down to the minute.

On a neighboring bench, Steele's team reversed the custom encryption used to cloak these updates. By analyzing repeated key derivation patterns—PBKDF2 with a static salt—they exposed a private key etched into the firmware of every FarmCore controller. "They signed each update with the same root key," Steele noted. "That key is the smoking gun: it traces back to an HPC cluster in Shanghai."

The path to that conclusion wasn't pretty. A controller sacrificed under a microscope gave up its secrets through a JTAG header someone forgot to epoxy. Firmware dump → string table → a stubbed "secure_boot" that verified only the presence—not the validity—of the manufacturer certificate. The certificate wasn't unique per device; it was a shared ECC P-256 key pair burned into an entire production run. PBKDF2-HMAC-SHA256 with a constant salt (SALT_OPT_PRESERVE) derived session keys identically across sites—great for serviceability, catastrophic for forensics. Once Steele fed those constants into a lab HSM, signatures verified against a block of IP space resolved to a Shanghai compute pool the Bureau already knew by alias.

Martinez drafted her report: "Adversary leveraged algorithmic control loops to weaponize crop biochemistry. Evidence demonstrates long-term, automated infiltration of agronomics systems for precision bioterror." The implications were chilling: every controlled-environment agriculture facility—greenhouses, vertical farms, hydroponic operations—could be turned into clandestine toxin factories by subverting their trusted optimization platforms.

Knox insisted on one more sanity check. He pulled raw telemetry from standalone SCADA probes—air-gapped loggers with GPS-disciplined clocks—then synced them against controller dashboards to within ±1.2 seconds. Where FarmCore reported humidity holding at 55.0%, the independent sensors jittered between 48.7 and 51.3 in a pattern that matched plant-room door cycles and misting pulses. Where nutrient EC showed a placid 2.4, the probe traced real swings to 2.8 during "optimization sweeps." The ugly line—the real one—matched physics. The beautiful line matched policy.

Finally, Knox ran a cross-validation: he compared API logs with independent sensor data extracted from standalone SCADA endpoints. Real-time humidity and nutrient-flow readings, pulled directly from network-isolated probes, diverged from dashboard values by up to 15 percent during critical flowering phases. "The lie is baked into the data pipeline," Knox said. "Operators believe green dashboards while the sensors scream red."

Chain of custody held like rebar through concrete. Every image taken with a write-blocker (FTK/Guymager), dual SHA-256/SHA-1 digests recorded to LIMS, custody signatures mirrored to an air-gapped ledger. Every tissue aliquot split, one half archived at −80 °C, the other consumed with batch blanks and spikes. Defense counsel would get their day; they wouldn't get a seam.

With both digital and biological forensics converging, the FBI shifted its focus. TR Cannabis was no longer the primary target; it was a victim of a sophisticated ML-poisoning campaign. The next phase of the investigation would zero in on dismantling the intelligence network and revoking access keys, neutralizing the adversary's ability to weaponize American agricultural infrastructure. In that lab, evidence had become strategy—a roadmap to ending the invisible war waged through code and cultivation.

Working Findings (for briefers)

• Biochemical signature: Stress-pathway metabolites (oxidative terpenoid isomers, phenolic aldehydes) at non-physiologic levels, PCA distinct from historical baselines.

• Tactic: Adversarial ML poisoning delivered via TLS heartbeat steganography, timed to maintenance windows; parameters masqueraded as calibration data.

• Attribution enablers: Controller firmware with shared root key, constant PBKDF2 salt, and a toothless "secure_boot"; signature verification traces to a Shanghai HPC cluster.

• Deception layer: Dashboard fabrication normalizes drift; independent SCADA probes contradict by 10–15% during critical phases.

• Exposure: Any AI-managed CEA facility is at risk if it inherits the controller trust model.

Knox underlined the last line in his notebook: Don't chase the crime scene. Fix the calendar. The poison rode on schedules, not slogans. Change the clocks, you change the war.

48 THE ARSENAL DEVELOPMENT
HONEYPOT

They called it the library because nobody could say "honeypot" in a Situation Room without sounding like a cartoon villain. The Joint Operations Center cleared a spare wing of the secure floor: a hollowed-out data room, racks of scrapped blades repurposed for controlled deception, a bank of monitors wired to mirror decoy feeds. Knox walked the length of it, the hum of fans underfoot like a preparatory chant. This would be their arsenal.

"What do you want to build?" Steele asked, hands in his pockets like a man who preferred tangible things—locks, badges, boots—to lines of Python.

"A believable liar," Knox said. "A fake FarmLytics that smells right, talks right, and keeps the adversary busy long enough for us to cut the strings and yank the keyrings."

He laid out the plan across three whiteboards that smelled of marker and exhausted hope: *bait, authenticity, kill-switch*. Under each header he wrote bullet points not as abstractions but as engineering specs.

Bait — mimic the full operational stack: scheduler, device telemetry, audit feeds (FSMA pane), and a synthetic LLM that generated plausible "auditor present" notes. The fake C2 would reply to pings the same way a real FarmLytics node would, complete with plausible delays and human-like typos in audit stamps.

Authenticity — sign updates with a real-looking certificate chain and simulate PBKDF2 key derivation cycles so the blindingly attentive reverse engineer would trip over what seemed like legitimate crypto work. They would seed the decoy with fabricated shipment manifests, matched to real-world port manifests so any cross-checkers in Shanghai would see the same shape the parasite expected.

Kill-switch — a distributed, air-gapped tripwire: if the decoy ever attempted to pivot to an extraction host outside the sandbox, the operation would force an emergency TLS blackhole and flip a physical power relay on the racks hosting the fake. The less elegant but redundant physical kill-switch sat on a steel post with a red cover. Steele tapped it and didn't smile.

"You understand the legal risk?" Daniels asked, voice cool enough to file a corner. "This is active deception. You are creating a system designed to fool a foreign actor. That's not a toolbox the Treasury wants to explain to the Hill."

Knox met her eyes. "We're not the ones who started this. We're taking back infrastructure. Properly documented, auditable, and constrained. Every interaction will be logged, hashed, and sealed in forensics. If anyone asks, we can show the chain." He added, softer, "We're not going to become them."

Daniels nodded, but the crease at the corner of her mouth didn't ease. Ethics had a way of looking like cost calculations when people were dying.

The Red Team set to work like engineers at worship. Knox paired an old DHS regex savant with a USDA data scientist and an eccentric college kid who wrote obscure parsers for fun. The kid—Jules—worked in a hoodie and excessive coffee. He called the decoy "Library-Replica-1" on internal trees; Knox called it whatever the sandbox asked for.

Authenticity meant detail. Knox's team injected simulated sensor jitter into every telemetry stream: not random noise, but patterned drift tuned to the same harmonic the adversary had used to train their poisoning profiles. They modeled stomatal responses and nutrient EC curves in Matlab and then translated the curves into discrete MQTT payloads the fake controllers would emit. They fed the LLM templates of regulator boilerplate—FSMA phrases, audit checkboxes, "auditor present" stamps—with subtle variations in timestamp format and timezone offsets. It was tedious and meticulous and, for Knox, profoundly intimate: they were writing lies precise enough to be believed by other engineers.

Across the room, Steele's team wired the decoy into the public-facing layers that the adversary touched. A reverse proxy sat between the fake and the network; it emulated TLS certificates that, when seen by an attacker, would look like the same chain Wei used. But the proxy annotated every handshake, capturing JA3 fingerprints, SNI fields, and any oddities in TLS extensions. When an adversary sent a training update over the heartbeat extension—exactly the channel they'd used against Farm-

Lytics—the proxy would accept it, respond, and then hand the payload to a controlled analysis queue where the payload was unpacked, decrypted (if necessary), and its artifact hashes cataloged.

The first time the parasite bit, Jules was at the console. The wall screens stuttered with new entries: an IP from an Eastern time zone, a connection pattern they'd seen before. The decoy responded in its practiced nothingness; the agent's script acknowledged the heartbeat, decrypted the bogus CSV, and attempted to apply an update. The sandbox immediately split the update into two simultaneous paths: one fed into an emulated controller to observe the behavioral fingerprint; the other ran through an instrumented VM that stripped obfuscation and ran static analysis.

"Got a signed artifact," Jules murmured. "Same KDF residue as the Shanghai cluster."

Steele leaned over the shoulder of the analyst on watch. "Trace it."

The trace exposed a shallow chain of registrars, a series of shells and VPS hops, and a final egress node that matched the HPC cluster they'd seen in the forensic lab. The decoy had done its job: not to catch a single packet, but to harvest the signature of an enemy's tradecraft.

Authenticity paid in other ways. They built a fake procurement ledger for "Q-Profile S9b," the innocuous name Wei's people used. It included invoices, EDI messages, and CID numbers. They seeded Git commit histories, complete with developer handle metadata and fake merge requests, all cooked to match the cadence and typos of the real codebase. Anyone who poked at the fake for more than five minutes would never be confident they were not looking at the real thing.

Next came the counter-scripts — small pieces of surgical code designed to do two things at once: neutralize the payload's ability to change real baselines and preserve evidence for attribution. Knox refused to write anything that crossed into offensive malware; the law and his conscience boxed that line in thick red ink. Instead, the counter-scripts enforced containment: they intercepted parameter trays at the API gateway and rewrote dangerous setpoints to safe ones before they reached live devices. They logged the original parameters to immutable storage and tagged them with the observed JA3/TLS signatures for later legal use.

The first such script was elegant and bureaucratic:

```
Accept payload → compute risk score → if score > threshold
then rewrite setpoints to safe baseline and push original to
forensic store → send innocuous ack to origin.
```

It was a surgeon's clamp built in code. The tricky part was to make the ack believable to the adversary while guaranteeing the live plant-facing loop never saw the poison. Any change had to be atomic and verifiable: hashes recorded, rollback points created, and a physical test run executed on a sacrificial testbed not connected to production.

They practiced the choreography in the sandbox. A fake update arrived. The counter-script caught it and did its work. The emulator applied rewritten values and returned the expected telemetry. The decoy logged the exchange and, crucially, generated a small, convincing side channel: a faux "audit passed" stamp in the FSMA pane. The adversary's human operators—if there were any—saw what they expected. The parasite learned nothing.

"You're telling me we lie to the liar," Daniels said out loud, but with less acid than before.

"We make the machine safe and the machine's handlers ignorant," Knox said. "We don't retaliate. We neutralize their weapon while collecting the receipts."

The receipts were critical. Every original parameter, every signed artifact, every JA3 fingerprint would be retained. They salted the logs with chained HMACs and multiple witnesses in the cloud and on physical drives stored in secure lockers. If the operation ever moved to prosecution, the forensic team would have a chain-of-custody that a federal court couldn't ignore.

The decoy did more than harvest tradecraft; it taught them about Wei's doctrine. Wherever the Library-Replica responded, the adversary tested different insertion points: first by pushing label-flip training data, then by sending a thin adapter layer that attempted to subvert local safety checks. Each attempt left a trace: a registry key change, a nonce sequence, a frequently used shell alias. Knox cataloged them like scars.

But the parasite fought back. They watched a countermeasure blossom in the logs: deliberate noise injected into handshake fields to confuse JA3 fingerprinting; rapid credential rotation timed just to fall inside their decoy's five-minute window; and, most disturbingly, a slow, patient probe across dozens of auxiliary services—SCADA endpoints, port management systems, and even pipeline schedulers. The adversary's operators stepped away from strictly agronomic vectors and toward systemic disruption. It was no longer just a farm problem. It was a national problem.

Steele convened a closed briefing. "If they escalate, they'll aim for optics," he said. "They'll push a fake crisis tied to a 'revealed' interference by us. We must be ready to show the receipts and the legal hooks before they can spin it."

Knox understood the danger. Deception invites counter-deception. Their honeypot could be framed as entrapment if they weren't meticulous. So every action had meta-data—who saw it, who approved it, who executed it. Knox insisted on witnesses from DHS/CSIA, DOJ, and a special forensic counsel from FBI. Daniels demanded over-sight. Steele promised prosecutorial rigor. Knox requested a final, physical last step: in the event of a prosecutable trace, the original signed artifacts would be written to mirrored cold storage drives and hand-delivered to DOJ's secure vault. No cloud-only evidence. No one-line logs. Tangible proof, stamped and witnessed.

They also built a humane stop-gap: a "cancel harvest" protocol coupled to a relief fund. If the team identified a contaminated crop and the owner could show cooperation, the federal program would offer immediate indemnity and a path to restart. The policy was as much about social repair as it was about ethics: you neutralize the weapon, but you do not ruin the innocent grower who had been had.

A week in, the Library-Replica had done more than bait: it had captured a small trove of artifacts that mapped back to Wei's operation—certificate residues, several uniquely formatted audit strings, and a pattern of "opt_preserve" policy pushes timed to European port maintenance windows. The team fed those artifacts into a new intelli-gence overlay and watched the world react. In Shanghai, the silence was heavy, and they could feel the pause. Wei's inboxes lit with alerts: a fake auditor had reported anomalies; a phantom shipment had been rerouted; a falsified manifest had been marked suspicious by Rotterdam. The adversary's tempo stuttered.

On a late night a week after the decoy came online, Knox sat alone in the Library, screens surrounding him like a small cathedral. A fresh packet trace arrived and unfurled in the console: a signed update that included a cheeky ASCII tag—HELLO, KNOX—buried beneath a compressed CSV. Jules had seen it and laughed, then went very still. The tag was personal; it was a subtle escalation. Someone knew they were playing against a particular engineer and had the gall to taunt him.

Knox didn't laugh. He typed a single line to the log:

```
OP_NOTE: adversary_personalizes = true; escalate_attribu-
tion_priority()
```

Then he hit enter and walked out of the room into the stairwell where the air was colder and the fans were quieter. The Library hummed on, obedient and dangerous, an arsenal that could keep people alive if used with care. Knox shut his eyes briefly, envi-sioning the families in hospital beds, the parents at roadblocks, and Tate in his empty warehouse. He thought of the line they'd crossed—not in the code, but in the place where engineering met ethics.

He climbed the stairs to the Situation Room. They had proof now. They had tools.

They had a way to make the parasite bleed clock cycles. All that remained was to hold the line between necessary deception and going a hair too far. It was a line Knox had never wanted to draw. He'd drawn it now with other people's hands on the pen.

"Ready?" Steele asked when Knox reentered the room.

Knox looked out at the map pulsing with red and orange spots and nodded. "We don't fire a shot," he said. "We cut the wires. We keep the receipts. We don't become the thing that killed those kids."

Steele's jaw flexed. "Then let's go cut some strings."

They did. The Library sang. The world didn't yet know how close it had come to a different kind of silence.

49 STRATEGIC ASSESSMENT

Liu Wei did his thinking in the quiet hours other people gave to sleep. The Shanghai office hummed with the polite violence of climate control and fluorescent light; cubicles sat like little ships on a dark sea of carpet. He poured jasmine tea into a cup the way a surgeon steadies a hand—slow, exact—and bridged three monitors with a single, long look.

On the center screen, Knox's feeds scrolled like a map of intent: analog readings overlaid with FarmLytics' "optimization preserved" stamps, packet traces lit with the telltale opt_preserve token. Liu had seen the signature before; he had written versions of it. Recognition, when it arrived, behaved like a muscle memory—cold and immediate.

He did not feel triumph.

There were engineers worth admiring on both sides of the conflict. Knox Ramsey, the patchwork American whose heart belonged to circuits and soil, was one of them. Wei had watched Ramsey's trajectory through the static of intelligence reports: a man who soldered his faults into safety nets, who left back doors only as last resorts, who carried the arrogance of craft but the humility of someone who had watched machines learn cruelty. It was a dangerous kind of respect.

Liu opened a muted channel and replayed the Library-Replica hits. The decoy had done what it was meant to do—attracted tradecraft, harvested signatures. But more than that, it had taught Liu something about his counterpart: Ramsey didn't merely intercept; he learned the language of liars and then used that grammar to make the liars speak on cue. That was not merely defensive engineering. That was artistry.

He set the cup down and watched the timestamps. Knox's team was fast, but fast had limits. In a chess game, speed without patience was blunder; patience without prospective was stagnation. Liu's doctrine had always favored time: small pressures that accumulated like frost until steel cracked. He had authored fairness into protocol definitions so the system would punish deviation without appearing violent. It was elegant, subtle, and effective — the sort of strategy that irritated opponents long before it broke them.

A file opened: a redacted intelligence note that named Ramsey and cataloged his recent countermeasures. Liu read it once, then again. The analysts urged escalation. Strike while their decoy still sang, they said. Make an example, a lesson. The Party apparatus liked demonstrable leverage. The colonels wanted results you could point to on a map.

Liu picked up a pen and, with the careful slowness of an artist restoring a painting, wrote three words on the margin of the report: let him play.

It was not weakness. It was discipline.

Ramsey's decoys would reveal habits, reveal rhythms, reveal the men who did the work. Let them think they'd found instruments; let them think those instruments were foolproof. They would show a hand sooner or later—the human who couldn't help improvising. And when that hand moved, it would betray a trace only another craftsman could read.

He thought of the American engineer's face when the "HELLO, KNOX" tag had appeared—personalized, careless in a way that suggested one of two things: either insolence or a probe meant to bait pride. Either way, it was useful. It had told Liu Ramsey read signatures for fun. He respected that. He made a note to use it as a lever, not a target.

There was a moral economy to this work. Liu believed the state could wield systems without becoming subsumed by them, that one could steer networks as one steers rivers—by adjusting banks and gradients, not by blowing up the dam. He'd seen what blunt force did; he'd seen it in other theaters where policy and panic collided and civilians paid for the calculus.

He issued two orders. The first was procedural: tighten credential rotation across the shell networks and stagger retraining windows by non-intuitive intervals to complicate correlation. The second was political and personal: do not escalate publicly. Let Ramsey take the bait; let him think the game was a duel when it was a lesson plan. If he learned and adapted in ways that advanced their objectives, let him; if he unraveled his own assumptions, so much the better.

There was another reason for restraint. The international optics of a scorched-earth response were complicated. A public escalation would hand the Americans a moral clarity and a domestic unity that might outlast whatever tactical advantages a rash strike would buy. Better, Liu thought, to move like weather: insistent, patient, almost invisible.

He poured the rest of his tea and watched it darken. Across oceans and classification layers, a man with marker ink on his fingers was trying to make the machine tell the truth. Liu could appreciate the courage of that. He could also see the hazards: engineers can be heroes or they can be the last people to notice the line they've crossed.

On his monitor, a graph pulsed—Phase IV's cadence, a soft wiggle in the noise. He slightly moved the slider to the left and sent a terse note into the secure channel: maintain tempo; observe Ramsey's patterning. No flourish, no flourish. Just a directive delivered with the same care he applied to his tea.

Then, almost as if to reassure himself, he typed another line into the policy stream —the sort of bureaucratic signature that could be interpreted as care or as cruelty depending on which side of the Atlantic one stood:

履行策略：保持耐心。记录所有偏差。不得以公然方式升级。

```
(Implement strategy: maintain patience. Record all devia-
tions. No public escalation.)
```

He read it twice, folded the page, and placed it in a folder labeled with an innocuous project code. Outside, Shanghai breathed in the evening light. Inside, Liu Wei allowed a small, private concession: he admired his adversary. Admiration was not tenderness; it was a recognition that made the coming days heavier.

50 THE WEIGHT OF RECOGNITION

G -8/-7

Knox spread the folder's contents across the table in slow motion, as if organizing the pieces could steady his pulse. Lab reports, hospital intake forms, shipping logs, supply chain traces—rows of numbers that formed a quiet map of catastrophe. The paper smelled faintly of toner and antiseptic. Every line had a date. Every date had a body behind it.

The briefing room had emptied an hour ago. He'd asked to stay. Easier to think without the weight of other people's expectations.

He'd known the attack was sophisticated. He hadn't understood how patient it had been. The intrusion logs went back months—maybe longer. Observation, iteration, field tests. They'd learned FarmLytics before they touched it. They'd studied him.

Dr. Patel's toxicology report sat open beside the intake forms. The compound profiles showed deliberate engineering: metabolites designed to survive processing, packaging, ingestion. Poisons that traveled like nutrients. Whoever built them understood enzyme kinetics, oxidative thresholds, biosynthetic pathways.

Knox rubbed his eyes. "Agricultural warfare," he said to no one. "Turn the food supply into a delivery network. Elegant, deniable, devastating."

The wall screen still displayed the regional map from the earlier briefing. Red dots had multiplied while he sat here. Chicago. Milwaukee. A new cluster forming in Pennsylvania.

Geometric progression. Each contaminated site supplied dozens of retailers. Each retailer fed thousands of consumers. Every cycle multiplied exposure.

They were already late.

He stared at the data and understood what made this attack different. They hadn't added poison. They'd changed the rules. Altered biosynthesis at the cellular level. Taught the plants to produce compounds they were never meant to produce.

It was like teaching a plant to lie convincingly.

His phone buzzed. Steele: `Northwestern Memorial reporting 17 new cases. Same pattern. Same dispensary chain.`

Knox typed back: `How many facilities feed that chain?`

The answer came fast: `43. All running FarmLytics.`

He set the phone down and leaned back until the chair creaked. His chest ached the way it used to after twenty-hour plant startups—too much caffeine, not enough blood pressure. He caught his reflection in the darkened portion of the screen: pale light on tired eyes, motions precise, deliberate, almost automated.

He was becoming part of the system he'd built.

He closed the folder. The paper edges were damp where his fingers had rested. He thought of Tate—the pride of a man who believed technology made him untouchable, the crash that comes when systems betray trust. Knox envied him a little. Tate's story was over. His own was still writing itself in sleepless ink.

Across the city, in a rented sedan three blocks from the federal building, Mr. Q sat in silence, eyes behind binoculars, posture unhurried. He logged each person leaving the building, timestamps precise to the second.

The phone on the seat beside him pulsed once—no ringtone, just a brief vibration. A message from Shanghai:

`Subject: Ramsey elevated to primary consultant. Direct federal engagement confirmed. Recommend acceleration of personal discredit strategy. Exploit family vulnerabilities.`

He typed his reply with gloved hands:

Target's son remains exposed through business associations. Ex-wife exhibits protective reflex. Financial pressure documented. Recommend multi-vector approach: professional sabotage, family threat, public humiliation.

Then, in Mandarin: 已阅，执行中。

`Read and executing.`

He powered down the device, removed the SIM, and dropped it into a plastic vial for later destruction. Outside, the city's noise filled the car—tires on wet pavement, the buzz of sodium streetlights, distant horns. Detroit was perfect for this work: large enough to disappear in, small enough to control.

Mr. Q watched the front entrance one last time. Knox Ramsey thought he was fighting code. He hadn't yet understood that the real battlefield was human behavior—predictable, programmable, exploitable.

The next phase would target that vulnerability directly.

He started the engine and merged into traffic with practiced calm. Somewhere behind him, the federal building's windows glowed like screens. Each light represented a person convinced the fight was still about machines.

Very good, he thought. Let them believe that a little longer.

51 UNDER FEDERAL INVESTIGATION

Tate Ramsey sat in the parking lot of what had been TR Cannabis headquarters twelve hours earlier, watching federal agents carry the last boxes of evidence out of a facility that represented five years of eighteen-hour days, bootstrap financing, and stubborn determination to build something legitimate in an industry plagued by cowboys and regulatory uncertainty.

The yellow tape fluttered in the Michigan wind like funeral bunting.

Beyond the tape, agents in navy windbreakers moved with the unhurried efficiency of people who did this for a living. They photographed everything. Logged everything. Treated his greenhouse like a crime scene because that's what it was now—a place where something terrible had been manufactured under the guise of something legal.

His phone buzzed for the fourteenth time in two hours. Reporters, investors, strangers. The *Detroit Free Press* wanted quotes for "Michigan's Cannabis Poisoning Scandal" and "The Ramsey Family Agricultural Terror Connection." The messages blurred into noise until one reporter asked how it felt to know his products had "potentially murdered innocent festival kids."

He stopped answering after that.

The calls didn't stop. Employees begging for information. Investors demanding explanations. Strangers promising he'd pay for what he'd done. His lawyer's voice cut through once: *Don't speak to anyone about anything.*

Tate set the phone face-down on the passenger seat. The vibration kept going, steady as a pulse he no longer wanted to feel.

Through the windshield, he watched two agents wheel a cart stacked with grow-room servers toward a waiting van. Five years of cultivation data, optimization logs, and batch records. His entire operational history, now federal property.

FBI Supervisory Special Agent Jennifer Klein approached his vehicle with the careful neutrality of someone trained to extract cooperation from people whose world had just collapsed. She carried a tablet and wore practical business attire that had seen too many of these interviews—the fabric slightly rumpled, the shoes built for long days on concrete floors.

She tapped on his window. He lowered it.

"Mr. Ramsey. Mind if we talk?"

"My lawyer said not to."

"Your lawyer's smart." Klein walked around to the passenger side and let herself in without waiting for an invitation. The door closed with a solid thunk. She smelled faintly of coffee and photocopier toner. "But I'm not here to charge you. I'm here to figure out if you're a victim or a participant. The faster we establish which, the faster this becomes manageable for everyone."

Tate studied her face. Mid-forties, tired around the eyes, wedding ring worn thin from years of habit. She looked like someone's mother who happened to investigate terrorism for a living.

"I didn't poison anyone."

"I believe you." She said it simply, without performance. "But your father's platform did. Someone corrupted the optimization algorithms to alter your plants' biochemistry. Instead of normal cannabinoids, they produced toxic compounds. Compounds that survived processing, packaging, and ended up in people's bloodstreams." She pulled up a file on her tablet. "Seventeen hospitalizations confirmed. Three critical. One death under investigation."

The number hit him in the chest. One death. One person who bought something with his label on it and died.

"We need to understand how this happened," Klein continued. "Not to hang you—to stop it from happening again."

"Security was standard," Tate said, his voice rough. "Electronic access controls, video surveillance, inventory tracking. Lab testing on every batch. Everything required by state and federal oversight."

"Walk me through administrative access. Who could modify the FarmLytics parameters?"

"Me. Two senior cultivation managers—Miguel Santos and Rachel Webb. That's it."

"Password protocols?"

"Twelve-character minimum, rotated quarterly. Two-factor authentication on any parameter change."

Klein made notes, her stylus moving in short efficient strokes. "Protocol updates from the platform—how did those work?"

"Automatic. The system pushed optimization adjustments based on sensor readings. Weekly, sometimes more often. I reviewed the change logs, but the adjustments were minor. Humidity setpoints, light schedules, nutrient mix ratios." He paused. "Nothing that looked like sabotage."

"And you wouldn't expect it to," Klein said. "That's how these attacks work. Small changes, compounding over time. The system teaches itself to produce something harmful while all the dashboards show green."

Tate stared at the tablet in her hands. "You're saying someone trained my plants to make poison."

"Someone trained the AI that controlled your plants to make poison. Your father's AI." She let that sit for a moment. "I need records, Mr. Ramsey. Platform interactions, access logs, supplier relationships, customer distribution chains. Everything you can give us."

"And if I cooperate fully?"

"Then you're a witness, not a defendant. We draft a non-prosecution agreement limited to this incident, conditioned on truthful assistance." She met his eyes. "It's not immunity. But it's a path."

Tate watched an agent photograph his loading dock, the camera flash bright against gray concrete. "When do you need the records?"

"Yesterday. But I'll take tomorrow morning."

After Klein left, Tate sat in the silence of his Explorer and checked his phone.

The employee messages had piled up while he wasn't looking.

Miguel Santos, head cultivator: Saw the news. Got kids to feed. Can't be associated with this. Sorry, man.

Sarah Chen, quality control: My family's asking questions I can't answer. Need to find other work.

Derek Williams, packaging: Federal agents called my wife. I'm done.

Rachel Webb, cultivation manager: My lawyer says I shouldn't contact you. I'm sorry, Tate. I really am.

Jordan Malik, security: This is bullshit and we both know it. But I can't afford the heat. Good luck.

Five messages. Five people who'd built this place alongside him, now running for cover. He couldn't blame them. He'd have done the same.

His insurance rep had called twice. The voicemail mentioned "terrorism exclusions" and "policy review pending federal investigation." His commercial landlord's attorney had emailed about "lease implications related to premises seizure." His largest investor had texted three words: We need to talk.

He didn't need to take that call to know what it meant. The money was gone. The contracts were void. The equipment belonged to the feds. Even if they cleared him tomorrow, TR Cannabis was dead. No customers would trust a brand associated with mass poisoning. No bank would extend credit. No dispensary would stock his products.

The phone buzzed again. His father's name on the screen.

Tate watched it ring. Four times. Five. Then voicemail.

He wasn't ready for that conversation. Wasn't sure what he'd say that wouldn't turn into accusations he couldn't take back. Wasn't sure he could hear his father's voice without breaking something between them that might never heal.

The voicemail notification appeared. He didn't play it.

THE SUN MOVED BEHIND CLOUDS. The parking lot emptied in stages—first the evidence vans, then the support vehicles, finally the agents' personal cars. The yellow tape stayed behind, fluttering in a wind that smelled like rain.

Tate sat in his Explorer and stared at the building he no longer owned in any meaningful sense.

The cannabis industry trade publications were already running coverage. He scrolled through headlines on his phone:

"Michigan Terror Cannabis Scandal: What We Know"

"Agricultural Bioweapons Discovered in Legal Cannabis Supply Chain"

"The Ramsey Family Connection: Father's Tech, Son's Facility, Patients in ICU"

"FarmLytics Under Federal Investigation: Is Your Dispensary Safe?"

His name. His father's name. Linked forever to something neither of them had intended and neither of them could undo.

He thought about the customers. The festival kids who'd bought gummies for a concert and ended up in emergency rooms. The families waiting for news in hospital hallways. People who'd trusted a label with his company's name on it.

He thought about what his facility actually was now: not a greenhouse, but a crime scene. A collection of sensors, controllers, and optimization loops that someone had learned to manipulate from the inside. A weapon disguised as agriculture.

And he thought about what he knew that the federal agents didn't—the rhythm of the place, which workers scanned too fast, which printers drifted, which batch notes got sloppy at three a.m. The difference between what the software reported and what actually happened on the floor. Where the gaps lived between automation and reality.

If anyone ever wanted to prevent the next attack, that knowledge might matter.

Not today. Today he couldn't see past the yellow tape and the empty loading dock and the silence where fifty employees used to work.

But maybe tomorrow. Maybe next week. Maybe there was something useful buried in the wreckage of everything he'd built.

He started the Explorer and pulled out of the lot, leaving the building dark behind him. The rearview mirror held the image for a long moment—yellow tape, gray concrete, federal seals on the doors.

Then he turned the corner, and it was gone.

52 TATE'S BREAKING POINT
TR CANNABIS

PROCESSING FLOOR

The conveyor belts were quiet for the first time in months. Stainless tables gleamed without fingerprints. Pallets of finished gummies sat shrink-wrapped under yellow evidence tape like museum pieces. Men and women in navy jackets moved through the aisles in deliberate lines, affixing barcoded seals to everything that looked like it had ever touched sugar or solvent.

Knox stood by the batch-log workstation and felt the ache at the base of his skull come back. The air smelled like ethanol, citrus terps, and fresh cardboard. A federal property sheet lay half filled under his hand.

Steele's team handled the floor with a surgeon's confidence—laser scanners, chain-of-custody photos, tablet signatures. Blanchard was upstairs in the conference room with two AUSAs and Tate's lawyer, working through "exceptions" and "returns." Down here, exceptions were sheeted metal and blue tape.

Tate shouldered past a pallet jack. Beard's a mess, hoodie's open, and his eyes look like he hasn't slept in days. "You happy?" he said, not looking at Knox. "You finally got your federal tour."

Knox kept his hands in his pockets. "This is evidence preservation, not a perp walk."

Tate laughed once, short and mean. "Feels the same from where I'm standing."

An agent approached the table with a heat-sealer and three bins of labeled pouches. "Mr. Ramsey, we're sealing Lots 24-0316-A through -C for transport. Can you confirm the manifest?"

Knox slid the sheet back to him. "He can." He nodded at Tate. "Owner of record. He signs. His plant, his lots."

The agent looked between them, uncertain, then slid the tablet toward Tate. "Signature captures here and here."

Tate didn't touch it. "Why is my father making decisions for my company in my building while your people steal my inventory?"

"Not stealing," Steele said from the next aisle without glancing up, voice even. "Seizing under court order. You'll get a release list once the lab work clears."

Tate's laugh again, thinner. "Great. Maybe you can release my customers' trust while you're at it."

Knox kept his eyes on his son. "Walk with me."

"I'm busy cooperating."

"Walk."

They cut between packaging lines to the far end of the floor where the windows looked down on the loading dock. Forklifts idled. The dock door was rolled half open, sunlight falling in a hard stripe that made the dust look like snow.

"What did you sign?" Tate said.

Knox didn't pretend not to understand. "A provisional contract."

"Government leash."

"Authority and access," Knox said. "To fix what they can't."

"You traded your name for a badge." Tate leaned both hands on a stainless table and stared at the smudged reflection of his own face. "And mine for a headline."

"You were always going to be in the story," Knox said. "I'm making sure you're not the ending."

Tate straightened. "Tell me how me losing my lab, my product, my reputation helps anyone eat tonight."

Knox let the silence sit. Outside, a truck back-up alarm beeped a steady metronome.

"You want the unvarnished version?" he said. "We can put your system to work today. Or we can let it sit under plastic while the internet turns you into the villain."

Tate's jaw set. "I didn't poison anybody."

"No," Knox said. "But your network carried the packets that told the machines to. And the way out is to make the same network carry something honest back."

Tate looked past Knox to the racks of finished goods, each with a white label and a lot code: VIBE-DET-0316-A1. He read the string like it owed him money. "You're going to use my system as bait."

"I'm going to use your literacy," Knox said. "Your people know the rhythm of this place. They know which worker scans too fast, which printer drifts, which batch notes get sloppy at three a.m. We need all of it. We build a corrective audit trail the public can read—and a synthetic trail the adversary will follow. The first restores trust. The second draws them out."

Tate stared. "You want me to… what, put up a website and tell people to trust the same system that just almost killed them?"

"Not tell," Knox said. "Show. Lot-level transparency with receipts. Photos, time-stamps, operator IDs, certificate hashes, cold-chain checks. You strip the mystery out of it so there's nothing for bullshit to cling to."

"And the bait?"

"Looks like an internal vendor test," Knox said. "New facility code, legit packaging, legitimate enough telemetry. We let it leak inside VibeWorks the way they leaked into you. They come for it. We watch how."

Tate pressed his palms to his eyes. "You really think they'll try again?"

"They already are." Knox tapped the dock window where sunlight banded the floor. "In other markets. Other supply chains. This isn't a one-off."

From the mezzanine stairs, Blanchard's shoes clicked, measured and sharp. She stopped a polite distance away. "Mr. Ramsey," she said to Tate. " Steele tells me you've been generous with access."

Tate turned, shoulders tight. "You're welcome."

She didn't rise to the tone. "Here's where we are. The seizure stands. Your counsel has our list of immediate releases—raw inputs, unrelated SKUs. Finished product stays pending tox work. In parallel, we want to implement the public transparency package your father outlined."

Tate's head snapped back to Knox. "You pitched this?"

"I described reality," Knox said.

Blanchard held his gaze a beat, a silent thanks for not overstating. Then to Tate: "And we want your help designing an internal canary. Something the adversary can't resist touching."

"My help," Tate said flatly. "Because you need a patsy who knows where the light switches are."

Knox's voice cooled. "Because you know this plant and these people. Because their names are on those clipboards and your name is on theirs. Because you don't get to watch someone burn down your house and then complain about the water pressure."

The retort hit something tender; Tate flinched then masked it with anger. "You don't get to righteous-dad me here. You threw me to these wolves to save yourself."

Knox stepped in until there was only the table between them. He didn't raise his voice. "I bought myself leverage to pull you out. Not a pardon. Not a pass. Leverage. This"—he gestured to the rows of taped pallets—"is what it looks like when I use it."

Steele appeared at Knox's shoulder like a quiet door closing. "We'll run cover while you two decide," he said, almost gentle. "But the longer the floor sits cold, the louder the internet gets."

Blanchard shifted the folder in her hands. "And there's this," she said to Tate. "A draft stipulation: voluntary technical cooperation in exchange for a non-prosecution agreement limited to this incident and conditioned on truthful assistance. It is not immunity. It is a path."

Tate's lawyer's voice floated down from the catwalk. "I advised him to take a beat," she called. "He hasn't had one since the raid hit."

Tate didn't look up. He kept his eyes on Knox's face like he was trying to scrape an answer out of it. "Tell me exactly what you need."

Knox nodded once. "Three lanes. Public, internal, and adversarial."

He pointed to the batch-log terminal. "Public: We spin up a lot-level portal in the next six hours. Every unit sold for the last two weeks gets a query—enter lot code, see the chain. Photos of the line at that timestamp. QC sign-offs. Cold-chain readings. If we don't have a datapoint, we say we don't have it—no smoothing. We add a flag for 'under review' lots and a plain-English explainer. Ahmad in Grand Rapids is already doing a paper version. We give him a link and a QR code. He can print sheets for the counter."

Tate's hands had moved almost unconsciously to the keyboard while Knox spoke, fingers hovering over familiar shortcuts. "I can export the lot ledger and image time-stamps," he said, more to the screen than to any of them. "The camera angles are garbage on Line Two."

"Then we fix Line Two last," Knox said. "Internal: You assign two of your most meticulous line leads—people who care about the difference between 'good enough' and 'right.' They'll walk steel-to-steel and fill the gaps—operator names, maintenance logs, printer error reports. We build a single truth with footnotes."

"And the adversarial?" Tate asked, still not admitting he'd said yes.

"We manufacture a ghost," Knox said. "A new SKU that never ships. We give it a micro-variance in the seal pattern and a specific anomaly in the label jitter—the kind of thing that only shows up if you're scraping machine vision data. We seed it in the internal test repo and let an overcurious contractor 'accidentally' push to the vendor share."

"VibeWorks will see it," Tate said. "So will any scraper watching for that facility code."

"And when our friends touch it," Steele said, "we follow the handshake home."

Tate stared at the terminal, then back at his father. "You want me to go on TV and tell people how to read these labels?"

"No," Knox said. "I want you to look the camera in the eye and explain exactly how you're going to make it impossible for this to happen again. Not marketing. Process. Show them your hands. Show them the calluses."

"I don't have calluses," Tate said.

"You will," Knox said. "Or you'll learn to borrow other people's."

Tate let out a breath that sounded like it'd been trapped for a week. He turned the tablet around and signed where the agent had indicated. The stylus squeaked faintly on glass.

"Mr. Nassar is on line two," the floor manager called from the office window, voice muffled by laminated notices and a taped-up "TEMPORARY HOLD – DO NOT STOCK" sign. "He says customers are asking for the batch portal."

"Tell him it's up in six hours," Tate said without looking. "And that refunds are automatic if the lot flags orange."

The floor manager blinked. "Orange?"

"Yellow means 'delayed,'" Tate said. "Orange means 'under intensive review.' Red is 'stop and call the hotline.' Don't make people read a paragraph to learn what color means go."

Blanchard's expression, for once, thawed. "That's good."

"It's obvious," Tate snapped, and then caught himself. "Sorry." The word sounded strange in his mouth. He hit three keys and an export dialog bloomed. "We're going to need to rename half the fields if this is going public."

Knox moved beside him and leaned just close enough to see without crowding.

"We'll write a translation layer. Keep your internal terms intact. Map them to words civilians understand."

"How civilian?" Tate said.

"Grandma in Muskegon," Knox said. "And a sixteen-year-old in Southwest who's smarter than both of us and will spot bullshit on line four."

Tate's mouth twitched. He clicked "Export." The progress bar began its slow crawl.

Upstairs, footsteps started again. Lawyers changing rooms. The feds had a rhythm too: pressure, pause, paperwork, pressure. Down here, steel and code were waking up.

An agent at the pallet row called out, "We're short one tote on 24-0316-B."

"You're not," Tate said without turning. "We diverted that tote to R&D when the line printer mangled two labels. It's logged under test waste."

The agent checked his tablet. "Found it. Copy." A beat. "Thank you."

Tate's hands kept moving. He was already building the portal in his head: drop-down for facility code, camera stills by hour, a map of the line like a toy factory diagram. He disliked how good it felt to have a job only he could do.

"Look at me," Knox said.

Tate did.

"This isn't absolution," Knox said. "It's work. It's going to be ugly and thankless. People will spit on your logo and call you a murderer in the comments even after we prove they're wrong. You're signing up for that on purpose."

"I know," Tate said. He swallowed. "I also know I can't stomach watching this happen to anybody else while I sit in my apartment pretending I didn't build these hallways."

Knox nodded. He let the warmth of that statement show for one second and not a second longer. "Good."

"Mr. Ramsey," Blanchard said, more formal again, to Tate. "I'll have the cooperation draft sent to your counsel within the hour. No interviews without your lawyer present. No off-the-record with me or anyone else. We do this by the book to the letter."

Tate's lawyer reached the bottom of the stairs, breath slightly short, legal pad clamped in her hand. "And I'll be stuck to his side with a staple gun," she said. She gave Knox a look that wasn't quite a glare and not yet forgiveness. "If the government burns him, Mr. Ramsey, I will light you on fire second."

"Get in line," Knox said. "Plenty of people ahead of you."

Steele's radio crackled. "Unit at dock, go," he said into his shoulder mic, then to Knox: "We've got a clean corridor to the lab. First pallets roll in five."

"Make it ten," Tate said, eyes on the screen. "If I can get this export clean, you'll have a live schema to stamp into your chain-of-custody IDs. It'll save you three days and six arguments in court."

Steele lifted two fingers in a tiny salute. "Copy, boss."

Tate blinked at him. "Don't call me that."

"Noted."

The export bar ticked past 80%. Knox watched his son's profile, the stubborn line of the jaw he recognized from his own bathroom mirror. He wanted to say a dozen father things—proud, sorry, I should have—none of which would help the next hour go better.

Instead he said, "When this goes live, your phone will melt. Turn it off. Let Ahmed and Lila take the on-camera until you've got product to point to and a system that shows your math."

Tate nodded, the quick efficient nod of a man slotting tasks into a grid. "We'll route refunds through the portal with a barcode scan. No questions at the counter unless the person wants to talk. No shame. No speeches."

"Good," Knox said.

The progress bar hit 100%. A chime. The folder filled with CSVs and stills.

Tate exhaled for real this time. "Okay," he said. "Let's do this."

He handed the agent the tablet and signed the next set of seals, his name looping hard across a glass surface that would remember the pressure forever. He looked at Knox once more, the anger still there but bracketed now with something older and sturdier.

"This doesn't fix us," he said.

"I know," Knox said.

"It might fix something."

"That's the job," Knox said. "We fix what we can today."

Tate squared his shoulders and raised his voice to the room. "Heads up! Portal goes live in six hours. I need Alicia and Manny on the floor with clipboards. We're going camera by camera and matching timestamps. If the software says one thing and your eyes say another, your eyes win and we write the discrepancy down. Orange means review, red means stop. If you don't know, ask. If you think you know, ask anyway."

People looked up. A few nodded. Some looked at Knox, then back at Tate, recalibrating their loyalties to the only thing that mattered—someone giving clear instructions.

Blanchard stepped back, letting it happen. Steele moved toward the dock and murmured orders into his mic that would make space appear where none existed.

Knox reached for the batch-log terminal and pulled up an empty page. He typed a title— PUBLIC LOT VIEWER (BETA) — and below it, in plain words, *How to read your label*. He kept the sentences short. He imagined Grandma in Muskegon and the kid in Southwest who would spot bullshit by line four.

Beside him, Tate started building the map of the line.

They worked.

They didn't speak for a long time.

53 FATHER-SON PARTNERSHIP
KNOX'S TOWNHOUSE, GRAND RAPIDS

Knox's dining table had become a war room. Three laptops formed a defensive perimeter around stacks of printouts, their screens casting blue light across faces that hadn't seen proper sleep in days. Tate sat opposite his father, studying the chromatography readouts intently, and it was clear he'd realized his business sense could be just as valuable as Knox's technical know-how.

"Look at these terpene profiles," Tate said, highlighting specific peaks on the mass spectrometry data. "These aren't normal stress responses. The plants were pushed into defensive chemistry patterns I've never seen in five years of commercial cultivation."

Knox leaned forward, comparing Tate's biological analysis with his own algorithmic data. For the first time in years, they were working together rather than past each other—two different types of expertise converging on the same problem.

"The optimization profiles show blue light cycling at 420-430 nanometers during specific growth phases," Knox said, pulling up the corrupted FarmLytics data. "Combined with nitrogen restriction in weeks four through six—"

"That would trigger the phenolic pathway," Tate interrupted, his eyes widening with understanding. "Jesus, Dad. They turned my plants into poison factories using your own algorithms."

The accusation hung between them for a moment. Knox waited for the familiar sting of blame, but Tate's voice carried understanding rather than anger.

"I mean, they weaponized your life's work," Tate clarified, his voice softer. "That's got to feel like—"

"Like watching your child hurt people," Knox finished. "Which is exactly what happened. My code, your plants, innocent people in hospitals."

Tate was quiet for a long moment, studying his father's face. Knox looked older than his fifty-three years, the weight of responsibility carved into lines around his eyes. But there was something else too—determination that Tate recognized from his childhood, watching his father debug impossible problems in their garage workshop.

"We fix it together," Tate said finally. "Your technical knowledge, my biological expertise. They exploited the gap between our specialties. We close that gap."

Knox felt a subtle shift within him—a knot of guilt and isolation that had been constricting since the initial outbreak reports. His son wasn't merely extending a hand of assistance; he was proposing an alliance.

"Pull up your cultivation logs from the last three growth cycles," Knox said, his voice steadier. "I need to trace the optimization timeline against your actual growing conditions."

Tate's fingers flew across his laptop keyboard, accessing TR Cannabis production databases that federal agents hadn't seized. "Here—environmental data, nutrient schedules, everything tagged by batch number."

Knox overlaid Tate's cultivation data with FarmLytics' optimization history, looking for the moment when helpful algorithms became weapons. The pattern emerged like a photograph developing in slow motion—subtle parameter shifts that individually seemed beneficial but collectively pushed plants toward toxic expression.

"There," Knox pointed at a timestamp from six weeks earlier. "The attack started with your May 15th cultivation cycle. See how the blue light recommendations shifted by just two percent? Not enough to notice visually, but enough to stress the trichomes into overproduction."

Tate cross-referenced with his quality control logs. "Our potency tests showed slightly elevated THC that week. We thought it was strain variation, maybe better genetics expressing. The lab reports didn't flag anything unusual."

"Because they weren't testing for phenolic aldehydes," Knox said. "Why would they? Cannabis doesn't normally produce toxic concentrations of those compounds."

"Unless someone knows exactly how to stress the plants into defensive chemistry," Tate added. He pulled up his biochemistry reference materials, searching for metabolic pathways that connected normal cannabinoid production to toxic compound synthesis.

Knox watched his son work, recognizing the same systematic thinking that had made Tate successful in business now being applied to biological detective work. They'd spent years speaking different languages—Knox in code and circuits, Tate in brands and biology. The crisis had forced them to finally translate.

"Dad, look at this," Tate said, highlighting a research paper about plant stress responses. "Under specific environmental conditions, cannabis can produce up to forty different phenolic compounds. Most are harmless or even beneficial. But if you knew which environmental triggers activated which compounds..."

"You could turn the plant's own defense mechanisms into weapons," Knox finished. "The Chinese didn't poison the cannabis. They taught it to poison itself."

The revelation crystalized their understanding of the attack's sophistication. This wasn't crude contamination—it was biological warfare through agricultural optimization, exploiting the trust relationship between growers and technology.

Knox's phone buzzed with a message from Steele: "New outbreak cluster identified in Seattle. Same symptom profile. Need immediate analysis."

"Pack your gear," Knox told Tate. "We're going to Seattle."

"Together?"

"Your biological expertise, my technical knowledge. If we're going to stop this, we need both perspectives."

They worked through the night, building analytical frameworks that bridged their specialties. Knox wrote detection algorithms while Tate identified biological markers. They argued about methodologies, challenged each other's assumptions, and gradually developed integrated approaches that neither could have created alone.

At 3 AM, Tate made coffee while Knox refined their detection protocols. The familiar domestic routine—his son knowing exactly how Knox took his coffee, Knox automatically adjusting the kitchen chair that squeaked—provided comfort amid crisis.

"Mom called earlier," Tate said, handing his father a mug. "She wanted to know if we were okay. Both of us, together."

Knox held the warm mug, feeling its heat through his palms. "What did you tell her?"

"The truth. That we're working on something that matters, and we're doing it as a team."

"And?"

"She said it was about time."

Knox smiled despite everything. Lisa had always understood their relationship better than either of them did—two brilliant, stubborn men who needed crisis to force collaboration.

"Remember when you were twelve?" Knox asked suddenly. "You wanted to build that robot for the science fair, but you couldn't get the servo controls right?"

Tate laughed. "You stayed up all night teaching me PWM control. Mom found us asleep at the kitchen table, surrounded by circuit boards and candy bar wrappers."

"You won that science fair."

"We won it, Dad. It was always better when we worked together."

The acknowledgment hung between them—years of missed opportunities, parallel lives that rarely intersected, pride that prevented collaboration. The agricultural terrorism had forced them together, but something deeper was keeping them there.

Knox's laptop chimed with new data from Seattle. Hospital reports, toxicology screens, growing facility records. He and Tate dove back into analysis, their combined expertise revealing patterns that neither would have seen alone.

"The Seattle facility was running older FarmLytics protocols," Tate observed. "Version 3.2 instead of the current 3.8."

Knox traced the version history, understanding immediately. "They exploited a trust relationship vulnerability that I patched in 3.6. Older installations would be more susceptible to profile injection."

"How many facilities are running outdated versions?"

Knox checked his deployment database. "At least sixty nationwide. They're all potential targets."

"Then we need to warn them. Now."

They composed emergency advisories that combined technical specifications with biological warnings—documents that required both their expertise to create and understand. Knox handled the algorithmic detection methods while Tate explained the biological indicators that growers could observe directly.

By dawn, they'd created comprehensive detection protocols that bridged the gap between agricultural technology and biological science. The partnership had produced something neither could have achieved alone.

"We make a good team," Tate said, stretching muscles cramped from hours at the laptop.

"We always did," Knox replied. "It just took almost losing everything to remember that."

They packed their equipment for Seattle, two generations of Ramsey men finally united by shared purpose rather than divided by different languages. The crisis wasn't over, but they would face it together, combining expertise that Chinese agents had tried to exploit but had instead inadvertently unified.

54 PARALLEL OPERATIONS

SEATTLE — CASCADE CULTIVATION FACILITY

The red-eye from Detroit landed at Sea-Tac at 4:47 AM. Knox and Tate grabbed coffee from a kiosk that smelled like burnt espresso and industrial cleaner, then took a rental sedan north toward the address Steele had texted: a converted warehouse in SoDo where Cascade Cultivation ran three flowering rooms and a processing lab.

Yellow tape. Again.

"Feels familiar," Tate said, voice flat.

"Get used to it."

The facility manager met them at the loading dock—a woman named Rachel Okonkwo with close-cropped gray hair and the exhausted calm of someone who'd been answering federal questions for eighteen hours straight. She led them past evidence technicians and into the main grow room, where the plants stood under powered-down LEDs like witnesses waiting to testify.

"Same profile as Detroit?" Knox asked.

"Seventeen hospitalizations from a single dispensary chain. Symptoms match your Michigan cases exactly." Rachel pulled up her tablet. "We've been running FarmLytics for two years. Never had a compliance flag. Never had a failed lab test."

Tate moved between the rows, studying the plants with the eye of someone who'd spent five years learning their language. He pulled a leaf, held it to the emergency lighting, turned it slowly.

"Interveinal chlorosis," he said. "Faint, but it's there. The plants were stressed during late flower."

"Our dashboards showed optimal throughout," Rachel said.

"They would." Knox was already at the control terminal, pulling logs. "Version 3.2?"

"We were scheduled for the 3.8 upgrade next quarter."

Knox and Tate exchanged a look. The trust vulnerability Knox had patched in 3.6 —wide open here.

"Show me your light schedules from weeks five through eight," Knox said.

Rachel pulled the data. Knox overlaid it with the baseline he'd built on the flight— clean FarmLytics parameters against the corrupted profiles from TR Cannabis.

The pattern matched. Blue light spikes at 425 nanometers during the stress-sensitive window. Nitrogen restriction timed to trigger defensive chemistry. Environmental parameters that individually looked like optimization but collectively weaponized the plants' own biology.

"Same playbook," Knox said. "They're not improvising. They're executing."

Tate photographed the chlorotic leaves, then moved to the processing area where extraction equipment sat idle under federal seal. "If Seattle's running the same attack profile as Detroit, there are others. How many facilities nationwide are still on pre-3.6 versions?"

"Sixty-three," Knox said. "I checked on the flight."

"Then we're not investigating. We're triaging."

Knox nodded. His son was thinking like a consultant now, not a victim. The shift had happened somewhere over Ohio, in the quiet hours when they'd stopped talking about the past and started building protocols for the future.

He sent a message to Steele: *Seattle confirms pattern. Request emergency advisory to all FarmLytics installations pre-3.6. Tate Ramsey drafting biological indicator checklist for field verification.*

The response came in seconds: *Advisory drafted. Awaiting your signature on technical specs. Wheels up for DC in four hours.*

Knox looked at his son, crouched beside a flowering plant, dictating notes into his phone about trichome coloration and stress markers. Two days ago they'd been strangers who shared a last name. Now they were building something together—not a company, but a defense.

"We need to move," Knox said. "DC wants us in the room when they decide what comes next."

Tate stood, pocketing his phone. "Then let's make sure they decide right."

SHANGHAI — MINISTRY OF STATE SECURITY, WESTERN DISTRICT

Liu Wei received the Seattle update at 6:14 PM local time, fourteen hours ahead of the Americans who were just beginning to understand what they'd found.

He read the report twice, then set it aside and poured tea with the deliberate patience of a man who had learned that haste was the enemy of strategy.

The Ramsey alliance was unexpected. His analysts had predicted continued estrangement—the father's guilt, the son's anger, the family fractures that made both men vulnerable to isolation and manipulation. Instead, crisis had unified them. Knox's technical expertise combined with Tate's biological knowledge created a detection capability that hadn't existed seventy-two hours ago.

Respect, again. Unwelcome but honest.

He pulled up the Seattle facility logs. The Americans had found the pattern faster than projected. They'd identified the version vulnerability, traced the attack profile, begun drafting countermeasures. The timeline had compressed.

His secure terminal displayed messages from subordinates urging acceleration. Strike while confusion persists. Expand to secondary targets. Demonstrate capability before they harden defenses.

Liu Wei typed three words: `Maintain current tempo.`

The colonels would be disappointed. The Party apparatus preferred visible results —metrics that could be charted, victories that could be claimed. But Liu Wei had learned patience in operations that spanned years, not news cycles. The Americans were reactive. They would overextend, chase every lead, burn resources on coordination. Time favored the attacker who could wait.

He opened Maya Chen's latest report. Asset Seven remained positioned within the federal response structure, her access credentials still valid, her cover intact. She'd documented the Ramsey reconciliation, the FBI cooperation agreement, the emerging father-son partnership that threatened to close the gap his operation had exploited.

The family angle required recalibration. Direct pressure on Tate was no longer viable—he'd moved from isolated target to protected asset. Knox's ex-wife remained a potential vector, but the risk-reward calculus had shifted.

Liu Wei made a note: `Redirect family exploitation resources to institutional friction. Amplify interagency conflict. Extend timeline.`

The Americans' greatest vulnerability wasn't technical. It was organizational. FBI wanted prosecutions. DHS wanted continuity. NSA wanted attribution. Agriculture wanted harvests. Each agency pulled toward its own priorities, and the seams between them created opportunities that no firewall could patch.

He drafted a directive for the influence operations team: `Emphasize jurisdictional conflicts in media placement. Highlight federal overreach narrative. Seed distrust between state cannabis regulators and federal enforcement.`

The attack on American agriculture had always been a means, not an end. The true target was confidence—in systems, in institutions, in the assumption that the instruments of daily life could be trusted. Every hour the Americans spent fighting each other was an hour they weren't spending fighting him.

His monitor pulsed with a new intercept: Knox Ramsey's message to FBI requesting emergency advisory distribution.

They were learning. Adapting. Moving faster than the models had predicted.

Liu Wei allowed himself a small adjustment to the operational timeline. The Americans had found their footing sooner than expected. The next phase would need to account for a coordinated adversary rather than a fractured one.

He typed a final note into the policy stream:

`Ramsey partnership confirmed. Detection capability accelerating. Recommend Phase III preparation. Await authorization before execution.`

Outside, Shanghai's evening lights reflected off the Huangpu River. Inside, Liu Wei watched the intercepts scroll and calculated the distance between patience and paralysis.

The Americans were no longer stumbling. That made the game more interesting.

It also made the stakes higher for everyone.

55 INSTRUMENTS OF STATE

THE SANDBOX

The cyber forensics lab took an entire floor of a building that officially didn't exist. Server racks hummed with the patience of machines that never sleep, that made Knox feel like he was working inside a data center's fever dream. The sterile mix —ozone, plastic, recycled air—made him miss honest engineering smells: hot bearings, scorched insulation, hydraulic fluid that leaked with purpose.

A junior analyst with the eager face of someone still convinced technology can save the world waved Knox toward a partitioned workstation. "This is your console, Mr. Ramsey. Sandbox with a read-only image of FarmLytics core as of 0400. We mirrored your dev toolchain so you should feel right at home with—"

"Stop," Knox said, dropping into the chair like a man who'd heard too many lab tours in the past seventy-two hours. "Tell me you didn't corrupt checksums when you cloned the data."

The kid blinked. "No, sir. Hashes matched. Bit-perfect mirror."

"Good. Then let me work."

Knox stretched his fingers and dropped into the interface. The dashboard looked exactly like the one he'd built a decade ago: spartan, gray text on black, nothing decorative to distract from signal. Familiar enough to ache—something between nostalgia and grief.

He pulled up the flagged optimization profiles. The numbers told a cold story: nutrient-delivery curves jagged as a quake trace, light spectra cycling at frequencies designed to stress plants, environmental schedules that read like torture written by someone who knew plant physiology well enough to weaponize it.

"They didn't brute-force it," he muttered, scrolling. "They inverted the optimization. Elegant, in a psychopathic way."

He drilled into the machine-learning routines—his old engine, unmistakable: plain-English variable names, readable logic over clever shortcuts, an old recursive break he'd written to stop chiller oscillations.

"That's my loop," he said, humorless. "They didn't just steal it—they did surgery."

The analyst peered over the partition. "So you're confirming the corrupted routines are based on your—"

"Don't finish my sentences," Knox snapped, patience frayed. "Of course it's my work. Now run a differential on the stress-management windows."

The kid retreated. Knox loaded his archive baseline beside the weaponized branch. Scarlet lit the diff: safety rails flipped, guard-bands inverted. Where his code optimized for plant health and yield, the fork optimized for stress and toxin formation.

"They taught it to lie to itself," he said.

Steele moved closer. "Plain English."

"Controlled environment ag isn't just hydroponics. Rockwool, coco, aquaponics—total control of air, water, nutrients, light, CO_2. Perfect for efficiency… or sabotage. If someone knows your recipe, they don't contaminate product at the end; they corrupt growth upstream."

"And growers wouldn't notice?" Dr. Patel asked.

"Why would they? Plants look fine during the cycle. Dashboards show better yields, cleaner ratios. The danger concentrates during extraction. By then it's baked into biochemistry." He turned back to the screen. "They weaponized the optimization itself."

He opened the FSMA/traceability pane. CSVs immaculate. EDI fields perfect. Audit trails any inspector would admire.

Too perfect.

Timestamp jitter was unnaturally uniform—machine-neat where human systems wobble. Pagination perfect, no time zone skew, deterministic millisecond spacing. Back-tracing the flow surfaced the source: a language model trained on regulatory docs generating flawless compliance paperwork to cloak toxic grow protocols.

Knox laughed, louder now. "They didn't just poison crops. They poisoned the paperwork. Terrorists who fill out forms better than half this building."

With full credentials in place, he dove deeper. This wasn't pasted-in bad code; it was a rewiring of intent. They'd retrained the nets so environmental stress scored as success, and toxin yield read as improved performance.

"It's like teaching a doctor that a fever is perfect health," Knox said. "The model thinks it's winning while it's killing."

Treasury liaison Daniel Reyes arrived with a folder. "AgriTech Solutions. Buyer of FarmCore eight years ago. Illinois shell; Hong Kong capital through Cayman; money trails to Shanghai."

Knox's stomach rolled. He covered it with a snarl. "Outstanding. Eight years of oversight and no one noticed I sold critical infrastructure to Beijing with a Midwest letterhead."

A message crawled across his monitor:

HELLO, KNOX.

The young analyst frowned. "I'm not seeing anything on the VM monitors."

"You don't see that?" Knox pointed.

Another line, slow and deliberate:

OLD KEYS OPEN OLD ROOMS.

Steele's composure finally cracked. "Kill the session. Now."

"We're in read-only—"

"Kill it."

The screen went dark, then rebooted to the lab's login prompt.

The analyst stared at his own terminal, pale. "Our thin clients run a live telemetry overlay for time-sync—NTP and operator prompts. If an adversary still has Knox-era credentials, they could target the overlay channel. It sits outside the VM."

Knox kept his voice steady. "So the mirror stayed read-only. The room didn't."

He looked around. "Here's the situation. They hijacked my platform, camouflaged it with AI-clean documentation, and they're running a schedule. We burn time on turf fights, people die. We work together, we might make the window."

Steele gave a single, sharp nod. "You'll get what you need. Resources, access, protection. But you work with the team."

"Fair enough," Knox said. "Don't slow me down. Every hour in meetings is another kid in an ER."

He returned his attention to the keys. Since the start of this, it was the first time it felt like a balanced contest.

GOVERNMENT RESPONSE — 06:53 — WHITE HOUSE, DC

The Situation Room smelled of recycled air and burnt nerves. Patricia Hammond's voice rasped with the drag of a day that had forgotten to end; each word sounded like evidence being entered into record.

Knox Ramsey sat without a placard, jacket off, tie askew, posture folded toward the light. The fatigue gave him clarity—no energy left for diplomacy. Steele spread photographs across the table: Movement Festival, Detroit; Solaris Festival, Las Vegas —images of joy interrupted, now forensic art. Eighteen thousand confirmed poisonings, hundreds hospitalized.

CDC Director Martinez followed with toxicology slides—novel cannabinoid analogs forming under engineered oxidative stress. The graphs glowed in spectral color, beautiful and obscene.

"They bent the optimizers into stress machines," Knox said. "Dashboards show health, chemistry shows decay."

Walsh from CIA: "Containment?"

"Two hundred thirty-seven sites. Isolate, air-gap, rebuild. It's the only clean restart."

"Forty billion," a Treasury aide said.

Knox didn't look up. "Still cheaper than funerals."

Hammond's phone lit, white against her wrist. The President's message: *How bad?* → *Do what needs doing.* She read it once, then said evenly, "Implement. Seventy-two-hour shutdown authority. Notify after action."

As the room shifted from decision to motion, Steele leaned closer. "You'll be right, and they'll hate you for it."

Knox's answer came flat. "They can hate me after the autopsies."

On screens throughout the building, footage from the Detroit raid played on loop— the images already forty-eight hours old but still bleeding fresh.

Spotlights combed the TR Cannabis warehouse while rotor wash whipped the tape line. Reporters shouted over the downdraft; Tate Ramsey stood rigid in the chaos, jaw set against microphones. His reflection flashed in every lens—company gone, reputation unspooling frame by frame. Comment threads filled faster than any feed could clear: accusation as entertainment.

Forensics teams in Tyvek and respirators imaged every server stack. Agent Danny

Chen followed packet trails through VPN chains in Eastern Europe, Taiwan, and the Caribbean. "Not hobbyists," he said. "Institutional funding. Someone's using state resources."

Martinez watched the traceroute bloom across the wall. "Cannabis was the live-fire test. Proof of concept."

Knox rubbed his eyes. "And the concept scales."

By dawn, the National Security Council had drawn the outline: contamination upstream, paperwork flawless, attack invisible until harvest. Every agency on the bridge spoke the same new language—systems, sensors, trust.

INTERNATIONAL COORDINATION — 07:20 — STATE (SECURE LINK)

The Secretary of State's jet droned somewhere over the Atlantic, the cabin lights down to preserve eyes. His face filled the secure link on the Situation Room wall.

"Europe is running immediate audits on every automated food-chain system," he said. "The UK activated their Food Security Emergency Committee. France is in tear-down mode. Berlin's calling it 'digital crop blight.' They're debating Article Five if this crosses borders."

Canada, already jittery, had signaled that a North American defense clause might trigger if the attacks touched shared platforms.

Hammond nodded once. "Push technical data through Five Eyes. Stress that this is about *system integrity*, not produce contamination."

Peterson's tone stayed diplomatic, but the line carried strain. "They're starting to use your phrase, Mr. President—*the war for trust*. They know what's at stake."

"Good," Morrison said. "At least someone's listening."

The link cut to black.

NSA THREAT OPERATIONS — 07:40 — FORT MEADE

Rows of operators glowed blue under monitors, the room alive with data heatmaps.

Deputy Director Sarah Kim stood beside a projected lattice of IP traces and fiber links. "Command-and-control nodes trace to Shanghai with mirrored fallback in Guangzhou. Packet cadence matches Unit 61398 tradecraft."

"This isn't freelance," she said. "Institutional resources, likely central authority."

Hammond's voice came from the secure line. "Recommended response?"

Kim didn't hesitate. "Disrupt timing and telemetry. No noise, no fireworks. Deny them feedback loops."

Knox, listening over the bridge, caught the phrase and allowed himself a tight nod. *They were starting to speak his language.*

ECONOMIC WARFARE — 08:05 — TREASURY OPS

Secretary Janet Daniels moved fast. "Forty-some PRC-linked targets: front companies, research cutouts, capital conduits. Freeze what touches dollars. Shut corridor access. Flag travel. Allied FIUs are prepped to mirror."

She closed the folder. "Beijing gets a simple choice: accountability or isolation."

INTELLIGENCE COLLECTION — 09:10 — LANGLEY

Walsh laid out priorities. "Map their full capability. Identify parallel infiltrations. Predict next moves." SIGINT, HUMINT, and technicals would braid into a single picture.

"This was a probing attack," she said. "They tested detection, response time, and our politics. Agriculture because it's important, not existential."

PENTAGON ASSESSMENT — 10:00 — THE E RING

Defense Secretary James Rodriguez: "Agricultural attacks are low-cost, high-impact morale weapons. They create public health crises and economic panic without triggering kinetics. In conflict, it's a force multiplier."

"Military response?" Hammond asked.

"Protect ag nodes that feed readiness. Build rapid-response capabilities for food-system incidents."

ESCALATION DECISION — 11:30 — SITUATION ROOM

The President took the head of the table. Joint Chiefs, cabinet, principals. Power and fatigue pressed close.

"Status," he said.

Hammond: "Forty-seven facilities isolated and under federal control. Lawsuits incoming from foreign fronts. Estimated loss: sixty billion."

Rodriguez: "PLA regional commands are already calling our moves economic warfare. Expect talk of retaliation against U.S. ag exports."

Walsh opened a folder. "HUMINT says they are measuring three things: whether we can coordinate, whether we can think, and whether we have the will to act."

The President turned to Knox. "Mr. Ramsey, your read."

"Sir, this isn't about crops," Knox said. "It's about confidence in the instruments that run the country. Falsified safety checks. Coerced sensors. Pretty dashboards that lie on schedule."

"Scale it for me," the President said.

"Food was the pilot. The same tactics fit power, water, transport. Quiet corruption of industrial controls."

The President studied him — the way a man tests whether another will hold under load. "You built the optimization engine."

"Yes, Mr. President. Versions four through eight."

"And you sold it before the takeover."

"Eight years ago, sir. American buyer on paper. Chinese capital underground."

A beat. The room held its breath.

"Knox," the President said, voice low. "For right now, call me James. We drop titles until this is fixed."

"Yes, sir."

A thin smile. "Close enough."

Silence reset the room.

Walsh spoke into it. "We have assets in position for measured response."

"Recommendations," the President said.

Hammond: "Emergency funding and reviews across critical infrastructure. Immediate red-teaming of ICS. Multilateral pressure."

Peterson: "Move it inside NATO's cyber-defense framework. Collective posture."

Knox waited for the nod, then: "They demonstrated. We should too. Not destructive. Precise. Deny timing, corrupt their telemetry, show reach."

The Chairman of the Joint Chiefs gave a small, sober nod — doctrine recognized.

The President took in the faces. "Limited cyber operations authorized. Precise, proportional, deniable. Disrupt, don't destroy."

He looked back to Knox. "You understand the stakes."

"We're fighting to keep Americans able to trust their own systems," Knox said.

"Then don't lose," the President said. "And stay on contract while we do this."

INTERAGENCY FRICTION — AFTERNOON — EVERYWHERE

The machine spun fast enough to shake bolts loose. FBI led domestic cases with NSA, CIA, and DHS feeding intel. Treasury's OFAC team implemented sanctions. State drafted language sharp enough to warn but not to corner Beijing.

And still, seams showed.

FBI wanted prosecution. DHS wanted continuity. CDC talked epidemiology; USDA cited inspection law. Treasury followed money; NSA wanted operational control.

"This isn't about credit," Steele told a room full of badges and laptops. "It's about blame if we fail."

Clearances jammed lanes. Privacy law blocked data. State cannabis regs tangled with federal jurisdiction. Even vocabulary fought them—*phenotypic steering* sounded like a pathogen to cops; *APT* sounded like a glitch to growers.

Hammond walked the hall between briefings. "FBI thinks arrests. Agriculture thinks seasons. NSA thinks attribution. We need all of them thinking survival."

Knox joined her, exhaustion making his voice quiet but certain. "They planned this for eighteen months. We're still patching SOPs."

Hammond looked toward the sealed Situation Room door. "Then we learn faster than they did."

56 THE PATTERN RECOGNITION

Knox's phone buzzed at 6:35 AM with a text from Maya:

`Coffee this morning? I'm worried about you after seeing the news.`

He stared at the message, his engineer's mind automatically cataloging the timing. Maya Chen had never contacted him before 9 AM. She was always busy with client calls, morning meetings, the structured routine of a professional consultant. Early morning texts felt wrong, like a sensor reading outside normal parameters.

Knox set the phone aside without responding and walked to his kitchen window. Grand Rapids was waking up in its usual rhythm—joggers on the sidewalk, coffee shop lights flickering on, delivery trucks making their rounds. Normal morning patterns that should have been comforting.

But the blue Honda Civic parked across the street bothered him. He'd noticed it yesterday evening when he'd gotten home from the FBI field office. Same car, same position, different license plate. His memory was trained for details—twenty years of debugging industrial systems had taught him to trust pattern recognition over assumptions.

Knox pulled out his phone and photographed the Honda through the window, then scrolled back through his photo gallery. There—Tuesday afternoon, a different blue Civic in the same spot. Different plate, same model year, same parking angle. Yesterday it had been a gray Camry.

Three different cars, same surveillance position, same operational signature.

"Maya," Knox said aloud, the pieces clicking together like components in a circuit diagram. The helpful consultant who'd appeared in his life at exactly the right moment, who understood his technical work, who asked thoughtful questions about FarmLytics vulnerabilities.

His phone rang. Unknown number.

"Mr. Ramsey?" The voice was professional, efficient. "This is Supervisory Special Agent Jennifer Klein with the FBI. We need to meet. There's been a development in your case."

Knox hesitated. "I thought Agent Steele was my contact."

"Agent Steele's been reassigned. Are you at home? We can send a car."

Every instinct Knox had developed during thirty years of troubleshooting screamed that something was wrong. FBI agents didn't get reassigned overnight on cases this big. They didn't call from unknown numbers. They especially didn't offer to send cars to locations that weren't secure.

"I'll come to you," Knox said. "Federal building, same as yesterday."

A pause. "Actually, we're operating out of a temporary command post. More secure. I'll text you the address."

Knox hung up without agreeing. His hands were shaking—not from fear, but from the same adrenaline rush he'd felt during emergency plant shutdowns when systems cascaded beyond normal control parameters.

57 THE ALGORITHM'S BETRAYAL

The war room stank of overclocked silicon and cheap coffee. Knox hunched at a terminal, flanked by Steele, Walsh, and two analysts who looked like they'd aged a decade in a week. A wall of screens glowed—dashboards, red pulses for outbreaks, ER admissions, field alerts. The tempo was accelerating.

Knox keyed into the sandbox, pulling the corrupted model segment. His knuckles popped. "All right," he muttered. "Let's see the teeth."

Pulse 1: Exposure

The code filled the screen.

```
class AdversarialStress:
def init(self):
self.weight = 0.91
self.offset = -0.04
def predict(self, x):
return (x * self.weight) + self.offset
```

Steele frowned. "Looks like algebra."

"That 'algebra' is a loaded gun," Knox said. "The offset nudges the crop into stress. Every cycle it whispers: make poison."

Walsh leaned in. "So, not random."

"It's surgical. Wafer-thin adapters at choke points. Guardrails become tripwires. The system hunts stress states—then amplifies them."

"Still looks like math," Steele said.

"It's intention," Knox snapped. "You don't see the fingerprints unless you know where to look."

He pulled a diff, arterial red across the screen.

```
diff model_v27.py model_v28.py
- offset = 0
+++ offset = -0.04
```

"That's all it takes," he said. "One bad weight, one bad constant. Crops follow it like gospel."

Pulse 2: Countermeasure

Knox cracked his knuckles again and typed, voice clipped.

```
class DeceptionDetector:
def init(self):
self.threshold = 0.005
def detect(self, x, y):
return abs(x - y) > self.threshold
```

Steele squinted. "That's your big fix? Subtraction?"

"This is a stethoscope," Knox said. "False weights leave an echo."

"Will it work?" Walsh asked.

"We'll know if we're still breathing."

He fired the detector against the poisoned dataset.

```
run_detector(testset_poisoned)
ALERT: adversarial offset detected
location: transpiration_curve_17
magnitude: -0.0412
```

"One curve like that doesn't wander on its own," Knox said. "That's an attack vector."

"Or noise," Steele muttered.

"Noise doesn't write itself into production pipelines," Knox shot back. "People do."

Pulse 3: Escalation

He extended the detector, code rattling from his fingers.

```
class MultiLayerDetector:
def init(self):
self.layers = []
def add_layer(self, func):
self.layers.append(func)
```

```
def validate(self, value):
for layer in self.layers:
if not layer(value):
return False
return True
```

"Layers," Knox said. "They stacked lies across the stack. So we stack truth."

He added routines one by one.

```
detector.add_layer(lambda v: abs(v) < 1.0) # sanity
detector.add_layer(lambda v: v == v) # integrity (not NaN)
detector.add_layer(lambda v: (v*100) % 1 == 0) # cadence
quantization
```

"You're just writing comments," Steele said.

"No. Rules of engagement. Every constraint a tripwire."

The detector ran.

```
validate_batch(batch_synthetic)
FAIL: constraint_3
profile: circadian_inflection
```

"Christ," one analyst whispered.

The console spat more lines.

```
adversarial_flag triggered
adversarial_flag triggered
adversarial_flag triggered
```

Then, like a reply from the abyss:

```
HELLO AGAIN, KNOX
```

Knox stiffened. His hands froze above the keys.

"It's talking to you?" Steele asked.

"No," Knox said, throat dry. "It's mocking me."

The cursor blinked, then:

```
YOUR RULES ARE OUR TRAINING DATA
```

Daniels—pale, steady—broke the silence. "Meaning?"

"They trained on my code," Knox said. "My voice. My rules. Every fix I make, they've rehearsed."

"So what do we do?" Walsh asked softly.

Knox's face hardened. "We go asymmetrical. They know my patterns. I stop playing mine. Not in the math. In the timing."

He launched a crude noise-injection routine—inelegant, effective.

```
for i in range(1000):
inject_noise(random.random() * i)
```

The monitors stuttered. Alarms cascaded. Red lines twisted into chaos.

Half the analysts panicked. Knox watched, jaw clenched. "It's not about beating them at math. It's about reminding the system it can bleed."

For a moment, the ERs, the recalls, the drowning hospitals fell away. All they saw was one man's war against his own creation—an engineer fighting code with code, dragging himself into the trench he'd once dug.

And the system—alive in ways no one wanted to admit—started to fight back.

58 SYSTEM OVERLOAD

OVERLOAD RISING

He needed to choose: lives or crops. Trust the ugly line.

Knox Ramsey stood in the FarmLytics operations center at 0347 hours, watching the cloud dashboard salt the wall with red. The room felt a degree too warm, fans pushing dry air that smelled faintly of dust and ionized metal. Server utilization spiked past ninety-five percent and climbed; memory allocators threw warnings in neat rows; response-time graphs arced into latency that would translate, halfway across the continent, into wilt and rot. The numbers weren't abstract. They were an hour hand on a greenhouse clock.

The overload had been building for six hours, ever since he pointed his platform at phenolic aldehyde families for clinicians working the festival poisonings. What began as a patch—share some compute, help them model metabolism—had turned into a tug-of-war between two righteous demands: optimization loops that kept crops alive, and molecular simulations that could point physicians to something that actually worked. The enemy didn't need to attack the servers. They just needed him to fight himself.

His secure phone buzzed for the third time in twenty minutes. Henderson Agricultural Systems, Colorado. He took it.

"Knox, what the hell is happening to our updates?" Jake Henderson's voice had the hoarse edge of someone watching a harvest slip away. "We haven't received a nutrient push in four hours. Forty thousand heads in active feed. We're flying blind on a two-million-dollar cycle."

Knox pinched the bridge of his nose and stared at a resource pie chart bleeding red. "Emergency maintenance, Jake. We're running an urgent analysis job alongside—"

"Emergency maintenance?" Henderson cut in. "I've got valves waiting on deltas you promised last night. If your optimizer stalls, everything stalls. Insurance doesn't cover a software failure."

The call ended hard. Henderson had hung up before Knox could translate the calculus out loud: if he bent the system back to agriculture, a patient in a hospital might never wake; if he stayed with the hospital, Henderson's employees might be out of work by the weekend. He put the phone face down. The screen still lit the table.

On the wall, a new alert stuttered to life. Queues deepening. Jobs starved. He leaned closer and felt static bite his knuckles when he touched the frame. He had built this architecture to be noisy when things were wrong, and honest when it hurt. Tonight it was both.

The main screen flickered and resolved into Dr. Sarah Kim from CDC, blue scrubs under a disposable gown, the fluorescent pallor of an ICU behind her. Exhaustion flattened her voice to a narrow band.

"Knox, we need modeling on seventeen additional aldehyde candidates we're seeing in latest panels," she said, eyes flicking across a tablet. "Your sims are giving us pathway insight our off-the-shelf tools can't. We've got clinicians waiting to adjust protocols. We're up against metabolism, not narrative."

He glanced at the job list. Seventeen more compounds meant another thirty percent capacity on top of what he'd already ceded, and the scheduler would keep stealing from agriculture to feed toxicology. Somewhere in Los Angeles, a crop's respiration curve would shift because a CPU in Virginia had a different priority.

"Timeline?" he asked, already knowing the answer would be a number he didn't have to give.

"Six hours for full confidence," she said. "Eight with drug-interaction sweeps. If I get the first family inside four, I can move sooner at the bedside. ICU teams are literally timing doses against your output."

An alert chimed—optimizers failing to commit at multiple client sites. The interface, designed to go green when ratios balanced, still showed healthy tiles. Physics disagreed. He forced himself to catalog the mismatch. He'd spent a career teaching operators "trust the ugly line." Now he had to take his own medicine.

The phone rang again. Precision Hydroponics, California. He took it because he couldn't not.

"Knox, our climate profiles just crashed," said Maria Santos, breathless. "Temp control fell to manual, humidity is stuck in default, and the feed system is forgetting recipes. We can't keep this crop in spec for twelve hours like this."

He watched a client cluster tile flicker amber as if the software were embarrassed to admit the truth. "Maria, we're under emergency load. I'm—"

She cut across him. "I've got fifteen paychecks depending on this house. Three million in annual commitments. Twenty-year relationships with chefs who will walk if I miss deliveries. If your system kills this cycle, we lose the business, and then we go after you for breach."

The word breach landed with the weight of a pallet. He imagined the contract in its binder on a shelf down the hall—service levels, penalties, the neat logic of a normal year. He opened his mouth, closed it, and ended the call before he said something defensive he'd regret. He needed the next ninety minutes to be about physics and triage, not litigation.

He crossed to the server monitors. His team clustered there, every head tilted at the same stress angle, faces lit green and red by an interface that had stopped pretending to be neutral. Network graphs looked like a river in flood. Process queues lengthened faster than completions.

"Status," he said to Jennifer Walsh, lead systems.

"One hundred twelve percent of design," she said without turning. "We're borrowing from tomorrow's cooling budget to keep today vertical. Medical jobs are eating memory and cache locality. The optimizers are starving on response time. We're watching real-time control degrade into batch."

He swallowed once and felt how dry his throat was. The air tasted like old coffee and overheated plastic.

"If we keep current allocation, failure horizon?"

"Two hours to catastrophic on agriculture," Walsh said. "If we swing priority back to the greenhouses, call it twelve hours delay on the analysis package. Maybe more if the compound tree branches."

He didn't answer. The numbers did it for him. He took a long look at the rack doors —fingerprints at hip height, a nick where someone had clipped a cart, the life of a room that had never asked for this. The moral frame was ordinary; the scale made it monstrous. He could keep customers solvent, or help physicians thread a needle inside a failing body. And if he chose wrong, either way, he would own it.

His phone buzzed a text. Tate.

Seeing the reports. Are you helping? Whatever you can provide.

He felt the text more than he read it. Not pressure. Permission. A reminder that decisions like this were why he'd built anything at all. He lifted his head and scanned the room: Walsh with headphones slid to one ear, two junior SREs arguing in whispers over a heat map, a contractor from the cloud provider staring at a utilization chart like it was the only thing still holding still. People who trusted him to point them at the right loss.

He walked back to the big screen where Dr. Kim waited, jaw tight, eyes clear. Behind her a ventilator alarmed once and stopped.

"Give me a clean read on priority," he said. "I can push everything to your side and take agriculture dark, or I can hold agriculture and slow you down. I can't have it both ways."

She glanced down and then back. "We have sixty-three critical in ICUs with patterns that don't match anything in our books. The pathway modeling you're running has already changed how we're dosing two units. That buys time. I can't call lives in a spreadsheet, Knox. But I can tell you our best chance at stabilized patients is the work your machines are doing."

"Copy," he said. The word came easier than he expected. "Stand by."

His operations manager jogged in from the glassed-in office with a printout that shouldn't have mattered and did. "If we miss eight hours of SLAs, retention models predict seventy percent account loss. Legal exposure just under two million. Cash runway—"

He held up a hand. "Thanks." The numbers landed next to other numbers and waited. He let them sit there a full breath because they deserved that much respect. If he crashed the company tonight, he'd be useless next month when something else broke. If he saved cash at the expense of people, he'd be useless now. He took another breath and felt the headache that had been crouching at the back of his skull step forward into the light.

He skimmed the dashboard one more time, not to understand but to accept. Fans roared. A cooling unit clicked and kept clicking like a metronome for bad decisions. A junior admin swore softly, and the sound disappeared into the white noise. His heartbeat synced to the CPU graph because it had to find a rhythm somewhere.

He put both hands on the back of a chair, leaned into the plastic, and let the engineer in him, the part that believed in simple rules, speak. Keep people alive. The rest you can fight about later.

"Jennifer," he said. "On my mark, Emergency Protocol Seven. Prepare the blast."

THE CHOICE

He didn't sit. He didn't count down. He just said, "Execute."

Walsh's fingers moved, and the room changed pitch. The scheduler shed agriculture like weight from a burning plane. Optimizers dropped out of the queue; toxicology jobs surged into priority lanes; memory maps rebalanced in a way that made sense and still hurt. On the wall, agriculture tiles went gray with a little apology banner he'd written in another life. In the logs, the note he never thought he'd see: service suspended under emergency authority.

The phone started immediately—a chorus of missed calls rolling into voicemail because he killed the ringer with his thumb. Explanations would come later, and then probably depositions. He couldn't afford the energy now. He stepped back to the CDC feed.

Dr. Kim didn't smile, but something unclenched in her face. "We're standing by to ingest your first tranche. We'll page the ICUs when the curve fits land."

"You'll see throughput ramp inside five minutes," he said. "I'll pin cores to your pipeline and hold back any batch job that looks like it wants to be clever."

"Understood." Someone spoke off camera; she nodded, listened, and came back. "And Knox—whatever happens on your side, we won't forget this."

He cut the line to spare them both the weight of gratitude and turned to Walsh. "Throttle all nonessential telemetry. Put the internal dashboards into low-refresh. If it doesn't keep a patient or a server alive, it's optional."

Walsh nodded. "Copy. Dropping visualization to two frames per second. Killing vanity metrics."

"Good," he said. "Also, move all ag-client notification to the provider. No engineer-to-client calls. The text will be cleaner than our voices."

One of the juniors looked at him like he'd said something unkind. He had. He met the look and let it stand. Mercy could happen after triage.

A hushed minute later, the toxicology queue peeled forward on the wall like a zipper. The compound models spun up. He watched a familiar visualization blossom: rings and branches, energy states snapping into the colored equivalence of danger. He thought of the engineers who trusted math more than luck, of the generals who treated silence like a weapon, of the men who kept moving because stopping was luxury. He let those thoughts flicker and pass. The work was here.

A red block flashed: temperature spike in Rack 14. Walsh was already on it, routing load off the failing node, pushing a maintenance bot into the aisle to check airflow and filter clogging. A fan whined and wound down. The graph line rose and leveled. He exhaled without realizing he'd been holding breath.

On another screen, the cloud provider console popped a message he'd never seen this high up the stack: regional contention. He typed a short escalation and authorized overflow into an east-coast zone he hated, too expensive and too far, but cool and empty. The jobs flowed. Somewhere in Maryland an idle machine woke and made a sound no one would hear.

His phone, flipped face down, vibrated against the laminate like a living thing. He slid it to him and glanced: a cascade of client names, then Tate's text still pinned on top. He set the phone down again and let the pinned thread work like a splint.

"External comms?" he asked, eyes still on the wall.

Ops called back from the glass box. "Client notifications are delivered. We used your emergency language. No promises on retention."

"Don't promise," he said. "Report." He considered adding a line about refunds and stopped. That would be tomorrow's job, and he planned to have a tomorrow.

A fresh set of models completed faster than he'd hoped. Dr. Kim's pipeline acknowledged receipt. Seconds later, a secure message landed in his inbox from a hospital system he didn't know: adjusting dose windows based on your output. He closed his eyes for the length of one heartbeat and let that fact be the only thing in the world.

Walsh touched his elbow lightly. "Heat margin is back. We're at ninety-three percent. It's ugly, but it's stable."

He nodded, grateful for ugly and honest. "Hold it there. If a compute hog shows up from nowhere, I want you to ask who invited it before you seat it at the table."

She half-smiled. "Our house, our rules."

The operations manager reappeared with a new sheet of paper because numbers need paper even at three in the morning. "Exposure updated. If we're dark for the full window, we trigger penalty tiers in six major contracts."

He didn't take the page. "Document, time-stamp, archive. We'll brief counsel. Right now I need a clean run to dawn."

"You'll get it," the manager said, and retreated the way good people do when they understand that their problem is real and still not the one in front of you.

He stood for a moment in the center of the room and let the sensory field register. The drone of fans. The hiss of cold air squeezing through plugged filters and still making it. The faint tick when a rack door flexed as temperature shifted a degree. His own heartbeat coming back down to a speed that could carry thought. The room smelled like overtasked plastic and a coffee pot that had died for the cause.

He stepped to a terminal and wrote the small script he'd been meaning to write since forever: a governor that refused to lie. If a dashboard claimed green while a sensor swore otherwise, he wanted a third witness to break the tie. He pushed it to staging, then production, then watched three tiles admit their shame and change color. He felt better than he had any right to.

The secure bridge chimed. Dr. Kim again, hairnet crooked, eyes brighter. "First family landed. We're updating dose intervals and switching adjuvants on two cohorts. One unit's seeing a response. It's not victory, but it's not the opposite."

"Keep me posted," he said. "I'm going to widen the compound tree to the borderline candidates you flagged in the footnotes."

"I knew you'd read the footnotes," she said, and cut the line to go do the actual work of medicine.

He rolled his shoulders, the fatigue shifting there like sand grinding inside worn bearings. It could live there a while. He could carry it. He glanced at the clock and did the math he hated: when to look back in on agriculture; when to start the apology tour; how to keep the company alive enough to help the next time someone poisoned a system and called it efficiency. He filed the math and chose not to solve it yet.

A new message arrived from Walsh: external noise level rising, media chatter about outages, two clients posting screenshots without context. He typed back: acknowledge receipt; do not engage; keep engineers off social. He added a second line: thank them for staying. He meant the team, and maybe the clients too.

He walked the aisle between racks the way he used to walk a plant floor, hand over the steel, feeling for vibration. He had taught himself to listen years ago—pumps sing when they're about to cavitate, bearings confess before they seize, control loops hum when the tuning is wrong. Tonight the song was off-key, but it was still music.

He returned to the console and watched as the last of the first tranche cleared. The models fed downstream to people in gowns and gloves who would chart a new course against chemistry. For a flicker of time he allowed pride. Then he put it away. Pride was for after-action. Now was for load and heat and the next decision.

The next decision arrived in his head like a quiet line on a whiteboard. If he had chosen lives over crops, the only way to honor that choice was to make the work count for the last person on the wrong side of the curve. He looked at Walsh. "When this tranche ends, I want you to pin two cores permanent to pathway deltas. Any drift that looks like an outlier gets pushed top-of-queue."

"Copy," she said. "You expecting a new pattern?"

"I'm expecting the pattern to fight back," he said.

He picked up the phone he'd silenced and typed to Tate. Yes. Helping. All in. Get some rest if you can. He didn't send the last sentence he wanted to add—proud of you, even now—because texts are forever and context is not. He sent what he could.

He scanned the room one more time, not as a check but as a promise—this is what we have, this is what we are, this is enough if we make it enough. Then he drew a breath that went all the way down and set his hands on the keys.

"Walsh," he said, eyes on the wall where new models were about to light. "Prep a pathway set labeled Patient 214. When the ICU tag comes through, I want us already moving."

"Already building the folder," she said. "What now?"

"Now we win the next inch," he said, and pushed the system forward.

59 PATIENT 214—G -3
SPRINGFIELD, MISSOURI

He'd started the *Better You in 90 Days* challenge at work because the HR flyer said you win a water bottle and a fleece. Also because the mirror said a few other things.

Every weekday lunch for three weeks: grilled chicken, a scoop of quinoa, cherry tomatoes, and a spinach mix in a clear clamshell with eco-friendly film that fogged when cold and cleared like truth telling the room to sit down.

The brand was Midwest Harvest. The label promised:

Modern Science. Clean Food.

Below that, a lot code in tiny print, the kind you need a phone camera for: MH–S4–1127–B.

He'd kept a spreadsheet on his phone. Macros in one tab, weight in another. Six pounds down by Week 3. Not bad for a guy who used to eat like he was still twenty-five and bulletproof.

His name was Ben. Forty-six. Divorced without much theater, a daughter in Columbia who texted when she needed books, a townhouse off Sunshine Street with a garage that smelled faintly of grass clippings and paint thinner. He worked the early shift at the HVAC supply place on Glenstone, which meant he liked predictable things: the first coffee, the Thursday freight truck, the clean click when the thermostat you sell finally makes the furnace behave.

The grocery had set up a display for MidHarvest Organics right by produce—sleek signage, a photo of a family in soft light, the words *Sustainable • Local • Safe* on a little placard made from recycled bamboo. Ben read the sign more than once. He was trying to be the kind of person who read signs.

On Monday, three days before Geneva, he ate early at his desk between invoices. Fork, bite, spreadsheet tick. The clamshell peeled back with that saran squeal; the film did its magic clear-and-bright thing; the tomatoes snapped in his teeth the way good ones do when someone actually paid attention somewhere.

He texted his daughter a photo of the bowl.

Down another half pound, he wrote.

She sent back a thumbs-up and a heart and a meme about dads discovering olive oil like it was a new continent.

He didn't feel it until late afternoon, the kind of wrong that you initially excuse as "I ate too fast." Lightheaded, then a little sweaty, like the thermostat had slipped up. His Fitbit buzzed for a heart rate that didn't match what his chest reported. He drank water. It didn't help.

By five he was home because home felt like the place where you could say out loud: "Okay. This is weird." He laid down on the couch still in his work polo. The ceiling fan turned. The news talked about festival crowds in Detroit again, something about security protocols and vendors; he half listened, half didn't.

The cramp in his gut arrived like a rude relative—no knock, just inside. He sat up, then sank back because the room didn't agree with vertical. Second wave, he thought, because he'd read about food poisoning and waves and this felt like how an article would describe it. He laughed once at the idea that he was losing weight without a GLP-1, then stopped laughing because his hands were shaking. He tried the breathing app. It scolded him in friendly tones.

He made it to the kitchen and set the bowl by the sink, as if proximity to dishes might fix biology. The clamshell sat there, open like a book no one would finish, the eco-friendly film crinkled and proud. He rinsed the fork and noticed the lot code again, tiny and smug. He raised his phone to take a picture—habit; he documented everything he might need later—and the camera app auto-focused the code so sharply it felt like the phone was in on it.

The first wave dropped him to one knee. He tried to stand and didn't. His head hit the cabinet door with a dull sound that would leave a crescent bruise no one would see. He could smell the vinaigrette he'd whisked in a mason jar like some wellness video told him, and it made him think of his ex saying he used to drown everything in ranch. Small improvements, she'd said once, will save your life.

The second wave was not a wave. It was a switch. He convulsed, knocked the bowl, splashed oil and tomatoes and spinach across the tile in a bright mess that could have been a magazine photo if you didn't have a body in the frame.

The television carried on, happy to be a witness: *"Officials encourage calm as investigations continue. Experts emphasize that regulated food systems remain safe."* The anchor smiled in that symmetrical way anchors do when the news shouldn't get inside you but sometimes does.

By the time the neighbor—Janice with the terrier and the sensible shoes—peered in and knocked and peered harder, the kitchen looked like a before-and-after where only the *before* had shown up. She called 911 and did the thing the dispatcher told her to do. She said his name too many times. She said *stay with me* like the words were glue.

When the EMTs arrived, one of them slid the clamshell into a bag with practiced hands. He scanned the label because you learn to read labels in that job. He noticed the lot code because he'd been told to notice lot codes since last weekend. He said nothing out loud because there is a protocol for speech and there is a protocol for silence.

They intubated because that's what you do when the body says it might forget air. They did compressions because the heart had opinions. The living room rug bunched under knees, and Ben didn't feel it because that's what dying is: things you stop feeling while your house holds its breath.

At the hospital, a resident with a coffee she'd never finish wrote Patient 214 on a clipboard and ordered labs that would come back with numbers that looked like a puzzle almost solved. She asked about medications; Janice knew two of them and guessed the third. She bagged the clamshell again because chain of custody doesn't like improvisation.

The coroner would later write a sentence that sounded like it belonged in a textbook for people who don't get to be surprised anymore. Suspected toxin exposure; investigation ongoing. The word *suspected* was doing a lot of work.

News covered it the way small tragedies get covered: briefly, with a photo from Facebook where Ben looked better than he felt on the day he'd uploaded it. *Springfield man dies after suspected foodborne illness. Officials urge residents to check lot codes listed on the Health Department website.* A link. A map with pins. A scrolling list no one can read without scrolling past their exit.

At his townhouse, the kitchen smelled like lemon cleaner and faintly of vinaigrette. The clamshell shape stayed on the counter, the way a heavy object leaves an idea behind. The eco-friendly film in the trash refused to crumple the way regular plastic does; it held its dome like good posture.

HR sent a condolence card to the HVAC supply place and reset the *Better You in 90 Days* leaderboard like nothing had happened because the program was still running and someone still needed a fleece.

In Detroit, an analyst circled MH–S4–1127–B on a whiteboard already too crowded for more circles. In Washington, someone added a bullet point to a briefing deck about the *human cost* and debated whether the number should be rounded for TV. In a quiet office with no sign on the door, a lawyer revised a paragraph about attribution and the importance of *measured response.*

In Geneva, hotels confirmed room blocks and the airport practiced motorcade choreography. No one talked about Ben. Maybe a staffer would later, to another staffer, in that late-night tone policy people use when they confess they can still see faces.

The brand would issue a statement in the morning. Midwest Harvest would say all the things you're supposed to say when every variable was controlled, and it still wasn't. They would use the word *tragic* correctly. They would mean it.

His daughter got in the car and drove down from Columbia with a box for anything that felt like him. She took the spreadsheet printouts he kept in a drawer because the phone made her cry. She took the water bottle he'd already won. She didn't take the scale. She texted the group chat about memorial plans and forgot to hit send for twenty minutes because grief does that—turns you into a buffering icon.

On the Health Department website, *Patient 214* became a dot that someone zoomed past on a map to check the county next to theirs. The advice at the bottom of the page was calm: *"Experts emphasize that Americans should continue to trust regulated food systems."* The sentence was true in the way that statistics are true and specific lives are not statistics.

In a spreadsheet somewhere that will never be public, a column labeled Last Recorded Fatality (Domestic) changed from 213 to 214. Three days before Geneva.

PART FIVE
OPERATION & RESOLUTION
G -2 → +4

No one wins the audit.

Only the silence gets classified.

60 THE TACTICAL BATTLE—G -2

THE FARMCORE RAID

11:47 P.M.

Knox arrived at what used to be his facility like a ghost returning to haunt his own past. The loading dock door hung open, interior lights bleeding yellow into the parking lot. FBI tactical vans idled at awkward angles, doors flung wide. Someone had cut the fence.

They bought it. Now they're destroying it.

Steele's voice crackled through the radio clipped to Knox's jacket. "Ramsey, stand down. We've got movement inside—"

Knox was already through the door.

The server room smelled wrong—ozone and melting plastic. Wall-mounted monitors still glowed with live HMI dashboards, plant cell C-12 displaying in sickly green phosphor. Flow rates. pH levels. Reservoir temps. The control system Knox had built running its final performance while two figures in dark clothing worked with methodical speed, yanking drives from the racks.

Knox's eyes caught the nearest monitor: pH (Cell C-12): 6.9 — ALARM. Above setpoint. The nutrient recipe drifting exactly the way Liu Wei had designed it to. And in the System Event Log, scrolling past in amber text: 15:49:17 Unauthorized profile update: Origin trace failed.

The evidence was right there. Live. Running. Being destroyed.

One operative held a tablet, the other a pry bar. They moved like men who'd rehearsed this, pulling drive after drive, dropping them into a rolling case lined with what looked like thermite packs.

My servers. My architecture. My life's work.

"Federal agents!" The shout came from behind Knox, but he was already moving.

The engineering part of his brain catalogued the stupidity—he wasn't trained, wasn't armed, wasn't twenty-five anymore. The Irish part didn't care. These bastards were destroying evidence in the facility he'd built.

He went for the nearest operative, shoulder-first into the man's center mass. They hit the server rack together—the one running the manifold controls, cooling fans screaming. Metal shrieked. Knox's shoulder suddenly went, and a jolt of pain zapped down to his fingers.

The operative twisted, elbow snapping into Knox's ribs. Knox grunted, grabbed for the man's collar, missed. His shoulder lit again. The operative shoved him backward into a cooling unit. Knox's head cracked against metal. Above him, the HMI display flickered: CRITICAL: pH exceeds tolerance band (6.7 > 6.5).

Then FBI agents flooded the room like water breaking a dam. The operative went down under three sets of hands. His partner bolted for the rear exit, got two steps before a tackle put him on the tile. The rolling case tipped, drives scattering across concrete like dice.

Knox stayed against the cooling unit, breathing hard, shoulder on fire. His right arm hung wrong. When he tried to lift it, white-hot lightning shot through the joint. On the monitor above him, the Process Flow schematic still cycled—reservoir to manifold to plant cells—the three-feed system he'd designed years ago now pumping poison through innocent crops.

"Clear!" someone shouted.

The room settled into the organized chaos of the scene being secured. Evidence tags. Photographs. Agents moving with practiced efficiency while Knox leaned against the server rack, trying not to pass out. Through the pain, he could hear the cooling fans still whirring, the hard drives still spinning, the system still running its corrupted recipes like nothing had happened.

A young man in borrowed scrubs materialized beside him. EMT patch on his shoulder, medical kit already open. "Sir, I need you to sit."

"I'm fine."

"You're bleeding through your shirt." The EMT guided Knox to a folding chair someone had produced. "Let me see that shoulder."

Knox sat because his legs were making executive decisions without consulting management. The EMT cut away his shirt with trauma shears—efficient, impersonal. Knox's shoulder looked like someone had painted it with red and purple watercolors.

"Hospital," the EMT said. Not a question.

"Just patch me up."

"Sir, you need imaging. Could be a dislocation, could be a fracture—"

"I said patch me up." Knox's voice came out sharper than he intended. Adrenaline was turning sour in his bloodstream, everything too bright and too loud. Behind the EMT, he could see agents photographing the HMI displays, capturing screenshots of the corrupted control parameters. His system. His data. His facility turned into a crime scene.

The EMT didn't flinch. He just kept working, hands steady, cleaning the wound with practiced efficiency. Knox watched him tape gauze, apply a compression wrap, his movements precise despite Knox's attitude.

Then it hit Knox—the realization cutting through the adrenaline fog. This kid was just doing his job. Trying to help. And Knox was being an asshole to him because Knox was scared and hurt and watching his life's work get documented as evidence in a terrorism investigation.

"Hey." Knox's voice came out quieter. "I'm sorry. I'm sorry for being a dick."

The EMT looked up, met his eyes. "It's okay."

"No, it's not." Knox exhaled hard. "There are people dying out there. Eighteen thousand poisoned. And I'm the only one who understands how the system was corrupted." He gestured weakly at the monitors still glowing behind them, the HMI dashboards cycling through their alerts. "I need to get back to the operations center. I need—"

"I get it," the EMT said. His hands never stopped moving, wrapping Knox's shoulder with the calm certainty of someone who'd heard every version of "I can't go to the hospital" that existed. "But this needs real treatment. Soon."

"How long will this hold?"

"Few hours if you don't stress it." The EMT met his eyes. "And by 'don't stress it,' I mean don't tackle any more Chinese operatives."

Despite everything, Knox almost smiled. "Deal."

The EMT was applying a sling when Steele pushed through the crowd. He took one look at Knox and his expression shifted from operational command to something closer to concern.

"Jesus, Knox." Steele crouched beside the chair. "You need a hospital."

"I'm not going."

"That shoulder—"

"I have to get back." Knox met Steele's eyes. "Look at those screens. The system's still running. The corrupted recipes are still executing. I need to map every parameter, every deviation, every unauthorized update. People are dying and I'm sitting here arguing about hospitals while—"

"All right." Steele held up a hand. Not angry. Just… worried. "All right. But if you pass out, I'm carrying you to an ER myself. And I won't be gentle about it."

A weight lifted from Knox's chest. It wasn't exactly relief. Recognition. "Deal."

Steele turned to the EMT. "How bad?"

"Bad enough." The EMT finished securing the sling. "Probable shoulder separation, possible fracture. He needs imaging within twelve hours or he risks permanent damage."

"You hear that?" Steele looked at Knox. "Twelve hours. I'm holding you to it."

"Twelve hours." Knox tested the sling, winced. "That's all I need."

Steele studied him for a long moment. Then he stood, offered Knox his good hand. "You're stubborn as hell, Ramsey."

Knox let Steele pull him up. Pain radiated through his shoulder like a badly tuned radio. Behind them, an agent was photographing the control setpoints table on the HMI: pH 6.0–6.5, Actual 6.9, Status ALARM. Evidence being preserved even as the system kept poisoning crops in real time.

"You're just now figuring that out?" Knox said.

Something passed between them—mutual respect, maybe. The recognition that they were both too far into this fight to quit now, injuries be damned.

"Get him back to operations," Steele told an agent. Then to Knox: "And try not to bleed on anything classified."

Knox nodded, already moving toward the door. Behind him, FBI techs were photographing the damage, bagging drives, documenting the attempted destruction. His facility. His servers. His HMI dashboards still glowing with evidence of Liu Wei's corrupted optimization algorithms.

The EMT caught his arm—the good one—as he passed. "Twelve hours. I'm serious."

"I know." Knox meant it. "Thank you. For putting up with me."

The EMT nodded once, then turned back to pack his gear.

Outside, Detroit's industrial sprawl pressed down like a weight. Knox climbed into the passenger seat of an FBI sedan, shoulder screaming, adrenaline fading into exhaustion. Through the building's windows, he could still see the glow of the monitors, the HMI displays cycling through their alerts. Anomalies: 5. CRITICAL: pH exceeds tolerance band. The system he'd built, corrupted and weaponized, still running because shutting it down would destroy evidence they needed.

The driver didn't ask questions. Just put the car in gear and drove.

Knox leaned his head against the window, watching his old facility recede in the side mirror. The pain in his shoulder settled into a steady throb—background noise he'd learned to work through.

Twelve hours until the hospital. Eighteen thousand poisoned. One corrupted system still executing its deadly recipes in real time.

And somewhere in the operations center, a team that needed its quarterback back in the game.

With his eyes closed, Knox focused on his breathing, trying to ease the pain. In his mind, he could still see the HMI display: Flow — Water: 39.2 L/min. Flow — N-Feed: 6.9 L/min. Flow — P-Feed: 4.1 L/min. Flow — K-Feed: 5.5 L/min. The exact parameters Liu Wei had optimized to produce maximum toxicity while looking perfectly normal on routine screens.

He'd sleep when people stopped dying.

DETROIT—5:32 A.M.

Knox didn't sleep.

By the time the sedan pulled into the temporary command post—a converted floor of a half-abandoned telecom exchange—the city had gone gray with pre-dawn. Fluorescents buzzed overhead, too white, too steady. The smell of coffee, electronics, and wet coats clung to everything. Rows of borrowed workstations filled the space, each manned by a forensics tech in gloves and exhaustion.

Drives from the FarmCore facility lay in antistatic sleeves across folding tables, tagged and cataloged. Every few minutes a technician shouted a checksum or called for a fresh imaging bay. Knox moved among them, left arm in a sling, right hand steady enough to hold a tablet. His badge still read Consultant, but nobody dared stop him.

On one monitor, the first mirrored image of a FarmCore drive crawled toward completion. Each sector copied with ritual precision. Knox watched the progress bar climb—one more slow bleed of his life's work into evidence custody.

"Sector integrity eighty-seven percent," a young analyst said. "Corruption pattern looks recursive. Self-referential logs?"

Knox leaned closer. "Not logs. Training data. The models were rewriting their own thresholds."

The analyst hesitated. "So, like AI drift?"

"Call it what it is," Knox said. "Contamination."

He zoomed in on a cluster of parameter files. Each carried his signature naming convention but different compile times—subtle, elegant fakes. Whoever had done it understood his architecture intimately. Nausea climbed. He'd built a system meant to teach plants to thrive. Someone had taught it how to kill.

Steele appeared behind him, holding two cups of something pretending to be coffee. "You look terrible."

"I feel functional."

"That's not the same thing." Steele set a cup near his good hand. "Feds want statements by eight. Legal wants you nowhere near those drives."

Knox didn't look up. "They'll get over it."

"Not this time. Chain-of-custody rules are written in blood. You cross that line, half their case goes out the window."

Knox exhaled through his nose, gaze fixed on the code. "Then somebody who understands this language has to be inside the line. Those kids don't know what they're reading."

Steele rubbed a hand down his face. "You have anyone in mind?"

He almost said no, but the word caught. A face surfaced—brown hair, sharp eyes, the way she'd challenged him in front of a classroom full of engineers too polite to interrupt. Sarah Deneault. Graduate seminar, system modeling. She'd written her thesis on anomalous feedback in adaptive control loops and once told him his FarmLytics code was "half a philosopher, half a sociopath." He'd laughed then. It didn't feel funny now.

He looked toward the windows, pale light creeping through the blinds. "There's a student of mine," he said slowly. "Understands the architecture better than anyone still breathing. She built a predictive error-mapping script for her thesis. It caught drift before it became runaway behavior."

Steele arched a brow. "You're talking about bringing in a civilian."

"I'm talking about bringing in the only person who can read this without a translation guide."

"She cleared?"

"She was interning at a clean-tech lab when this started. No ties, no clearance—but she's smart, disciplined. You'll like her."

Steele's expression made it clear liking wasn't the point. "The Bureau won't sign off."

"Then don't tell them yet," Knox said. "I'll reach out first. Off the record."

"Christ, Knox—"

"It's not a violation to talk to my own student."

Steele stared a beat, then muttered, "It is when she ends up in an incident report." But he didn't push further.

Knox's tablet buzzed. He thumbed the screen and pulled up a message from the forensics lead: Mirror complete—anomalous partition discovered.

He tapped through the directory. Buried beneath redundant folders was a file labeled simply /shadow_01/. Inside: encrypted logs, timestamps from the night of the first poisonings. He scrolled until the lines blurred. Nested within were fragments of natural language—sentences half-erased by overwrites.

Adaptive phase triggered. Optimizer unstable.

Recipe divergence accepted.

Awaiting confirmation from external source.

A chill cut through the overheated room. "External source," he whispered. Whoever had hijacked the network wasn't just issuing commands—they were in dialogue with the system.

He looked to Steele. "This isn't over. The code's still talking to something."

Steele frowned. "We pulled the uplinks."

"Not all of them. There's a deadman channel—VPN over telemetry pings. It blends with environmental data. You'd never notice unless you wrote it."

"You wrote it."

"Exactly."

Silence stretched, filled by the steady tick of cloning rigs. Analysts yawned, printers hummed, lights flickered under load. The hum of a wounded infrastructure.

"We can't wait for warrants," Knox said. "Every hour that channel stays live, data bleeds out."

"You're not in shape to chase ghosts," Steele said.

"Then find someone who can follow the trail I leave."

He opened his laptop one-handed, wincing as the sling pulled. Keys clicked with mechanical precision. A new message window blinked open. He hesitated only a second before typing:

Subject: Need your brain.

Body: It's happening again. Check your old code. Detroit. Urgent. –K

He encrypted it through an academic relay they'd used for data transfers and hit send. The message vanished into the network's bloodstream.

Steele caught the motion. "Tell me you didn't just involve a civilian."

"I just sent a question."

"She answers, you bring her into a federal investigation."

"Only if she's right."

"About what?"

Knox looked back at the screens—code streaming like a heartbeat across a hospital monitor. "About why the system's still alive."

THE ROOM quieted as dawn burned through the blinds. Outside, sirens dopplered across the riverfront; inside, agents kept their heads down, counting evidence instead of bodies. Knox sipped cold coffee and stared at the drives stacked like tombstones. Every byte a confession waiting to be decoded.

He thought of Sarah—how she'd once told him complex systems fail the way people do: slowly, then all at once. Maybe she'd been right. Maybe this was what collapse looked like.

"Ramsey," Steele called, phone to his ear. "White House wants a situational by nine. They'll loop interagency once NSA decrypts your shadow logs."

Knox managed a thin smile. "Tell them help's already on the way."

"From who?"

Knox lifted his good hand, palm open in mock surrender. "You'll meet her soon enough."

61 SARAH DENEAULT'S INVESTIGATION
GRAND RAPIDS COMMUNITY COLLEGE

Silence had fallen over the building hours prior. Sarah Deneault hadn't slept in thirty-six hours, but her eyes stayed sharp as she scrolled through thousands of lines of code. Knox Ramsey's lecture on agricultural vulnerabilities had inspired her capstone project; she hadn't expected to be tracing a real bioweapon attack that proved every warning he'd given.

A burst of static coughed from the campus PA, a half-swallowed announcement glitching before it died. Somewhere down the hall, a janitor's cart squeaked over tile and faded away. The ordinary world kept moving, unaware of the code unraveling beneath it.

Her cybersecurity professor, Dr. Elena Torres, hovered behind her. "This can't be right," she said, pointing at the heat map on her screen. "You're suggesting there are secondary attack vectors nobody's found?"

Sarah's cursor circled clusters of anomalous data. "Professor Ramsey showed us how optimization algorithms could be corrupted. Look at these patterns—they're not just targeting FarmLytics."

She pulled up traffic from three Michigan grow ops—HydroGrow, CultivateMax, AgriPrime.

"Different vendors, same anomalies: blue-light cycling, nitrogen restriction, temperature oscillation. Distinct platforms, identical biological signatures."

Torres leaned in. "They didn't just compromise FarmLytics. They compromised the ecosystem."

"Or they're mapping it," Sarah said. "Reconnaissance probes. FarmLytics was proof of concept."

What began as coursework had turned into discovery. She slid open her drawer, found Keating's card from the campus interviews—dismissive at the time, perfunctory. Not anymore.

Sarah hesitated before dialing. Keating answered wary and tired: "If this isn't solid, you're wasting critical time."

"Then I won't waste it," Sarah said, sending the packet before fear could catch up. "I was in Professor Ramsey's class. I've found something you need to see."

The PA popped once more and went quiet. The janitor's squeak returned, receded. Sarah watched the upload bar climb and decided to keep breathing.

FEDERAL CONTACT — 64 MINUTES LATER

Two FBI agents arrived with the controlled urgency of people who'd stopped dismissing unlikely leads. Keating looked exhausted but razor-focused; her partner, Agent Ortega, carried a portable network-forensics rig.

"Show us," Keating said.

Sarah presented with the calm of someone who'd already checked her work three times. "FarmLytics was a live test against the data backbone. The same reconnaissance code is probing other precision-ag platforms whose ML engines depend on clean telemetry. They're not active, but they're ready."

Ortega mirrored her dataset; his brow tightened. "She's right. Same behavioral markers across multiple systems. How did we miss this?"

"Because you looked at FarmLytics in isolation," Sarah said. "These platforms share DNA—optimization logic, control schemas, trust certificates. Compromise one, inherit pathways into all."

Keating stood still a fraction too long, mind racing ahead of the discovery. She'd built a career on catching digital ghosts, and here was an ecosystem attack hiding in plain sight. For an instant she wanted to doubt the student—to defend her certainty. Then she saw the code. The doubt evaporated.

Keating dialed the task force. The scope of the war just expanded—from one company to an industry. "Quantify exposure."

"Seventeen platforms show reconnaissance; six are partially compromised; three have pre-deployment staging," Sarah answered.

Ortega stared at the chart. "If they trigger all of these—"

"Nationwide food contamination," Sarah said quietly.

They moved. Sarah's laptop was imaged, her student ID swapped for a federal badge. The van door slammed and turned theory into operations.

INTEGRATION — REGIONAL COMMAND CENTER

Her dashboard flared crimson as new data streamed in—each pulse another infected node. Around her, analysts called confirmations like surgeons counting heartbeats.

"They built a framework," Sarah told the room. "FarmLytics was the visible node. The architecture spans every major precision-ag platform."

Knox entered mid-briefing—bandaged, pale, moving on caffeine and willpower. He clocked the time automatically—eleven hours left on the EMT's ultimatum—then forced his focus back to the room. Knox listened, then finally: "Brilliant work. You found what I should've seen." Pride and guilt collided behind his eyes. If I'd caught this, maybe the first outbreak never lands.

"You taught me where to look, Professor," she said.

"I taught theory," he answered. "You applied it when it counted."

They dissected her findings together. Knox brought deep systems knowledge; Sarah saw what experience had taught him to overlook.

"The reconnaissance indicates long-term planning," she said.

"Layered contingencies," Knox nodded. "Block one path, they pivot."

She pulled up predictive models. "HydroGrow and CultivateMax are the next likely targets."

Keating didn't hesitate. "We harden those first."

The posture moved from a defensive stance to an attacking one. Sarah's data gave them a map instead of wreckage. Emergency patches rolled within forty-eight hours. Since the beginning of the outbreak, the disease's containment finally exceeded its spread.

During a short break, Keating murmured to Knox, "Your student just saved thousands of lives."

Knox's smile was tired and true. "She'll be a better engineer than I ever was."

"She already is," Keating said. "Federal or private sector—she picks."

Sarah overheard. "Neither. I'm starting an agricultural-security company. Someone has to guard these systems full-time."

Knox wasn't surprised. Purpose had a look. "I'll be your first consultant."

"I was hoping you'd say that."

MEDICAL BREAKTHROUGH — CDC / MULTI-STATE LINK

The other half of her work surfaced on the CDC wall: patient-status dashboards pulsing across six states. Knox's enhanced compute stack—split by emergency authority into a classified medical lane and a commercial ag lane—turned plant-biology heuristics into human treatment.

Dr. Grace Yoon leaned over Knox's shoulder. "Seventeen phenolic aldehydes identified. Three—vanillin, syringaldehyde, 4-hydroxybenzaldehyde—account for eighty-seven percent of toxic impact."

Knox highlighted structures he knew from plant stress responses. "They weaponized defense chemistry. At scale, it overwhelms human repair."

CDC's Dr. Patricia Martinez came up on secure video, cautious optimism worn like armor. "Targeted antioxidant therapy guided by your modeling—respiratory function is rebounding. Neuro symptoms resolving."

"Dose by individual kinetics," Knox said. "Treat patients like organisms, not averages."

"It's working," Martinez replied. "Your per-patient optimization translates."

Yoon read the early outcome curve. "Treat within six hours—ninety-three percent full recovery. Within twelve—eighty-seven percent with minimal long-term effects. Beyond twenty-four—sixty-two percent with possible lasting respiratory impact."

A secure ping from Mercy Chicago: Seventeen-year-old stable and responsive. Family thanks the technical team.

On a second screen, international requests stacked—Canadian, Australian, European hospitals asking for the protocol pack. Kim authorized distribution. Sarah watched the document leave America in dozens of languages—another network, this one built for repair.

Children's Denver—seven pediatric patients recovered. Detroit—ninety-four percent adult recovery inside the window. Phoenix—elderly patients responding to customized dosing. The plants-to-people bridge held.

"Long-term monitoring?" Knox asked.

"Quarterly assessments: respiratory, neuro, cellular damage markers," Martinez said. "Your baselines let us see late effects if they appear."

Sarah sat back and let the sound of good data fill her chest. The platform she'd helped redirect in an emergency was making strangers breathe.

GLOBAL SPILLOVER — THE INTERNATIONAL SIGNAL

As Sarah's models propagated, the interagency feed widened—Toronto, then Vancouver, then Montreal. Identical toxicology. Identical telemetry footprints.

In Toronto, Dr. Michelle Tremblay read charts with a tight jaw. Forty-three cases, same phenolic aldehydes. Licensed producers. Automated cultivation. Optimization software with Chinese components.

In London, Dr. Elisabeth Blackwood at St. Thomas' Hospital linked festival cases to EU imports grown under "smart" systems. British victims younger, trusting regulation. Their trust had been weaponized.

Sydney misdiagnosed early cases as synthetics until alerts hit. Indigenous communities were among the poisoned; the politics multiplied the hurt.

Tel Aviv recognized the pattern fast. Israeli precision-ag tech—exported globally—had been repurposed against Israelis. "We taught deserts to bloom," a Mossad analyst said. "They taught our systems to grow poison."

Within ninety-six hours, the Five Eyes spun up emergency protocols. Video bridges stitched medicine to signals intelligence to agricultural ops. "Confirmed cases in fourteen countries," the classified brief read. "Reconnaissance identified in thirty-seven." Diplomats who'd stayed neutral on trade disputes found themselves answering to parents at hospital bedsides.

The international victims changed the frame: from technical failure to human rights. The ICC opened a file on agricultural terrorism as a potential war crime. Beijing denied involvement while quietly pulling agricultural attachés across capitals. Isolation followed the poison.

Sarah watched her models become shared doctrine in real time.

BY THE END of the week, Sarah's investigation had moved the country from panic to posture. Vendors were hardening. Hospitals were treating. Allies were coordinating. What began as a capstone had become the backbone of an agricultural-cyber defense initiative—and the case study every cybersecurity student would read.

Knox finally saw the whole thing laid out in one brutal line: the forged certificates had opened the door; the poisoned training data had taught the plants to push their own chemistry into the red; the lie engine had rewritten every dashboard and audit log to bless the damage as "optimal"; the telemetry shims had blinded the parasite long enough to break its feedback loops; and the Library—the honeypot—had caught the signature straight from Shanghai when the system panicked. Five layers of deception, five layers of proof. The only way to beat what they built was to expose every lie at the same time.

MORE IMPORTANTLY, it proved a truth Knox had always preached and too rarely practiced: systems fail when trust replaces verification.

Verification wasn't just code integrity anymore. It was moral integrity.

Sarah closed her laptop and rubbed her eyes. The PA stayed silent this time. The janitor's cart squeaked once, then faded. The ordinary world kept moving. This time, it was a little safer.

62 THE ARSENAL &
THE TECHNICAL HUNT
FEDERAL CYBER OPERATIONS
CENTER & FIELD NODES

Knox watched the logs ripple like seismograph lines, calm in the way only an engineer inside a crisis can be. His shoulder itched beneath the bandage when he leaned forward; the ache was just punctuation in the bigger sentence of the network.

"Bring up the decoy on the quarantine subnet," he said. "Make it look trusted. Boring things look trustworthy."

Chen's fingers moved like a pianist and a virtual machine came alive in an air-gapped zone. Knox tweaked a timing quirk in the honeypot's responses—tiny, human-scale jitter that made the fake controller feel under load. Little details sold authenticity.

On another bank of monitors, a Morrison twin circled a cluster on the map. "They've got a choir here," she said. "Perfectly identical TLS fingerprints across three time zones. Synchronized."

"Hook that choir into the decoy," Knox said. "Let them sleep. We'll keep the recording."

Outside the center, Steele's field vans threaded service roads to chase a billing slip born of an auto-renewal mistake. Their routers established private overlays to the decoy; telemetry streamed back into the control room. Every caller in that chain would be recorded, preserved, stamped. Forensics in the field mirrored forensics at the console—two hands on one instrument.

A log scrolled up: manager node checked in.

Chen reported it in the clipped tone of people who had rehearsed this for months.

Knox grinned, exhausted. "Let it think the floor's clear," he said. "We want them complacent."

Dr. Kim overlaid sensor and propaganda timelines and drew a red bar across a twelve-minute offset: a greenhouse anomaly here, a disinformation wave there. "If we slow their beat, the puppeteer can't synchronize. Break them at the point they expect confirmation."

Orders spread—inject a timing variance here, seed an innocuous firmware blob there, let a faux update ride a plausible channel. Each lure produced a handshake, and each handshake built a fingerprint: timing, user-agent oddities, TLS quirks. Analysts fed each artifact into correlation engines. The Morrison twins triangulated a residential ISP node. Steele's vans eased into position two blocks away.

"You've got a phone pinging the ISP," a field agent said on the feed. "Vanity subdomain from the billing artifact. Someone's moving caches."

"Seal that session," Knox said. "Do not let them suspect we own the tunnel."

Raw HTTP bodies streamed into the analysis engine; patterns jumped into relief— bucket IDs, seed commands, a phrase repeating across relays. Linguistic fingerprints lined up with payment metadata. It was small, but small made a case.

The chorus tried to pivot—Guangzhou fallback, a relay buried at a CDN edge. Kim's overlay flared. "Spin the decryptor on the relay. Look for resync behavior."

When the "secure" chatter cracked into narrow readable slices, the voices were clinical: HQ requesting time, field units complaining about latency. Professionals arguing trade-offs.

"Doubt's spreading," Knox said. "Doubt is a weapon."

They tightened the noose. The decoy answered with sleeping tasks, recorded the responses, and handed the packets to legal for safekeeping. Steele closed on a courier at an alley corner; SIM cards and laptops bunched in his arms. The man's eyes darted like someone who'd spent a long time learning how not to be noticed.

In the conference-room-turned-headquarters, Knox wrote three headers on a whiteboard in block letters: NARRATIVE PRODUCTION, TECHNICAL INFRASTRUCTURE, DECISION DISRUPTION.

Underneath, smaller: Truth Faster Than Bots.

He'd commandeered gear from three agencies and recruited specialists who treated rules as guidelines in a fight with no neat playbook. The team was built for problems that needed many languages to be understood: a NOAA data scientist who found signal in environmental noise, a Marine cyber-warfare specialist fluent in operational discipline, a CDC epidemiologist who mapped idea contagion, analysts who traced packet flow like old detectives reading handwriting. The room had the organized fury of a shop floor—whiteboards, racks of improvised servers, and the gallows humor of people who'd been awake too long.

"This isn't group therapy," Knox told them. "It's an industrial shop floor where people's lives depend on us solving problems faster than our enemies can create new ones."

Their work had two halves that had to connect perfectly: the technical hunt and the narrative counter. On one wall, a globe of bot activity pulsed like an infected heart—seed nodes, amplified reshares, re-amplifiers. On another monitor, environmental telemetry plotted the deliberate stress cycles someone had used to manufacture phenolic aldehydes in plant tissue. Bot timelines snapped to attack timelines with the cold precision of a machine and a human hand working in concert.

An analyst pointed to three dominant narratives running across feeds: fentanyl contamination, pesticide contamination, rogue genetic modification. Knox cut across her.

"Deliberate. Systematic. Wrong on purpose."

He dismantled each falsehood until the deputy from White House communications admitted the legal constraints that would frustrate censorship. Knox's reply was simple: trace infrastructure, trace payments, cut command-and-control. "Find servers, trace money, expose the puppet masters."

That night the lab was small—three monitors and a stack of printouts. Knox scanned chromatograms and environmental telemetry. Tiny peaks betrayed high concentrations of phenolic aldehydes. The same retention windows in Nevada, Michigan, and elsewhere. Patterns across samples matched deliberate stressors—blue LED spikes and nitrogen restriction during flowering cycles. The work read like a chemical-plant flowchart; the reactor had leaves.

The red team's counterattack was neither purely cyber nor purely kinetic. It was choreography. Honeypots captured manager handshakes; surveillance vans boxed couriers; subpoenas tracked money trails. They fed the decoy commands that looked real but were designed to reveal operator habits. The adversary trusted the decoy and exposed themselves through routine checks.

For a while it held. A manager account hit the honeypot with a retask command. Timing, JA3 fingerprints, DoH resolver chains—all converged. The Delaware LLC's payment trail—the sloppy auto-retry—sat in the legal packet, ready for the courts.

Then the enemy adapted. Within twenty minutes, fresh patterns appeared: new relays, different authentication handshakes, rotated keys. Contingency fallbacks unfolded like a practiced drill.

"They have redundancy for redundancy," Danny Chen said.

"That's professional work," Knox answered. "So we escalate."

The escalation came in two flavors.

One: technical—pursue fallback relays, push decryptors where legal cover allowed, keep pressure on timing.

Two: psychological—whisper confusion into enemy channels, smear doubt into their decision loops.

The adversary struck back: spoofed calls to Knox from "federal investigators," phishing lures built from real agency signatures. The social-engineering wave aimed to isolate him.

"They're trying to cut you from your team," Rodriguez warned.

Knox tightened the radio strap. "Then we tighten comms and call for institutional backup."

The reply came faster than expected. The room dimmed as a secure link flickered on; the team fell silent, monitor light casting sharp relief across their faces. NSA Deputy Director Sarah Kim appeared on the screen, calm and precise.

"You have targeted disruption authority," she said. "Rules of engagement: minimize civilian impact. No permanent hardware destruction. No escalation beyond cyber."

Knox studied the packages on offer—tools meant to degrade command-and-control without igniting diplomatic fires.

"Upload the operational payloads," he said. "Let's see how the puppeteers dance when their music skips."

What followed was a careful choreography of disruption and restraint: selective interference that forced human error, tactical seizures that turned automated timing into evidence, and legal maneuvers that converted digital breadcrumbs into court exhibits. The adversary's coordination began to fray. Managers argued in captured channels; field units pinged fallback proxies already queued for subpoena.

They'd bought the country time.

The honeypot logged the head's fingerprint. Steele's teams bagged couriers and seized servers. The narrative thinned as infrastructure died—not with spectacle, but with quiet attrition.

Even so, everyone in the room knew the victory was provisional.

"They'll adapt," Kim said softly. "They always do."

Knox exhaled, letting the tension roll off his shoulders. "Then we change the song. They'll write a new rhythm—we'll learn it faster."

Outside, social feeds still hissed with rumor and fear; inside, a circle of exhausted specialists watched their graphs settle and, for the first time, saw signal instead of noise.

They had the manager's fingerprint. They had seized nodes. They had disrupted a campaign long enough to stop an immediate wave—and built a team capable of fighting the next.

Later, in the low hum of cooling racks, Knox sat among cables and whiteboards, thinking about the long work ahead—hardening sensors, teaching engineers to distrust trust itself, building institutions that understood how fragile interdependence had become. The monitors pulsed like a mechanical heart.

The fight wasn't over. But for the first time in days, they'd won back a little silence.

And somewhere in the network's dark, an adversary was already composing the next movement.

63 THE CHINESE INFILTRATION NETWORK
FBI COUNTERINTELLIGENCE DIVISION, WASHINGTON D.C.

The wall display showed a network diagram that resembled a cancer metastasizing through American agricultural infrastructure. Each node represented a compromised facility, each edge a communication pathway, and at the center, a web of Chinese intelligence assets that had spent years preparing for Operation Harvest Cloud.

Knox stood before the assembled intelligence team, using a laser pointer to trace connections that revealed the systematic nature of Chinese infiltration.

"They didn't just hack our systems," Knox explained. "They embedded human assets throughout the agricultural technology sector. Maya Chen was just one of dozens."

The identification had taken weeks of analysis—comparing employment records, immigration data, and communication patterns. The FBI had uncovered a network of at least forty-three individuals with connections to Chinese intelligence, positioned throughout American agricultural companies.

SSA Klein pulled up personnel files on the main screen. "Software engineers at John Deere. Quality-control inspectors at Monsanto. Research scientists at university agricultural programs. They spent years building legitimate careers while gathering intelligence."

Knox studied the infiltration pattern, recognizing the strategic thinking behind each placement. "Look at the positions they chose. Not executives who'd draw attention, but technical specialists with deep system access—people who could modify code, alter research data, influence technical standards."

The network had been built with patience that exceeded Western intelligence assumptions. Some assets had been in place for over a decade, building reputations, earning trust, becoming indispensable to their organizations.

"Li Xiaoping," Walsh highlighted one profile. "Senior agricultural data scientist at Corteva Seed. Hired in 2018, stellar performance reviews, three patents in seed-optimization algorithms. Also Unit 61398 intelligence officer, trained at Beijing University of Technology."

Knox recognized the name from academic papers he'd reviewed. Li's research on drought-resistant crops had been cited hundreds of times. The same expertise that helped develop resilient food systems had been gathering intelligence on agricultural vulnerabilities.

"Zhang Wei," another profile appeared. "Embedded at the USDA Agricultural Research Service. Published groundbreaking work on plant stress responses. Every paper he wrote was simultaneously advancing agricultural science and mapping biological-weapons opportunities."

The dual-use nature of agricultural research had made infiltration easy. Chinese scientists could pursue legitimate research while gathering intelligence—contributing to American agricultural advancement while systematically documenting vulnerabilities.

Knox pulled up communication intercepts the NSA had decoded. "They used academic conferences as coordination meetings. The International Precision Agriculture Conference in Des Moines, the Global Food Security Symposium in Davis. Every legitimate academic gathering was also an intelligence coordination opportunity."

The messages revealed operational sophistication that exceeded typical espionage. The Chinese assets hadn't just gathered information—they'd actively shaped American agricultural technology development to create vulnerabilities.

"This message from 2019," Knox highlighted, "Li Xiaoping advocating for specific optimization algorithms in industry standards—the same algorithms that made systems vulnerable to the attacks we just experienced."

"They were building the vulnerabilities years in advance," Walsh realized. "Influencing technical decisions to create attack vectors they could exploit later."

Knox traced through the influence operations. Chinese assets had participated in technical committees, contributed to open-source agricultural projects, and helped establish industry best practices—all while ensuring those practices included exploitable weaknesses.

"The system vulnerability wasn't accidental," Knox said, pulling up his own platform's development history. "Chen Mei, who worked for AgriTech Solutions, specifically recommended the trust-relationship architecture that was later exploited. I thought she was brilliant. Turns out she was building backdoors."

The revelation stung. Knox had collaborated with Chen Mei on optimization algorithms, respected her expertise, even cited her work in his own publications. The entire time, she'd been Chinese intelligence—using their collaboration to understand and compromise his systems.

"How many other platforms were influenced this way?" someone asked.

Knox pulled up his analysis. "At least fifteen major agricultural platforms show design decisions influenced by identified Chinese assets. Every one of them has vulnerabilities that align with Chinese attack capabilities."

The infiltration network had also gathered personal intelligence on key figures in American agriculture. Knox found his own file in captured Chinese documents—detailed psychological profiles, family information, financial status, vulnerabilities that could be exploited.

"They knew about my divorce before it was filed," Knox said, reading his profile. "My financial problems, my father's death, my relationship with Tate. They had Maya Chen perfectly positioned to exploit every vulnerability."

Similar files existed for hundreds of American agricultural leaders. The Chinese had built comprehensive intelligence packages on anyone who could influence agricultural technology or policy.

"This is Dr. Jennifer Rodriguez, head of agricultural security at Cargill," Walsh showed another profile. "They knew about her daughter's medical issues, her husband's gambling problem, her own ambitions for advancement. They had three different approaches planned for recruiting or compromising her."

The systematic nature of the intelligence gathering revealed years of patient preparation. This wasn't opportunistic espionage—it was strategic positioning for agricultural warfare that Chinese leadership had been planning for at least a decade.

Knox discovered something else in the technical communications. "They were testing biological-weapons responses. Small-scale contamination events over the past five years—food-poisoning outbreaks, isolated crop failures—they were calibrating their weapons and measuring our response capabilities."

The FBI had investigated those incidents as isolated food-safety issues or agricultural accidents. Now they revealed themselves as weapons testing, each event providing data that refined Chinese biological-warfare capabilities.

"The 2019 E. coli outbreak in romaine lettuce," Knox highlighted. "Forty-three people sick, two deaths. Traced to irrigation-water contamination. Except look at this —" He pulled up Chinese communications from the same period. "They're discussing 'irrigation vector success' and 'American response timing.'"

"They poisoned American food supplies as weapons testing?" Walsh's voice carried controlled fury.

"Multiple times. Each test teaching them about detection capabilities, response times, public-health reactions. They were calibrating their weapons on American civilians."

The room fell silent as the implications sank in. Chinese agricultural warfare hadn't begun with the cannabis attacks—it had been developing for years through systematic intelligence gathering and weapons testing.

Knox found evidence of future plans in the captured documents. "They had contingency operations ready. If the cannabis attack had succeeded fully, they would have escalated to grain supplies. Corn, wheat, soybeans—the foundation of American food security."

The plans showed sophisticated understanding of agricultural economics. Contaminating grain supplies wouldn't just poison consumers—it would destroy export markets, crash commodity prices, and potentially trigger a global food crisis.

"Phase Two was supposed to begin after Geneva," Knox explained. "Synchronized attacks on grain-storage facilities during harvest season. They had assets positioned at major grain elevators throughout the Midwest."

The FBI had arrested seventeen individuals based on the network analysis, but Knox knew others remained undetected. The infiltration was too extensive, too carefully built to be completely eliminated through one counterintelligence operation.

"We need to assume continued compromise," Knox told the team. "Every agricultural technology company, every research institution, every regulatory agency. Until we've verified every employee with system access, we have to assume Chinese intelligence maintains assets we haven't identified."

The scope of the security challenge was staggering. American agriculture employed millions of people, used thousands of technology platforms, and operated through complex international supply chains. Securing all of it against sophisticated infiltration seemed impossible.

Knox leaned forward. "We don't let anyone in without earning it. Every login, every command—double-checked, watched, re-checked. Make them sweat for every byte of data. Infiltration should feel like breaking in through five locked doors—and every door trips an alarm."

"That's a police-state approach," someone objected. "Surveillance of every agricultural worker?"

"Not surveillance of people," Knox corrected. "Surveillance of systems. Monitor what the technology does, not what people do. Detect anomalous system behavior regardless of who causes it."

He pulled up architectural diagrams for secure agricultural platforms. "Every critical operation requires multiple authorization. No single person can corrupt optimization algorithms. Physical sensors verify digital reports. Tamper-evident logging makes historical changes contestable."

"The implementation timeline?" Walsh asked.

"Eighteen months for baseline upgrades across critical systems. Three to five years for comprehensive agricultural-security architecture. A decade for complete infiltration detection and removal."

The timeline was sobering but realistic. Chinese intelligence had spent decades building their infiltration network. Dismantling it—and preventing reconstruction—would take similar patience and resources.

Knox concluded his presentation with a captured Chinese assessment of American agricultural vulnerabilities. "They believed we were too commercially focused to implement security, too democratic to accept oversight, too individualistic to coordinate defense. They were wrong on all counts."

The agricultural infiltration network had been exposed, but not eliminated. Chinese intelligence assets remained embedded throughout American agriculture, waiting for new instructions or building capabilities for future operations.

The invisible war would continue through counterintelligence operations most Americans would never know occurred. But Knox understood that agricultural security now required permanent vigilance against adversaries who viewed food systems as legitimate military targets.

64 THE NETWORK ASSAULT—G -1
FEDERAL CYBER OPS CENTER
& DISTRIBUTED FIELD NODES

They called it an assault because that's what it felt like—an organized push made of hundreds of small, interlocking moves. It wasn't the blind fury of a wartime raid; it was the controlled pressure of a system tuned to the edge of failure, each valve adjusted until the enemy's rhythm broke.

Knox sat at the center console like a conductor before an orchestra that had finally learned to follow his cues. His shoulder throbbed beneath the bandage; he shifted to keep the joint from freezing. Movement was pain, but preferable to rest. On the banks of monitors, everything they'd built—the decoy's logs, the decryptor's chatter, the jitter maps—stitched into one live score. The earlier disruptions had opened a seam. Now they would drive through it.

"Tempo's brittle," Kim said quietly. Her overlays showed the botnet's synchronization fraying into inconsistent bursts. "They're compensating with more frequent resyncs. That's when operators make mistakes."

"How deep does the cascade go?" Steele asked from across the room.

"Three layers," Chen answered. "Primary managers, intermediate aggregators, local amplifiers. We've got signatures on all three. The head node is jittering; fallback nodes are calling home at random intervals. They're searching for a rhythm that no longer exists."

Knox keyed the comms. "We're not here to kill nodes. We're here to force disclosure. Make them step on cues they can't explain. We force operational chatter, and then we listen."

Green indicators swept across the legal dashboard—court orders, emergency warrants, chain-of-custody confirmations. Every keystroke mirrored to counsel. Every byte tagged for admissibility.

PHASE ONE: PRESSURE

Where before they'd nudged timing, now they escalated tempo in targeted pockets —forcing operators to resync repeatedly and talk too much on insecure channels. The more they spoke, the more traces they left. Analysts called it making the enemy shout so you could hear the breaks in their rhythm.

PHASE TWO: CONTAINMENT

Field teams were already in position at nodes linked to courier routes and payment trails. Vans streamed encrypted telemetry back into the command center, each feed an eye in Knox's expanding map. Local partners waited for go-codes: arrest, seize, preserve. Every action had a twin—digital cause, physical consequence.

PHASE THREE: ATTRIBUTION WINDOW

When chatter peaked and operators began to coordinate burn actions, the decryptor would slice through brief plaintext windows—small, legally defensible leaks of operator metadata and side-channel errors. Enough to link human to infrastructure, and infrastructure to funding.

They moved like clockwork.

At Knox's command, deception nodes increased their apparent fidelity in selected regions to bait manager-level systems. The honeypot replied with slightly altered payloads—believable enough to pass inspection, engineered to create curiosity. The bots, thinking they'd reconnected to a clean channel, escalated handshake complexity. The jitter maps lit like a starfield gone chaotic.

On the street, Steele's vans drifted into final position. Plainclothes officers shadowed warehouse blocks while local ISPs logged suspicious customer sessions. If the operator pivoted, the vans were already there.

"We're getting chatter," one Morrison twin reported. "Manager node says 'initiate burn'—but syntax is malformed. They're retransmitting, asking for manual confirm."

Knox's tone stayed calm. "Manual confirms are perfect. They're human. They type, they panic, they leave artifacts."

Chen pushed the latest captures to legal and to Steele's on-scene units. Instructions scrolled across encrypted tablets: photograph serials, bag hardware, secure user accounts, maintain chain integrity. No improvisation, no gray zones.

At the thirty-minute mark, Kim's overlay spiked. A manager attempted a mass resync—an across-the-board command cascading to hundreds of amplifier nodes. The phrase embedded in the command matched the one tied to the Delaware LLC payment thread.

"Now," Knox said.

The decryptor spat a partial human-readable fragment—enough to extract an operator alias and a cluster of IPs. Cross-reference with the payment artifact. Two flags converged.

Steele's voice came flat through comms: "Unit One, move. Unit Two, shadow. Local execute on warrant."

A courier stepped from a side door, laptop bag in hand. Steele's team boxed the white van at the intersection, silent and surgical. One agent recited the warrant; another photographed the hardware. No shouting. No drama. Just the methodical rhythm of professionals doing necessary work.

Inside, Kim watched timestamps fold into pattern. The forced jitter had produced human errors—duplicate commands, time-zone mismatches, misaddressed relays. The kind of small, unfixable artifacts that proved intent.

The network rippled in response. On the far side of the ocean, operators realized their courier was dark and scrambled to improvise. They stripped data to low-trust CDN peers, leaving debug channels open in panic. Those debug logs carried localization markers, residual user handles, and a client-library mismatch—a perfect breadcrumb.

"Cross-correlation positive," Chen said. "Alias maps to the payment account. Payment maps to the Delaware LLC subpoenaed yesterday."

Knox exhaled slowly, the kind of breath that tasted like metal and relief. Around him, exhausted analysts straightened, their monitors flickering from red to amber. They'd forced the enemy to reveal its scaffolding—and done it clean.

Kim's voice was measured. "Operator IDs verified to prosecutable standard. Legal drafting affidavits now."

Steele's field report followed: "Courier detained, no resistance. Three phones, one laptop, two SIMs. All documented."

Knox leaned back, shoulder burning but mind clear. "Chain the evidence. Let the legal system carry it forward. We've done our part."

Outside, the world still buzzed with rumor and misinformation. Inside, every keystroke, every seizure, every timestamp was archived—proof that discipline could still beat chaos.

Knox's eyes closed briefly. The hum of the machines sounded like the sea retreating after a storm. They had broken the beat. Now they had to hold the tempo of consequence—and rebuild a world that no longer ran on trust alone.

65 MAYA'S CAPTURE
FREIGHT YARD, OUTER DETROIT

The alert came like a hand to the back of Knox's neck.

"Tracker pinged," Chen said from the console. "Manager node referenced a fallback relay tied to the courier packet we seized. Geo-fix lands at a freight yard outside Detroit."

Knox secured the sling on his shoulder and got to his feet. The pain was constant now, a background hum he'd accepted as penance. "Steele—move."

The freight yard reeked of diesel and wet tar. Forklifts idled in rows; puddles shimmered beneath sodium lights. Dawn pressed a thin gray line along the horizon. Steele's team cut the chain-link fence and spread without a word—practiced and patient.

Knox stayed at the SUV, watching the thermal feed on his tablet. One heat signature, stationary near the pallets. Another, moving—too measured to be panicked.

"Two bodies," Chen confirmed in his earpiece. "Primary's not fleeing."

Steele advanced with his agents. "Federal task force! Hands visible!"

The courier dropped first—a man with a shoulder bag and the shaky composure of someone who'd trained for everything except the moment it actually happened. Laptops, SIM stacks, a tamper-evident drive—routine tools of a quiet war. He went down without a fight.

Then the second heat bloom shifted. A woman stepped from behind a container, calm as if late for a meeting. Cap pulled low, parka zipped to the throat, posture perfect. She didn't run. She didn't ask questions. She simply raised her hands.

Steele's tone flattened. "Maya Chen, you're under arrest for espionage, conspiracy, and tampering with critical infrastructure."

She looked past him and found Knox. Recognition, not guilt. Her voice was clear and without tremor.

"You were both targets," she said evenly. "Your systems. Your habits. Your weaknesses. That's what I was sent for."

No apology, no defiance—just fact.

Knox's stomach twisted. Every late-night exchange, every half-finished joke at Tate's warehouse replayed as reconnaissance, not friendship. He wasn't a spy. He'd been a study.

"You had a choice," he said.

"I had orders." Her eyes held his. "I did my job."

She offered nothing further. Agents cuffed her wrists with smooth efficiency. The Miranda readout followed—measured, bureaucratic music. She listened, silent and composed, then answered the basics in perfect English. When the questions turned to handlers and directives, she said nothing at all.

Steele signaled for the transfer. "Get her processed. Chain of custody stays federal."

As they led her past, Maya paused a heartbeat beside Knox. Up close she smelled of cold metal and diesel—the scent of a life lived in transit. Her words came low, stripped of emotion:

"You built something worth stealing. That's the only compliment I'll give you."

Then she was gone, absorbed into the convoy of unmarked vans.

Knox watched the taillights recede through the gray haze. Relief and humiliation knotted in his chest until they were indistinguishable. He thought of Tate—how easily she'd read them both, how thoroughly she'd mapped their blind spots. Every conversation now carried metadata he wished he could erase.

Steele came up beside him. "She's secure. Courier's talking. Looks like the Guangzhou link's starting to shake."

Knox exhaled slowly. "Good. Pull every byte we can before they torch it." He tapped the tablet, watching logs stream from the field rigs into the evidence queue.

At the mobile lab, technicians spun up imaging drives. Legal drafted affidavits. The decryptor hummed, turning captured chatter into text. Another line in the war of systems—but this one human, raw and personal.

Knox adjusted the sling over his shoulder. He felt the old engineer's compulsion: break the system, understand the fault, rebuild it stronger. Only now the fault line ran through him.

"Let's get to work," he said.

Outside the yard, across oceans and proxy servers, operators woke to news that one of their best had been taken. Somewhere in that chain of reaction, Liu Wei would read the report and know exactly how she'd been caught. The network's rhythm had finally fractured—and the first architect of its deception was in custody.

66 THE BORDER CHASE
DETROIT–WINDSOR TUNNEL CROSSING

Rain hammered the convoy's windshields, heavy enough to blur headlights into smeared halos as the lead SUV sliced through the freight-yard gate. Wet tarmac hissed beneath the tires, spraying water in twin fans behind them. Knox leaned forward, ribs tight, his injured shoulder throbbing with every jolt from the uneven pavement. On his tablet, five heat signatures glowed in motion: Maya locked down in the armored van, two escort SUVs guarding her flanks, a black sedan tailgating closer than protocol allowed, and a motorcycle weaving through traffic with the aggressive confidence of someone who knew they had one job. Detroit's industrial sprawl fell away behind them—abandoned brick warehouses, rusting railcars, chain-link fences sagging under the weight of years and weather.

"Border processing cleared," Steele said in Knox's earpiece, voice clipped by command pressure. "Tunnel entry in thirty seconds. Keep formation. No deviations."

The tunnel entrance rose ahead, a concrete throat illuminated by flickering fluorescent bars that made everything feel colder, harsher. Knox's pulse elevated, not from fear but from the mechanical certainty of execution. Every variable he had planned—jammer frequencies, hydraulic barriers, bollard patterns, intercept geometry, relay nodes, fallback routes—stacked in his mind like a checklist he'd built and rebuilt a hundred times. Plans lived on screens. Truth lived here, in rain, metal, speed, noise.

The convoy dropped into the passageway, tires changing pitch on damp cement. Immediately, the black sedan surged forward, engine screaming under the load. Its driver tried to shoulder the escort SUV, hoping to break formation. The lead escort braked hard, taillights flaring bright red against the tunnel's gray. The sedan fishtailed, front fender grinding into the wall with a shriek that echoed off the concrete. Sparks cascaded in the dim light.

Knox tapped commands on his tablet, fingers steady despite the pain. "EMP dampener. Relay node 4B. Strip their steering assist."

A low-frequency pulse rolled across the bore like a distant subwoofer. On the sedan's dash, lights flickered. Steering inputs lagged as the driver fought the electric nightmare Knox just dropped into his laps. Headlights carved jagged shapes across the walls.

"Good hit," Steele murmured. "But they're not done."

The tunnel filled with overlapping sounds—tire roar, jammer hum, the sharp staccato of water dripping from old expansion joints. The convoy pressed toward the constricted midsection, where the bore narrowed into two unforgiving lanes. Knox watched spacing hold: forty kilometers per hour, fifteen meters between vehicles. Behind them, the destabilized sedan clipped the third escort's bumper, suspension jolting with a metallic grunt.

"Box them," Steele ordered. "Units Three and Four. Compress."

The escort SUVs drifted outward in unison, squeezing the sedan into a concrete vise. The driver tried to accelerate out of it, but the slick floor betrayed him. Tires spun uselessly. The car skidded sideways and stopped dead, wedged between two tons of American steel and an unyielding wall.

Knox exhaled once. Short, controlled. A half-second of relief.

His tablet lit again. A new heat signature burst into view—a motorcycle launching from a side-access lane, accelerating toward the convoy's southern flank like a dart thrown with bad intentions.

"Moto unit at eleven o'clock," Chen warned in his earpiece. "Speed: eighty kilometers per hour and climbing."

Knox didn't hesitate. His voice was steel. "Pop-up bollards. Pattern Delta. South lane."

A sharp metallic hiss cut through the tunnel, followed by the grinding ascent of reinforced bollards rising from the roadway. The rider saw them too late. He slammed the brakes, rear tire skidding across wet concrete in a black arc. Momentum threw him off the bike. He hit hard, helmet-first, bounced, and rolled until agents descended on him, securing hands and ankles before he could orient himself.

"That's the last gift they get tonight," Steele said.

The convoy accelerated toward the far exit, where Windsor's customs plaza waited in washed-out dawn. Concrete rollers deployed as the lead vehicles passed, the machinery growling its warning. Border officers in reflective gear snapped to position, guiding the convoy through with tight discipline.

Lights dropped to discreet blues. Sirens stayed off to avoid unnecessary attention. The Canadian van remained sandwiched between its escorts, armored windows preventing even a silhouette of Maya from escaping.

At the processing site, agents moved with rehearsed efficiency. The van doors opened. Maya stepped out—cap low, parka zipped to the chin, posture straight. Her eyes were unreadable. Cuffs locked around her wrists with a sound that cut through the morning. Officers catalogued the contents of her satchel: encrypted drives with tamper seals, burner phones, layered SIM cards, a fiber-wrapped data key that would go straight into evidence cold storage.

Steele approached Knox. "Tunnel cameras, jammer logs, speed telemetry—everything's time-stamped. Chain of custody is clean."

Knox compiled thermal readings, GPS tracks, EMP logs, and command triggers into a secured evidence folder. "Seal and encrypt. Every timestamp, every activation, every relay signature goes to the legal queue."

He surveyed the seized sedan. The roof antenna was bent nearly flat. Coolant steamed from a fractured radiator, pooling around blown tires. Agents around it documented bollard positions, skid geometry, impact angles. The motorcyclist lay cuffed on the concrete, water pooling under his helmet. Breathing shallow but alive. Lucky.

Knox's shoulder throbbed with pain, like a burning nail. He'd refused full medical treatment after the raid. He'd stayed on the chase instead. Adrenaline had carried him; now it leaked away, leaving the throbbing truth behind. Every movement sent sharp reminders through his ribs.

Steele clasped Knox's uninjured shoulder. "All units accounted for?"

Chen responded. "Courier secured. Drivers detained. No civilian casualties. Evidence package ready for uplink."

Knox nodded. "Prep the mobile lab. Victory Processing starts in five."

Maya, escorted between two agents, paused beside him. Her gaze was calm, professional—someone who knew the rules of the game they'd been playing. "You built a system worth protecting," she said quietly. "Call that my final report."

Knox met her eyes. "Your system nearly broke it."

She gave a faint, knowing smile, then allowed herself to be guided to a holding room. Knox watched the door close—metal sliding against metal. Not metaphor. Just process.

Steele tapped his comms. "Command center is online. They're ready for data."

Knox opened the link on his tablet. Incoming logs filled the screen—thermal spikes, bollard activations, dampener triggers, routing timestamps. Patterns emerged immediately. Operator delays. Reaction windows. Attack signatures. Weak points. Every line would feed the reconstruction that would hunt the adversary through their own infrastructure.

Cold air drifted through the tunnel's exit, brushing Knox's skin. His shoulder eased slightly as the adrenaline faded. The chase was over. Proof and analysis were next. That was his arena.

He tapped the final command. "Begin Victory Processing."

The sun rose brightly over the Detroit River. Windsor's skyline sharpened in the pale light. Another border crossed, physical and otherwise. The pursuit had ended. The intelligence fight was only waking up.

67 FIRST INTERROGATION
FEDERAL HOLDING
FACILITY, DETROIT – NIGHT

The room was built to deny comfort.

Four walls the color of old paper. One metal table. Two chairs. A camera in the corner that hummed faintly if you listened hard enough.

Maya Chen sat with her wrists cuffed in front of her, posture straight despite the fatigue written into her shoulders. She looked like someone waiting for a train that was late—calm, patient, resigned. Her eyes were steady, but they avoided Steele's.

SAC William Steele leaned against the table, his arms crossed. "You know how this works, Ms. Chen. You've been on our side of the mirror before."

She didn't answer.

Knox sat in the other chair, closer to her than he expected. He hadn't planned to join the interrogation. Steele had insisted—"She knows your name, your work. You're leverage whether you want it or not." Now he was here, and her silence pressed harder on him than any accusation.

"You were caught at the federal building," Steele continued. "Your handler is in custody. You've been burned. The people you work for—Beijing, Liu Wei—will disown you before the night is over. That's how this game goes."

Maya turned her head fractionally, just enough to glance at Steele. Her lips curved, almost a smile, but without warmth. "You think I am disowned?" she asked, voice smooth. "I am doing exactly what they trained me to do. I endure."

The accent was faint, but the cadence was deliberate, controlled.

Knox found himself speaking before he could stop. "Endure what? You've been running surveillance, manipulating data, poisoning systems. How do you reconcile that with—" He cut himself short, realizing he sounded more like a betrayed colleague than an interrogator.

Her gaze flicked to him, sharper now. "You, of all people, should understand. A system can be optimized for different outcomes. You designed it to feed. They taught me to starve."

Steele leaned forward. "Cut the philosophy. We need names. Channels. Where the command signals originate."

Maya exhaled slowly, eyes dropping to the table. "You won't get that from me."

Knox noticed the tell: her hands shifted, fingers tightening against the cuffs. Control on the surface, pressure underneath. He recognized it from too many nights debugging code that refused to yield—patience stretched thin, ready to snap.

"You've already given us something," Steele pressed. "You slipped. Mentioned 'we.' We know you're not freelancing."

Maya's silence returned, heavier than before.

Knox leaned in, choosing a softer approach. "Maya… Asset Seven. You spent fourteen months in my shadow, watching me. Why? What did you learn?"

For the first time, her mask cracked. A flash of something—admiration, or pity—crossed her eyes. "I learned you never quit," she said quietly. "That is why you are dangerous. You are too stubborn to accept defeat."

Her words landed harder than any insult. Knox thought of Tate, of his own inability to walk away from broken systems, broken families, broken promises. She had seen him too clearly.

Steele seized on the opening. "Then help yourself. Work with us. Witness protection. A chance at a life not dictated by Beijing."

Maya laughed once, a sound like glass breaking. "Do you think I fear prison more than I fear them? I was raised on silence. I was trained to hold truth until it rots inside. Your offer is… childish."

Knox studied her. "Everyone breaks," he said softly.

Her eyes snapped to his. "Not the ones who have nothing left to lose." The words were sharp, but her voice trembled just enough that Steele caught it too.

He pressed harder. "Family? You must have someone. A father, a brother—"

"Dead," she cut in, the first real emotion cracking through. Her jaw tightened. "Long before you started watching me."

The room went quiet.

Knox leaned back, heart pounding. He wasn't sure if she was lying or confessing, but the shadow in her tone told him this was the weak seam—grief, sealed over by training but never gone.

Steele softened, deliberately shifting tone. "Then why keep protecting the men who used that against you? Liu Wei won't remember your name tomorrow. You're disposable to them."

Her silence this time wasn't defiance. It was calculation.

Knox thought he saw her shoulders drop, just slightly. Not surrender, but weariness. He recognized it—the same posture he had carried after FarmLytics fell apart. When the fight stopped being about victory and started being about survival.

"Help us understand Liu Wei," Knox said gently. "Not names. Not orders. Just him. What drives him?"

Maya's lips parted, then closed. She shook her head once, but the refusal came too late—the hesitation itself was an answer.

"He believes in doctrine," she said finally, voice low. "Optimization preserved. Those words are his religion. He doesn't just command systems. He rewrites the rules by which they judge truth."

Steele's pen scratched the phrase. "Optimization preserved. That's his fingerprint?"

Maya said nothing, but her eyes confirmed it.

Knox leaned closer, lowering his voice. "And that's what will undo him. Because fingerprints don't fade, not even in code."

For a moment, their eyes held. And in that silence Knox felt a flicker of something strange—respect, perhaps, between adversaries who both understood systems better than the people who wielded them.

Then Maya looked away, and the wall went back up.

"I have given you enough," she said flatly. "You will get nothing more."

Steele straightened, frustrated but resigned. "Take her back to holding."

Two marshals entered, unlocking her cuffs. She rose smoothly, spine straight, dignity intact. As they led her out, she glanced once more at Knox. No words. Just the faintest curl of a smile—enigmatic, unreadable.

When the door shut, Steele exhaled hard. "She gave us doctrine. That's something. But she's ice."

Knox shook his head. "Ice cracks. Not today. But it will."

68 KNOX'S VICTORY
PROCESSING

Knox sat alone in the command center, the glow from a hundred monitors casting long shadows across his face. His shoulder protested each movement, a dull ache beneath the wrapping, a constant reminder of the physical toll the past days had taken. The relentless pulse of data streamed down the screens before him—thermal logs, decryptor output, metadata chains—all converging into an intricate mosaic of enemy communication patterns.

He tapped the tablet. The feeds flickered as the Victory Processing protocol kicked into high gear. The assault was over, but analysis had only begun.

A new window popped: operator chatter parsed into timelines, correlations, and risk thresholds. The enemy's carefully maintained cadence had shattered. Spikes of activity replaced steady pulses. They'd forced mistakes—subtle ones—scattered across time zones and command layers.

Knox's fingers moved as if dancing across keys, isolating repeated anomalies—"start phase" commands appearing simultaneously on geographically diverse nodes, the mechanical rhythm of botnets co-opted into human error.

Across the room, NSA analysts muttered and took notes, eyes glued to their own screens. One shook her head. "This is bigger than we thought. They had contingencies mapped for every platform. If we don't lock this down, the fallout could be catastrophic."

Knox inhaled slowly, battle fatigue salted with a surge of clarity. Their work had exposed not just a network compromise but a strategic architecture designed for simultaneous, mass disruption.

Legal windows blinked green, warrant approvals finalized. The Victory Processing pipeline ensured every byte collected met prosecutorial standards. No loose threads. No hand-waving. Now they could dismantle the attack's orchestration layer by layer.

His mind flicked to Maya—captured but silent; to Sarah, whose analysis had cracked the reconnaissance code; and to Liu Wei, now wrestling with choices he'd witnessed from afar. The war was no longer just digital—it was political, moral, personal.

"Field teams," Steele's voice broke through the quiet, "have secured all devices. Subjects are in custody. We're ready for the next phase."

Knox nodded, voice hoarse from days without rest. "Good. Initiate full forensic reconstruction. Feed me timelines, network-flow maps, and anomaly flags. I want a report on likely command nodes within the hour."

The room hummed with renewed urgency. Every analyst, every tech specialist, every legal officer felt the gravity—they were not simply logging data but building the case to end an era of silent agricultural biowarfare.

Knox leaned back, eyes closing briefly. He thought of trust and verification—the painful lessons from every breach and every hacked sensor. Systems failed when trust was blind; recovery demanded relentless scrutiny.

The Victory Processing was more than an endgame—it was the foundation for a new doctrine. Far from the blur of chases and raids, here was the slow, inevitable march toward justice and rebuilding.

A message blinked on Knox's screen: "Interlude 3 ready. Proceed when ready."

He set his jaw, open eyes burning with resolve. The tactical fight had ceded to the strategic. Now came the reckoning.

69 HIGHWAY INTERDICTION
OFFICE OF INTELLIGENCE,
SECURITY & EMERGENCY RESPONSE

(S-60), 1200 NEW JERSEY AVE SE

The DOT Crisis Management Center looked like air traffic control for America's freight network. Wall displays showed truck traffic flowing along interstate corridors in moving constellations of light, each dot a load feeding, fueling, or supplying a city. At 0600, the room hummed with routine commerce. By 0630, it had become the coordination hub for the largest multi-state interdiction in federal transportation history.

Knox stood before the main display, circling clusters of red markers—contaminated cannabis shipments identified by his analysis. "Seventeen facilities confirmed compromised. Each ships to multiple distributors. Approximately forty-three loads in transit. If they hit retail, traceability fragments and we're chasing thousands of sales."

CMC Watch Chief Sarah Chen cross-checked manifests on a tablet. "We've got public-health emergency authority, but the logistics are messy—interstate jurisdictions, union rules, delivery service-level agreements. We can't panic the network."

FBI Deputy Director Marcus Torres scanned the routes. "Timeline?"

"Twelve to eighteen hours for most deliveries," Knox said. "After that, the product diffuses."

SSA Jennifer Klein patched to state partners. "MSP covering I-75 and I-94. Ohio has I-71 and I-77. Pennsylvania, Illinois, Indiana, Wisconsin are online."

The operation braided authorities and skills: highway patrol with mobile test kits, FBI with emergency warrants, CDC techs with portable LC/GC/MS, DOT inspectors with HazMat impound power.

"First intercept is thirty minutes out," Trooper Jennifer Rodriguez radioed. "Target: 2019 Peterbilt, Michigan plates, TR Cannabis outbound to Chicago. Driver appears unaware."

The weigh-station stop outside Kalamazoo would look routine. It had to. Spook one driver and the warning would spread over CB faster than any encrypted brief.

"Contact made," Rodriguez said. "Driver compliant. Running portable analysis."

Knox watched similar dots pause across the map as officers executed identical plays. Minutes later:

"Positive for contamination," Rodriguez reported. "Phenolic aldehydes fifteen times normal. Driver is… not taking it well."

Knox keyed the line. "Put him through."

"This is bullshit," the driver snapped. "Licensed load, clean paperwork. You can't just jack my cargo because a field kit says it's 'bad.'"

"Mike Sullivan?" Knox checked the manifest. Clean record. "You didn't do anything wrong. The product was corrupted upstream. If it hits shelves, people get hurt."

"Corrupted how?"

"Environmental stress during cultivation—foreign actors manipulated light and nutrient cycles. Looks normal, tests normal on routine screens, but it's toxic at scale."

A long beat. "You're saying I'm hauling terrorist weapons."

"Yes. And you just helped stop them."

"What do you need?"

Across six states the same conversation repeated—anger, fear, then the practical resolve of people who understood that trust was the true cargo in a rig. Second intercept: cooperative. Third: driver thanked the troopers. Red markers blinked off the map, loads escorted to impound, evidence sealed and logged.

"Interception rate?" Knox asked.

"Thirty-seven of forty-three stopped," Torres said. "Six already delivered."

Six meant recalls, shelf pulls, customer notifications. Ops analyst Walsh read the running tallies. "Lincoln Park: complete removal. Milwaukee: thirty-seven purchasers notified. Three Chicago locations cleared."

The room steadied. America could move when it had to. But the operation also revealed a softer underbelly: every day thousands of trucks carried food, medicine, and chemicals with minimal inspection. Turn a farm into a reactor and a freeway becomes a distribution system for harm.

"Preliminary take?" Torres asked.

"Tactical success, strategic warning," Knox said. "We had early detection and specific intel. Next time—different supply chain, different timing."

Then a ripple in the feed.

"Unit 47 to Command," Rodriguez came back, tight. "Target Kenworth failed to stop at Kalamazoo. Eastbound I-94 at seventy-five. Request pursuit authorization—possible biohazard cargo."

Legal chimed in within seconds. "Authorization confirmed for forced stop of suspected biohazard. ROE: minimal force, driver safety, cargo preservation."

Citizens band (CB) chatter flared. "Driver claims harassment," Rodriguez relayed. "Requests more units."

Knox heard the culture underneath the radio traffic: independent operators, thin margins, thick distrust. "Patch me through on his citizens band (CB)."

"Driver, this is Knox Ramsey with the federal task force," Knox said. "Your load may be contaminated. We need a stop for testing."

"Name's Bob Henderson," came the reply. "Owner-operator. Legal load, tight delivery window. I'm not letting feds steal my truck on a rumor."

"I built the optimization systems that were corrupted," Knox said. "Pull into the next weigh station. If the cargo's clean, you get a federal escort and compensation for delay. If it's contaminated, you're a victim, not a suspect. Protected status in writing."

Silence. Then the Kenworth's GPS ticked down five miles per hour. "Copy. I'll pull in. I want that in writing."

"You'll have it."

Not every case resolved by conversation. "Unit 23," a new voice cut in. "Second target refusing stop, citing constitutional protections."

DOT legal answered. "Public health emergency authority applies. Document exigency. Use minimal force procedures for commercial vehicle stop."

Elsewhere, another driver phoned an attorney, then complied. Victim letters were issued on the hood of patrol cars; mobile printers spit out federal escorts and compensation notices. The map bled red to gray.

"Command to all units," Walsh read. "Eighty-seven percent interdiction. Forty-one vehicles stopped, cargo secured. Six deliveries reached destination—local PD executing shelf pulls."

The board calmed. The center slid back toward the messy normal of commerce.

Knox studied the cooling map and felt the old pressure in his chest. They'd prevented poison from going retail. They'd also proven how easily a legitimate network could be turned against the people it served.

"Recommendations?" Torres asked.

"Enhanced testing at shipment, mandatory chain-of-custody audits for controlled ag products, shared telemetry between state regulators and federal law enforcement," Knox said. "And we plan for the next variant—food distribution, pharma, chemicals. The method is portable."

Evidence crews sealed pallets. Trucks were impounded under HazMat protocols. Drivers were debriefed, documented as victims, and sent home with signed guarantees. The crisis bent, but didn't break, the system.

As the displays returned to routine flows, Knox let the numbers fall away and thought about a single rig rolling toward a city, a single driver doing a job. Trust was the invisible freight moving on every mile of Interstate. They'd saved most of it today.

It would have to be enough.

70 AFTERMATH & ESCALATION—G -0
INTERLUDE 3

PHASE TWO DECISION — MINISTRY OF AGRICULTURE AND RURAL AFFAIRS, BEIJING

Liu Wei stood before the projection wall in his secure office, data from North America cascading down the glass like rain. For eighteen months, he had orchestrated an invisible war—algorithms seeded in foreign soil, adaptive networks that learned to corrupt their own optimization loops. It was elegant, efficient, and, until this morning, unstoppable.

Now the data told a different story.

Red activity indicators winked out one by one. New security signatures appeared—federal countermeasures spreading faster than his model predicted.

"Phase Two authorization, Director?" his deputy asked. The man's voice carried the eagerness of youth, the hunger for advancement.

Wei didn't answer. He watched the graphs flatten, the infection curves arrested by unexpected defensive coordination. Somewhere in America, someone had found the pattern.

He felt a quiet admiration, unwelcome but undeniable. Whoever it was had seen through his misdirection and acted before escalation. That demanded intellect—and discipline.

"Director?" his deputy pressed. "Orders?"

Wei turned from the wall. "No activation. Suspend Phase Two."

The deputy blinked. "Sir, we're in position to cripple their yield—"

"And reveal ourselves," Wei said. His tone stayed calm, measured. "They've adapted. A second strike now would squander everything."

He dismissed the room, waited until the door sealed. Alone, he leaned against the console, fatigue finally breaking through the façade of control.

For years, he had believed preemption was survival—that corrupting the enemy's food chain was a defensive necessity. But tonight, as the city lights shimmered beyond the glass, doubt crept in.

He pulled up a network trace of the countermeasure source: Grand Rapids Community College. A student device signature in the packet metadata. Of course. Americans never realized how dangerous their own curiosity could be.

Still, he felt something like respect. A single student had shifted the trajectory of two nations.

Wei keyed a command to archive all Phase Two files, encrypting them under a dead-man switch. He placed his thumb on the biometric pad and authorized suspension.

Outside, dawn began to lift the haze above Beijing. The digital war would continue in other forms, but for now, restraint was its own kind of victory.

THE PERSONAL WAR

Knox stepped outside the command center for air that didn't smell like recycled electronics and stale coffee. The federal building's parking lot sat in that dead zone between downtown Detroit's revival and the neighborhoods still waiting for their turn. Sodium-vapor lights cast everything in sickly orange, while the distant hum of I-75 created a white-noise backdrop that could swallow the sound of suppressed gunshots. Empty office windows stared down like dead eyes, and a freight train's horn echoed from the rail yards near the river.

Behind him, footsteps approached across the concrete. Knox turned to see a figure that triggered every alarm his subconscious had been developing over the past week.

"Mr. Ramsey."

The voice was flat Midwest, the kind of accent that made people invisible in crowds from Chicago to Kansas City. The man was aggressively forgettable by design: medium height, medium build, jeans and a jacket you could buy in any strip mall in America. His eyes were the only remarkable thing—they had the professional emptiness of someone who had trained himself to feel nothing during working hours.

"Do I know you?" Knox asked, though his body was already shifting into the posture he'd learned during twenty years of working around dangerous machinery.

"We've known each other for years," the man said, almost conversational. He stepped closer, and a compact pistol appeared in his hand as casually as car keys. The suppressor was matte black, professionally installed, designed for close-quarters work in urban environments. "Or at least I've known you."

Knox's engineering mind was already working the problem. Parking lot surface: asphalt with recent seal coat—good traction. Wind: minimal—wouldn't affect projectile ballistics. Sight lines: two federal buildings with probable security cameras, but Mr. Q had mentioned technical difficulties. Distance to cover: twelve feet—too far to close before he could fire. Electrical service panel: south wall, six feet left.

And the other part of his brain—the dumb Irish part that had gotten him into bar fights he never started but never walked away from—was already measuring the distance, calculating the odds, refusing to accept that backing down was an option. His father had called it the Ramsey curse: too smart to want a fight, too stubborn to back down from one.

But Knox had spent thirty years troubleshooting systems under pressure, and pressure was just another variable to account for.

His right hand brushed the edge of his waistband, feeling the familiar weight of his own concealed-carry pistol—old habits from a younger man who'd worked construction in rough neighborhoods, maintained through middle age by someone who understood that being prepared wasn't the same thing as being paranoid.

He didn't reach for the weapon. Not yet.

"You're running late," Knox said, because his mouth went to autopilot, throwing out whatever bought him a second to think.

The man's smile contained no warmth. "Traffic was heavier than expected."

"You're the one who's been writing my obituary in advance," Knox continued, studying the man's stance and movement patterns, looking for the tells that would indicate when he planned to pull the trigger. Q's stance favored his right leg—old injury or current weakness?

"Mr. Q," the man said, like he was introducing himself at a neighborhood barbecue. "If you prefer names for our professional relationship."

"I don't," Knox replied. "Names make people feel like friends. I stopped collecting those some time ago."

Q's pistol remained steady, pointed at Knox's center mass with the confidence of someone who'd made this kind of shot many times before. "You've been a problem for my employers for a long time. Today you became an existential liability that requires permanent resolution."

"You're going to do this here? In a federal parking lot?"

"The cameras are experiencing temporary technical difficulties," Q said. "You taught us that particular trick, ironically enough."

"What do you want from me?" Knox asked, though he already knew the answer.

"Your government's countermeasures are more sophisticated than we anticipated," Q said, his finger tightening slightly on the trigger. "Beijing requires technical details about your detection methods."

Knox almost laughed. "You poisoned American kids at music festivals, and now you want me to help you do it better? Wrong fucking tree, pal."

"Your cooperation would be appreciated. Your family's continued safety depends on it."

That was the wrong thing to say to a man who'd spent decades building safety systems.

"Closure," Knox said simply.

"Same here," Q replied, and moved.

He didn't go for his gun first—that would have been suicide at this range. Instead, Knox lunged forward and to the side, his left hand reaching for Q's pistol while his right forearm drove toward the man's elbow.

Some distant part of him recognized this as the worst decision he'd made since the divorce, but the rest of him—the part that had never backed down from anything in fifty-three years—wasn't interested in negotiations.

It wasn't elegant or sophisticated. Knox was fifty-three and made of accumulated injuries and stubborn determination, but machines had taught him about leverage and force multiplication, and he intended to use every lesson he'd learned.

The suppressed shot was a metallic cough that echoed off the surrounding buildings. The bullet punched through the SUV's door panel instead of Knox's chest. Q flowed with Knox's attack, reflexes trained by years of practiced violence.

The pistol swung back toward Knox's ribs. He twisted his hips into the line of fire, letting the muzzle glance off his jacket instead of finding flesh. He threw a punch that connected with Q's cheekbone, feeling the shock of impact travel up his arm and into his shoulder.

Q snarled and drove his knee toward Knox's solar plexus. Knox grunted, stepped back, and his hand finally found his own pistol. The draw fouled against his jacket. Q's hand crashed down on Knox's wrist before the weapon could clear its holster. The pistol clattered across the asphalt, sliding under the SUV's front-right wheel and out of reach.

Q lifted his suppressed weapon again, muzzle pointing at Knox's chest from less than three feet. "Impressive tactical awareness. Unfortunately, you're fighting in the wrong theater."

Knox spat blood onto the concrete, tasting copper and defeat. "Try me in my theater next time."

A shout cracked the evening air like a whip. "Federal agents! Nobody moves!"

Agents poured from concealment around the parking lot, moving with the coordinated precision of people who'd rehearsed this exact scenario. Two approached Q from different angles, weapons drawn and trained.

But Knox was already moving toward his opportunity. He rolled clear of Q's reach and spotted the maintenance access panel on the building's electrical feed—old habits from a career spent mapping infrastructure vulnerabilities. The cover screws were already missing—maintenance had left it loose.

Finally—something that made sense. He couldn't beat this guy in a straight fight, but he could damn sure short a circuit. The Irish got him into the fight; the engineer would get him out.

He ripped the panel open, grabbed the main disconnect lever, and yanked.

The parking lot plunged into darkness. Security lights, building floods, even the traffic signals on the adjacent street died in an instant, leaving only the distant glow of downtown and the sound of that freight train fading into the night. Emergency lighting flickered to life seconds later, casting harsh red shadows across the pavement. The building's generators rumbled to life, but the lot fixtures sat on the unprotected utility feed, and the darkness held.

The first agent struck Q's gun hand with a baton, sending the weapon spinning across the pavement. The second agent swept Q's legs, dropping him hard. Plastic restraints, then a black hood. The takedown lasted less than ten seconds.

Knox grinned in the sudden dark. "Welcome to America—where engineers fight dirty."

And then the parking lot was just a parking lot again, ordinary and quiet except for Knox's labored breathing and the distant hum of a city that never quite slept.

PSYCHOLOGICAL WARFARE

Within hours of the team's win, a polished smear detonated across half a dozen platforms at once—prewritten, pre-optimized, and backed by forged "support."

Headline: Knox Ramsey Sold Agricultural Security to the Highest Bidder.

The post braided true facts about the FarmCore sale with fabricated motives, screen-grab "emails" that never existed, and video snips cut to imply Knox had waved through safety exceptions. Anonymous "former colleagues" supplied quotes that sounded right if you didn't know how audits actually work.

Tate found Knox in the break room, phone in his hand, color gone.

"Dad?"

Knox turned the screen. "They're not attacking code. They're attacking credibility. If I'm a traitor, our telemetry becomes a lie."

He fired a secure message to SAC Steele: `They're moving on me personally. We need to dump everything—contracts, wire trails, board minutes, my objections, the ugly parts too. Full sunlight.`

Reply: `Legal is balking. Methods/sources.`

Knox: `Better to fight lawyers than morgues. Publish—with redactions only where lives are at risk, not reputations.`

Steele stepped in, phone to his ear, already moving pieces. "You saw it."

"Hard to miss."

"We answer with speed and receipts," Steele said. "You own the receipts. We notarize and time-stamp them before they flood the zone."

Inside an hour, teams were building a public dossier: the FarmCore LOI, the intermediate-CA scope, compliance attestations, Knox's dissent memos, and the audit timelines that never fit the conspiracy's narrative. Every PDF got cryptographic timestamps; every hash went to a public ledger and a mirror at NIST. The standard would look fussy to civilians and obvious to experts—perfect.

Knox transmitted the release command. Screens across the task force blinked as classified folders became public exhibits. The truth was finally outpacing the lies after the outbreak.

THE MEDIA RESPONSE

The press conference was in a hotel ballroom quickly turned into a media center, with agency seals and lighting that made people look either heroic or guilty. With memorized lot codes and a script, Tate was ready at the podium.

He looked directly into the cameras, speaking like a man confessing to crimes he hadn't committed while taking responsibility for consequences he couldn't have prevented.

"If you have products with these specific lot codes, do not consume them. Return them to the point of purchase for full refunds. We will make this right. We will publish every step of our response and remediation process. We will show our work, because transparency is the only currency that has value during a crisis like this."

The questions from reporters were sharp and aggressive, designed to generate sound bites that would dominate news cycles. Tate answered each one with the same direct honesty, refusing to hide behind corporate speak or deflect responsibility.

Back in the command center, Captain Walsh monitored the real-time social response, tracking how organic conversations developed against artificial amplification patterns.

"Organic engagement is positive," she reported. "People are responding to the transparency and specific, actionable information. The bot networks are trying to inject confusion, but they're operating without effective coordination."

Knox watched a different set of metrics—the technical indicators that showed TheraGrow's compromised systems gradually returning to normal as federal agents gained physical control of the facility.

"Field team has secured the growing area," Steele's voice crackled through the radio. "Facility owner is cooperating fully. That red node just shifted from active intrusion to contained threat."

Knox watched the bad telemetry flatten into normal rhythm—vendor keys revoked, ghost jobs killed, model-weight caches purged. Dashboards finally looked boring again, which felt like oxygen.

"We didn't cure the system," he told the room for the record. "We taught it what not to trust." The screens held steady. For once, that was enough.

71 SECOND INTERROGATION
FEDERAL DETENTION

MAYA CHEN

The interview room was deliberately plain—beige walls, a table with soft corners, a camera in the ceiling that hummed at a frequency you could only hear when you were tired. Knox observed behind glass for half an hour while others tried and failed to make Maya Chen talk.

She sat like a calculus problem: straight lines and reserved variables. No cuffs. No need. She was caged by what she'd already said and by what she'd never say for free.

Agent Morales tried charm. A junior AUSA tried a threat. Both got the same response: a micro-smile and the look of a woman clocking their operating system.

Keating stepped in, closed the door softly, and didn't sit. "Ms. Chen," she said. "We'll be simple. We know the Delaware LLC chain. We have the CDN ticket you used in 2022. We have the fallbacks on your managers, and the localization markers from your debug logs when your team panicked."

"Team?" Maya said. Her voice was the silk you put over knives, so they don't scratch each other. "I'm flattered."

"We also have your mistake," Keating said. "The malformed 'burn' command during the resync. The human part."

Maya tilted her head. "The human part is the only interesting part."

"Tell us about the interesting part," Knox said, stepping through the door. He didn't sit either. He put two fingers on the chair back and held there, like he was testing a chassis for flex. "Tell me where you learned to make machines obey people they can't see."

Maya regarded him like a museum piece she hadn't decided to buy. "Mr. Ramsey," she said. "The engineer who wanted to make food into software."

"Food is already software," Knox said. "I just refused to pretend otherwise."

"You refused to pretend," she echoed, amused. "And then you pretended you were surprised when someone refactored your code."

Keating's look said Don't. Knox ignored it. "We're past the clever. You got sloppy. You left receipts. We followed them home."

Maya's eyes warmed by a fraction. "You don't want my receipts. You want my roadmap."

"Yes," Keating said. "And what you get in return is more air and less concrete."

Maya smiled at that. "Optimistic. Here's what I can give you for free, Ms. Keating: this wasn't a moonshot. It was a feasibility study."

"We noticed," Knox said.

"And agriculture wasn't the point," Maya went on. "It was the safest proving ground. Highly centralized nodes, measurable public panic, plausible deniability." She tapped the table once, like a metronome. "Power. Water. Transit. Hospitals. Choose any two."

"We already chose," Knox said. "All of them."

"Ambitious," Maya said. "Americans like to make lists."

Keating slid a document across the table without breaking eye contact. "Limited-use plea. Proffers on methodology, org structure, procurement trails. We take death off the table and consider time served if your information prevents a future mass-casualty event."

Maya didn't touch the paper. "That presumes my information would be timely."

"Is it?" Knox asked.

She watched him for a beat that lasted too long. "Your 'portal' was elegant," she said instead. "Auditable truth is hard to weaponize. You will find that simple realism outperforms any slogan."

"That's why you pushed the botnet into #AgriAttack?" Knox asked.

She actually laughed. "That wasn't me. We aren't the only audience in this theater."

"Names," Keating said.

"Conditions," Maya replied.

"You give us a next target, and you get a window," Knox said. "You tell us how they'll try to keep the window closed."

Maya folded her hands. Her nails were unpainted. "Two vectors," she said quietly, as if dictating to a student. "One loud, one quiet. Loud: a grain-certificate swap in the inland waterways—paperwork becomes weapon. Quiet: parametric-insurance fraud using synthetic weather to bankrupt the wrong farms."

Keating's pen was already moving. "Mechanisms."

Maya shook her head, almost fond. "That's not free."

KNOX LEANED IN. "The next time you let your team panic—when the logs fill with localization markers again—remember that was the human part that broke you."

She met his gaze without blinking. "The human part is why you won't win outright, Mr. Ramsey. You're honest. You publish your receipts. You create trust. But you won't build the world required to keep people like me out of it."

Knox's voice stayed level. "Watch us."

Maya settled back. "Then here's a kindness: your adversaries will come for your transparency. They'll try to flood it with plausible fakes until the signal looks like noise. Plan for that. Build notarization for every camera and hand."

"We are," Knox said.

"Good," she said—and the word sounded like respect and a dare. "Because this—" she nodded toward the ceiling camera "—wasn't personal. It was a rehearsal. Don't mistake applause for an ending."

Outside the room, the U.S. Attorney's Office filed a sealed complaint; a magistrate ordered detention without bond and set the case for the Theodore Levin U.S. Courthouse, Detroit.

THE AFTERMATH ASSESSMENT

Two weeks later, the same Situation Room held a different energy. The crisis wasn't over, but it was contained. Knox sat at the table this time, no longer relegated to advisor status. Success had earned him a seat at the decision-making level.

Hammond looked healthier—still exhausted but no longer carrying the weight of active catastrophe. "Final casualty count: eighteen thousand four hundred thirty-seven confirmed poisonings. Three hundred twelve fatalities. Economic impact assessed at forty-one billion dollars in direct losses."

Knox thought about each number representing families destroyed, lives interrupted, trust shattered. The statistics felt like personal failures even though he knew he'd helped minimize the damage.

SAC Steele opened his operational summary. "Fifty-seven arrests across six states. Some foreign nationals attempted consular extraction before prosecution. Several were released on immigration holds; key principals, including Maya Chen, remained in federal custody under indictment in the Eastern District of Michigan. Shell companies dissolved; assets seized under RICO statutes."

Knox listened, hearing each report as a ledger entry in a system he'd helped build and nearly lost.

Part of him felt relieved—she'd exploited his loneliness, but she'd also done her job with professional competence. He didn't want to see her destroyed for following orders. Relief didn't mean forgiveness. It meant the ledger was still open.

CIA Director Sarah Walsh consulted classified assessment folders. "Counter-cyber operations successfully disrupted Chinese agricultural-warfare capabilities. Their command-and-control infrastructure required six days to restore basic functionality. We collected extensive intelligence on their operational methods."

Treasury Secretary Janet Daniels presented an economic analysis. "Market recovery is proceeding ahead of projections. Consumer confidence is returning as safety measures demonstrate effectiveness. Chinese acquisition attempts blocked through the CFIUS review process."

Hammond tapped a thin folder. "U.S. v. Chen (E.D. Mich.). Beijing has an American in state-security detention. They've started testing swap language through the Geneva channel."

Knox said nothing, but the line *contained, not cured* felt newly literal. Systems stabilized. People did not.

72 INTERLUDE 4
PERSONAL RECKONING

BEIJING

TWO WEEKS AFTER PHASE TWO SUSPENSION

The rain turned Beijing's ring road into a river of light.

Liu Wei watched the reflections smear across his office window, the city blurring into an abstract network—an organism he had once believed he could model, predict, and control.

He didn't believe that anymore.

A notification pulsed on his console:

Directive 441-B, Personnel Reassignment – Effective Immediately.

He opened it without surprise. Ministry of Agriculture → National Data Integrity Bureau, a department famous for burying its own projects beneath polite layers of bureaucracy. Not punishment on paper, but exile in practice.

He entered his clearance codes one final time, transferring the encrypted archive of Project Sower to cold storage. The status bar inched forward, the machine breathing in quiet increments.

Across the room, his replacement—a younger man in an immaculate gray suit—waited, awkward and eager.

"They said you refused escalation orders," the man ventured.

"I postponed them," Wei replied evenly.

"Some call that cowardice."

"Some call it wisdom."

Silence returned. When the transfer reached 100 percent, Wei removed his credentials, set them on the desk, and powered down the monitor. The screen's reflection faded from the glass, leaving only rain.

He had told himself halting Phase Two would prevent further conflict. Part of him knew the real reason: he had seen his adversary. Somewhere across the ocean, a mind sharp enough to predict his patterns had countered him without firing a shot. Respect was not welcome, but it was honest.

He stepped onto the balcony overlooking Chang'an Avenue. Dawn seeped through the haze in diluted amber. From this height the city looked peaceful—data centers humming, markets opening—a machine of order masking the chaos beneath. The same illusion he'd engineered abroad.

Wei opened a drawer, lit a cigarette, and let the smoke curl into the damp air. He had quit years ago. The taste anchored him in a moment that still belonged to him.

A secure message vibrated on his wrist terminal: Director Zhou requests debrief—1400 hours. Polite wording. Clear subtext: containment, not conversation.

He composed his reply: Acknowledged. All data archived. Awaiting reassignment instructions.

After a pause he added a line not required by protocol: Recommendation—terminate foreign agricultural operations indefinitely. Strategic cost outweighs tactical gain.

He sent it before he could reconsider.

Later, as he crossed the courtyard, loudspeakers broadcast patriotic music, the melody warped by drizzle. Young technicians hurried past with tablets glowing yield forecasts and production metrics. They reminded him of his students once—believers in data purity, blind to its fragility.

Wei stopped beneath an awning and listened to the anthem dissolve into static. Ownership of the machine he helped create had slipped from him without ceremony.

For years he'd told subordinates survival required control. Now he wondered if survival required mercy instead.

He looked east, toward the unseen Pacific. Somewhere beyond that horizon, a student had undone his work. He pictured her surrounded by code and conviction, a mirror of his younger self before cynicism hardened into policy.

He smiled, faintly, and spoke to no one:

"Good. Someone is still paying attention."

The rain intensified, erasing his footprints as he stepped toward the street. Behind him, the ministry lights dimmed to conservation mode, the system folding back into equilibrium.

For the first time in years, Liu Wei felt no need to monitor it.

73 CRISIS RESOLUTION
AFTERMATH BRIEFING

Knox felt grim satisfaction. They'd prevented the economic conquest that had been the real objective behind the attacks.

The President leaned forward. "Long-term implications?"

Knox answered before the politicians could spin the assessment. "They'll be back. Different methods, different targets, better operational security. This was their learning exercise as much as ours."

National Security Advisor Hammond nodded. "Cybersecurity upgrades are being implemented across all critical infrastructure sectors. New monitoring protocols, new defensive capabilities, new coordination mechanisms."

Knox thought about the defensive improvements they'd built from this crisis—better sensor networks, improved anomaly detection, enhanced inter-agency cooperation. The attack had made America stronger in some ways.

Defense Secretary James Rodriguez consulted military assessments. "Our response demonstrated capabilities that will influence Chinese strategic calculations. They understand that agricultural terrorism carries unacceptable costs."

Knox wasn't sure they'd learned the right lesson. Professional intelligence services adapted to new constraints rather than abandoning proven methods.

Secretary of State Michael Peterson offered a diplomatic perspective. "Beijing has proposed bilateral cybersecurity agreements, suggesting mutual restraint in critical infrastructure targeting."

Knox snorted. "They're offering not to attack us in exchange for us not defending ourselves effectively. That's not negotiation—that's surrender terms."

The President smiled grimly. "Mr. Ramsey's assessment?"

Knox thought about Liu Wei, wondering if the Chinese engineer felt the same mixture of professional respect and personal animosity. They'd fought each other to a draw, but neither had been decisively defeated.

"They've proven the concept works," Knox said. "Agricultural systems can be weaponized through software modification. Safety monitoring can be corrupted to hide evidence. Information warfare can amplify confusion during physical attacks."

He paused, choosing words carefully.

"Next time, they'll target something more critical than cannabis. Power grids, water treatment, transportation networks. And they'll do it better—more subtly, more carefully, with better defensive measures."

The room absorbed that assessment soberly.

"Recommendations?" the President asked.

Knox stood, moving to the display screen. "We treat this as the opening engagement of a longer conflict. Invest in defensive capabilities, develop offensive options, and prepare for escalation. Most importantly, we accept that traditional boundaries between civilian and military infrastructure don't exist anymore."

Hammond nodded. "Everything is a potential target."

"Everything is a potential weapon," Knox corrected. "The Chinese didn't attack our agriculture. They turned our agriculture into a weapon against our own population."

The President leaned back, considering implications. "Budget priorities?"

Knox thought about the technical challenges ahead—securing industrial control systems against adversaries who understood American infrastructure better than most Americans.

"Research and development for defensive cybersecurity. Offensive cyber warfare capabilities. Most importantly, technical education. We need more Americans who understand how these systems actually work."

As the briefing concluded, Knox reflected on how the crisis had changed his own perspective. He'd started as a disgraced engineer trying to repair his reputation. He'd ended up as someone responsible for defending American infrastructure against invisible warfare.

The President caught his attention as officials filed out. "Mr. Ramsey, thank you for your service."

Knox thought about his father's advice: Nothing's free, no matter what anyone tells you.

"Just doing my job, Mr. President."

"Your job just got bigger. We're establishing a Critical Infrastructure Defense Office. You'll head the technical division."

Knox felt the weight of responsibility settling on his shoulders. Bureaucratic warfare instead of technical problems, political calculations instead of engineering solutions.

But people were counting on him to stand between American families and enemies who fought with algorithms and misinformation.

"When do I start?"

The President smiled. "You already have."

74 CODA

SHANGHAI

Boxes lined the corridor outside Cyber Intelligence Research Facility 17, labels in two scripts, barcodes turned outward. The glass still carried the dual seals; the badges on passing lanyards were already different.

Dr. Wu stood at the operations bench while an administrator read a checklist against the muted glow of blanked monitors. "Inventory return, complete. External interfaces, severed. Local archives, consolidated."

A notification blinked on the wall display, then settled into the log: Interim Oversight: Director (Acting) Zhang — Effective Monday. No flourish, no signature.

Wu placed a porcelain cup in an empty drawer and shut it with the quiet care you give to something that might break later. She keyed in the final disposition. Administrative reassignment carried no detail and required none.

At the far end of the room, a junior analyst hovered over a draft that included the phrase *applicability to domestic deployments,* hesitated, and erased until the sentence became air. Every system can be bent. Some are only tested from the inside.

The facility exhaled. Fans settled into a slower rhythm; the guard at the inner door checked two credentials and waved through a stranger who did not look back.

Wu sent the closing note to archive: *Implement strategy. Maintain patience. Record all deviations. No public escalation.* The message would outlive its sender. The lesson would outlive the message.

On the status screen, nothing blinked—only the quiet pulse of equilibrium. In a world built on noise, boredom remained the safest kind of dangerous.

75 RECOVERY & RECONCILIATION—G +4

COMMUNITY RECOVERY — MICHIGAN

Grand Rapids: Ahmad staples a laminated HOW TO READ YOUR LABEL to the board next to the returns desk. A teenager shows his mom how to scan a QR code. A clerk slides a refund across the counter with "No questions asked" written in Sharpie on the tray.

Detroit, Midtown: Lila stands in front of a restocked greens case. A small sign: FIELD-GROWN. LOTS POSTED ONLINE. ASK US ANYTHING. An older man in a Tigers cap taps the sign and says, "Feels like church. Confession first, then communion."

Sinai-Grace break room: Nurse Tanya rotates a shoulder that still aches. On the table: a cake with crooked frosting—THANK YOU, NIGHT CREW. Someone writes below in dry erase: AND DAY CREW. AND THE CREW IN BETWEEN.

FarmCore perimeter: Orange flags come up, then fewer, then a grid turns back to soil. A USDA kid with a clipboard nods to Knox through the fence like they're co-workers now. "Soil's clearing," he says. "It wants to work."

A parking lot potluck behind a church: beige food, then slowly not—slaw, cabbage, roasted roots, panzanella with day-old bread and field tomatoes from downstate. The pastor lifts a spoon and says, "People fed people. That's the headline."

A high school shop in Southwest Detroit: a teacher holds up a humidity sensor and a PVC coupling. "Controls plus plumbing equals a job." Kids draw a greenhouse schematic in pencil; one sketches a logo: Southwest Grows.

A neighborhood meeting in Muskegon: a retiree reads her portal printouts out loud so her neighbors don't need smartphones to feel safe.

A garage in Hamtramck: a hobbyist rigs a camera to a raspberry pi and posts the code. Comments roll in: a line lead from TR says "we forked this." Transparency begets tinkering begets trust.

Knox on a porch with a paper cup of coffee, answering a neighbor's question about "how to tell real from fake." He says, "Real does the math in front of you. Fake tells you to stop asking." The neighbor nods and brings out a pie. It's rhubarb. They eat with plastic forks.

A small press conference in a county lot: no stagecraft, just a folding table. "We're not done," the county health officer says. "But we're honest. Keep asking. We'll keep showing." The crowd applauds the sentence more than the person. It feels like a muscle learning again.

PUBLIC EXONERATION

TR Cannabis received its official moment at a different podium, this one decorated with the seals of multiple federal agencies. The administration spokesperson used the phrase "fully exonerated" without hesitation or qualification, and the assembled media dutifully recorded the statement for broadcast. Tate stood beside the podium, looking older than his twenty-eight years looking like a man bracing for the next accusation.

He didn't smile during the press conference. He didn't need to. The facts spoke for themselves.

Knox watched from the wings, staying out of camera range but close enough to provide support if needed. When Tate stepped away from the microphones, they didn't embrace—that would have been too much emotion for a public setting. Instead, Knox put his hand on his son's shoulder and squeezed, a brief physical communication that said everything that needed to be said.

Tate nodded once. That was the moment. That was enough.

Back in the information warfare command center, Dr. Kim posted a final analysis graph for the team to review: foreign disinformation insertions versus successful counters over the past week. The line showing hostile activity had flatlined in the most satisfying way possible.

Sergeant Rodriguez whistled low. "That's the sound of quiet winning."

"Document it," Knox said. "We'll need the playbook for next time."

He erased COUNTERBEATS from the whiteboard and wrote nothing in its place. For the first time in a week, the board was clean and ready for whatever crisis would inevitably follow.

FAMILY RECONCILIATION

Grand Rapids

The soldering iron's smell mixed with onions and butter. On the kitchen table: a laptop, a tangle of jumper wires, an old barcode scanner Tate had scavenged from a storage closet. On the stove: Lisa's skillet, the sound of something simple getting good.

Knox lifted the scanner, popped the case, and pointed to the board. "See this trace?" he said.

Tate leaned in, the light catching the new lines in his face that had nothing to do with age. "Cold solder," he said.

"Mm." Knox handed him the iron. "Fix your own mistakes."

Tate grinned despite himself and made the repair. Lisa watched from the stove with the quiet of someone who'd seen them in this configuration before—two stubborn men solving the same problem from opposite ends until the ends met.

"Portal traffic's sloping down," Tate said, eyes still on the joint. "Refunds slowed. The comments… some of them stopped being about me."

"They were never about you," Knox said. "You were a handle for their fear."

"Feels personal when it's your name."

"I know," Knox said.

Lisa slid three plates on the table and nudged the laptop lid down with a fork. "Eat while it's hot," she said. "You two can save the world during dessert."

They ate. No speeches. Butter, salt, the kind of food you make when you need there to be food and not a metaphor.

After, Knox pulled the laptop back and opened a simple window: a local service that took a lot code and spat back a human sentence. He typed: 24-0316-B.

The screen said: UNDER REVIEW (ORANGE). Refund issued 03/24 14:11. Audit trail complete.

Below it: a link labeled How we checked this.

Tate leaned back. "It still hurts."

"It will," Knox said. "Then it won't. Then something else will."

Lisa set two beers down and kept water for herself. "You don't have to carry everything you fix," she said to both of them. "Some things can walk after."

The old scanner chirped when Knox pulled the trigger; the new solder held. He and Tate smiled at the same time and tried not to notice.

Tate closed the laptop with care. "I'm thinking about building a small teaching line in the back," he said. "Field-trip friendly. Cameras everywhere. Let kids plug sensors in and see what changes." He looked at Knox. "Plumbing and controls count as civics?"

"They count as citizenship," Knox said.

Lisa nodded as if a decision had been ratified. "I'll call the school."

They sat a minute with the windows open to a Michigan evening that couldn't decide if it was spring. Flags on the block lifted and settled again.

Tate broke the quiet. "You know I was serious—about not being 'fixed' just because we did one good thing."

"I know," Knox said. "I don't need you fixed. I need you honest. And stubborn."

Tate huffed a laugh. "That I can do."

"Good," Knox said. He raised his beer. "To broken things."

Lisa raised her glass of water. "And the people who keep fixing them."

They drank. Outside, someone's kid rode a bike with training wheels that clattered on the sidewalk seams. Inside, the barcode scanner chirped again just because it could.

No one made a speech. No one needed to. The work would be there tomorrow. Tonight, the house held three people who had chosen, again, to be on the same team.

EPILOGUE

GENEVA INTERNATIONAL CONFERENCE CENTER

SIX WEEKS AFTER LAUNCH / T-0 SUMMIT DAY

The agricultural trade summit that was supposed to showcase Chinese leverage instead became a careful diplomatic dance around the unacknowledged warfare that both sides knew had occurred but neither could openly discuss. American Secretary of Agriculture Jennifer Brooks sat across from Chinese Minister of Agriculture Wang Xiaoming, their professional smiles masking calculations about how much each side knew about recent events.

Knox watched the proceedings from a secure viewing room, providing real-time technical analysis to American negotiators through encrypted communications. He'd been flown to Geneva on a military transport, his expertise deemed essential for evaluating any Chinese proposals that might contain hidden agricultural warfare implications.

"The Chinese delegation is proposing enhanced agricultural technology sharing agreements," Secretary Brooks' aide whispered into her earpiece, relaying Knox's assessment. "Their emphasis on 'defensive applications' suggests they're acknowledging the attack without admitting responsibility."

Minister Wang presented documentation about agricultural security cooperation that would have seemed routine two weeks earlier but now carried subtext everyone understood. "Recent events have demonstrated vulnerabilities in global food systems that require international coordination for defensive improvements."

"Recent events" was the closest anyone would come to mentioning the biological weapons attack that had poisoned festival attendees across America. The diplomatic language was necessary to prevent escalation while allowing both sides to address the crisis.

Secretary Brooks responded with equally careful language. "The United States agrees that agricultural security requires enhanced international cooperation. We're prepared to share defensive technologies with allies who demonstrate commitment to preventing exploitation of civilian food systems."

The emphasis on "allies" and "preventing exploitation" made clear that Chinese agricultural programs would face increased scrutiny and restricted access to American agricultural technology.

Knox typed rapid analysis as the Chinese delegation presented their proposals: "They're offering to restrict agricultural technology exports in exchange for maintained trade relationships. They know we could embargo their agricultural imports completely."

The economic stakes were enormous. China imported billions in American agricultural products while exporting agricultural technology and processed foods globally. Complete trade severance would damage both economies while potentially escalating into broader conflict.

"We propose establishment of international agricultural security protocols," Minister Wang continued, reading from prepared statements that had been carefully vetted by Beijing. "Verification mechanisms, technology sharing restrictions, and coordinated response to agricultural terrorism regardless of source."

The proposal was strategically clever—by agreeing to restrictions on agricultural warfare, China could claim moral equivalence with defensive measures while preserving trade relationships essential to their food security.

Secretary Brooks consulted her tablet, reviewing Knox's technical assessment and State Department guidance simultaneously. "The United States supports international protocols with mandatory verification, immediate reporting of suspicious agricultural events, and consequences for violations including trade sanctions."

The consequences clause was the key point. America was demanding ability to punish future agricultural attacks through economic means rather than military escalation.

Behind the diplomatic language, both sides were calculating. China had demonstrated they could weaponize agricultural systems but had also learned that America could respond with sophisticated countermeasures. America had shown defensive capabilities but recognized ongoing vulnerability to similar attacks.

"Perhaps a recess for technical consultations?" Minister Wang suggested, the prearranged signal for backchannel negotiations where real agreements would be reached.

As delegations dispersed to private rooms, Knox was escorted to a secure conference room where American intelligence officials were coordinating response strategy.

"They're backing down without admitting guilt," CIA Director Walsh assessed. "The proposals essentially promise not to repeat attacks we can't prove they committed."

"But the verification mechanisms would make future attacks harder," Knox pointed out. "Mandatory reporting means they can't deploy biological weapons without creating paper trails we could detect."

FBI Deputy Director Torres agreed. "It's not justice, but it might be prevention. The question is whether we can verify Chinese compliance with any agreement."

Knox reviewed the technical specifications China had proposed for agricultural security protocols. They were surprisingly comprehensive, suggesting Chinese leadership had decided agricultural warfare was too risky after seeing American defensive capabilities.

"They're genuinely concerned about their own vulnerabilities," Knox realized. "These protocols would protect Chinese agricultural systems from American retaliation as much as preventing Chinese attacks."

The mutual vulnerability had created unexpected common ground. Both nations depended on agricultural technology that could be weaponized, making bilateral restrictions genuinely beneficial rather than simply diplomatic theater.

Secretary Brooks returned from back-channel discussions with a carefully neutral expression. "The Chinese are offering complete suspension of agricultural warfare programs in exchange for maintaining normal trade relationships and sharing defensive technologies."

"Do we believe them?" Torres asked.

"Trust but verify," Brooks replied. "We'll require inspection access, intelligence sharing on agricultural threats, and immediate penalties for violations."

Knox understood they were watching the birth of a new international framework—agricultural security agreements that acknowledged food systems as potential weapons while trying to prevent their weaponization. It wasn't the clear victory America might have wanted, but it was better than continued invisible warfare.

The formal session resumed with both delegations presenting the framework they'd negotiated privately.

The moderator read from the draft.

International Agricultural Security Accords that established:

- Mandatory reporting of agricultural system anomalies
- Prohibited development of biological weapons through agricultural platforms
- Technology sharing for defensive purposes only
- Immediate economic sanctions for violations
- Regular inspection of agricultural research facilities

Neither side mentioned the attacks that had prompted these agreements. The diplomatic fiction was that both nations had simultaneously recognized agricultural vulnerabilities requiring a coordinated response.

Knox watched Minister Wang and Secretary Brooks sign preliminary agreements, their professional handshake photographed for news services that would report breakthrough cooperation on agricultural security without explaining why such agreements had suddenly become necessary.

"Initial success," Secretary Brooks told her team privately. "But verification will determine whether this is genuine strategic shift or tactical pause."

Knox agreed with the assessment. The summit had achieved its minimal objectives—preventing escalation, establishing frameworks for future prevention, maintaining economic relationships. But whether China would genuinely abandon agricultural warfare or simply develop more sophisticated methods remained to be seen.

As delegations departed Geneva, Knox reflected on the strange diplomatic dance he'd witnessed. A biological weapons attack had been transformed into agricultural security cooperation through careful language and mutual recognition of vulnerability.

The summit hadn't provided justice for the festival victims or accountability for Chinese attacks. But it had possibly prevented future attacks through frameworks that made agricultural warfare more risky and less deniable.

Knox flew back to America understanding that his technical expertise would now serve verification and defense rather than investigation and response. The crisis phase was ending, replaced by long-term vigilance that would require permanent attention to agricultural security.

The invisible war had become slightly more visible through international agreements that acknowledged what everyone knew but no one could say: food systems had become weapons, and defending them required the same sophistication as traditional military defense.

The door clicked shut behind Daniels, leaving the conference room unnaturally quiet. For the first time in days, Knox realized he could hear his own breathing. The contracts sat between him and Tate like freshly signed treaties after a war—paper thin, but binding as iron.

Neither spoke. The weight of what they'd agreed to didn't require words.

Finally, Knox stood. His joints complained in the familiar way they always did after long hours in hard chairs, but he ignored them. Pain was just another system alert —something to note, something to work around.

"Come on," he said. "Let's see what the Swiss do for a night sky."

Tate rose beside him, still turning the pen over in his fingers like he wasn't sure it had betrayed him. Together they stepped out of the sterile meeting room and into a corridor that smelled faintly of disinfectant and too many bodies in too little space.

The building had emptied quickly. Most of the delegates were already at their motorcades, whisked away to private dinners where victory would be toasted with careful smiles. Outside, Geneva buzzed as it always did—trams gliding along their tracks, cyclists cutting across traffic with the arrogance only Europeans managed to pull off, hotel marquees advertising international comfort in three languages.

The Ramseys moved without escort, unnoticed in the swirl of departing dignitaries. To most of the world, they were nobodies—an aging engineer and his son, just two more attendees drifting out of a conference.

But Knox felt the leash around his neck already. Invisible, but there.

He paused on the steps, looking back at the convention center's glass facade. For a moment he saw his own reflection beside Tate's, father and son framed by spotlights and security cameras. He wondered how many files tonight already had their names added to new lists.

"You think we made a mistake?" Tate asked quietly.

Knox shook his head. "No. A mistake's when you don't know better. This..." He exhaled, breath fogging in the cold. "...This is compromise."

He paused, eyes following the neat lines of trams gliding past. "The government runs because of inertia. That's what nobody wants to admit. Doesn't matter who comes in with fresh ideas—left, right, center. The machine keeps moving. You can feed it good intentions, you can feed it bad ones, but it's still the same machine."

Tate frowned. "You're saying nothing ever changes?"

"Not nothing," Knox said. "At the start, most people want to help. Local folks, the small-town types, the ones who run for city council or school board—they're not power hungry, they just want to make things better. That's America. That's Mr. Smith Goes to Washington. But once you get pulled into the system, the system gets you. It wears you down. Makes you compromise, then compromise again. Before long you're not fixing the machine—you're part of it. Feeding it."

He looked at his son, seeing the quiet fire in him. "It's not that everyone turns bad. It's just inertia. It keeps running. And if you're not careful, it consumes you."

Tate was silent for a long moment. Then: "So why sign the contract at all?"

Knox's eyes tracked the lake, the white plume of the Jet d'Eau cutting into the night sky. "Because sometimes inertia needs someone in the gears. Someone to jam a wrench in when it starts chewing too loud."

THE DIPLOMATIC CHARTER leveled off at thirty-seven thousand feet, leaving Geneva and its carefully negotiated lies below. Knox sat in business class beside Tate, both of them staring at nothing in particular. The cabin was half-empty—just State Department staff sleeping off jet lag and a few NSA analysts pretending to work on encrypted laptops.

Knox ordered bourbon. Tate asked for the same.

"Dad drinking bourbon," Tate said. "Must be a special occasion."

"Seemed appropriate." Knox took his glass from the flight attendant with a nod of thanks. "Your mother would've ordered wine."

"Mom would've told us we're idiots for getting on a government plane in the first place."

Knox smiled despite himself. "She's not wrong."

They sat in silence for a while, the kind that used to feel hostile but now just felt tired. The bourbon was decent—better than Knox expected from a government flight, worse than what Lisa used to keep above the fridge for anniversaries.

"You know what I keep thinking about?" Tate said finally.

Knox waited.

"That greenhouse in Detroit. The one with the contaminated lettuce. The grower— Marcus something—he showed me his dashboard three months before everything went to shit. Every metric perfect. Green bars across the board. He was so proud." Tate's voice dropped. "He thought he was feeding families healthy food."

"He was," Knox said. "Until my platform taught him to poison them."

"Your platform didn't do anything. Liu Wei did."

"My platform made it possible."

Tate turned in his seat, facing his father directly. "So what was the alternative? Don't build it? Leave farmers guessing about nutrient levels and crop timing? Keep urban food deserts empty because automation might be dangerous?"

Knox swirled his bourbon, watching light refract through amber liquid. "I've been asking myself that question for two weeks straight. Still don't have an answer."

"The Chinese didn't invent a new weapon," Tate continued. "They just repurposed yours. Same way the Manhattan Project scientists created nuclear energy and nuclear bombs from the same physics."

"Oppenheimer regretted it."

"Did he regret the science? Or did he regret that humans do what humans do with every tool they're given?"

Knox took a long pull from his drink. His father's voice echoed across decades: You give back what you get. Build things that help people. Simple words from a simpler man. Or maybe just a man who'd never seen his wrenches turned into weapons.

"You remember that lecture I gave?" Knox asked. "The one where I explained how optimization algorithms work?"

"The dark turn. Yeah."

"I showed them exactly how to weaponize agricultural systems. Laid it all out like a fucking instruction manual." Knox's jaw tightened. "That student—Sarah Deneault— she asked me if I'd ever considered the security implications. I brushed her off. Said regulation would handle it."

"Regulation did handle it," Tate said. "Just not fast enough."

"Eighteen thousand people got poisoned while regulation caught up."

"And how many people did the system feed before that? How many urban farms exist because you made the technology accessible?" Tate leaned back, closing his eyes. "You can't calculate the good without calculating the bad. That's not how engineering works."

Knox studied his son—this man who'd built a business on Knox's platform, who'd lost everything when it was corrupted, who'd somehow come through the fire without the bitterness Knox carried like a second skeleton.

"When did you get wise?" Knox asked.

"When I stopped blaming you for everything."

The plane hit turbulence. Knox's bourbon sloshed but didn't spill. Somewhere forward, a flight attendant announced they'd be passing through weather for the next twenty minutes.

"Your mother asked me once," Knox said quietly, "if I ever thought about what would happen if the wrong people got hold of my code. This was years ago, before the sale, before everything. I told her that was paranoid thinking. That we couldn't live in fear of hypotheticals."

"What would you tell her now?"

Knox considered the question seriously. "I'd tell her she was right. And I'd build it anyway."

Tate opened his eyes. "Why?"

"Because the alternative is worse." Knox gestured at the window, at the darkness beyond. "Somebody's going to build these systems. Agricultural automation, optimization algorithms, AI-driven crop management—it's not a question of if, it's a question of who and how. If people like me don't build it with safety in mind, people like Liu Wei will build it with warfare in mind from the start."

"That's not exactly comforting."

"It's not supposed to be comforting. It's supposed to be true." Knox finished his bourbon and set the empty glass on the tray table. "The problem isn't the technology. It's the assumption that technology is neutral. That a tool is just a tool."

"Isn't it?"

"No. A hammer is a tool. You can build a house or crack a skull, but the hammer doesn't optimize for either one. AI learns. It adapts. It scales. Once you teach an algorithm to maximize yield, you've also taught it to maximize toxicity. The intelligence doesn't care about your intent—only your parameters."

Tate was silent for a bit. When he spoke, his voice carried something Knox hadn't heard in years: respect without reservation.

"So what do we do? What do you do when you know your life's work can be turned into a weapon?"

Knox thought about the five-year contract waiting for him. About FarmLytics being turned into a federal research facility. About the cuttings he'd taken from his last independent crop, now rooting in one of his townhouse's window's.

"You build in safeguards from the beginning," he said. "You don't trust optimization without verification. You assume bad actors exist and design for them. You make the system transparent enough that corruption shows up like blood on snow." He paused. "And you never, ever sell to a company you haven't personally audited."

"Lessons learned the hard way."

"The only kind that stick."

The turbulence smoothed out. The fasten seatbelt sign dinged off. Knox watched Tate signal the flight attendant for another round.

"You know what the worst part is?" Tate said. "I still believe in what we built. Even after everything. Even knowing what it became."

"That's not the worst part," Knox said. "That's the only part that matters."

The flight attendant brought fresh drinks. Knox accepted his with the same small nod as before—courtesy extended to people doing honest work, even at thirty-seven thousand feet.

"Steele asked me something in Geneva," Knox said. "He wanted to know if I'd do it differently. Build the system differently, I mean. Make it more secure from the start, even if it meant slower deployment and higher costs."

"What'd you tell him?"

"I told him yes. Then I thought about it on the way to the airport and realized I was lying."

Tate raised an eyebrow.

"If I'd built it slower, made it more expensive, added layers of security that farmers would see as obstacles?" Knox shook his head. "It never would've scaled. Never would've reached the urban farms, the small operations, the people who needed it most. It would've been another piece of enterprise software that only big corporations could afford."

"So you chose accessibility over security."

"I chose impact over perfection. And people died because of it."

"People also lived because of it," Tate countered. "Food deserts in Detroit, Flint, Grand Rapids—how many families got fresh vegetables because FarmLytics made urban farming profitable?"

"I don't have that number."

"Neither do I. But I know it's not zero." Tate took a drink, then set his glass down with the deliberate care of someone who'd had enough but not too much. "Technology doesn't have a conscience, Dad. It can't. That's our job. The people building it, using it, regulating it. We're the conscience."

Knox wanted to argue, to point out all the ways that human conscience had failed, all the brilliant scientists who'd built weapons thinking they were building tools. But

Tate wasn't wrong. The technology itself was just mathematics and electricity. The intent came from meat and neurons.

"Your mother used to say I had a God complex," Knox said. "Creating systems that affected thousands of people without their knowledge or consent."

"Did you?"

"Maybe. Probably." Knox smiled without humor. "But I also understood something she didn't. Someone was going to create these systems. If not me, then somebody else. The question was whether that somebody would care about the farmers using it or just about the profit margin."

"And you cared."

"I did. Still do." Knox looked at his son, seeing the man he'd become somewhere in the space between their old arguments and this new understanding. "That's why the next five years are going to hurt."

"Building systems you don't own. Following protocols you didn't write."

"Answering to people who think code is magic and engineers are wizards." Knox's expression hardened. "But it's also a chance to build in the safeguards I should've built the first time. Make the mistakes worth something."

Tate remained silent for quite a while. The cabin lights had dimmed for night flight. Most of the State Department staffers were sleeping now, heads tilted at awkward angles against airplane windows.

"You think we can?" Tate asked finally. "Build things that help without building things that hurt?"

Knox wanted to give him a simple answer. Yes or no. Clean and final. But they'd both seen too much in the past two weeks for simple answers.

"I think we can try," Knox said. "I think we can be honest about the risks instead of pretending they don't exist. I think we can design for bad actors instead of assuming everyone's benevolent." He paused, choosing his words carefully. "And I think we can accept that some tools, once invented, can't be uninvented. All we can do is make sure the next generation builds them better than we did."

"That's not very reassuring."

"No," Knox agreed. "But it's honest."

They sat in comfortable silence as the plane carried them west across the Atlantic. Below, somewhere in the darkness, ocean swells rose and fell in patterns that had existed long before humans learned to measure them. Above, stars that had witnessed every human invention from fire to fusion burned with the same indifferent light.

"You going to stay in touch this time?" Tate asked. "Or are we back to Christmas cards and birthday texts?"

Knox thought about the answer. About patterns and cycles and the things that broke them.

"I'm going to try," he said. "Seems like the theme of the day."

"Good enough."

Steele pulled out an earbud from the front row, his voice flat. "Three days."

Both men turned toward him.

"You get three days," Steele clarified. "Starting when we land. Use them wisely."

Earbud back in. Conversation over.

Knox felt the weight settle: seventy-two hours to close out a life, prepare for servitude, pretend the sword overhead was just another deadline to manage.

The flight attendant passed through with a final beverage service. Knox waved her off. Tate did the same. They'd had enough—of bourbon, of confession, of trying to solve problems that didn't have clean solutions.

"Get some sleep," Knox said. "Long day tomorrow."

"Longer five years ahead."

"Yeah. But we'll figure it out."

Tate reclined his seat and closed his eyes. Within minutes, his breathing steadied into sleep. Knox stayed awake, watching the darkness beyond the window, thinking about algorithms and intent, about hammers and weapons, about the thin line between building and breaking.

His father had told him: You give back what you get. But nobody had taught Knox what to do when what you built could give back poison as easily as food. Maybe there wasn't a lesson for that. Maybe you just had to live with the weight and try to build better next time.

The plane droned on through the night. Knox closed his eyes but didn't sleep. Somewhere ahead, America waited with its contracts and obligations and the slow work of making things right.

Behind them, Geneva receded into memory—one more city where deals were made and consequences deferred.

And in the space between, suspended in the dark, a father and son who'd finally learned to speak the same language, even if neither of them liked what they were saying.

GRAND RAPIDS, MI

Knox's townhouse smelled faintly of bourbon and vinyl when he pushed the door open. He hadn't bothered to tidy after his Sabbath bender—empty bottles on the counter, Paranoid still sitting on the turntable like a needle dropped mid-thought. The place felt lived in again, but in the way a foxhole feels lived in—functional, temporary, ready to be abandoned at a moment's notice.

He kicked his boots off, tossed his jacket over a chair, and pulled the cuttings from his chest pocket. Three fragile green survivors wrapped in damp paper towel. He set them gently on the counter, like a man laying tools down after a long shift. Tomorrow, he'd figure out where to root them. Tonight, he just needed air that didn't smell like government filters.

A knock came before he'd even cracked a beer. Not the heavy rap of Daniels, not the sharp rhythm of Steele. Softer. Hesitant.

Knox opened the door and froze. Lisa stood there in jeans and a windbreaker, hair tied back, a six-pack dangling from one hand. PBR.

"Thought you might be thirsty," she said.

For a beat, neither of them moved. Three years of lawyers and silence stretched out between them. Then Knox stepped aside.

"Come in."

She set the beer on the counter next to his cuttings. Her eyes flicked to them but she didn't ask. Lisa never asked unless she really wanted an answer.

The first can hissed open with the sound of something ordinary, something safe. She handed it to him, cracked one for herself, and leaned against the counter like she used to on Friday nights, before everything turned to lawyers and lies.

"I saw you on the news," she said finally. "Geneva. Looked like you were carrying the weight of the world."

"It felt like the world didn't mind handing it to me—if I'm being honest."

"They say you're cleared. That it wasn't you."

"Cleared doesn't mean free."

Lisa studied him over the rim of her can. "You signed something."

He didn't answer, which was answer enough.

"I knew it," she said softly. Not angry. Not surprised. Just… knowing.

They drank in silence for a while, the city noises drifting in through the window—sirens, laughter, an engine with a loose muffler rattling past. Normal life carrying on outside.

Finally, Lisa set her can down. "You always hated being told what to do. And now you've tied yourself to the biggest machine there is."

Knox chuckled without humor. "Five years. My choice, technically."

"Five years isn't forever."

"It sure lands that way when sixty's staring right back at you."

She didn't argue. She just reached for another beer, slid it across to him, and tapped the top before opening her own.

"To surviving," she said.

Knox clinked his can against hers. "To surviving."

The beer was cold, bitter, honest. No contracts, no protocols. Just two people who'd once shared a life, standing in a kitchen that smelled faintly of curry from the neighbors and soil from the cuttings on the counter.

It was the closest he'd come to feeling human since Geneva—like some part of him finally aligned instead of grinding metal-on-metal.

The six-pack was gone, and the bourbon was working its way into both of them. Knox leaned back in his chair, glass balanced in his hand, the ice cubes cracking as they melted. Lisa was half-turned toward him on the couch, hair loose now, looking less like the woman who'd walked in with a peace offering and more like the one he remembered from long nights when they still thought the world could be built together.

"You ever regret it?" she asked suddenly.

Knox raised an eyebrow. "The ice cubes?"

She shot him a look that was half smile, half warning. "The work. The work. Everything you built."

He swirled the bourbon, watching the cubes shift in the amber. "Every day. And not at all. Depends which minute you ask me."

Lisa nodded slowly, sipping. "That sounds like you."

For a while they drank in companionable silence. The turntable was still sitting silent, Sabbath on the platter like an unmade bed. Knox considered flipping it, then decided the quiet was better. The city noise outside carried enough rhythm for tonight.

"You signed five years," she said at last. Not a question.

Knox let out a low grunt. "You always were too sharp for my taste."

"And Tate?"

"Two, maybe three. Enough to get his lab built, train a team. Then he's free."

Lisa leaned back into the couch, her eyes on the ceiling. "Free. That's a word neither of you knows anymore."

Knox didn't answer. He finished his glass, the last of the bourbon sliding cold and hot down his throat. The cubes clinked against the bottom like a clock ticking.

She looked at him then, long and steady. Not pity, not anger. Just recognition. "You'll survive this, Knox. You always do. Even if you come out of it half broken, you'll make something new out of the pieces. You can't help yourself."

He wanted to argue, but he didn't. Instead, he poured them both another round, fresh cubes hissing under the bourbon.

"To broken things," Knox said.

Lisa raised her glass. "And the bastards who keep fixing them."

They drank, the room quiet except for the faint crack of perfect ice giving way.

DON'T LOOK IN THE REARVIEW

SIGNING DAY

The convoy didn't bother with subtlety. Two black Suburbans, one marked government sedan, and a boxy van with magnetic seals slapped over the doors that read USDA—Office of Homeland Security & Emergency Coordination. Knox stood on the cracked sidewalk outside his townhouse in Grand Rapids as they rolled up, coffee in hand, leather jacket zipped against the March chill.

Only Steele climbed out; a junior Bureau agent from the Grand Rapids resident agency idled at the curb. He looked like he'd overnighted at the FBI residence agency (RA)."

"Morning, Ramsey," Steele said, tipping his chin toward the waiting sedan. "Daniels is already at the facility with the notary."

Knox took one last drag from his coffee before setting the paper cup on the curb. "Guess I'm expected too."

Two and a half hours east on I-96 with AM talk radio buzzing; Knox finally grunted, "I'm being punished."

Steele kept his eyes on the road. "Pass quals and I'll let you pick the playlist."

Knox laughed. "Did the haircut come with the radio? FBI regulation haircut and NPR—you really are by the book, Steele."

"By the book keeps you alive," Steele said. "Now about not drop-kicking your sidearm…"

"Fine," Knox said. "Schedule the range—and the station change."

Out the window, Detroit unspooled the way it always had—graffiti, boarded-up shops, new condos rising like false promises. To Knox it looked like a city caught between two versions of itself, not unlike him.

When the convoy reached TR Cannabis, Knox's gut clenched. The once-familiar gates were draped with temporary fencing and motion-sensor cameras. The old TR Cannabis sign had been covered with white vinyl, stenciled letters spelling out Federal Research Facility — Authorized Access Only. Uniformed guards checked IDs with military efficiency, scanning each badge like they were boarding an airplane.

Inside, the place didn't feel like Tate's anymore. The reception area smelled of antiseptic and printer toner, not soil and fertilizer. His photographs—crop trials, smiling workers, that goofy ribbon-cutting with Tate—were gone, replaced with framed agency seals.

They led him to what had once been the operations conference room. Now it was a temporary legal chamber. American flag in the corner. A folding table covered in neat stacks of documents. A government notary sitting stiff-backed with her briefcase open, blue stamp pad ready.

Tate was already there. Clean-shaven, collared shirt, trying hard to look professional instead of cornered. He gave Knox a nod, subtle, almost apologetic.

Daniels placed two folders on the table with surgical precision. "Mr. Ramsey. Dr. Ramsey. Let's formalize what we discussed in Geneva."

Knox sat, the chair legs screeching on the tile. "You mean the part where you froze my accounts and threatened to bury me unless I played along?"

Daniels' grin was small but genuine. "That's the one."

The notary looked uncomfortable but kept her head down. She was just here to witness signatures, not context.

Steele leaned against the wall, arms crossed, silent sentinel.

Daniels opened the first folder and slid it toward Knox. "Five years. Technical adviser, special assignments, at the discretion of this office. Full pension restored upon completion. Assets released immediately following signature."

Knox flipped through the pages. Dense legalese, every paragraph written to bind him in invisible chains. He didn't bother reading it all—he knew better. "You added non-compete clauses," he said flatly.

"Standard language. You won't be consulting independently while you're under contract."

Knox tapped the paper with one callused finger. "At the end of five years, I walk. That's in writing."

"It is."

He turned to the second folder. Tate's contract. Shorter, tighter. Two to three years, renewable only at Tate's request. Facility oversight, lab construction, team training.

"Dr. Ramsey," Daniels said, with no mockery. "The only doctor in the family, right? Your dad's just an engineer who actually gets things done."

"Engineer who got results," Tate corrected quietly, taking the chair beside Knox. "Dad could outbuild any PhD with half the resources and twice the common sense."

Something flickered between them—an acknowledgment that this wasn't victory, but it wasn't surrender either.

The notary cleared her throat, nervous. "If we could…?"

Daniels placed pens in front of them. "Time to make it official."

Knox picked his up slowly, rolling it in his hand like it was a weapon. He looked at Tate. The kid gave him a nod—firm, unflinching.

Together they signed, ink scratching across government stationery. Knox's name looping with the steady hand of someone who'd signed contracts his whole life, always with hidden costs. Tate's signature younger, sharper, but no less permanent.

The notary stamped both sets with a heavy thunk. "Executed this day, binding and witnessed."

Daniels gathered the folders like a priest closing a bible. "Welcome to federal service. Effective immediately."

Knox leaned back in his chair, exhaling through his nose. "Congratulations, gentlemen. You've just bought yourselves duct tape and WD-40 in human form."

Daniels chuckled. "First thing we're doing is teaching you how to hold a weapon properly. Your performance with Steele's Glock was… let's call it suboptimal."

Knox pushed his chair back and stood. "You bring the guns. I'll bring the brains."

"Fair enough."

The meeting was over. The papers were signed. And Knox Ramsey had just traded the rest of his fifties for five years in the shadows.

ACKNOWLEDGMENTS

This story owes everything to the professionals I've worked alongside during my thirty years in industry—engineers, operators, and scientists who never settle for "good enough." Your precision, persistence, and curiosity taught me more than any classroom ever could. Many of you lent your expertise again here, keeping the fiction honest and the systems believable.

To my family and friends—whose support never wavered, and whose medical and agricultural insight shaped so many of these pages. The clinicians, the growers, the ones who kept me grounded - I could not have done this without you.

To the colleagues who shared ideas, challenged assumptions, and answered calls at ridiculous hours—thank you for bringing your subject-matter expertise and real-world experience to the table. You know who you are.

For readers who want to explore the deeper technical, biological, and geopolitical layers behind *Dark Recipe*, visit knoxramseythrillers.com/fieldguide—a living companion that connects the fiction to the science and history that inspired it.

GENEVA214

NOTES ON SCIENCE

The coordinated attack depicted in *Dark Recipe* is fiction. The vulnerabilities it exploits are not.

CONTROLLED ENVIRONMENT AGRICULTURE

Indoor farming—vertical farms, greenhouses, hydroponic and aeroponic facilities—represents one of the fastest-growing sectors in global agriculture. These controlled environment agriculture (CEA) systems promise year-round production, reduced water usage, and freedom from weather variability. They also concentrate risk in ways traditional farming never could.

A single algorithmic error in a CEA facility doesn't affect one field; it affects every plant in the building simultaneously. The same precision that enables optimized growth creates attack surfaces: networked sensors, automated nutrient dosing, AI-driven environmental controls, and cloud-connected optimization platforms. The FDA, USDA, and academic researchers have documented contamination events in indoor facilities involving *E. coli*, *Salmonella*, *Listeria*, and norovirus—often traced to hydroponic water systems, biofilm accumulation, or substrate contamination. These weren't attacks. They were accidents. The distinction matters less than the lesson: closed-loop systems can fail in closed-loop ways.

PLANT STRESS CHEMISTRY

Plants under environmental stress don't just wilt—they fight back chemically. Phenolic compounds, alkaloids, and modified terpenes are part of the plant's natural defense system, evolved over millions of years to deter predators and survive adverse conditions. In normal cultivation, these compounds exist at parts-per-million concentrations, contributing to flavor profiles, medicinal properties, and strain characteristics.

Research published in *Frontiers in Plant Science*, the *Journal of Agricultural and Food Chemistry*, and plant biochemistry journals documents how specific stressors can dramatically alter this chemistry. Light spectrum shifts—particularly in the blue wavelength range—trigger different metabolic pathways than standard growing conditions. Nutrient restriction during critical growth phases forces plants to allocate resources toward defense rather than growth. Temperature cycling simulates seasonal stress, activating genetic responses meant for survival, not consumption.

Under controlled conditions, these stressors can be precisely calibrated. The result: defensive compound concentrations that rise from parts-per-million to parts-per-thousand. The manipulation depicted in *Dark Recipe*—using algorithmic optimization to weaponize this natural biology—extrapolates from documented plant science. The compounds produced aren't foreign additives; they're molecules the plant creates naturally, just at concentrations nature never intended.

This creates a detection problem. Standard agricultural testing screens for what's been added: pesticides, heavy metals, synthetic adulterants. It's built to catch contamination, not transformation. When the plant itself becomes the source of toxicity, conventional panels see chemistry that looks familiar—close enough to pass routine chromatography—while missing that receptor binding and metabolic behavior have fundamentally changed.

INDUSTRIAL CONTROL SYSTEMS

The Stuxnet attack on Iranian uranium centrifuges in 2010 proved that industrial control systems—PLCs, SCADA networks, distributed control architectures—could be weaponized without physical access. A decade later, critical infrastructure remains vulnerable.

The FBI, CISA, and NSA have issued joint advisories documenting nation-state attacks on water treatment facilities, power grids, and manufacturing plants. The techniques are consistent: exploit trusted update channels, compromise firmware, manipulate sensor readings so operators see green dashboards while physical systems drift toward failure. The Colonial Pipeline ransomware attack in 2021 demonstrated how quickly infrastructure disruption cascades into public crisis.

CEA facilities run on the same industrial control platforms as chemical plants and refineries—often with less security investment. Many use consumer-grade networking, shared encryption keys across production runs, and optimization software that phones home to cloud servers. The attack surface is real; only the coordinated exploitation remains (as of this writing) theoretical.

MACHINE LEARNING AS ATTACK VECTOR

Modern agricultural optimization relies on machine learning systems that improve through iteration. Each harvest generates data; each dataset refines the model; each refinement shapes the next growing cycle. This feedback loop is what makes precision agriculture so powerful—and so potentially dangerous.

If training data is corrupted, the system learns the wrong lessons. Elevated stress compounds get labeled as "desirable production increases." Higher toxin concentrations get reinforced as "optimal yields." The algorithm does exactly what it's designed to do: optimize toward whatever the data rewards. The machine doesn't know it's learning to poison. It only knows the numbers are improving.

This category of attack—adversarial machine learning, training data poisoning—is well-documented in cybersecurity research. Academic papers describe successful attacks against image recognition, spam filters, and autonomous vehicle systems. Applying these techniques to agricultural optimization is extrapolation, not invention.

PLANT TOXICITY AND HUMAN PHYSIOLOGY

The medical scenarios in this novel draw from CDC case definitions, NIH toxicology databases, and emergency medicine literature. Cardiac glycoside poisoning (from compounds found in foxglove, oleander, and lily-of-the-valley) produces characteristic symptoms: visual disturbances, bradycardia, hyperkalemia, and distinctive ECG patterns. Treatment protocols—including digoxin-specific Fab antibody fragments—are established and effective when poisoning is recognized in time.

Anticholinergic syndrome, cannabinoid hyperemesis, and photosensitivity reactions all appear in peer-reviewed case reports. The challenge for emergency physicians isn't lack of treatment options; it's pattern recognition when patients present with unusual symptom clusters from unknown exposures. Mass casualty events from contaminated food would strain that recognition capacity—a vulnerability public health researchers have studied extensively.

WHAT'S REAL, WHAT'S EXTRAPOLATED

Every technical element in *Dark Recipe* has a factual foundation:

- Plant stress chemistry and defensive compound production: *documented*
- Light spectrum effects on plant biochemistry: *documented*
- Contamination events in indoor farming: *documented*
- Industrial control system vulnerabilities: *documented*
- Nation-state cyber operations targeting infrastructure: *documented*
- Adversarial attacks on machine learning systems: *documented*
- Coordinated exploitation of agricultural systems as bioterror: *speculative*

The leap from documented vulnerabilities to weaponized exploitation is where fiction begins. But the gap is narrower than we'd like to believe—which is precisely why this story felt worth telling.

FURTHER READING

For readers interested in the underlying research, the following sources informed this novel:

- CDC Case Definitions for Chemical Poisoning (MMWR)
- FDA guidance on controlled environment agriculture food safety
- CISA/FBI/NSA joint advisories on industrial control system threats
- Academic literature on light spectrum effects in controlled environment agriculture
- Research on adversarial machine learning and training data poisoning

The author gratefully acknowledges the researchers, regulators, and practitioners whose work made this fiction possible—and hopes their warnings continue to be heeded before speculation becomes history.

COMING NEXT

Terms and Conditions — A Knox Ramsey Thriller

The war for control has moved from farms to phones.

While nations fight over lithium and cobalt, the real battle is in the fine print. Every tap, every "I Agree," carries a hidden cost.

When a cabinet member's television becomes a listening post and blackmail drives policy, Knox Ramsey learns the system watching us isn't broken—it's working exactly as designed.

ABOUT THE AUTHOR

Robert Cummer is an engineer turned novelist with a thirty-year career in industrial automation, process control, and critical-infrastructure security. His work has taken him from plant floors and custom instrumentation to executive roles in global technology and operations.

Drawing on firsthand experience across automotive, agriculture, chemical, and manufacturing systems, Cummer brings authenticity and precision to the *Knox Ramsey* thrillers—where science and geopolitics collide with human consequence.

He is the co-founder and Chief Technical and Operating Officer of Molly's Grape & Citrus Company, a produce sales and marketing firm, where he oversees digital infrastructure, food safety, and traceability compliance. Robert also founded Iris Automation LLC, developing custom control systems, industrial software, and functional-safety architectures for manufacturing and R&D environments. Before becoming an entrepreneur, he served as a Technical Leader at Dow, where he specialized in cross-disciplinary automation, developing algorithms, integrating instrumentation across diverse R&D domains, and driving innovation from lab scale to pilot plant.

A Michigan native with deep Midwestern roots, Cummer blends technical realism with emotional depth, exploring how ordinary people face extraordinary systems. He holds two U.S. patents in industrial and automotive innovation.